THE TRAITOR IN US ALL

OTHER FIVE STAR TITLES BY ROBERT S. LEVINSON:

Ask a Dead Man
Where the Lies Begin
In the Key of Death

THE TRAITOR IN US ALL

ROBERT S. LEVINSON

FIVE STAR

A part of Gale, Cengage Learning

GALE
CENGAGE Learning™

Detroit • New York • San Francisco • New Haven, Conn • Waterville, Maine • London

GALE
CENGAGE Learning™

LIBRARY OF CONGRESS CATALOGING-IN-PUBLICATION DATA

Levinson, Robert S.
　The traitor in us all / Robert S. Levinson. — 1st ed.
　　p. cm.
　ISBN-13: 978-1-59414-852-1 (alk. paper)
　ISBN-10: 1-59414-852-X (alk. paper)
　　1. Teenage girls—Crimes against—Fiction. 2. California, Southern—Fiction. 3. Germany (East)—Foreign relations—United States—Fiction. 4. Mielke, Erich—Fiction. 5. Diaries—Fiction. 6. Traitors—Fiction. I. Title.
PS3562.E9218T73 2010
813'.54—dc22　　　　　　　　　　　　　　　　　　　2009042257

First Edition. First Printing: February 2010.
Published in 2010 in conjunction with Tekno Books and Ed Gorman.

FOR SANDRA, OF COURSE

CHAPTER 1

The three high school girls waltzed into Dino's Pizzeria as they had twice a week since he arrived in Eden Highlands, Mondays and Fridays, never later than fifteen minutes after their last class, no way of knowing what made today different, but—

He knew.

Today, one of them would not be leaving.

He checked his wristwatch and smiled at their punctuality.

He lit another cigarette, soaked his lungs with a heavy hit, and pushed a fat jet trail of blue smoke out the driver's window of the delivery van, reciting to himself the words he had made his mantra since pulling into the parking lot five minutes ago:

Whatever will be will be.

Words he remembered from a song in an old Hitchcock movie.

Whatever will be will be.

He drew an approximation of the tune from memory and hummed the lyrics to the light breeze infiltrating his beard as he eased from the van and took his time covering the twenty-two steps to the entrance.

He killed the butt under his boot heel and pushed open the swinging door, inhaling the smell of pizza freshly pulled from the giant bake oven.

A few feet to his left was the order counter, past the arch to his right two lines of wooden picnic tables and benches in a narrow, windowless sitting area whose austere white walls were decorated in cheaply framed movie posters. The sitting area was empty.

The three girls stood at the counter, giggling and arguing among themselves over what toppings to choose. Mushrooms and sausage appeared to be winning out, although a debate over anchovies kept the final selection inconclusive as he stepped up behind them, within arm's reach.

He answered a nod of recognition and a *Just a minute* smile from the guy behind the counter with one of his own while reaching for the snub-nosed .22 tucked under his Hawaiian shirt, inside his belt.

He revealed the weapon, nozzle pointed at the fiberglass drop ceiling, causing the counterman to widen his eyes in confusion, wider with alarm, then dodge his head like he was looking for ducking room.

The counterman held out his palms and backed away, inching left toward the pizza chef whose back was to the counter, flinging dough by second nature while watching a soap opera playing out on the small TV mounted above the double oven.

"Fuh Cri'sake," the pizza chef said, taking a hard bump. Turning, he saw the .22, knew what it meant, and threw up his hands. The motion sent the raw dough wheel flying. "Fuh Cri'sake," he said again, his Hispanic accent more pronounced this time.

The three girls swung around to see what had caused the clerk and the chef to act as they had. The snub-nose was now aimed at the girl in the middle. Amy was her name, Amy Spencer, who looked like she'd already eaten a million too many slices of pizza in her lifetime. She was the one who had been lobbying loudest for sausage.

Fear registered on their faces in equal measure and he wondered who'd be the first to muster enough courage to say something to him.

Just as he'd have guessed, it was Betsy, Betsy Wheatcroft, who as usual had led the threesome inside. She said, "I know you. You've been here before, when we've been here."

The third girl, Tracy Collins, clutching her arms in a way that accentuated her well-developed breasts, her thighs pressed hard against an accident, hypnotized by the .22, said through spurts of breath punctuating every word, "Are you going to hurt us?"

He answered her by squeezing the trigger.

Betsy Wheatcroft looked surprised when the bullet hit her, like she was too good to die, especially since he'd been aiming the .22 at Tracy Collins. What she was was too smart for her own good, showing off that way: *I know you. You've been here before, when we've been here.* Like Betsy was hankering for an A in Memory I. The problem he'd always noticed with all self-anointed leaders, the need to be one step ahead of everyone else. Only now she was taking a step back, grabbing for the counter with one hand while her other gripped the hole in her chest that was spilling blood and staining her white lambswool cardigan a lusty burgundy.

She whimpered, said a word that sounded like "Mommy," slid to the floor and into a sitting position against the counter wall.

Amy Spencer threw her chubby hands over her face and began crying.

Tracy Collins gave him a look as deadly as one of his bullets. She dropped to her knees to minister to Betsy, although anybody with half a brain could see the girl was gone for good.

The counterman and the pizza chef had turned their heads away, either to let him know they'd seen more than they wanted to remember or to blind themselves to the bullets that might be coming for them. The counterman, his hands still reaching for

Heaven, said something about God. The pizza chef crossed himself.

Neither meant anything to him or they'd already be heading for that Great Pizza Kitchen in the Sky. He awarded himself a smile for that one: *Great Pizza Kitchen in the Sky.*

Tracy was easing Betsy down onto the ceramic tile, as if to make her friend more comfortable in death, indifferent to the blood staining her hands. He ordered her to her feet. When she hesitated, like she was about to confuse *brave* with *stupid,* he said, "You get on up by the count of one or I shoot your other friend." *The count of one.* Another good one, he thought. His sense of humor always seemed sharpest at times like these.

Amy Spencer howled and her body broke into a spasmodic dance strong enough to register on the Richter Scale.

He said, "We're out of here, the three of us," and told the counterman and the pizza chef, "I see or even think one of you is doing something stupid like grabbing the phone for a 911 before I disappear from the lot, the police will find two more bodies parked outside when they get here."

"I hear you," the counterman said, shouting the words to be sure he'd been heard.

The pizza chef crossed himself again and said, "Me, too–me, too–me, too–me, too," turning the words into a stutter still running at mach speed while he ordered the two girls out ahead of him and to his van.

The van was used and bruised, a ghastly white no wash and wax could ever correct, the plates obscured by a thick layer of mud he'd lathered on earlier in the day, so it would be crusted long before he drove into Dino's. A sliding rear door. No side doors or windows to worry about.

He moved on Amy, burying the .22 between them, pressed hard against her spine as an incentive for Tracy to obey his order: slide the door open and get inside. She did so, and at once Amy tried stepping forward to follow her.

"No," he said, restraining her, digging the gun into her spine. He jammed a key into her hand. "I need you to shut and lock the door, then give me back the key." She gave him a look that put fear to shame. "You're going to be riding up front with me," he said, letting go of her.

Amy nodded and did as she was told.

She turned from him to head for the passenger door on legs that verged on collapse. Before she'd taken a third step, he had stashed the key in a pocket, pressed the .22 against the base of her skull, and put a bullet through her brain.

At once, there was banging from inside the van, Tracy Collins' voice, a series of indistinct screaming demands.

He stuck the weapon back under his Hawaiian shirt, climbed behind the wheel and pulled out of the parking lot, Tracy Collins pounding on the cabin wall like it was going to make a difference to him.

The smell of fresh pizza lingered in his nostrils. He wished there'd been time to down a slice or two. Double-cheese and pepperoni, with the extra-thick crust. That's what he called real pizza pie. None of those fancy trimmings for him.

After a few miles he trained his thoughts on Shane Vallery, wondering what she might taste like now, so many years later.

Delicious, of course.

Absolutely delicious.

He had never heard anyone say less of Shane, so why should now be any different?

CHAPTER 2

Later that day, sunset closing in, Margaret Collins stepped away from the bank of microphones and out of the harsh glare of the lights being used to illuminate the front of the Eden Highlands Police Department by the horde of television crews that had swarmed into town intent on turning tragedy into a media circus.

She averted her eyes from the cruel stares of condemnation she was getting from Phyllis Spencer and Eleanor Wheatcroft, sitting like they were joined at the hip on folding chairs outside camera reach, their arms entwined, their tears and wails of anguish beyond the tentacles of the press corps.

Before it became Maggie's turn, the two of them had displayed their common grief for all America to see, wounds that would likely never heal, that festered like open pus sores on every word they'd used to condemn the madman who had killed their daughters.

Maggie was no less sad.

She felt their pain as if it were her own.

Her tears were for them, their families, their dead daughters, as much as for her own plight, but she didn't expect them to understand, any more than she would have understood if Tracy had been murdered like her best friends, instead of being the one the killer drove away with.

Did they expect her to feel guilty because Tracy was still alive and their daughters were not?

Did they expect her to apologize to them, beg forgiveness, because Tracy was still alive and their daughters were not?

If Tracy was still alive—

Maggie realizing again that her daughter could be lying dead in a ditch somewhere between here and wherever that lunatic was fleeing to in his van, her use to him as a getaway hostage invalidated by time and distance.

For hours afterward, every vulgar, obscene possibility she remembered from other crimes involving the children of other parents—regularly documented in intense detail by a media that routinely brought its own obscenities to the misfortunes of others—weighed on her mind.

She kept returning to an image of the ditch—

Filled with the decomposed body of her fifteen-year-old—*Oh, Mother. I'm fifteen and a half and I wish you'd remember that*—and she woke up time after time throughout the night, drowning in sweat, pulled from sleep by the sound of her own nightmare shouts for Tracy.

The morning brought no relief.

Only a succession of phone calls, the news people sending ingratiating smiles and dialogue through the line, hoping for an exclusive interview, some comment they could use to "freshen up the story."

She lost track of how many times she heard that expression or its cousin:

Freshen up the sound bite.

All received the same answer, a turndown dressed as a click in their ear.

As her fears and frustration mounted, she wanted to pull the phone from the jack, but she couldn't risk that.

What if the bastard who stole her child called, demanding ransom money? *Yes, yes, whatever it takes. I'll find it somehow.*

Telling her how to proceed. What to do. Where to go. When to—

Or the police, telling her they had found Tracy. *Thank God. My baby safe? Is she okay? Did that bastard harm her? I'm coming to get her now; where are you?* Or, calling to tell her—

No!

Maggie shut her eyes to visions of the ditch, foxed her hands over her ears to silence the echo of invented sounds—

Her child begging for her life.

Screaming for her mommy to come save her.

Yes, darling. Yes, yes, yes!

The phone again.

Maggie leaped for it.

"How you holding up, kid?" The voice familiar this time. Welcome. Detective Glen Traylor of Eden Highlands' eight-man police force.

"Lousy. What?"

"Nothing new, but I needed to make sure you were okay."

"The Amber Alert?"

"Running on every freeway marquee up and down the state. What little description of the van we got from the kid works at Dino's. If the van's on the road, somebody'll ID it and call it in, so hold yourself together best you can, okay?"

"I'm dying, Glen. If it's not on the road. If nobody sees the van. If—"

"Maggie. Turn it off. Please . . . she's going to be fine. If he'd wanted to kill Tracy, he'd have done it same time as Amy and Betsy."

"They hate me, Phyllis and Eleanor. Like I'm responsible for what happened. Did you see it, the way they looked at me yesterday?"

A moment's pause, then, "I'm coming over."

"No. I need you to look for Tracy."

"Fifteen minutes. Maybe twenty. Some follow-up here."

"I said no, Glen."

"Need to make sure the news people cleared away from your house, like I ordered them. Anyone still there, outside, bothering you?"

"I don't know. I haven't looked since last night, when they were camped out front and I phoned you. The damn phone. Even calls from New York, wanting to fly me there for interviews. Like I'm some freak in a goddamn sideshow."

"Twenty minutes, a half hour max," Glen Traylor said, disconnecting before she could respond.

Maggie's legs ached and felt like anchors as she moved to the picture window in the living room. Her body unable to reach a compromise between hot spells and a chill turning her hands clammy and her mouth dry. Her stomach upset, verging on another need to race to the toilet bowl, as she had twice during the night.

She attributed this to the tablets Dr. Ayres had forced on her yesterday, threatening to tie her down and administer them himself if she didn't cooperate, ignoring her reminder that she habitually boycotted pills of any type, even aspirin, saying it would take the edge off the fear-driven anxiety she was drowning in.

"Having my daughter back will do that," she'd told the doctor.

"Maggie, I wish to Heaven I had a pill for that," he answered.

Her ability to concentrate fogged by confusion, she stared at the curtains blocking out the daylight, wondered what had brought her here. *The press, that's why. Still outside?* She stepped to a corner of the window and peeked out. The vultures were all gone. Only a blue Lexus there, parked directly across the street, in front of Carolyn's. Empty. Probably another of Carolyn's overnighters.

Maggie went through the ritual of showering. She threw on a robe and slippers, dabbed on some lip gloss and ran a brush through her hair. Decided the house needed a cleaning beyond the twice-weekly run-through it got from Anna, who charged too much for too little effort—*No laundry, Missus Maggie, or that's extra, and also no dishwasher*—but Anna had come with the house, inherited along with the wallpaper and the furnishings; no thought of replacing her, no matter what the cost. Tracy had grown up with Anna and adored her.

Maggie found the vacuum cleaner and moved it to the living room, ran it over the plush lavender carpeting like she was mowing a lawn until it coughed and sputtered to a stop. The dirt bag was full. She dumped it in the kitchen waste bin, but couldn't locate the drawer where Anna kept her fresh cleaning supplies. The kitchen linoleum was soiled. She got the squeegee mop and mop bucket from the broom closet, filled the bucket with warm, soapy water, and was sorting out the best starting point when she remembered she had not yet spoken with Roxy.

Roxy had been there yesterday, watching when the press blitzed her with cameras and microphones and questions, some of them ugly, like, "Do you fear for your daughter's safety?" *Why, no, what's to fear, you unfeeling, insensitive moron? That my daughter was taken away by somebody who'd just killed two of her best friends? Of course not. Hell, no. I'm having the time of my life.* What she didn't say, because her throat by then was clogged with tear snot and phlegm and fear that her world was over.

Roxy, Roxy, Roxy.

Roxy hugging her, letting her squeeze her hand a bloodless white, whispering support, urging, *Keep hold of yourself, Sweetie Pie. You just go out there and say it like you feel it.* Roxy, dabbing away the mascara stains, freshening up her makeup and finger-combing her hair. Roxy, ready with outstretched arms and a mama bear hug after she had broken down for all the world to see. Disintegrated. Fled the cameras and the microphones and questions after begging for Tracy's return, her head in a tailspin as bad as the one she felt now. Worse.

Maggie leaned the mop against the stove and almost tripped over the bucket aiming for the wall phone.

She tapped in the number for The Garden of Eden.

A pickup on the sixth ring.

A wrong number.

She had misdialed a number she'd been dialing two and three and four times a day for almost sixteen years, since coming back home, the number she and Roxy shared with no one.

Maggie dialed again, exercising more care.

Roxy picked up on half a ring, saying, "I'd have called, but didn't want to run the risk of waking you if you were sleeping, Sweetie Pie."

That was Roxy, always putting the other person's interests in front of her own.

Although not at first with Maggie, after Maggie returned to Eden Highlands.

Eden Highlands.

In years past, it had been tucked like somebody's dirty secret inside the rambling hills above the San Luis Rey Valley, closer to San Diego than to Los Angeles, a whispered-about patch of flatland populated by a couple hundred farmers and merchants and maybe as many whores, what back then they were still calling *Women of Easy Virtue,* back then being the late 1800s. Brothels had lined both sides of a narrow main street laid out about the time General Phineas T. Banning was blazing a trail from the desert to the ocean, while other, far less bawdy communities were springing up around revered Padre Juan Crespi's mission in the San Luis Rey Valley.

Thriftiest and most cunning among the ladies of the day and night who found cash money more stimulating than virtue as its own reward was Pilar Eden, the area's dominant madam and leading dominatrix, who invested her gross proceeds in additional houses of ill repute and, when the need for more petered out, began buying up the acres she wasn't able to acquire in trade. It wasn't long before she had acquired enough territory to turn her wish into reality and give birth to a small but stylish city.

Wagging tongues of the time shared a joke that played well in the barrooms along General Banning's stagecoach route to the Blue Pacific: If Pilar had given it another couple years, not retired from the profession to raise breeding goats, she would have wound up owning all of the damn state and maybe a large chunk of Tia Juana across the border.

The Garden of Eden was the first and grandest whorehouse built by Pilar, the one on which she'd built her reputation and her fortune. Modeled on a Victorian mansion Pilar had seen in *Harper's Weekly,* it was constructed in the Queen Anne style, entirely of redwood; three-and-a-half floors tall; a series of perfectly balanced windows on the ground level; an assortment of steeples; a spire as visible as a church tower; lights always glowing behind gossamer curtains in the uppermost windows, to help anxious customers, first-timers, or visitors from out of town find their way.

Pilar's marriage to a defrocked priest, Father Melchoir Couts, begat seven children, two boys and five girls. The boys grew up to enter the military and both rose to the rank of two-star general before retiring with special commendations from the White House. Three of the girls grew up to become nuns. The two other girls followed Pilar's tradition of begetting, and so it happened that years later the family tree came to include a twig named Margaret, who inherited her Eden Highlands home as a birthright and as Margaret Collins, "Maggie" to her relatives and friends, fled from the tight-knit community not quite sixteen years ago, when the happiness in her life turned desperately elusive, then impossible.

Roxy Colbraith had been running The Garden of Eden before Maggie showed up to claim her rightful inheritance as the last of Pilar Eden's direct descendants.

That Maggie got the family residence, that was okay with Roxy, who had created a lavish residence for herself at The Garden of Eden, but—

The Garden?

Not so okay.

Roxy had come to think of The Garden of Eden as her own.

She read Maggie's return to Eden Highlands as a demotion, somebody whose mere presence undermined her half-dozen years of successfully and profitably operating The Garden as an exclusive bed-and-breakfast, an ultra-luxurious retreat catering to newlyweds, celebrities playing secretive games far away from prying eyes, and anyone else who could afford what was frequently reported as the most expensive resort rates west of the Rockies. East of the Rockies, too.

Maggie understood this at once and was determined to set the record straight. She locked them in a room and insisted they would stay there until Roxy understood she would continue to be in charge of day-to-day operations and receive a substantial raise in salary and commissions, in addition to her free residence at The Garden of Eden and any other perk she'd rewarded herself with.

"You hear yourself?" Roxy had said. *"You're already giving me orders."*

"Never in front of anyone. My solemn promise."

"My staff would know. I give in, you wait. You'll see. They'll be laughing behind my back faster than any of Pilar Eden's whores could ever have faked an orgasm."

"Only if you let them, Roxy. Look. Are you looking at me?"

"What's that supposed to mean?"

"I'm a kid next to you, a kid with no experience running any kind of business, where you've proven yourself to be a great managing director. I need you."

"Twenty-nine to my thirty-five. Big effing deal."

"I'm fat. Pregnant. A belly as big as a blimp. I want to devote myself to raising my child."

"Until the day comes you decide otherwise and send me packing. Wouldn't be the first time that happened to me, Mrs. Collins."

"Call me Maggie."

"Quits. That's what I'm calling it."

Roxy relented after more than an hour of give-and-take shouting that climaxed in hugs and tears and a kiss that became more passionate and intense than either probably intended, an early clue to what their relationship would become.

Maggie asked into the phone, "What's that, Rox?"

"I said I didn't want to wake you if you were sleeping, Sweetie Pie."

"Awake as possible, Rox." Maggie settled onto a serving counter stool, ran a finger across the ceramic surface and checked it for dust. Frowned. Moved the napkin dispenser closer to the salt and pepper shakers.

"Worried sick about you, Maggie. Kept me up all night."

"Thanks. How's the store?"

"Busier than usual. The staff and the old familiar client faces send you their love and prayers."

"Do you think the bastard will call, Rox? That, not—"

She couldn't finish the thought.

"Sweetie Pie, you have to keep on thinking positive thoughts. Sounds like you can use company. I'll finish up a few things and head on over, how's that?"

"Glen'll be here any minute."

Silence, then, "Oh. Okay, sure, Sweetie Pie. Call if you need me for anything, you hear?"

"Thanks, Rox," Maggie said, then realized she'd already racked the receiver. She rubbed at the dust on her index finger with her thumb, smelled the back of her hand, and wondered if there was time for another shower before Glen arrived.

The door chimes answered the question for her.

She shuffled to the front door, wondering why he hadn't used his key, a question answered on first sight of the man on her porch, a stranger, an expression revealing nothing about him until he said, "I'm sorry to see you again under these sad circumstances."

"Again?" Maggie shook her head violently. "I don't know you. Who are you?"

"I'm Jack Sothern and you're Meg Boone, yes, Mrs. Collins? It's been a long time, our meeting in East Berlin, but I'm right, aren't I? We weren't together for long that night at Café Munchausen, but I knew it was you the minute I saw you on the news."

She examined his face for confirmation. "I'd managed to forget all about you, you lousy, lying, hypocritical bastard." Her face turned beet red. She whipped her palm across his face and caught his other cheek on the rebound with the back of her hand. Not satisfied, she spat in his face.

Sothern toweled off the spittle, used a sleeve to wipe his palm dry and accepted her verdict for what it was, saying, "Why I came down here to Eden Highlands. To try to make amends. To save my soul and your daughter. I can help find Tracy for you."

His words staggered her. She grabbed the doorjamb for support.

"Help how? Help me the way you helped my husband? My husband died thanks to your help. Find Tracy how? The same way they found Danny after you helped him? Dead, dead, dead, God damn it, dead?"

"Alive, Mrs. Boone. Find your daughter alive. Get Tracy back to you."

CHAPTER 3

Jack Sothern's home in Los Angeles was at the Westlake Court, a three-sided rectangle of wood frame bungalows, twelve in all, that he'd stumbled onto six years ago on Chandler Avenue in the Mid-Wilshire District, when his declining fortunes and an unfeeling building manager obliged him to vacate his high-rise, high-rent condo on the Westwood Corridor for a place he could call, at the very least, a hovel.

The Court, a few blocks removed from MacArthur Park, looked like a movie set left over from *The Grapes of Wrath*. His place had a bedroom the size of a linen closet, bad plumbing that caused the toilet to overflow on a schedule of its own making, and an entry port for the mice who visited regularly from the beggars' alley outside his back door.

Deep into last night, Sothern had sat transfixed in front of the TV watching the Eden Highlands murder and kidnapping coverage as if the rest of the world did not exist, switching channels whenever the reporting grew stale on repetition, always with the hope he'd stumble onto something new.

His eyes felt like someone had poured molten lead into them, but his focus was as pure as his memory for faces.

That was her.

Yes.

For certain.

By any name.

She was calling herself Collins, Margaret Collins, but he

knew better.

She was in her mid-forties now, overweight by five or ten pounds, but no less movie star gorgeous. A flawless peaches-and-cream complexion on the face of an angel dominated by luminous emerald-green eyes capable of lighting a moonless sky. Powder-puff lips. Hair freshly laundered and worn in a pixie cut more appropriate to her age than the windblown shoulder-length style he remembered, the Harlow platinum replaced by a far more subdued shade of blonde.

Margaret Collins was Meg Boone.

She was Dan Boone's widow.

She was, please God, the key to his redemption.

Jack Sothern's redemption.

A long time in coming, God.

A long time.

Through all the bad times, bad luck and bad fortune that had followed him since he betrayed Dan Boone, he had never lost faith, never lost hope that the opportunity to redeem himself would come one day, just as he'd always believed his personal and public downfall resulted from going back on his word to Boone.

The decision brought him temporary rewards and glory, but soon after put him on a downhill slope to the failure and despair from which he was yet to emerge.

God willing, come tomorrow, there'd be a new beginning—

Opportunity to atone for his sin, and, maybe, with it, rescue from the junkyard life he'd brought upon himself.

That night, for the first night in hundreds of nights, he slept with the memory, not the nightmare, of what began in 1987, when he was banana green as a journalist, barely hanging on to his gig at *L.A. Inside/Out,* a weekly news rack freebie staffed entirely by young, underpaid writers and reporters who, unlike him, were making their mark with investigative pieces that once had been the exclusive, prize-winning province of the twin Goliaths of Los Angeles newspaperdom, *The Times* and the *Daily.*

Frequently, when one of the guys scored, he got stolen away to the *Times* or the *Daily,* in a few cases to the *New York Times* or the *Wall Street Journal,* or onto the staff of one of the big-time glossies. *Vanity Fair. Esquire.* Craig Kelsoman to *Rolling Stone,* for a three-parter on the inner city's street gangs that almost got him killed and barely lost out on a Pulitzer, or so Craig Kelsoman was fond of telling anyone who'd listen.

Going on two years of cranking out good copy on pedestrian subjects, Jack began sensing signs his editors were ready to trade him in for a newer model, someone who might catch the big stories that were eluding him.

Not that he didn't have the touch.

He had the touch.

What Jack didn't have was the connections or the clout to take a piece of gossip and run with it, develop a rumor into the leadoff piece on page one. He came close a few times, but for different reasons the sizzle became a fizzle before he could keyboard in his byline, what was leading to his prick of a city editor getting ready to write –30– to him.

Jack Sothern, over and out.

Bye, Jack Sothern instead of *By Jack Sothern.*

This particular night, he was bemoaning the sad state of his life at the old Phillip 'n' Bobby Joynt on the Strip. PB's was one of the "in" places, an oasis for movers and shakers, where he might barstool into a hot rumor or, more often, a hot chick, a starlet or singer-type, out skimming the long bar for career advancement.

How Jack happened on Shane Vallery.

She was an angel-faced brunette with ambition as big as her boobs, nursing a beer on the next stool and eyeing him like a kennel club judge with watery green eyes that tied with her brightly painted bee-stung lips as her next best feature.

She ran fingers as slender as her five-five figure down the shoulder-length hair she wore like stage curtains, first one side and then the other, and branded him with a smile bright enough to light Times Square.

"Why the bottle of Cutty Sark in front of you, with a paste-on label that has your name written on it?" she said, her voice a whisper of sexuality, like she'd practiced a lot of Marilyn Monroe. "Derick Trevino. Your name?"

"A buddy. We hit Los Angeles together from the Bay area a few years ago. San Francisco. Derick buys it by the bottle here. Says the shots work out cheaper that way. I'm allowed to poach from it, even when he's not around." Sothern pointed an invitation at her.

"Sure, Scotch more than I can afford right now, why this bottle of Dos Equis. *Olé.*" He signaled the bartender to set her up with a drink from the bottle. "Your buddy? That all, or is there more to it? Being from San Francisco and all? No offense, although I happen to prefer my men same as my liquor—straight." She told the bartender, "Rocks and a hint of H_2O, as usual, Georgie. And don't be stingy."

"Like a ruler," Jack said.

"I can get you straighter," she said, raising her glass for a toast. After the clank: "No offense, it's just how I get when I notice someone interesting, like you, even though you're younger than me."

"Not so that I can see."

"Flattery will get you everywhere, preferably your place. What? Twenty-two or three, I'm guessing."

"You're not supposed to ask a gentleman his age."

"Don't be such a smarty, smarty. And I hope you're kidding when you say you're a gentleman."

"Not necessarily."

"Good answer. Are you in show business?"

"A writer."

"Screenplays? Television?"

"Newspaper. I work for *L.A. Inside/Out*. Derick is the screenwriter. Movies of the week." Although she was clearly the aspiring actress type, she didn't seem disappointed by what she'd just heard, so he figured she'd soon be angling and wangling for him to give her an intro to Derick.

She surprised him. "I don't give a flying frig about your friend Derick, except for his bottle. You're the one who interests me. Something about robbing the cradle that's more intoxicating than this stuff." She held out her hand. "I'm Shane. Shane Vallery. One night with me and for sure it's, *Shane, come back, Shane.*"

"Jack Sothern. You an actress, Shane?"

She tasted her Scotch-rocks, wrinkled her nose. Reached for the Cutty and gave the drink a booster shot. "In a manner of speaking, but I'm not acting with you, Jack Sothern. Unless you're allergic to older women, what say we trade this place for a warm bed?"

His place was closer.

Shane had made him promise, *No questions,* so a week later he knew hardly more about her than she'd confided in him that first night. "Apart from chemistry," she had said, "which you and I have up the gazoo, Little Boy, what matters to me is honesty, the ability to communicate honestly. And passion. And friendship. Spontaneity is important, because it helps keep a relationship fresh and new and exciting. And compromise. *Our* way is always better than *your* way or *my* way."

Their nights almost every night after that for two weeks were always spent at his place, her argument always its convenient location, but never revealing hers. Revealing little about herself, in fact, while pushing and probing to learn everything about him.

Shane Vallery's concept of *compromise*.

Their last time together, their last night of making love, he pushed her a little harder on the subject.

She rolled closer and stroked his hair, his face, rubbed his chest, eked out a sigh of remorse telling him, "Oh, Jack, I'd love for it to be possible to answer your questions, only I can't."

"Why can't you?"

"That's a question, Little Boy." She wagged a naughty-naughty finger at him.

"Nothing significant. Maybe a little something to hang my hat on."

Her hand tracked down his leg. "How about little this to hang your hat on?"

"You're changing the subject again."

"Doesn't it bring us closer together, your knowing what to expect?"

Sothern moved her hand aside and rolled over with his back to her.

She found him again and said, "If I could, I'd tell you I love traveling. My last time, it was through the Austrian Alps, hiking up from Salzburg, Mozart's home, and ending up in Germany. Beautiful weather. Beautiful scenery. Germany, not so beautiful. Maybe we'll travel one day. Paris? Rome? Spain? I've never been to Spain, but I kind of like the music."

"Tomorrow night? Your place?"

There was a stretch of silence. "Okay, yes, but only because you've turned out to be special in my life. Don't let me drive off without leaving the address. Deal?"

"Deal."

They made love again, and once more to celebrate the rising sun.

She showered and threw herself together because of the job she couldn't be late for, and so much for what he knew about her job. Or, anything at all about the type of work she did.

"Tell me something," he said, blocking the door, the urgency showing on his face, disengaging the humor in his voice.

Shane said, "I take brisk walks in the morning and I work out with weights. I love all kinds of music, especially rock. Old movies, *film noir,* the best. Disneyland. Big Sur. A beautiful High Mass. I love vegetables and fruits and salads made with flowers. Anything about the Royal Family. Dominoes. Backgammon. Gin rummy. Clothing that sparkles. I love light chocolate and dark chocolate. I love antique cars. Dogs that are so hairy, you want to run through them with your feet. I love history, American history and European history. Any history that's made at night, like ours." She bopped his nose with a finger. "You're not careful, Little Boy, I might be adding you to the list." She shuffled Jack out of the way, blew him a kiss, and disappeared from the apartment.

And his life.

Sothern phoned Shane during the day, got no answer on a dozen attempts. Her message machine wasn't picking up. The operator said there was nothing wrong with the connection. The address she'd given him, on Sparrow Road in the Hollywood Hills, off Outpost Drive, turned out to be an empty lot. A posted sign directed potential buyers to a married pair of realtors working out of the Beverly Hills office of Coldwell Banker: *The Gladds. So Gladd to Be Your Guides to Gladder Living.*

He reached the Gladds.

They'd never heard of Shane Vallery.

Nobody at Phillip 'n' Bobby's had seen her since the last

time they were in together. He hung out until closing, wishing through one Scotch after another that she'd fly through the entrance and into his arms, her explanation one he could accept. Hell, he was prepared to accept any explanation she wanted to fit on him. The next morning, when he awakened, he had no idea how he'd gotten home.

He made a nuisance of himself with the police.

Nothing. Not for two and a half months, during which time Sothern would often wake up nights damning vegetables and fruits and salads made with flowers. Anything about the Royal Family. Dominoes. Backgammon. Gin rummy. Clothing that sparkles. Light and dark chocolate. Antique cars . . . But not Shane Vallery.

Never Shane.

Never.

She was an unsolved mystery, an unfinished chapter in his life.

He wondered if she knew that, if she even cared.

The cleanly typed letter was postmarked East Berlin:

Dear Mr. Sothern,

My name is Dan Boone and maybe you've heard of me. I've heard excellent things about you from a mutual friend of ours, Shane Vallery. Shane says you're the right person to tell my story to. It's a story I'm anxious to share with the world for reasons best left for when and if we meet. If you haven't heard of me, please check me out. If what you learn is of interest and value, be advised a round-trip airline ticket in your name is being held with Delta Airlines, pre-paid, Los Angeles International Airport. It will be valid for two weeks from the date of this letter. You'll be met upon your arrival. Thank you for your time, for which I hope to return full value.

Sincerely—

And it was signed *Dan Boone,* handwritten in blue ink in a strong hand, a fancy scrawl under the signature that could have been borrowed from John Hancock.

Sothern had no idea who Dan Boone was outside of the history books, but seeing Shane's name—

In his mind, he was already packing for Germany.

By the time he boarded the flight, Sothern knew far more about Dan Boone than he knew about Shane Vallery, the result of a few hours at the main library downtown, pouring over back issues of the *Times* on microfiche. The motivating force remained the possibility of finding Shane, but even without that possibility he knew it was a trip he had to make.

Dan Boone was a major story in the making, one that had the potential of springing him from *L.A. Inside/Out,* to someplace Big Time enough to house his talent, maybe even pay a premium to land Sothern and the exclusive he'd be bringing there.

Dan Boone was the biggest star going in the Communist Bloc, but—

That wasn't the story.

Dan Boone was an *American* who had gone to East Berlin and become the biggest star going in the Communist Bloc.

That wasn't the story, either.

That had been revealed a few years ago, when Dan Boone was exposed as "The Turncoat Rebel" in the international edition of the *Herald-Tribune* and the story carried onto the AP wire, then to *Newsweek,* where Boone was branded "an anathema to what America stands for, a disgrace dishonoring the name of a genuine American hero for all ages," and to *Time,* where it was suggested, "We'll take our Boone in a coonskin cap any day over this Commie-sympathizer parading around Red Square in Moscow in a military ushanka, spouting the

Commie party line like he owned it."

The other part?

The hook?

Sothern had no idea, but he could smell it.

Why else would Boone have summoned an American journalist, any American journalist, to a meeting in East Berlin?

The scent would not go away, no matter how many times he reviewed his Xerox copies of the stories over the unlimited wining and dining in the First Class compartment. More wining than dining, and a storehouse of the miniature bottles of Scotch in his attaché case by the time the Delta 747 broke through a foreboding cloud bank and landed at Tegel Airport in West Berlin, as far as the ticket took him.

He exited into the terminal feeling lost, but only for another minute, until he felt a hand on his shoulder to go with a questioning voice: "Herr Sothern? Jack Sothern?" Jack turned to find himself being smiled at by a man smaller than him by half a head, wearing a mismatched black suit, the jacket too tight, the pants too baggy, a black cap with a plastic brim, running a well-used handkerchief over his sweat-drenched face. "Yes, I can tell it's you. I almost missed you. Sorry. Traffic. You know how that is, Mr. Sothern, like in the States. Like New York, I hear, and Los Angeles." Talking nonstop.

"How'd you know it was me?"

"You look like your description. I have a keen memory and a good eye for faces."

"Described?"

"Shane Vallery. Her eye, also good, although not so good as mine."

"Shane. Is she here?"

He shrugged and checked the ceiling with a sideways glance. "She minds her own diary. Shares it with nobody." Stuffed the handkerchief in a hip pocket. "She tells me who and where. I go where and find who. Life, so simple when it doesn't call for complications, yes?" He finger-patted down his wispy hedge of black mustache. "Herr Grass, I am. Emil Grass, Herr Sothern. You go now through customs. When you come through, I'll be on the outside waiting for you. A Jaguar, that's me." He pronounced it *Jag-you-are.* "Already too many Mercedes on the roads. A Jaguar. Tops." Almost smacked his face with a vibrating thumbs-up.

Sothern had more questions, but Emil Grass had wheeled around and was speeding up the crowded terminal concourse.

"I suppose you're one tired hombre, the long plane from Los Angeles, unless you slept on the flight? I hear about people who can do that. I don't know how. I need my two good feet solid on the ground. Why it's the Mother Earth, not the Mother Sky. The sky is full of tricks, it wants to be, like the clouds now. Packed for rain, but who knows? Maybe blue tomorrow and smiling at me. You. Who knows? The good earth, never any tricks."

Emil Grass prattling on as fast as he was powering the Jaguar through a maze of crowded streets, delivering disjointed commentary like a tour guide on speed, never answering the few questions Sothern threw him about Shane, about Dan Boone— anything. His grammar was shaky, but not his American accent, barely tinged with a clue to his German roots. "A proud German," he had explained earlier. "Yes, ashamed of the history brought to us by Adolf and Company, but only that. Too young to be part of it, in my twenties now, like you, Herr Jack. The mustache, I think it makes me look older, good in a country that respects its grandmothers and grandfathers, unlike over in the States, or so I hear. But the States, too much good about the States to complain. You think I look older, do you? Everybody else I know says so."

He checked over his shoulder for an expression from Sothern, who was sucking up the passing scenery from the back seat.

"Distinguished," Sothern said, not meaning it. *Foolish* would have been the better choice of word. "Emil, you still haven't explained where we're driving—"

"Yes, almost there." The Jaguar took another turn, onto Gitschiner Strasse. "You see how the Wall is ugly? Ugly people put up ugly walls. Not the graffiti, that is what we on this side of the Wall, the freedom side, think of the Russky rats who make prisoners of our family and our friends in the east sector. *Scheisse.* Shit. I would spit on them, but it would only be stopped in flight by that damn Wall."

Another five minutes and Emil Grass pulled a turn, weaving in and around strings of BMWs and Mercedes to where Gitschiner Strasse met Oranienstrasse. He double-parked with the motor running and hurried from the Jag to open the door for Sothern.

"You see up ahead, Jack? That's the famous Checkpoint Charlie. You go through there now." He handed over an envelope. "Then what to do when you cross over, it's all explained in there."

"You're not coming with me?"

"I go in there, on wheels or on foot, that is the finish for Emil Grass." He drew a finger across his throat. "Besides, you get where you're going, Dan Boone himself will be waiting for you." Two thumbs up.

Emil Grass settled back behind the wheel.

Sothern bent over to wonder, "Shane Vallery? I asked you about her before."

"Yes. I remember," Emil said. "I'll be here waiting when you get back, Jack. Spit on a Russky for me, you see one."

With that he slipped the Jag into gear and glided away.

Sothern pushed the envelope into an inside zipper pocket of his thick windbreaker, the collar turned up against the mid-afternoon chill, adjusted his Raiders cap, and covered the twenty yards that would get him to Checkpoint Charlie.

CHAPTER 4

Passing through Checkpoint Charlie, one of four entry points into East Berlin's Russian-dominated German Democratic Republic, Sothern thought of the times he cruised through U.S. Customs into Tijuana, from San Diego. Only, where Tijuana with its blatant sex-and-sin attractions always reminded him of a hellhole, he sensed now he was heading into Hell itself.

The weather seemed to agree. Maybe it was only his imagination that the sky was darker on this side of the Wall, as grim as a ghost story, but no debating the pregnant black rain clouds that trailed him to a GDR clearance bungalow, where he joined a modest line of visitors passing through a series of inspection stations under scrutiny of stern-faced, iron-eyed paper-pushers in police uniforms out of a costume designer's sketchbook.

He took the propaganda-ridden rigmarole with a good-natured smile, scribbled his name on documents he didn't bother reading, traded in fifty dollars in American bills for GDR money that would have no value outside the GDR, and followed the trail out and across the vehicle lanes to the station guarding the walk-in gate to East Berlin, manned by armed Russian troops. More of them were in turrets overlooking the wall, a couple aiming rifles downward and, unless it was his imagination, licking their lips at the prospect of bagging a tourist.

"American," said the soldier decked out for a Russian winter. An olive greatcoat, the bars on the red shoulder boards and collars identifying him as an officer; his high black boots, spit-polished beyond damage by the rain; black fur gloves and a fur hat, the ears pulled down. His face, like his voice, frozen against emotion. He tapped Sothern's passport again and pointed at him.

"American, yes."

"Sad," the soldier said, handing back the passport. He pointed to the gate. "Here you see true democracy at work." The words sounded memorized, phonetically imperfect.

Sothern moved on and grinned hearing the soldier say to the man tracking behind him: "American . . . Here you see true democracy at work." He had the urge to laugh loud, turn and say something, but was struck with a vision of a trigger-happy sentry answering with a well-placed shot.

He scooted through the gate and onto Friedrichstrasse, the main drag, hoping to find someone who might be waiting for him and at the same time looking for a roof against the downpour. He found an overhang first, hunched his shoulders against the rain, his hands under his arms for warmth, and waited a few minutes.

"Excuse me?" It was the American who'd entered behind him. Dressed warmly, a porkpie hat over a full-length mink coat; Kris Kringle eyes twinkling behind out-of-date horn-rimmed frames; two rows of teeth too perfect to be real. A stocky six-footer. Probably late forties. "I hear you say you're an American?"

Sothern nodded.

The man lobbied for a handshake. "Crews. Burt Crews. Minnesota. Minneapolis." He sounded it. "Taking a few hours away from business to see true democracy at work." Putting a Russian spin on the words. Making a face, rolling his eyes.

"Jack Sothern. California. L.A."

"Los Angeles. Sothern from Southern California. Appropriate. Why, we're almost neighbors." Chuckling under his breath. "You also in Berlin to make a little jack, Jack?"

"Manner of speaking."

"Manners, you bet. Smart to mind your manners whenever you're here in this God-forsaken cutout from civilization. You watch out for patrols on foot, dogs the size of the hound of the Baskervilles rarin' to be turned loose and leap straight for your jugular, you so much as give cause to raise suspicion."

"You've been before?"

"Not to speak of," Burt Crews said. He dug a Polaroid camera from a pocket and offered it to him. "Jack, be a good Samaritan and take my picture. I'll stand over there, so we don't get anything in the background to make the Russians nervous. You peek, you'll see they still have their eyes on us." He ignored the rain and moved to *over there*. Relit his tooth-heavy smile. He said, "Thought it had to be you passing through, Jack," chapped lips barely moving.

"*Had to be?* Who the hell are you?"

The camera whirred and buzzed and the photo slid out.

"Burt Crews. Minneapolis, Minnesota. Enough with that look. They're watching. Hand over the picture and the Polaroid, like it's my turn to take your picture. Two tourists collecting a souvenir of their visit to East Berlin. Remember to smile like you mean it."

"I mean, who the hell are you, really?" Sothern said, trading places with Burt Crews.

Crews gestured him to adjust his position. "They got a lip reader somewhere, we don't need them reading yours or mine. Edgar Bergen, remember? Charlie McCarthy? He was the worst ventriloquist, his lips always moving, but he counted on everybody's eyes being glued on Charlie, the dummy. Or Mortimer Snerd. Effie Klinker. Smart, no dummy himself, that Edgar Bergen." Pursing his lips. "Me? Your welcoming committee,

Jack. A friend of Shane Vallery. She told me what to look for. Spot right, that woman."

"Is she here? Shane Vallery?"

"Edgar Bergen's daughter, Candace. Pretty blonde girl. Been in some movies. You get an envelope when you landed at Tegel?"

"Yes."

The Polaroid spat out a photo. Crews studied it and nodded aggressively, like it was a prizewinner. "Good. Emil, Emil Grass. Not the most reliable of people. Like the White Rabbit from *Alice in Wonderland*. Late, late, late for important dates, like he's aiming for a spot in the *Guinness Book of World Records*. So out of character for a German in a country prides itself on the trains running on time."

Crews took a second shot, gave it a similar stamp of approval, and turned it over.

"We'll shake hands and part company now, Jack. You head up Friedrichstrasse for a distance, maybe as far as over to the Opera Palace. Someplace where you can check out the contents in private, clear of prying eyes. You'll be almost there."

"Where?"

"You bet."

"Dan Boone?"

"Yes, he is a big star here. Russia. China. Quite the entertainer. Hurry off, Jack. Have a nice visit."

With that, Burt Crews pulled his porkpie down over his forehead and waved himself off, too fast for Sothern to try again about Shane.

The rain stopped as abruptly as it had started falling by the time Sothern reached the Opera Palace, one of the few decent structures inside East Berlin that wasn't designed to be visible to the other side of the Wall. What he mostly passed was evidence of a city crushed by Allied bombs and bullets or hastily, shabbily built post-war structures, their concrete facades toppling onto streets that looked and felt as dead as yesterday. Block after block off the main drag was lined on both sides with towering, Soviet-style apartment complexes that had as much personality as a dish of cottage cheese.

A few times, he sighted buildings that talked of history and happier times. Architecture imitative, but worthy. Ornate exteriors paying homage to the Greeks. Imposing statuary towering overhead on pedestals, mainly heroic male and female nudes, indifferent survivors in the rubble of history. Silent witness to a government run by fear and containment. And a wall, *the* wall, the Berlin Wall that divided a city already divvied up once, after World War II, by the Russians, the United States, England, and France.

That was in August 1961.

East Germany closed its borders to West Berlin on the morning of August 13.

Citizens awakened to find barbed wire, barricades, and armed guards denying passage from East to West. A day later, the historic Brandenburg Gate entrance to the central city was closed. A day after that, workmen in East Germany began construction of the infamous wall. Less than two weeks later, every crossing point to West Berlin had been closed, even to West Berliners with work and family in the East.

Divide and conquer?

The Russian squatters and their East German cronies celebrated, confident they had accomplished half the equation.

Sothern did a quick mental count—

1961 to the present.

More than twenty-five years ago, going on thirty.

In that time, more than two hundred people killed attempting to cross the wall.

He wondered how many back home were aware of that history. Guessed not many by now, maybe not even by the two wars since, Korea and Vietnam. Maybe the Kennedy words when he visited here in '63, *Ich bin ein Berliner. I am a Berliner.* Sothern knowing what he did only through researching Dan Boone and getting ready for the trip here.

Dan Boone, as in *Ich bin ein East Berliner.*

He wondered how Dan Boone could sacrifice America for this cesspool.

It was one of the questions he intended to ask him.

Sothern settled on one of the cement benches in a modest grassy area outside the Opera Palace. Some of the other benches were occupied and there were couples out for a stroll. His provided enough privacy for a look at the contents of the envelope. He pulled it from the zipper pocket and in a moment was staring at a blank sheet of paper.

A rustling sound.

A heavyset woman wearing a cheap wool coat with frayed cuffs, her frizzy gray hair protected by a babushka faded through too many washings, settling on the opposite end of the bench. Holding tight rein on an undernourished dog. Leaning over to apply a series of gentle strokes down its hairless back, saying, "You go on back to the street five minutes after I'm gone, Herr Sothern. A hundred yards to a cross street, then you turn to the right and walk until you see a café, the first and only one, and you take a seat inside."

The woman cooed a few loving words at her pet and stood.

Pressed a hand against her side and stretched her shoulders back.

Exhaled satisfaction and wandered off, never once having looked at Sothern, who by now was certain he was on his way to a story as big as he'd imagined, maybe bigger, or had stumbled into a John le Carré novel.

Café Munchausen occupied the entire ground level of an apartment building that had survived the war. The rains had emptied a generous terrace full of white plastic tables with pole umbrellas jutting from their centers, but through the picture window he got the impression it had pushed all the customers inside. He was right.

Stepping inside to a mushroom cloud of tobacco smoke that promptly clogged his nose, stung his eyes and addled his temples, Sothern found almost all the tables occupied and drinkers three deep and chatting noisily, like old friends, at a small bar; music blaring from overhead speakers, the finish to Madonna's "Open Your Heart" segueing to U2 and Bono on "I Still Haven't Found What I'm Looking For."

How appropriate, he thought, almost as if the place was welcoming him personally.

The café was furnished in tables and chairs out of the Black Forest, some operetta, *The Student Prince* or maybe *The Merry Widow.* The walls were full of framed posters of German movies, some titles familiar to him, like *Metropolis* and *M, The Way of All Flesh* and *Pandora's Box,* American movies with German titles but the usual suspects, Swanson, Astaire and Rogers, John Wayne, Gable, Harlow, Bogart; a batch of the later unforgettable faces: Brando, Dean, Monroe, and, of course, Elvis. In a place of honor above the elegantly framed mirror behind the bar, a poster for some Western movie, the title in German, but the American face he recognized from his research: Dan Boone. Boone brandishing a pair of six-shooters and his narrowed eyes staring straight into the lens, challenging all comers.

He crossed the room and settled at an empty table for four, in the chair facing the entrance, uncertain what to expect next.

He didn't have to wait long to find out.

"Lager." Sothern was giving his order to a barmaid in a skimpy outfit that showed off hips meant for motherhood, supported by thighs that belonged on a cow, as the young woman who had just entered hurried over, waving a greeting.

"The same," she told the barmaid, then, "Jack, how marvelous to see you again."

She leaned over and gave him a kiss on the forehead before sliding onto the chair next to him and taking his two hands in hers.

Sothern returned her smile and said, "Who the hell are you?"

The smile stayed, but her eyes crisscrossed the room anxiously. "How the hell am I? Great, and how about you?"

"I asked *Who.*"

"Ever the kidder, aren't you, you old sweetheart." She dropped her voice under the din and said, "Meg Boone, Dan's wife. Play along, for God's sake." The edges of her false smile reaching for her cheeks.

"Meg, I'm so embarrassed. No makeup or the way you're wearing your hair, that has to be what faked me out."

She ticked an appreciative smile, relief filtering down to her shoulders. "And ever too much the gentleman to mention I am no longer the sleek, svelte maiden I was when I visited the States and barged in on you, that it, Jack?"

"No Weight Watchers here? Or is it too much of that marvelous German bread and butter and—" He raised one of the lagers the barmaid had delivered. "—Too much of this?"

Meg Boone raised her stein. "Cheers. Dan is due any minute. I'll let him break the news . . . speaking of the devil." She indicated the entrance.

Dan Boone had arrived inside Café Munchausen and was searching around, his arrival evidenced by a depletion in the noise level, replaced by admiring murmurs of his name; some finger-pointing; eyes trailing him as he marked his discovery of their table with a grand, two-armed *There you are!* gesture and hurried over, smiling and slapping hands along the way, like the Lakers' Magic Johnson and James Worthy heading into the locker room tunnel.

He exuded a natural charisma that added inches to his small stature. A head out of proportion to the rest of him and a bushel of golden-brown hair contributed to the illusion of height, but Sothern judged him to be five foot six or seven at most, on par with so many other stars who made up in fame what they lacked in stature. Redford. Pacino. Cagney and Ladd before them. Bogart not so tall, either. Dustin Hoffman.

Boone carried himself with cock-of-the-walk assuredness and a dancer's grace on legs supporting a muscular upper torso, a broad chest, and broader shoulders that bespoke regular hours spent in the gym.

He settled a quick kiss on Meg's generous lips before moving on Sothern, locking his cheeks and planting a far more generous kiss on his lips. "Jack, so damned pleased you didn't let me down. Stand up and let me get a good look." Sothern stood. Boone took a step back and studied him for several seconds. "Still taking good care of yourself, you are." He moved in for a shared embrace, pounded Sothern's back with gusto while muttering in his ear, "They're watching me like hawks." Louder: "A sight for sore eyes, you are."

"You, too, Danny."

Boone draped his brown leather bomber jacket across the back of the empty chair between Sothern and Meg and sat down. He pinched her cheek, caught her bundled hands and brought them to his mouth for a kiss, generating another undercurrent of approval from patrons tracking him. His smile had enough wattage to light the world.

Meg pried her hands loose. Reached for his beard and stroked it lovingly, leaned in, and settled a kiss on the base of his ear, where it melded into the top of his strong jaw line. He had just enough of a left lobe to allow the gold pirate's earring Meg tugged at playfully, a twin to the gold ring she wore in her right ear.

Boone gave hers a tug and said, "Sorry I was tardy, Jack. My bride and I aren't up from the farm that often nowadays. Meetings with my business associates. The next movie. Recording sessions. Why I sent Meg on ahead." To her: "Goldilocks, you tell my best pal why we wanted him here?" His voice as mellow as a choice Bordeaux.

"Waiting for you, Danny. You should be the one."

"Here's your first clue," Boone said. He locked his hands on his wrists and rocked the cradle.

The patrons who'd been sucking in the star's presence along with their lager and ale broke into thunderous applause and shouts of *Bravo!* that drowned out the music, currently what sounded like Madonna again. "Papa Don't Preach."

Meg was blushing.

Sothern let out a whoop, extended her his congratulations, and joined the clapping that by now was synchronized to the music.

Boone sprang to his feet. Bowing. Flinging out his arms like a victorious general. He climbed onto his chair, earning another crescendo of congratulatory sounds. Signaled for quiet. When he had it, he declared in flawless German that translated as, "Thank you, my wonderful friends. Come, celebrate with us. Drinks for everyone on me."

With that, Boone could have been elected president of the GDR.

He took some handshakes, signed some autographs before settling back at the table inside the invisible glass wall stars carry with them, privacy protection that fans somehow know to respect when it's raised.

Meg took some last swallows of her lager and rose. "I'm going to head back to the hotel and leave you two boys to catch up," she said, adjusting her overcoat.

"Goldilocks, no."

"Superstar, yes. I'm tired, my ankles ache, and there are some woman things I can only do there." She aced Boone's pleas with an open-mouthed kiss that caught his tongue, patted Sothern's shoulder, saying, "See you later, Jack," and hurried away—

The first and last time he'd encounter Meg Boone in East Berlin.

He and Boone finished the round and had one more over what anyone watching could read as engaging small talk between old friends before Boone suggested, "Up for a walk, Jack? Enjoy some night air now that the rain's stopped?"

The half moon had broken through the cloud banks and was casting light off the rain-sopped pavement as Sothern and Boone wandered aimlessly through the poorly lit streets of East Berlin, which they had almost to themselves, hunched against a cold wind biting at their faces.

Uniformed Russian soldiers appeared occasionally at intersections, their growling guard dogs straining at the leash. Otherwise, East Berlin felt to Sothern like a ghost town that even the ghosts had abandoned.

Boone broke their silence after about a half mile, saying, "They're watching, Jack. They see us, even if we can't see them. Hearing us, that's something else, we keep it to this level. Why we're outside. I felt them inside Café Munchausen the instant I arrived."

"Who are *they*, Mr. Boone?"

"Dan. It's still 'Dan' to you, Jack. We're friends now, although not as good as we can be down the line. . . . They? From Stasi, the East Germany secret police agency. Spies. Herr Erich Mielke's murderous thugs tracking me day and night. The letter you received? You would not believe how many hands it had to pass through to get to you."

"Why? I still don't know, Dan."

"Because it's time for me to go home, Jack. Home to America. I need your help for that."

"Why me?"

"Because Shane Vallery said I could trust you. She said you're the man who can get done what has to be done."

"She here, Dan?"

"Don't be silly, my friend. Have you ever known Shane to sit still for long in one place?"

"I haven't known her long enough to know anything much about her, Dan."

"Yet, you're here. That speaks to her. That says you may know more about her than you realize. She does that to people she meets, Shane. . . . You think you want to help me out, Jack? I'm the 'Turncoat Rebel' puppet of the Commies, after all. A traitor who traded in his country to be the big star he couldn't become back home. So say 'no' and I'll understand. I'll shake your hand and see you on your way with no hard feelings."

"And if I say 'yes'?"

"Meg will return to the United States. Our child can be born there. Afterward, I'll be able to escape from this nightmare once and for all. Join them. Explain through the stories you'll write why I did what I did and how I have truly felt playing the Commie dupe through all those years. Given the American public's sense of fairness and willingness to forgive, be able to continue my career back home at a level I'd never been able to achieve before I made the dumbest, damnedest mistake of my life and pretended to buy into the party line and the Commie bag of tricks. But, Jack, you need to believe—I was seduced by fame, not by the Commies."

Sothern recognized at once what the story could do for his career. He was going to say yes, of course, but first there was something he had to know.

"Dan, this business with people watching and the secret police?"

"They somehow got an inkling of what's going through my mind. Snitches all over. They don't want to lose one of the biggest propaganda tools they have. Me. My travel has been cut off, where I used to travel freely anywhere I wanted, whenever I wanted. I try getting out, back to the West through other means, they're only a few feet away. I'm not afraid for me, but I absolutely won't endanger Meg or our child, you understand?"

"I understand, Dan, and my answer is, 'yes.' Tell me what it is you want me to do."

Chapter 5

Tell me what it is you want me to do.

Sothern's dream ended here this time—

Saving him from reliving the nightmare events that followed their first meeting, back in '87, Meg and him, and Dan Boone, when Sothern was chasing after a future, not hiding from his past.

He clicked on the TV to catch the morning news.

The brutal murder of the two girls and the kidnapping of Tracy Collins was still the lead story. Nothing new beyond stakeout footage. Mainly a rehash of yesterday's press conference, providing Sothern the opportunity to reconfirm it was Meg Boone.

He pressed the mute button and went after his cell phone.

Marty Baldwin, the most recent in a line of short-term ex-bosses, wasn't happy to hear from him. "When I fired your ass, threw you out of here, didn't I tell you to forget my phone number?" he said.

"What man forgets, auto-dial corrects, Marty."

"You sound like you're on something again, Jack. You on something again?"

"My cell, Marty. Better on one than in one, I always say."

"Hah-hah."

"Been there, done that. It sucks like a five hundred dollar a night hooker."

"You've been on a few of those, too."

49

"Something else I'm on, Marty. I'm onto a big story. Right now. This minute."

"For real, I'm supposed to suppose? Unlike all the bags of crap you were shoveling here before I got wise to you? Almost got my own ass sliced and diced because of—"

"That was then, this is now, Marty. Coming off our history together, would I lie to you now?"

"Let me take a minute to think on it. Yes. And here's your sixty seconds change."

"Marty, Marty, Marty. Old friend. Old boss. My act's so clean now, if I were a dog, the noise you'd be hearing would be me licking my balls. I'm offering you first refusal, for old time's sake."

"Jack, if it's a few bucks you need, come over later. For old time's sake. As far as I'm willing to go."

"The other thing, Marty. I'm currently short on wheels. A rental as part of our deal? Nothing exotic. I can get by with something along the lines of a Lexus. One of those sleek little two-door sports mothers—Marty? You still alive, Marty? I don't hear you breathing."

The SOB had hung up on him.

Sothern snapped the cell phone shut and rolled into a sitting position on the sofa. He leaned forward to recapture the bottle of Jack Daniels on the coffee table and drained what was left, barely a shot and some raindrops.

He stroked his lips dry, studied the two lines on the table—the last of his stash—and with cavalier indifference welcomed the nose candy through a rolled dollar bill. He stretched the buck and licked it clean, tongued the mirror, and restored sound to the TV picture.

Slapped his knee and pointed at the screen.

Cut loose with a gleeful screech.

Margaret Collins?

No way, José, he addressed the wall. *Meg Boone, that's who. And you, Marty, you can keep your damn charity. You hearing me, Marty? You listening? I'm onto something big here and you ain't coming along for the ride.*

Sothern went for his cell again, tapped down to Jimmy Bugle's special number, and left the usual message.

Jimmy was back to him fifteen minutes later.

"How they hanging, bro?"

"By the short hairs, Jimmy, so credit's still my only game."

"What you did for my family when it mattered, man? Before you fell away for the duration? When nobody else would give me spit for soda pop? You're a decent dude and one class act, so it's open end and no end in sight until you're back on your size tens, Jack. Say the words. Same as before? I can have somebody there in sixty."

"All I need is a car, Jimmy. I have to be someplace and I'm four wheels short."

"Don't go nowhere, bro." The line turned quiet as dust before Jimmy Bugle was back saying, "Got a cousin on the other line, his line of work, asking what you had in mind, in particular; anything?"

"I was thinking a Lexus, one of those great-looking sporty jobs?"

"Hold your mouth . . . G, my man here's saying Lexus, one of those sporty jobs? . . . A particular color, bro?"

"No."

"Particular state on the plates?"

"Whatever's on the lot."

Jimmy Bugle gave him a *hah* and advised G: "My man says whatever's on the lot." Then, after a minute, to Sothern: "In an hour, maybe two. Out front your place. Keys under the floor mat, driver side. Full tank with G's compliments."

"I don't know what to say, Jimmy."

"Way we like it, bro, especially anybody come snaking around with questions."

Sothern gave it the full two hours before trooping barefoot through the courtyard complex, grimacing whenever he connected with loose pebbles on the cement walkway, but his irritation turned into a smile as bright as Broadway when he saw the Lexus parked by the curb. It was cherry red, sparkling like it had been waxed and polished a thousand times, and wearing Nevada plates. As well as the keys, there was an ounce of shit stashed under the driver's side floor mat. He hadn't asked for it, didn't want it, but couldn't bring himself to toss it away.

Three hours later, Sothern was in Eden Highlands and parked outside Maggie Collins' home, which he'd located by trailing after a television van rigged with satellite dishes.

He waited for the news-hungry crews to leave before approaching the door.

She took his name as an incitement to riot, her voice rising to screamer's pitch when Sothern proposed helping her find her daughter—

"Alive, Mrs. Boone. Find your daughter alive. Get Tracy back to you."

CHAPTER 6

She wouldn't let him into the house.

She drowned out the suggestion with shouted demands to tell her about Tracy, blurting out the question again and again, like a CD player on repeat, constantly turning up the volume until, finally, the words became a blur of unintelligible blather.

"We can discuss this more intelligently inside, maybe over some coffee?" Sothern said, when her voice failed her while she labored for breath. He made a move to enter. She pushed the door and caught his foot in the gap. "Any harder, Mrs. Collins, I'll have broken bones to go with my fallen arches."

She rejected his grin. "Tell me about Tracy," she said, and pushed harder. "Answer me about Tracy, damn you. You said *get her back alive*. Tracy is alive, is that what you're telling me?"

Sothern did what came naturally to him—

He lied.

"Yes, and I know where to find her, Mrs. Collins."

He felt like a son of a bitch for saying the words, but that was not unexpected. That also came with the territory. "May I come inside and we can discuss it?" He forced another smile and, while she debated with herself, pretended away the pain shooting up his leg.

The pain in the small of his back was new, though, something grinding against his vertebrae. As Sothern reached around to assay the cause, Maggie registered a monumental sigh of relief and said, like some desert wanderer discovering an oasis, "Glen, this man told me he knows where to find Tracy."

Whoever Glen was, he said, "Gone far enough, mister. What you are feeling is my Beretta, certain to kill you dead as you will ever be if you make one false move." His voice coming from behind, firm and decisive.

"My foot trapped in the door, I can barely make one real move."

"Glen, did you listen to me? He said he knows where to find Tracy."

"I heard him loud and clear, Maggie, better than he heard me coming up on him. That so, mister?"

Sothern edged his head around for a look. The guy was about the same height as him, five-eleven. Maybe six or seven years older, which would put him at forty-seven or forty-eight. He could stand to lose fifteen pounds if he wanted his snappy cashmere plaid sport coat to fit properly, not look like he'd shoplifted it off the rack at Barney's in Beverly Hills two sizes too small. Close-cropped black hair that blended well with a five o'clock shadow verging on seven o'clock, the distinguishing feature of a pie-shaped face that could pass for jovial until you dug into the close-set, threatening black eyes book-ending a nose that did not quite fit the format, as if it didn't originally come with the territory. The eyes, partner to his strident tenor, burning with an urge for menace.

He was nobody you'd want to meet in a dark alley or on the front porch of any one of the single-story Spanish-style haciendas dressing both sides of this tree-lined residential street within strolling distance of Eden Highlands' sleepy downtown district.

Sothern said, "You came on as quiet as a cemetery, like a cop or something, Glen."

"A cop and something else again, if you don't start cooperating in a hurry. I asked if that was so, about Tracy?"

"Don't I have the right to remain silent?"

"And I have the right to shoot you dead on the spot for resisting arrest, mister." The cop clamped a palm between Sothern's shoulder blades and slammed him hard against the door. It happened too fast for Sothern to angle his face. He knew the crunching sound. This wasn't the first time his nose had been broken, but usually it was by someone's fist finding his face during a barroom brawl or out in some parking lot, not by a door as dangerous as the one molesting his left foot. He stretched his tongue to catch some of the blood sailing from his nostrils to his lips and wished it tasted more like the Jack D.

Glen said, "Nice and easy now, I want you to get those hands behind you. I have some cuffs'll fit you just fine."

"Something in a nice sterling silver?" Sothern said, but he did as he was told. "They have to be so tight?"

"Still not as tight as you, mister. Anyone ever tell you you smell like a brewery?"

"All the time."

The cop squeezed the cuffs another notch. "Now turn around, wise ass, and let me have a look at you."

Sothern made a mental note he owed the cop one. Two. One for his nose, one for the cuffs biting into his wrists. "Easier said than done, Glen. Mrs. Collins, you mind?"

"He means release his foot, Maggie. Go on, it's okay now."

Maggie opened the door wide, saying, "Glen, make him tell about Tracy." Giving Sothern his first close look at her since her breakdown on television. She was hardly more composed, all the worry gullies still digging into her wide forehead and etching her mouth, her eyes. Her memorable eyes hotbeds of fear and frustration. New, a visible contempt for him. No question she figured he might be the bastard who'd abducted Tracy after gunning down the two girlfriends.

Glen said, "In due course, Maggie, trust me on that. He'll be telling us all there is to tell, won't you, mister?"

"I'm your encyclopedia," Sothern said. "Your *Book of Knowledge.*" He winked at Maggie and wondered, "I don't suppose you could spare a hankie, a dish cloth, something for this nose?"

The cop must have seen the wink. "No way to treat a lady," he said, and crashed the Beretta on Sothern's shoulder. The blow sent a lightning bolt coursing across his back, with a detour up his neck to an explosion in his head that suggested what Mount Vesuvius was like whenever it blew its cool, and let him write off as sissy stuff the agony derived from a previous preoccupation with his doorstop of a foot swelling to balloon proportions. "If you missed it, butt brain, I said for you to turn around, nice and slow-like."

"Butt brain, for sure," Sothern said. "I aim to please." He eased around. Measured the distance between them and lunged for the cop, who recognized the move but couldn't back off fast enough to avoid collision. The crack this time was Sothern's head connecting with the cop's nose. The blood this time was the cop's blood. The sound after that was the cop's Beretta sideswiping Sothern on the shoulder, which Sothern had managed to put in the way of a blow meant for his temple.

Sothern lashed out with a leg, aiming for the cop's balls, but the cop saw it coming and swung around, so the only damage was to his thigh and insignificant. The cop grunted, wheeled around, and pounded Sothern's bad foot with his boot heel. The pain immobilized Sothern long enough for the cop to move into a shooter's stance and take two-handed aim at his chest.

Maggie jumped in front of Sothern, ran her arms around him like she was Joan of Arc and he was the stake, demanding, "You can kill the son of a bitch, Glen, but not until I hear about Tracy."

The cop rolled his eyes Heavenward, one of those *For Christ's sake* expressions. He said, "For Christ's sake, Maggie, back away."

Sothern said, "Don't listen to him, Maggie. He looks crazy enough to do it."

Sothern forced open his eyes.

Eased himself up on his elbows.

Definitely not the Beverly Hills Hotel or even a Hilton.

Had to be a jail cell.

The wall of bars, the bars on the window, those were the clues.

Also, the bunk bed chain-riveted to the brick wall, bedsprings that creaked to his every move on a sagging mattress two inches thick.

Also, the smell, nothing like room deodorant or detergent, more like—

Something from the geezer sitting on the crapper in the corner, his head buried inside an old issue of *Unforgettable,* a magazine specializing in recycled celebrities so old they were new again. Sothern had been reduced to writing for it on occasion, to feed an outstanding balance on his Bar None tab, currently somewhere north of the National Debt.

The geezer was dressed in a brown buckskin outfit full of dangling decorative strips, the jacket open, revealing a shirt flap secured by ivory buttons that also reminded Sothern of Buffalo Bill. So did the geezer: Early seventies. His face and hands as dark and cracked as cured leather, contrasting sharply with an unruly snow white mustache that drooped to his sagging jaw line. A slightly lopsided salt-and-pepper goatee. Sideburns thicker than his thinning hair topside, pulled back from his prominent brow into a ponytail draped over a shoulder.

The geezer looked up from the magazine and caught him staring.

"What's it? Like yours don't stink?" he said. "Or are you one of them perverts on top of everything else you're in here for, that it? If so, don't figure to jump my bones, get on top of me, you know what's good for you, understand?"

Sothern answered him with a nod. His body ached liked hell. He studied the wrap job somebody had done on his swollen foot, touched his nose, and found it also bandaged. Smoothed out both sides of the bandage from the bridge down and got the sense that the bone had been reset.

Wondered when all this had happened.

The last he remembered was—

—Maggie Collins holding her ground, protecting him from Glen the cop.

—Glen the cop grunting his frustration. Moving on him. Gentling Maggie Collins aside and bringing down the Beretta on his head, like he was trying to crack a coconut.

—An explosion of light fading into black and the sensation he was diving down a bottomless pit.

—The sound of a siren, and—

The geezer said, "Your head twitching up and down like that? You mean yours don't stink or you're a pervert? Which is it?"

"I got farts worse than anything you're putting out," Sothern said, to shut him up.

The old geezer laughed liked he'd never have another chance. "There's nothing to beat a sense of humor," he said. After a few minutes, he flushed, hoisted his trousers, and headed over, his hand stretched for a shake. "Name's Mount, Vernon Mount."

Sothern took his hand without thinking, earning a two-note cackle of appreciation from Vernon Mount.

"I like you, Mr. Sothern. Jack, isn't it? I like you, that handshake alone. A man who goes straight for cordiality, you are, where others usually rail on about me not washing my mitts first after finishing a dump. Like sanitation is some *Get*

Out of Jail Free card."

He crossed over to the sink bowl, gave his hands a good scrubbing, and wiped them dry on his backside.

"Mr. Mount—"

"Vernon."

"Vernon, you have any idea how I got here?"

"Every idea in the world, Jack. . . . You up for a cup? I know you're a booze hound, but caffeine's the best I can do for the duration. Don't go 'way." Vernon Mount crossed the cell, pushed open the door, and stepped out to the corridor. He dug out a key chain from a trouser pocket, found the one he wanted, and turned it in the lock. "*Don't go 'way,* my little joke there. They don't come much littler than that. Saving the good ones until I get to know you better." Sothern gave him an incredulous look. "Probably not anything you're thinking, Jack. Actually, truth be known, I'm the chief of police here in this little corner of the world, population seven thousand and some, one of California's best-kept secrets and hoping to let it stay that way."

Sothern called after him, "Vernon, I have questions for you."

"Of course, you do, Jack. I'd be disappointed otherwise."

Settled again in the cell a few minutes later, Vernon Mount said, "I watered your coffee with a little hair of the dog. I hate to bark alone, so to speak, especially so early in the morning." Sothern turned a sip into a swallow before checking his wrist. "Unless you're checking for skin cancer, Jack, we got your watch. Your wallet. Your pocket change. Your belt. Your shoelaces. You name it. Nothing that might let you do damage to yourself, though, from the looks of it, my detective did a pretty good job of it, short of taking your breath away." He pulled his own watch to within a couple inches of wide-set eyes as blue as a Bunsen burner flame. "Nearing on six-thirty in the A.M., Jack. Too early to get the plumber over here to fix the department john, why you caught me with my britches down, so to speak."

Whatever Mount had laced his coffee with hit Sothern's stomach almost as hard as the blow from Glen, the detective who'd clocked him, but with a far more satisfactory result. "It's your detective should be in the cage, Chief. My foot. My nose. My head feels like the Liberty Bell before it cracked. His handiwork."

"Doc Ayers said no serious damage to your foot that time and plenty of soaking in warm water won't fix up. Your beak, at most a hairline fracture, something for Super Glue. Glen didn't get off so easy. Wait'll you see what you did to his beak yesterday."

"His fault. Your detective brought on the rough stuff. I want to file charges against him. Assault without provocation."

"What you should be worrying over instead is the sack of shit Glen's dumped onto your lap, my friend. Attempted home invasion, and that foot of yours—done by the lady of the house, not by Glen. Resisting arrest. Aggravated assault on an officer of the law. Drunk and disorderly. Extreme DUI—"

"Jesus! DUI? I was on the front porch of a private residence, for Christ's sake."

"Your car was parked out front. It didn't get there on its own. An opened bottle of hooch inside the vehicle, in violation of state code, and I should also mention possession of an illegal substance. A baggie stuffed under the driver's seat with enough crack cocaine to send you up the river without a paddle, Jack."

"Planted."

"You telling me you don't use?" His squint challenged Sothern.

Sothern knew *Not lately* wasn't going to cut it as an answer.

He took a mouthful of comfort from his coffee cup. "Illegal search, Chief."

"*Probable cause,* how our judge'll hear it, Jack. Besides, that's what they all say, them what come across Glen Traylor the wrong way. You think you got an exclusive on his temper?" Mount's hoot hit the ceiling. "He's especially like that with anyone looks cross-eyed at him or his woman."

"Margaret Collins. His woman? What would she see in a jerk like that? He's not much in the looks department, and that's just for openers. Someone like that belongs in a bull ring chasing after the red cape."

"No accounting for taste. Hear tell from my boys called to assist at the scene, bring you in, it was only Maggie kept him from inflicting more damage on you. Damn Glen, can't break him of all them bad habits he picked up and improved on during his years yanking chains in the discount districts of Los Angeles, like he was auditioning to play Dirty Harry Junior. You know the movies I mean? Clint Eastwood. Wouldn't never want to be Dirty Clint's partner. They never make it to the end of the picture show."

"How'd this Traylor wind up with you?"

"Luck?" The police chief sniffed at his cup and took a swallow, nodded approval. "Not far from the truth, you have to know. In Glen's case, paying back a favor to his late father. Bill and me, we did our twenty on the LAPD, through the Academy together and partners some of those years. He saved my life, but down the line I rounded a corner too late to save his.

"Glen followed in Bill's footsteps, but his pa's shoes were always going to be too big for him. He finally crossed the line once too often and was invited to resign from the force. A little over two years ago. He'd come here needing a shoulder to wail on about the time I lost a man, so I pinned a badge on him and he's been here ever since." A shrug. "For better or for worse." A sip from his cup. Another sip. "Now, Jack, maybe it's your turn to show and tell, you hope to get sprung from here anytime between now and a trial date? Maybe starting with what it is

61

poor Maggie Collins is saying you know about her missing daughter? You could tell her what she should hear to get Tracy back alive?"

The chief had been holding up a wall. He crossed to the wall opposite Sothern and settled down on the bunk with his arms at ease on his shelf of a belly, his coffee cup within striking distance of his mouth, which he'd worked into an expectant smile.

"I had nothing to do with those murders or Tracy Collins' abduction, Vernon."

"Wasn't my question, Jack."

Sothern rose and took Mount's old spot at the wall. "I'm a journalist. The story caught my interest. I think I can make a buck with it, so I drove down from L.A. I said what I said to Mrs. Collins hoping she'd open up to me. That's it. I lied. Plain and simple. Over and out." Thinking, *That's enough. All he has to know. My salvation none of his business.*

"Lied." A guffaw. "That's proof you're a journalist, alright, but there's more than I'm hearing. You also told Maggie you were seeing her again. *Again,* Jack, after a long time."

"Gilding the lily."

"I already know better'n that."

"Better than what?"

"This is a small town, but I ain't small *time,* my friend. While you were napping, I made some calls to buddies still hanging in at LAPD. You're no stranger to their computer system." Sothern held up his hands in surrender. "Now that we've settled that, what else is there I might want to know that might even convince me to drop all those pending charges and let you walk out of here today?"

"You'd do that?"

"Convince me."

"It's a long story."

The chief of police spooned the coffee cup with his finger and said, "World enough and time, Jack. World enough and time."

CHAPTER 7

Roxy was in the office she shared with Maggie, at the partners' desk preparing the biweekly payroll, when she heard Maggie pulling into her reserved parking space by the private side entrance to The Garden of Eden. She was up and to the door before Maggie finished keying in the security code that freed the triple Grosvenor safety locks.

Maggie moved inside, then froze, as if uncertain of her surroundings.

Roxy stepped behind her, wrapped her arms around Maggie, and gently wondered at her ear, "Sweetie Pie, you certain you should be here, not home? Roxy's got everything under control and—"

Maggie shook her head. "By myself there, I would go crazy. Put on call forwarding to my cell phone, just in case . . . you know."

"Sure, honey. A call could come any minute . . . I thought Glen was going to be with you, keep you company."

"Until he got this hurry-up emergency call, so he had to take off. He didn't want to, but I told him to go on. My cell rings, maybe it'll be Tracy who's calling? Saying she's safe and come get her? It's happened before, so it could happen now, don't you think so, Rox?"

"Everybody here's been praying for something like that to happen."

Maggie freed herself, turned, and gave her a suspicious look.

"Everybody? You really mean *everybody?*" Roxy finally shook her head and padded back to the partners' desk. "Phyllis and Eleanor. You're telling me they showed up?"

"They showed up, Sweetie Pie. Swallowing their emotions and, like you, paying me no heed. Saying the work is helping take the mind off their pain. Saying they needed all the money they could get now, to help pay for Amy's and Betsy's funerals."

"They say how much?" Roxy told her the amount. "Write them out checks for that much and add another five hundred apiece on top. Don't say it's from me. Say it's on your own hook."

"You should let them know. Let me tell them. Why make it a secret?"

"They'd only think I was trying to buy off their grief, trying to make them not hate me because my daughter is alive and theirs aren't. Give them the checks and tell them to go home. Tell them however long they need away, they'll be paid." Maggie pulled the cell phone from her jeans and centered it on her side of the desk. Sank into her chair and stared into space. "Who can take their shifts?"

Roxy thought about it and volunteered several names.

"Wanda Shoemaker? Wasn't she getting ready to retire and devote her life to the PTA and adding on some church Sunday School classes for the intermediate and junior grades?"

"Realized how much she'd miss her home away from home. Charles is on the road again, five months this time, so she'd have the hours. Besides, she's always been the kind of person you can count on in an emergency."

"Emergency." Maggie laced a grim smile to the word. "Elena Fernandez? Who I think she is?"

"The illegal who showed up on our doorstep last week, recommended by Aurora. Young and eager. Folds a mean bedsheet and earning rave reviews so far during her probation period."

"The one who said she needs to save up to pay off the ghosts and get her husband to our side of the border?"

"That's Elena, sweet as honey."

"Fine, then. Wanda and Elena. If it isn't going to work with them, you choose."

"Handled. Now will you go home?"

"I want the phone to ring, Rox. I want it to be Tracy. Or hear whatever it costs to bring Tracy back home. What's worse? Knowing that your daughter is dead or having to wait and be afraid of the other answer or no answer at all? You know what *closure* is, Rox? It's a word you get from people who don't understand the truth, that there is no such thing as closure. Ever. The end is only the beginning of something else that could be even worse."

Maggie talked down to her that way sometimes, but that was Maggie's way. Paying no attention was Roxy's way. Did she know what closure was? She could teach Maggie a thing or two about closure, she ever wanted to engage her in another one of those lose–lose philosophical arguments she had sworn off, given—laughing to herself—closure to a long time ago, when she was hurting as much as Maggie was hurting now.

Inwardly, she wasn't holding out hope for Tracy's safe return. A person who would shoot and kill two innocent teenagers in cold blood was hardly the type to release someone who could identify him, put him behind bars, into a courtroom, turn closure into a dead end for him.

The message beeper sounded on Roxy's computer, shutting down whatever else Maggie intended to say. Gerry Cotton was calling from the reception desk, reporting that Chief Mount and somebody with him, a Mr. Jack Sothern, were here, wonder-

66

ing if Maggie was around and could she spare them some time.

Talk about closure.

Something *open* was going on between Maggie and this Jack Sothern.

Roxy saw it the instant he limped into the office steps ahead of Vernon Mount, set his eyes on Maggie, kept them there crossing to a guest chair, almost stumbling over the bearskin rug that was rumored to date back to a trade-out for services between Pilar Eden and General Phineas T. Banning himself. His look appeared to be bred of awareness and curiosity, Maggie's stare of fear and suspicion.

Vernon settled into the chair alongside Sothern, who acknowledged Roxy with a smile when the chief introduced her. It was a nice smile, winking, unforced, on a haggard, handsome face not helped any by the bandage on his nose. He was the youngest person in the room, late thirties, she figured. Not quite six feet. Lots of black hair that could use a trim. Hooded brown eyes that could be sexy if they weren't so clouded by—guessing here—a thousand too many nights on the town and far too many drugs of choice. His suit showed as much wear and tear as the rest of him, but he was still straight out of the Hunk catalog.

"Nice making your acquaintance, Roxy," he said, his voice effortlessly sexy. The way his Adam's apple bobbed, a turn-on for her once upon a time. "The chief had a load of good things to say about you on our walk over." He drilled her with his eyes and turned back to Maggie: "Glad to see you again, Mrs. Collins."

Maggie was on her feet. She inched away from the partners' desk, arms locked across her body like she was protecting herself from imminent danger. "What's he doing here, Vernon? He's supposed to be in jail. He's—"

"—got an interesting story to share," Vernon said, interrupting her. "It's one I think you should hear, Maggie."

"No. What I want to hear is what he knows about Tracy."

Vernon said, "Part of the story, Maggie." He crossed his legs and moved his white ten-gallon hat to his lap, like he was using it to hide a giant woody, and winked at Roxy. "Sit down until you don't like what he's telling, if that's your mindset."

Maggie gave Jack Sothern a hard look and seemed about to settle back at the desk when some thought flashed across her face and sent her fleeing the office, Roxy thinking: *Maybe fear she's about to hear something about her daughter she doesn't want to hear, but needs to know.*

"She'll be back," Roxy said, indicating the cell phone on Maggie's half of the desk, at the same time resisting the urge to chase after her.

They filled the next several minutes with small talk, quit when Maggie stormed back through the door. She moved behind her desk, swept up the cell phone, and deposited it in a pocket. For a moment she seemed intent on taking off again.

Roxy said, "It can't hurt to listen, Sweetie Pie."

"How do you know?" Maggie said, but she sat down. Her elbows resting on the mahogany surface of the desk. Fingers laced. Chewing at a thumbnail.

Jack Sothern glanced over at Roxy.

Maggie recognized the reason.

"There's absolutely nothing you can tell me that Rox can't hear," she said.

Sothern tipped his head and found a comfortable position. "This goes back a number of years, Mrs. Collins, to East Berlin. It was the year before the Berlin Wall came tumbling down. At a café called Café Munchausen, where I'd gone to meet with a big star over there in Commie Land named Dan Boone."

"This here's the good part coming up," Vernon Mount said.

Sothern described the café in detail and how he was ordering a lager when he was joined unexpectedly at the table by a young woman he had never seen before, who ordered one for herself, planted a kiss on his brow, and clasped his hands in hers like the old friends they had never been.

Maggie massaged her fingers with her thumbs, like she was trying to expunge her prints.

"The natural scent she threw off was intoxicating as a rose garden in full bloom," Sothern said, and detailed how they were shortly joined by Boone, who turned out to be the woman's husband. "He also turned out to be the superstar and an American," he said. "Now, he wanted to go back home. He wanted my help in a dangerous plan to get his pregnant wife, Meg, back here in the states first." He quit the story long enough to be certain he had Maggie's complete attention. "I left East Berlin having seen Meg only that one time. Having seen you only that one time, Mrs. Collins. . . . You're Meg Boone, and, of course, that makes Tracy Collins Dan Boone's daughter." Maggie glowered at him. "Why I came hurrying down here to Eden Highlands, Meg. Why I said what I did to you when I came knocking at your door. Why I think I may be able to help find Tracy for you."

"Like you helped the last time?" she said.

Maggie pushed up and came around the desk. Her face was beet red, her body bursting with fury. She caught his face with her hand in two directions and escaped out the private side entrance.

Roxy raced after Maggie, calling her name, half-hearing Sothern say, "She sure has that move down pat," Vernon responding, "Jack, my friend, appears there's a lot of telling by you that remains to be told to me." Jack Sothern answering, "Bottom line, Vernon? I don't think Tracy is dead. Not yet, anyway."

CHAPTER 8

He tapped the attention bell at the reception desk, then again when it didn't get a rise from Gerry Cotton, whose attention was trapped by whatever had his fingers dancing on the computer keyboard. He was more successful on the third try. Cotton looked up, wondering, "Help you, sir? If it's registration you're after, that's just over there to your right, but we're full up right now."

Cotton was treating him like a stranger.

"Rooms top to bottom occupied by sightseers turned on and turning out by the terrible tragedy what's befallen Mrs. Collins, our owner, and two of our very best staff people, a story what you probably seen on the news?" Cotton said. "You one of them, too, maybe, or maybe one of them damn bloodsucking news people trading on other folks' sorrows?"

"What's with the *sir* business, Gerry?"

Gerry shifted his eyes away from the computer. "Hey! Sorry. Didn't recognize you there. Something different about you this time." He checked him over like he was studying for a pop quiz. Snapped his fingers. "That's it, you've grown a mustache since you first came by to check out the lodging here at the finest lodging establishment Eden Highlands has to offer."

"In two days' time? I don't think so, Gerry."

Cotton's faced knotted in uncertainty. He struggled to make a connection through eyes reduced to slits. Finally, his skimpy voice similarly tarred by failure, he said, "Guess you'll have to tell me."

"I shaved off my beard, Gerry." Cotton gave him an *Of course* reaction. "One of those spur of the moment decisions."

"Same as my latest date dump. The one I told you about the first time you dropped in, before we got hit by this terrible awful tragedy, and you should've taken a room, while we still had?"

"Shame I didn't fancy what was available. MsMatch, you said."

"Her, yeah, who I thought was the one for sure when we met over on the EvolDotCom Internet date and mate service. The reason I rid myself of LoveBumps and SmilingEyes. Big mistake doing that. Not my only goofs and not my last."

Cotton was in his mid-thirties, tall and rangy, stoop-shouldered and bow-legged, who looked and dressed like he belonged out on the open range herding cattle. He had sharp features on a lean, sculpted face that didn't bear a second notice, his best feature a dime-sized mole on the left side of his chin, but he viewed himself like every woman's secret desire.

On his first scouting mission here, he had discovered Cotton loved sharing his private life with anyone who'd listen. Off and on, he was taking continuation classes on the Internet, looking forward to completing twelfth grade and receiving a high school diploma, but he spent more time and a monthly thirty-dollar membership fee at EvolDotCom.

Cotton had a certain type of relationship in mind for himself. "They got to be in my age range or younger or older, it's not important, but I need them to be someplace near, like Beverly Hills or over to Newport Beach, Balboa, where it takes *dinero* to be," he had explained. "I need them to have something in common with me, me with them, so it's more than pretty faces and a bank balance the size of a lottery winner's that can spring me out of here and let me get back to earning my diploma. Look, see this one? What I have in mind for me. Read her rundown and see for yourself we're close to being the perfect match."

Her screen name was "SoleMate." She was a reasonably attractive brunette lying about her age, claiming to be fifty, but another ten years not entirely airbrushed from the half dozen portrait photos included with her profile.

She described herself as an ex-dancer "in great shape," recently widowed by a shoe manufacturer and now spending lonely nights at her Malibu Colony home. "I'm so sick and tired of the flakes and clueless dudes I have been meeting and am in search of someone hip who will be my best friend and lover for who I am, not for my inheritance," she wrote.

She described him as "a gentleman who is educated, literate, sophisticated, and hip to all the world has to offer, but who's as tired as I am of the snobbery and hypocrisy of his class. A muscular George Clooney type with marvelous blue eyes will do me fine, full lips and beautiful hands and feet, and you are financially well-endowed to steal me away to Paris or Rome or some tropical paradise."

Cotton said, "I'm setting this one up for sure, don't you think so? Like two peas in a pod we are."

He nodded agreement then, cultivating a friendship, and now, on this visit, he spurred their conversation by wondering, "What happened with you and MsMatch, Gerry? You were so high on her."

"Like with SoleMate before her, remember? MsMatch lied to me, man."

"About her age."

"That, also. Everything. She was broke as a clock chiming thirteen, thinking I was her free ride to the bank."

"What gave her that idea?"

"Something I must-a wrote," he said, his eyes checking the floor. "Besides, better fish in the sea. I'm sorting them out now.

Wanna have a look?"

"Short on time today, Gerry. Only dropped in to say hello and check again if my kind of room has come available."

"I've piggy-backed you up high on the wait list, since you don't mind staying elsewhere until whenever."

"Whenever."

Turning to leave after a few more minutes of inconsequential chatter, he caught a glimpse of Vernon Mount, Eden Highlands' police chief, heading out with somebody, the two of them too locked in an animated, mumbling conversation to notice him.

"See that?" Cotton said. "Our chief and the other fella? They been in a meeting with Mrs. Collins and Miss Colbraith, Roxy, our g.m. who really runs the show, for going on an hour. I'm betting dollars to donuts it's to do with them poor kids of Phyllis and Eleanor that got themselves murdered."

"The other fella? One of your chief's detectives?"

"Stranger to me. Name of South, Sothern, something like that. Imagine, Phyllis and Eleanor still working full shifts. Human nature. Sometimes I just don't get it. Misery loves company, you suppose that's it?"

He suppressed a smile. "Enough misery everywhere in the world to keep everyone from ever being lonely, Gerry."

When he returned from The Garden of Eden, he looked in on Tracy before he showered.

She had not moved since he left, not that the drugs gave her a choice.

As long as he remembered not to overwork the dosage, she'd pose no threat to him or to her own safety, awake or asleep.

The last thing in the world he needed was Tracy getting damaged before he was through needing her.

Then—

Forget about *Then.*

This was still *Now*.

In the bathroom, he kicked off his shoes, left his clothing in a pile on the floor, and tested the spray for temperature before climbing into the tub and drawing the curtain. The way he liked it, too hot for most. So hot, it felt like needles digging deep into his skin.

He doused himself with liquid soap, raised a thick, creamy lather, began scrubbing with the wire brush meant for filthy tile and linoleum.

By the time he was finished, he'd have rubbed away enough skin to draw trails of blood and get to feeling better about himself.

He always supposed there was some reason this had become his way, but he never gave it much thought or worried over it.

Purification, probably.

Doing for his body what he knew he was past accomplishing for his soul. His soul would be up to a greater power than he possessed.

God?

If he believed in God, that would be a satisfactory answer. He believed in himself, but he could only play God when it came to doing the work others were incapable of, like murdering Tracy Collins' two friends.

Did they have to die?

Of course not.

If they hadn't gone to Dino's Pizzeria with her, one or both could still be alive, at home crying their eyes out over their kidnapped friend, fearing for her safety, praying for her safe return; taking comfort from their whore mothers.

If they hadn't gone to Dino's Pizzeria with Tracy, he would have dropped the kid behind the counter, which would have been a shame. There was something about the kid he'd come to like, maybe the way he treated him, like an ordinary person who had a thing for pizza. He would have dropped the pizza chef, only because he was there, nothing to do with the quality of his work.

One more corpse in his graveyard of memory, what did it matter?

It didn't.

All he needed was a single body to make the point.

That was Betsy Wheatcroft.

The second body became an exclamation point he didn't need on the message he was putting out there, loud enough to guarantee shock, horror and attention and keep the plan in motion.

That was Amy Spencer.

All the way to the parking lot, he had thought about turning Amy loose once he had Tracy in the van. It was one of those unexplainable twinges he got once in a blue moon, his nerve endings connecting and jump-starting little sparklers of compassion.

They fizzled out fast, though.

Who was he kidding?

Sympathy was for simps, as in simpletons.

Compassion was a luxury he couldn't afford.

He should have bummed the counterman and the pizza chef as well.

Four for four, and Tracy Collins for the taking.

All this thinking—

It had rekindled a taste for pizza.

Maybe mushrooms and sausage, like the girls had been about to order. Double up on the cheese. Yes, that's what he needed. A pizza. He toweled off and strolled out of the bathroom after a cigarette. A large pizza. Thick crust. Mushrooms. Sausage. And don't be stingy with the cheese.

CHAPTER 9

Tracy Collins snapped open her eyes.

Her lids wouldn't cooperate.

They fell, sending her back into total darkness from the dim light that had briefly shown her she had no idea where she was. Her head ached and her body hurt. An itch on her nose was in desperate need of scratching, but she could not get her arm, her hand, to cooperate.

She wanted to call out to somebody, anybody, tell them her nose was itching and it needed to be scratched, only she couldn't move her mouth past mumbles and fuzzy words.

She willed her way out of the fogbank clouding her memory.

And what she remembered made her want to scream out in pain and in fear and for her mommy or for someone, anyone, who could come and find her and rescue her and take her home, or out of this nightmare, if that's all that it was.

A nightmare.

A bad dream.

Yes, what it was.

Any second now, she'd awaken to the morning light slashing through her bedroom window. School. Boy talk with Amy and Betsy, especially about the new, cute transfer in from Oceanside High, who couldn't take his eyes off her in homeroom. Maybe find a way to invite him to join them later for pizza at Dino's. That would be Betsy's job. Betsy was so good at that.

Yummy.

Tracy was already smelling the pizza.

Mushrooms and sausage.

No anchovies, the topping Amy was always begging for.

None of the pepperoni she liked best, although the sausage was almost as good.

She needed to pee, but the nightmare still had her trapped in her bed.

Her panties felt all of a sudden wet.

She couldn't believe what had just happened.

She didn't remember the last time she'd wet her bed.

She felt her face flushing with embarrassment.

She began sobbing.

A voice said, "Give me a minute, I'll clean you off, dear."

A man, a voice she didn't know, then thought she recognized.

She remembered, and knew the nightmare was no nightmare.

She wanted to scream out, but she couldn't.

Or open her eyes.

Or think anymore.

So she stopped trying.

CHAPTER 10

Glen Traylor was frothing at the mouth, spittle running down both corners; the detective too caught up in anger to bother with anything but the rabid outrage he was directing at his boss. "That pond scum busts my nose and you let him go, just like that, Vernon. Take him on over to The Garden of Eden. I can't believe you did that."

"Believe it, Glen," Vernon said. He was behind his desk, chair tilted back, his feet propped up, working a polishing cloth over his new treasure, an M9 Beretta he'd found on eBay and stolen on the cheap, getting in his winning bid less than thirty seconds before the bidding closed. It was your basic 92F, this version the Army's standard firearm. Explaining this to Glen and how the M9 was as good or better than Glen's Beretta, and certainly better than Vernon's stock-in-trade .45 pistol and .38 automatic.

"Don't you go changing the subject on me, Vernon." The detective rattled off the charges hanging on Jack Sothern's booking sheet. "You could've at least run him past the judge, paint bail on him, and let the asshole rot up to a trial if he wasn't able to make it."

"Yes, I could've," the chief of police said, as agreeable as Glen was argumentative. "You aware this beauty has safety features that keep it from accidentally discharging? Fires in double- or single-action mode? Uses a fifteen-round magazine, but it can fire without a magazine load?"

"Vernon, you're not listening."

"Place the thumb safety on the 'on' position, like this, and you can uncock the hammer without activating the trigger. . . . I listened real good, Glen, only I didn't hear you say anything to make it worth having Jack warming his heinie in a cell and running up a department budget that can't afford to saddle a flea when he can be out doing us some good."

Glen threw a *God help me* look to the ceiling, slumped into the visitors chair alongside Vernon's desk. He hated it when Vernon toyed with him this way. Growing up and, later, in his first years on the LAPD, his father was always using the same trick on him. He hated it. One of the reasons that led him to hating his father. "Maybe you need to tell me something that let's me understand otherwise."

Vernon blew on the M9's slick black barrel and polished it with his handkerchief. Satisfied, he offered the handkerchief to Glen, who used it to wipe his mouth and chin dry.

"For one, Glen—last I noticed, I was in charge here and didn't need to tell you a damn thing I didn't want to tell you. For another, Jack Sothern is not about to head anywhere outside Eden Highlands, so we got him anytime you find a better reason to hold him, besides your nose being out of joint. For another, Jack's been feeding me ideas that have me wondering if he's got a better sightline on why Amy Spencer and Betsy Wheatcroft were murdered and Tracy, your lady friend's daughter, only abducted than anything I'd been thinking or you were saying."

"Were you planning to share with me, Vernon?"

"Right after you calm down a hundred percent or show me proof your rabies shot is up to date." He pulled open an upper desk drawer and deposited the M9, trading it for an almost empty pint of Jim Beam. He took a healthy swig and offered the pint to Glen, who waved it off. He checked over his shoulder toward the cell corridor, calling, "Jack, last call before the next call for some hair of the hound, you got the thirst."

Glen did a double-take and swung around for a look. "Sothern?" Thinking: *Damn Vernon, anyway, for not having the courtesy, the decency, to tell me Sothern's still in the jailhouse.*

After a minute, Sothern popped into view. He gestured *Hold on* and disappeared back into the corridor. A toilet flushed. Sothern returned, explaining, "Your turn to catch me with *my* pants down, Vernon."

"Plumbers, uppity breed, about as reliable as a lawyer's word of honor. You happen to be tuned in on my conversation with Glen here?"

"Catching fifteen winks. I woke up around the time he was calling me an asshole. Time out for a dump." He took the pint from the chief and drained what remained, toweled his lips with his fingers. Patted his stomach and showed contentment.

Glen said, "You are an asshole, Sothern. In my mind, there's already plenty enough evidence to convict you."

"In your mind?" Sothern said. "That pretty much puts the odds in my favor in front of any judge and jury in the land."

Glen stamped his palms on the desk, for leverage out of the chair, but Vernon knew the move and cautioned him to stay put.

Sothern, recognizing what Glen had in mind, had balled his fists and was standing his ground.

Vernon used his fist to pound attention. "Save it for the playground." He pointed Sothern to the other visitors chair. "Settle down and settle in, Jack. If you're gonna be one of my detectives, start behaving like one. Don't be behaving like this ornery critter, who's got the way of a rhino in his blood, like his old man before him."

Glen scattered his amazement between Sothern and Vernon, settling on the chief. "One of your detectives? Jesus F. Christ. What the hell is that all about, Vernon?"

"You're the other one, the senior man, so stop rattling the

cage, Glen. Besides, it's only temporary. Easier for Jack to make a contribution, I give him some official status."

"I get to wear a badge," Sothern said. "Haven't done that since growing up I was one of Sunset Beaudry's Junior Range Ropers. Came inside my box of breakfast cereal."

"The Range Roper himself—a big fan myself," Vernon said.

Not to be outdone, Glen said, "Sunset Beaudry. He was the Law and Order North of the Border on television."

"Movies first," Vernon said. "See, boys, you already got something in common. I think you'll make a fine team of detectives, like that Jerry Orbach fellow was with the other ones on those *Law and Order*s."

"What kind of possible contribution from this alky, Vernon, besides drinking up your whiskey?"

"Jack holds it better'n you hold your tongue. . . . He'll be giving us an outsider's fresh perspective."

Glen wasn't going to let that pass without a challenge. "And we need that, a fresh perspective, because—?"

"Because he got me thinking your lady friend, Maggie, is into this a lot more than being a mama fearing for a loved one and aching something fierce right now. Not the kind of perspective I even expect you to have under the circumstances, Glen. It's okay to go on and tell him now that he's got a fix on the rules, Jack. You listen up real good and careful, Glen. Call it another learning experience."

Glen turned his thoughts into words after Sothern caught him smirking when he reached the part about Maggie slapping him, then running away with Roxy Colbraith on her tail. He said, "I'd also be ashamed, like her, somebody comes along and reminds me I was once married and had a daughter by a Commie turncoat shit-heel suddenly claiming he was a true-blue American all along."

Sothern said, "You know any of that before now, *partner?*" Taking pleasure in mocking him about their new relationship.

"So what?" Glen said, dismissing the question. "What I'd like to know is why she ran off blaming you for the shit-heel's death, although there's nothing I'd put past you, *partner.*" No way anyone could miss the sarcasm oozing from his twist on the word. "Did you?"

"Kill him? No. Responsible for Dan Boone's death—?"

Glen watched Sothern's mood go dark, his face sinking into gloom and looking for somewhere to escape scrutiny and judgment. He almost felt sorry for the asshole. Almost. The notion passed quickly.

Vernon said, "Tell him the rest, Jack."

Sothern filled his lungs, pushed out the used air, and began, reluctantly: "So, here's this American citizen who has become the biggest star the Communists have. Not only East Berlin. Everywhere in the Red Bloc. China. Cuba. Who gets a hero's welcome whenever he visits the Kremlin. Red Square filling up the day the regime's despots steered him onto a balcony to award Dan Boone the Order of Lenin, hundreds of thousands of fans who adore him from his movies and recordings and concert appearances applauding, screaming their affection, chanting his name. Dan Boone. Dan Boone. Dan Boone . . ."

The night they met at Café Munchausen, using a casual stroll in the dying light of early evening to mask their conversation from the ever-present danger of prying eyes and ears, Boone explained why he was anxious to get his pregnant wife, then himself, safely home to the States.

He asked Sothern to help, the pleading in his voice close to outright begging.

Once Sothern agreed, Boone described what had to be done.

He said, "I want you to write a story about Dan Boone believing more than ever in the eventual victory of Communism over democracy and how, in your exclusive interview, the Turncoat Rebel boasted how he returns the adoration and love of his fellow comrades without reservation or compromise."

"Hold on, Dan. You don't expect the United States to welcome you back with open arms after that kind of story gets printed, do you?"

"I expect Erich Mielke and his cutthroats to buy into the propaganda and back off their surveillance of Meg and me, maybe even lift the travel sanctions. I only need a little window of opportunity to spring her from here, get her past the Wall. I'll worry about me afterward. Come what may, I want Meg safely out of here and I want our child born in the country I never should have abandoned."

"What if the secret police don't fall for it?"

"Make the story you write ring true enough and they will, Jack. Can you do that? Write it so strongly? So powerfully they'll have no choice but to recognize it as the truth. Shane Vallery believes you can, or she'd never have pushed for you, telling me over and over, 'Danny, you ever believe me about anything, believe what I say about my friend Jack Sothern.' "

"Shane said that?"

Dan Boone raised his hand like he was taking an oath. "She said that and more. So what do you say, Jack? We still on?"

Glen said, "I hate admitting it, Sothern, but, Maggie being here, Tracy growing up here, you obviously earned yourself a Boy Scout merit badge."

"Except, they're not here because of me, detective. Vernon, I could use a little more hair of the dog."

The chief shook his head. "Not any near enough or big enough to help you over this mountain, Jack."

Sothern reached over and picked up a stray paper clip from

Vernon Mount's desk. He worked it like he was studying it before pulling it open, turning it into a slightly bent toothpick. When he couldn't get it straighter, he dropped it in the trash basket. The pinging noise the metal made hitting bottom encouraged him to go after another paper clip and repeat the process, all the while explaining, "What I did was sell him out. When I got back to L.A., I pitched the story Dan Boone wanted to every magazine and news agency, the TV programs like *60 Minutes* and *20/20*. The answer was always the same. *There's nothing new in what you're telling us, Sothern. It's a rehash of ancient history, Sothern. That Commie turncoat is begging for publicity and playing you for a sap, Sothern . . .*

"I was dying with a lie made on a promise, when I had the real story that everyone would want, be willing to pay big bucks for, put a fire under my career. It ate me alive for weeks that turned into months, in the meanwhile getting mail from Dan Boone that always came second or third hand from outside East Berlin. France. England. The Netherlands. A time or two from somewhere in the States. Vermont. Chicago. No return address. Typed, except for his signature. Single-spaced. Thin margins. Never a return address."

Sothern closed his eyes and recited from memory:

"Dear Jack, I hope that you are well and in good spirits when this letter arrives in your hands. As Meg grows bigger with child, I remain hopeful that you will find a source for printing our story in a process that I believe is more difficult than I ever presumed. I have not lost confidence or faith in you or in your ability in due course to overcome the obstacles or odds necessary to achieve our goals. Our future rests in your capable hands. Take care of yourself. Bye for now. An embrace. Dan Boone."

Sothern struggled to find a comfortable position in the chair. Failing, he rose and crossed to the jailhouse wall full of frames and citations. He studied and straightened one after the next.

"He always talked about *our* story. *Our* goals. *Our* future. Generalities, not any specifics that might come back and haunt him if one of his letters was intercepted by the Stasi, the GDR's equivalent of Russia's KGB.

"At the same time, my so-called career was idling in neutral, stranded somewhere in limbo, while others were lucking out and moving up. Nothing they found to write about could hold a candle to the real story about Dan Boone. It got me crazy and it got me drunk more than once. Finally, one night, dragging home from Phillip 'n' Bobby's bar on the Strip, where I'd first met Shane Vallery, who got me into this, I banged out a detailed account of the truth on my old IBM Selectric. A tell-all. The games Dan Boone played to become this big fucking star, how his dream now was to get his pregnant wife back to the States, and so on." He kicked the wall. "Shit!" Without thinking he'd used his injured foot. He grabbed for it and hopped around the office to a safe landing back in the visitors chair.

Glen and the chief waited for Sothern's moaning to subside, Glen certain where the rest of his story would go. He and Vernon locked eyes. Vernon showing he already knew, but open to hearing again.

Sothern said, "I sold the story first time at bat. *Glamour World*. Magazines don't come any bigger or more prestigious than that. A five-figure payday for the exclusive, the offer of a staff job in New York, after I showed them some of Dan's correspondence with me, to prove I wasn't peddling fiction. They ran Dan's picture on the cover. The story got picked up by the wire services. I became a hot commodity on the interview circuit. I scored option money for a movie based on the story that, Hollywood being Hollywood, never got made. All this time, me feeling like a rat for betraying Dan Boone. You calling me an asshole, partner? Not strong enough. I sent Dan a note apologizing, to an East Berlin address that I tracked down, Schmockwitzer Damm 8. I never got an answer.

"Not long after, the *New York Times* picked up on a story from Reuters and ran it on an inside page, how Dan Boone, the American actor and singer who became a big star behind the Iron Curtain, but longed to return to the United States, had drowned in a lake near his home in East Berlin. How officials were calling it a suicide. That's what you heard from Maggie, partner. Maggie. Margaret Collins. Meg Boone. Her. Blaming me for bringing on her husband's death." Sothern had found another paper clip to deal with. "After coming across the Reuters story, I also blamed myself. I drank heavier than ever. Drugs more than ever. More than that I'm too ashamed to mention. My career spiraled downwards. The penalty for letting ambition get the best of me—writing the exposé that inspired Dan Boone to weight himself with bricks and rocks roped to his body before taking one last look at the sky and rolling over the side of his fishing boat into the lake." Sothern's face grew a hundred years older.

Glen didn't try hiding his rage, his face seized by a blend of red and purple that almost radiated on his ears. "You are a world-class bastard, aren't you, *partner?*" His word filled with rattlesnake venom. He palm-slapped Sothern's face. "You son of a bitch!"

Sothern didn't flinch. He lit a small grin at the corners of his mouth and said, "Not to hear my mother tell it."

Glen ignored Vernon's demands to quit and came at him from the other direction.

His knuckles connected with Sothern's face, causing a small break at the right edge of his lower lip. Sothern wiped at the trickle of blood. "You hit harder than your lady friend," he said. "Both times."

"I get the chance, worse damage coming your way."

Sothern checked the fingertip stain, licked at it, and reapplied an index finger to the break. "Or maybe not, partner. You might feel differently, you let me finish."

"No question in my mind, you miserable excuse for a human being."

Vernon broke in: "Listen to the man, Glen. An order."

Glen took a heavy slug of air and stepped back.

The chief nodded approval. "Go on, Jack. Lay it on him."

"The Reuters story also reported that Dan Boone's wife, Meg, had been pulled from the lake, but unlike him, she was no suicide," Sothern said, nodding to the memory. "Someone had beaten her to a bloody pulp and crushed her skull with a blunt instrument before throwing her overboard. One guess who the authorities said that was, *partner.*"

CHAPTER 11

Sothern liked what he saw, the mind-busting confusion rampant on Glen Traylor's face, blue veins flexing at his temples while he digested the significance of what he'd just been told; Traylor's fingers laced, thumbs rotating around one another, his eyebrows glued to the bridge of his off-kilter nose. He wasn't out to bust the detective for brain-dead, only neutralize him, make it possible to pursue the story with some assurance Traylor would play fair with his unwelcome partner. It lasted several moments, until Vernon Mount raised the stakes, saying, "I don't know what to make of that. How about you, detective?"

Traylor gave the chief slits for eyes and one of those *I'm thinking* kinds of gestures.

Vernon, visibly enjoying the tease, said, "What's it say to you, Jack?"

"What it began saying the instant I saw her on the news and realized it was Meg Boone whose daughter had been kidnapped. She either made a miraculous recovery from being beaten to death and dumped in an East Berlin lake or the news stories got it wrong."

"Like you got it wrong on a lot of stories down the road and finally got junk-heaped from the news business?" Traylor speaking out, his hissing tenor taunting Sothern for all it was worth. "I got the full scoop on you from my old contacts at Parker Center and I know Vernon did, too, so there's no wool to pull here."

"Guilty as charged," Sothern said, "but *mea culpa* doesn't mitigate against what you heard. You understand what the word *mitigate* means, detective, or should I wait while you look for a clue in the dictionary? *Mea culpa* while you're at it."

"Screw you, too, you piranha."

"Also *pariah*." He turned to Vernon, as if Traylor no longer existed. "If Reuters and the others got it wrong, if Dan Boone's wife wasn't dead, if nobody else caught on to who Margaret Collins was back then—I knew I was onto a story that can get me back into the business, Chief."

"More'n that, I'm thinking," the chief said. "Like, maybe, you got some debt needs paying back. Something along those lines, Jack?"

It was nothing Sothern needed to reveal. He responded with a flick of the wrist and said, "I knew I had to get here pronto. Questions built on questions for every mile of the drive down. If not Meg Boone who got killed, who? Who was it they pulled from the lake? What happened between the time I met her at Café Munchausen and now? How did she get out of East Berlin? What's her life been like since? Why has she been hiding behind a different name all these years and—?"

Traylor got his thumb and middle finger into his mouth and piped a whistle.

"That one's easy," he said. "Because after all your scam stories were revealed for the lies they were, anybody who'd ever believed you in the first place about Dan Boone not being a tool of the Commies went back to understanding what that damn rotten turncoat stood for. No shame Maggie ever needed and no shame she'd want splashed all over Tracy."

"You know that for a fact, partner?"

"Common sense, Sothern. And I got a few questions for you. . . . Assuming all we've been hearing out from your mouth is true, how do we know that fishing boat business ever happened?"

"I didn't invent Reuters or the *New York Times.*"

Traylor ignored him and appealed to the chief. "How do we know anybody was murdered by Dan Boone before he committed suicide? *If* he committed suicide. Or that Dan Boone isn't still alive and kicking, like Maggie? Also escaped from East Berlin. Or that now and for the past sixteen years Boone hasn't been hiding somewhere, maybe even here in the United States?"

Finally, where he'd been steering the conversation. "Maybe you should ask your lady friend those questions?" Sothern said. "You and the chief saw she's not about to open up for me."

"Don't think I won't, smart ass."

"*Mr.* Smart Ass to you."

"Meanwhile, smart ass, I suppose the ideas you were feeding Vernon, about Tracy being taken off instead of being killed like Betsy and Amy were. You were trying to link current events to ancient history, to build yourself a better story?"

"Maybe because it could be true?"

"Saying you didn't think Tracy was also dead by now. Same reason?"

"Sherlock Holmes has nothing on you."

"You forgot about the two fellas working at Dino's who also didn't get themselves killed."

"But they weren't hauled away. Only Tracy. Why do you think that was? Why not them, partner?"

Traylor's look darkened. "Tracy's young, she's pretty, and you know the rest that happens with those kinds of perverts and crazies. Or maybe he's getting ready to make ransom demands on Maggie. Maybe both."

"Maybe because he was sending a message to her. Saying, *I got your daughter because you have something I want.*"

"Listen to him, Vernon, turning a horsefly into horse flesh.

And exactly what might that something he wants be?"

Sothern shrugged. "I don't know everything, partner. Let's go ask your lady friend. She may have the answer to that one."

Traylor flashed him a thumbs-up. "If only to bust your little bubble. You there to hear it go pop."

"Bust away," Sothern said.

Vernon applauded and said, "See, boys, you're already working together."

Traylor drove in his unmarked cop car, a dark blue Ford a few years old in serious need of grooming. Sinatra was selling Chicago, his kind of town, from a CD playing under the crackle of Traylor's two-way, interrupted a few times by patrol cars checking plates and drivers' licenses on motorists stopped on the main drag into Eden Highlands.

After about a mile, he turned onto a residential street and double-parked with the engine humming. "Here's where you and me, we part company," Traylor said, his mouth twitching, his midnight shades concealing anything his eyes might reveal.

"I don't think our chief is going to like you dumping your partner and going it alone to Maggie's," Sothern said, guessing at Traylor's destination.

"It won't matter none after Vernon hears it was at Maggie's request, when I called her."

"Was it?"

"It will be, once I get to her place." The twitching turned into a malevolent smile. "They teach you how to open a door in newspaper school? Nice hike back to the station house and your wheels while a real detective does some real detecting, partner."

"Vernon's already hired a replacement for you?"

"Here's the deal. You don't get in my way and I won't get in yours. Understood, partner? And while you're at it, steer clear of my woman."

"Don't you mean Dan Boone's woman?"

Traylor gunned the motor, then three more times. "You press that button, it pops the door lock. You pull that handle, it opens the door. I'll give you some credit, Sothern. You can figure out the rest from there."

CHAPTER 12

They sat over coffee at the kitchen table, Glen Traylor telling Maggie the part of Jack Sothern's story she had fled The Garden of Eden without hearing, Maggie a reluctant listener, showing scant emotion until Glen told her about the lake. About Dan's reported suicide by drowning. About his wife's body pulled from the water, but no suicide, her head bashed in.

Her hand flew to her temple, rubbing and rubbing while tears formed and stumbled from her eyes, squeezed shut against old memories she had hoped never to confront again. Her head nodding, as if a spring were loose.

When she'd found her voice, she said, "Yes."

Glen warmed his palms on the cup, struggling with the word.

Maggie aligned her thoughts, bracing herself for the questions she knew were coming; determined to let Glen know only what he needed to know. No more than that. Glen couldn't be part of the solution. She didn't want to make him part of the problem. Horrible enough already having Jack Sothern around, stirring things up, making noises that could get Tracy murdered if Sothern took public what he knew. Even if it were only what he thought he knew. What he might learn if he got to the right people the right way.

Sixteen years ago, Jack Sothern had seemed the answer to their prayers, hers and Dan's, only to turn into their worst nightmare.

She was not going to let that happen a second time—

Sothern endangering Tracy's life by asking the wrong questions.

She'd see Jack Sothern dead before she let that happen.

She had told that to Roxy earlier, when she told her the rest of the story, but it was nothing she intended to share with Glen. Taking the law into her confidence, not the same as taking the law into her own hands. She broke out a smile reflecting on Roxy's response, Roxy passionately assuring her: *I'll never allow anyone or anything to harm you, Sweetie Pie. Day or night, just say the word and I'm there for you.*

Glen thought the smile was for him. He reached across the table and gave her hand a squeeze. "Yes, what, Doll Face?"

"What you heard was true as far as it goes, but not the real truth."

"Take it farther?"

"I'm not dead. I didn't get my skull crushed by my husband or anybody else."

"I'm a good enough detective to have figured out that part by myself."

"Yes, you are, Glen." Careful in the selections drawn from her memory bank and her choice of words, she told him the parts he couldn't have heard from Jack Sothern, the parts Sothern never knew.

How Shane Vallery had come to them days before the real story about Dan—how Dan truly felt about Communism and his dream of returning to the United States—ran in *Glamour World*.

"We've been betrayed by Jack Sothern," Shane told them. "You have to get out of East Berlin now, before Erich Mielke dispatches his men to bring you in, closes all hope of you ever leaving. Disgracing the system is disgracing him. He'll have you denouncing the story as false, U.S. government fabrication, propaganda, and life will seem to go on as it was, for a while, before you fall off the pedestal and fade into obscurity or worse, Meg and your child with you."

Dan and Meg shared apprehensive looks. He broke into a cold sweat. She trembled. They clung to one another while Shane explained, "Dress warmly. Gather only what your pockets will hold. Your identity cards. Any Deutschmarks or other Western currency you've been squirreling. Be ready to leave in an hour."

"How—?"

"No time for questions, Danny. I have to complete arrangements," Shane said. She had a hug and air kisses for both, pats and a massage for Meg's belly mound before fleeing their home without a backward glance, only a whirling wave goodbye.

An hour later, to the minute, there was a knock at the door.

Meg did not know the little man dressed in shabby black who was talking at her before the door was fully open. Dan's expression said he didn't know the man either, but the man was already addressing them like lifelong friends, one word following the next at the speed of light.

"You are prepared to leave, I see, as Shane said you would be," he said. "Good, good, good. Outside now and fast. First, you alone, Meg, then after you by a few minutes will come Dan, my favorite movie star. I also have all your records, but sad to say no time now to get an autograph, Dan." His English falling to German structure and pronunciation with some of the words. "I see your concern, Meg, and it shouldn't be. No, no, no. Not. We have two different ways to reach our border destination, but the end result will be the same. Reunited. Safe and sane, you see? Better safe than sorry.

"From the road you will see a light mint-colored Fiat 128, a black stripe along the lower part of the body. One of the last made before production quit in nineteen hundred and eighty-five, or perhaps you know that already. About forty-five meters away, with the motor running. The driver's name is Wolf Haller-vorden. You say to Wolf my name. You say *Emil Grass*. That is all the reassurance Wolf needs. Get in and off you go to the West and freedom."

Meg protested, insisting she would not leave without Dan.

Emil Grass tapped the face of his wristwatch and said, "No time for discussion. Sorry. You're expected and to be late is to be trapped with no second chances likely, if Shane knows what she's talking. And she does. Always right, a good trait where trust can decide life from death." His head nodded agreement, one eye closed, an eyebrow up five notches.

Meg wasn't satisfied. "Tell me about Dan. Dan, make him tell."

Grass waved him off and said, "The black Trabant parked a few meters behind the Fiat? That is my shit piece of plastic Trabi, the best the GDR can make and nothing better, unless you're a diplomat and more equal than the masses in this society where all are equal. Workers save for years to afford one, then have to wait more years for theirs to roll off the assembly line. Crap car, the Trabi, but we love it this day, because it is the car taking Dan to freedom at the same time as you. Me at the wheel for Dan, as Wolf will be at the wheel of the Fiat for you."

"No. Together. Why not together?"

Grass said, "Nothing I know or need to know. I'd tell you if I knew. When you meet up with Shane, you ask her."

Meg's look beggared a better answer from her husband.

Dan threw away his hands, his star status of no value at this moment. "I'll see you on the other side," he said, stepping in for a kiss she shared eagerly, one hand firm on her belly, gently teasing, "You and our son."

"Daughter." The teasing game they'd been playing for weeks.

Giving Meg cause for a momentary smile. Easing the pain of separation, however temporary.

Wolf Hallervorden barely looked her way, directing her to the passenger seat with a gesture. She came around the front of the Fiat and paused with her hand gripping the door handle. "Hurry up, missus," Hallervorden said, his harsh voice a fit companion to a young, meaty, typically German face full of pockmarks and picking scars. After fifteen or twenty seconds, he repeated himself, but she was not about to move until she was sure about Dan.

She heard boots breaking the layer of snow that had frozen on the footpath since it stopped falling two days ago and, in the challenging light of a half moon carving patterns of indifferent visibility, Dan and Grass stepped free of the gate and the thick forest of towering, sweet-smelling lindens guarding the property.

Not until they got into the Trabant and she heard the engine start, shielded her eyes against the glare of the Trabi's headlights, did she settle next to Hallervorden in the Fiat. The Trabi shot past them before Hallervorden had geared out of neutral and eased his foot down on the gas pedal. She watched its back lights grow smaller as the distance between the cars steadily increased. Within fifteen minutes, the lights had disappeared entirely.

The taciturn Hallervorden sensed her apprehension. He said, "That Grass, he drives like a madman. Always in a hurry to leave where he doesn't belong." She tried questioning him about their destination, but all Hallervorden would say was, "We use the back roads, just in case."

"Just in case what, Herr Hallervorden?"

"Just in case just in case," he said, and turned onto another narrow, two-lane road as rutted as his face.

After a half hour, they were on a road paralleling the Elbe.

The GDR patrol boats that guarded the river during daylight hours against desperate East Berliners attempting a cross to freedom were moored along the east bank, leaving any movement to drifting ice floes that brought *Uncle Tom's Cabin* to her mind. Little Eva. Meg as Little Eva, making perilous leaps from one ice floe to the next in a brave-beyond-belief escape from Simon Legree and slavery.

Is that what they had in mind for her and Dan?

Was it a risk she was prepared to share with the child kicking inside her?

The Elbe disappeared, replaced after several miles of convoluted travel by brush-free flatlands lined with walls of razor-sharp wire.

Minefields filled with machine guns on tripwire.

Monolithic conning towers at measured intervals.

She half-expected tower lights to burst on any second, pull them from the night shadows, and issue a hail of bullets in their direction, but the towers remained as dark and as silent as her imagination stayed hyperactive.

Another half hour went by. The steady hum of the Fiat was on the verge of putting her to sleep when Hallervorden slammed hard on the brakes. The car fishtailed, almost slid off the road and down an embankment. She used an arm to guard her eyes against the beam of light crashing through the windshield.

Two *VoPo*, members of the German People's Police force, blocking the way. Both armed, the one with the flashlight fingering a Grach pistol at the hip. His mate ready to use some kind of machine gun on them, using it to motion them out of the Fiat. The fur collars of their greatcoats turned up for warmth against the frigid night air. Both of them emitting visible clouds with every breath.

"Come on," one of them said. He led them forward about a hundred meters, to a VoPo command post guarding the gated entrance to an otherwise unobstructed dirt path leading into the West.

She followed, hunting for signs of the Stasi, of Dan and Emil Grass.

Nothing.

The man who stepped from the guard post rubbing his gloved hands against the cold didn't look to be wearing a VoPo uniform under his fur coat. His fur hat was more Russian military ushanka than German People's Police, his rattlesnake boots straight out of a Neiman-Marcus catalog.

"About time," he told Hallervorden. "Why I sent out the search party." He gave Meg a smile and a two-fingered salute at the temple and adjusted his horn rims. "My name is Burt Crews, Mrs. Boone. I'm here to see you safely across." He turned to the VoPos and said something in German as perfect as his English. They holstered their weapons and marched back to the road, joined by Wolf Hallervorden.

"Where's Dan, Mr. Crews? Where's my husband? I'm not leaving without him."

"He's already safe in West Berlin and waiting for your arrival, I expect. Probably as anxious as you are to be reunited. We moved him up the line about three miles when our VoPo friends tried to hold us up for more money after they saw it was him we were taking across. The price of super-stardom. Four times what the going rate's been, the greedy SOBs. Bad enough we get skinned when it's nobody famous."

"How do I know Dan's safe?"

"The way I see things, Mrs. Boone, it's something we both have to take on faith. Emil assured him, same as I'm assuring you now, that he's never had a problem up the line."

"I'm not budging until I know for sure."

Crews dug his hands inside his coat pockets and gazed off into the distance. He said, "That does create a situation, I'm

afraid. You heard that? Hallervorden driving off. That means the
VoPo will be back any minute. The deal's always that we're
gone before they return. We're still here, all bets are off, for me
as well as you. Please don't ask me to explain the logic in that.
We're dealing with the German mindset here."

Maggie headed for the coffeemaker and a refill. Saw she'd barely
drunk from her cup. She spent a minute doing a reheat in the
microwave and rejoined Glen at the kitchen table. She swiped
at her eyes. They stung and were wet again before she managed
a swallow of the freshly ground and brewed black coffee.
Double-strength, the way Danny had taught her to like it.

Glen saw her distress mounting.

He said, "Take your time, we have all day." He could have
said *all night,* but she had made him understand, when he settled
in Eden Highlands going on two years ago and started showing
interest in her, that the best he was ever going to get was a kiss
to go with his wishful thinking.

He'd played by her rules ever since, but never missed an opportunity to let her see he was hoping for more and better one
day, no matter how often she made it clear she wanted Glen as
a friend, not a lover. The whole town thought otherwise. Neither
of them minded. They both wore the gossip for the same reason,
as a shield protecting her from the attention of other men. If
he'd noticed anything unusual about her relationship with Roxy,
he kept it to himself.

Maggie dried her eyes. "I never saw Danny after that," she
said. "I crossed over to the West and sat with Burt Crews for
hours, waiting for him. Do you know what it's like when you
know something has gone wrong and you're powerless to do
anything about it? It's like pulling the drawstring on your
parachute and the chute doesn't open. Your world crashes, not

only you. That was me, growing more hysterical the closer I fell to earth.

"Finally, I let Crews take me to the rendezvous point in the city, a modest pension off the Friedrichstrasse, hoping against hope Danny would also show up there, maybe be there already. Some prayers don't get answered, Glen. They fed me something that let me sleep. When I woke up late the following afternoon, there was an envelope propped up on the nightstand lamp. My name. Danny's handwriting. All these years and I can still recite his letter from memory . . . *My Dearest Goldilocks* . . ."

My Dearest Goldilocks,

The fates have conspired to keep me here in the GDR. More I cannot say in this hastily-penned note about the circumstances, but I have acted on your best interests, not mine, and the best interests of our son to be. Call it unfinished business. I know you will want to return to my side, but you must not. Please, Dearest One, continue on the journey we prescribed for ourselves and have faith I will join you at the soonest moment possible. Love recognizes no walls or borders and neither should we. Not now. Not ever.

Forever,
Your Daniel

"*Forever, Your Daniel* . . ." Maggie considered the sentiment. "Talking about our *son*, the joke between us, him carrying on about the baby being a boy and me insisting it would be a girl, but he was never ever a *Daniel*, Glen. Dan or Danny, but never Daniel. I knew he was sending me a message, that he was being held by the VoPo or, worse, by the Stasi. I wanted desperately to return to his side, but there was no denying the truth in the rest of his message. Within hours, I was on a plane bound for London and after that to the United States. Los Angeles. Eden Highlands."

She sought understanding from him.

Glen shook his head. "You did the right thing, Doll Face. Think of what life would have been like for Tracy, growing up over there in East Berlin."

"Only it wasn't East Berlin for long after that. The Wall came down and the borders opened up again. The country was reunified. No more GDR. No more Russian domination. No more Stasi. No more VoPo. By then—" She made two fists and banged her knuckles together, to a quiet beat that did little more than mark time. "No more Danny. Somebody saw the story in a newspaper and sent it to me, or I never would have known. No idea who or why or which newspaper, but knew to send it to me here. No note, just the story saying how Dan drowned in the lake near our home, a probable suicide, and how he had killed me first and dumped my body."

"This Burt Crews person? Or Emil Grass?"

"I don't know. It didn't matter then and still doesn't. All that mattered was Danny and a child that was going to grow up fatherless. I went crazy with grief. I holed up here and nobody could get me out for over a month, until finally, Roxy broke in and screamed and nursed me back to the world."

Glen said, "The woman pulled from the lake, if not you . . . ?"

"I think it was Shane Vallery. I think the Stasi found out Shane was behind Danny and me trying to get out of the GDR. They stopped him before he could cross the border, but I was beyond reach. Shane made the perfect stand-in for me when they decided how to punish Danny, in a way that would eliminate the chance of any future embarrassment and destroy forever his image as a superhero. They turned him into some crazy person who committed an unspeakable crime before taking his own life."

"Why didn't you come forward and say something, Maggie?"

"Because, maybe, if they knew where I was they'd come after me. I could not risk that, especially not with our child on the way—Danny's legacy. The same reason I stopped being Meg Boone and became Margaret Collins. Not even my maiden name. I borrowed it from my great-grandmother."

"Does Tracy know any of this?"

The question made her shudder.

She saw concern flash across Glen's eyes.

She signaled him she was okay.

"Tracy will one day," she said. "Soon, I think."

Glen let her see he understood there was more to the thought and waited her out.

Maggie looked past him to nothing in particular.

She said, "I received a phone call earlier today."

"The person who abducted Tracy."

"No . . . Tracy's father."

CHAPTER 13

Glen arched back and stared at Maggie in disbelief.

He locked his arms across his bulky chest and, sounding like he had to make sure he'd heard her correctly, said, "Dan Boone?"

"Danny, yes."

"Dan Boone." This time sounding like she should give him one of those wrong answer buzzes from *Jeopardy*. Tell him: *Sorry, Glen, the correct answer is, "Who is Dan Boone?"* His head didn't know where to stop. "That wasn't him in the boat, like it wasn't you?" She sat quietly and let him play with the thought. "Still alive after all this time?"

"It appears."

"Maggie, you're sure it was him who called? You're certain?"

"His voice has never left me, Glen, the same way I can still feel his touch. He didn't have to say it was him. I don't expect you to understand, but I knew it was Danny from his sigh— before he said hello."

"What else did he say? Did he say where he was calling you from?"

"I don't think so."

"You don't—?"

"All I could think was, *This can't be, this can't be,* but it was. It was, Glen. It was."

Glen leaned forward to make his fingers reach her mouth, urging, "Calm yourself, Maggie." He used his napkin to pat her eyes and face dry. Gave her another minute to pull herself together before asking in a calm voice that could have been a priest ministering to a member of his congregation, "What else? What do you remember?"

"He'd seen the news about Tracy, Glen. He said he was coming to the Highlands." She picked up the coffee cup, her hand trembling so badly she was unable to get it more than a few inches off the table. It splattered as she set it back down. "He said he'd be here as soon as he could. He said he couldn't stand for me to suffer through this awfulness alone."

"But not from where?" She shook her head. "And this, the first time he's contacted you since you got out of East Berlin?"

"No." Using her napkin to dab at the wet spot on her blouse caused by the coffee.

"No?"

"The first time since after the lake, after Danny supposedly murdered me and then committed suicide. A letter. Someone delivered it to me not long after I got here."

"Saying?"

Maggie crumpled the napkin and set it down, closed her eyes, and recited:

My Dearest Goldilocks,

Our friends tell me you're safely back in America and I can't thank God enough for that. I'm here for a while longer, but S.V. says the means for my joining you will soon be in my hands. The days without you are unbearable and this need to wait adds to my suffering. I have visions of a great life for us and our son, once America has fully forgiven my sins as a fair trade for what I'll be bringing back home. Stardom there is not out of the question, as long as . . .

Maggie interrupted herself. "He goes on to talk about finding an agent who won't be afraid of him politically. A record company. A movie production company. Maybe a producer who would be interested in his life story. *The Turncoat Rebel.* Danny playing himself, of course, and maybe somebody like Elia Kazan to direct it. He'd always felt a bond with Kazan. *On the Waterfront?* I don't know. But there is something I do know, Glen." He waited her out, his eyes shut down to an inquisitive squint, his brow wrinkles squeezing interpretation from her body language. "Danny's letter was too upbeat, looking too far ahead into the future to be written by someone who had suicide on his mind. From the beginning I didn't believe it. That he was murdered by the Stasi, yes. Suicide, no. Absolutely not."

"But alive?"

"Not that either."

"*Someone* delivered it, you said."

"Like the time before, in West Berlin. Waiting for me on the desk one morning at The Garden, on top of a pile of letters, mostly bills and solicitations. No stamp. No return address. Only my name on the envelope. In Danny's handwriting. After I got past my shock, I checked around. Nobody remembered anybody but the postman delivering letters or saw a stranger going in or out of my office."

"The postman?"

"Harvey, as usual. He was already a hundred years old, and you know how fussy he is about his mail pouch."

"Your husband wrote that the means for joining you back here would soon be in his hands. Any idea what he meant by that? *The means?*"

"No. Why are you asking so many questions, Glen?"

"He would be forgiven by America in trade for what he'd be bringing home. *In trade.* That strike any chords then or now?"

"No . . . Glen, I need you to stop. I'm sorry I ever said anything about this."

"When he called today, did he say when he'd be arriving in

the Highlands?"

"Glen!"

"Who else knows about any of this, Maggie? The letter. The phone call."

"Nobody . . . Roxy. You and Roxy . . . Glen, please. I don't want it to go any further."

"It won't. I promise. But I need you to promise me something in return . . . Promise you'll let me know immediately when he shows up on your doorstep or if he contacts you again before that. Will you do that for me, Maggie?"

"Why?"

"I think your husband may be the reason Tracy is still alive. Let's leave it at that."

She maimed him with a look and said, "Let's not."

Glen pushed up from the table and wandered over to the fridge. He studied the wall of photos and market discount coupons; Tracy's seventh-grade report card—the one with all A's—and her first-grade crayon drawing of three melon-headed stick-figures holding hands in front of a slant-roofed house, under a radiating canary-colored sun; photo booth shots of Maggie and Roxy hugging and mugging for the camera, their hairstyles dating the pictures by several years; a calendar from Romanin Realty; an invitation to a baby shower for Nina Hirschfeld, Fred's wife. He straightened the magnets before opening the door and came away with a quart container of milk.

"I'll never get used to your coffee," he said, heading back to the table. "Any stronger or thicker and you could use it to tar leaks in a roof."

"Why did you say that, Glen?"

"You could blacktop a highway with your coffee."

"I'm not into games, Glen. My husband the reason. Why?"

Glen laid in the milk and stirred the coffee, tried a sip.

"Better . . . a theory you can't hold me to, unless or until I find someone or something to back it up. . . . Back in East Berlin, Dan Boone got his hands on something so important to the government, he was confident he could use it to buy his way out of there and redeem himself here. Not to be. Something goes wrong, but he manages somehow to get out with the important something. The Commies cover up his escape with the phony suicide and have been after him ever since."

"For sixteen years?"

A shrug. "He's better at hiding than they are at seeking."

"That old world doesn't exist anymore, so why? What could be so important?"

Another shrug. "Maybe something that kept your husband in hiding and became so important all over again that they turned up the volume on finding him. They came to Eden Highlands because you weren't as difficult to find. They took Tracy thinking the daughter he's never seen—putting her life at risk—is what can draw him out. And it has, right? He's on his way here."

"Why kill those poor girls, Betsy, Amy, who had nothing to do with any of that?"

"To make it a bigger story, a greater tragedy, the kind that always makes it to the national news. Make sure your husband caught their message, that Tracy's alive, but in danger of losing her life. Setting the stage for a confrontation and a trade. Tracy for what they're after. Only—" He turned away from the fear building on her face.

Maggie bit down hard on her molars, took a deep breath. "Say it, Glen."

"There's no guarantee they won't harm her afterward. Or you. Anyone who doesn't matter anymore. They've killed twice, so what's one or two or three more bodies? Why you have to let me know the minute your husband shows up on your doorstep. The minute you get a phone call, a letter, any kind of contact from these people."

"What if your theory is wrong, Glen? What if it is what they keep reporting on the news—a maniac pervert running around loose?"

"There's more hope for Tracy in my theory, Doll Face." He reached for her hand.

She pulled it back, rose slowly, and said, "Thank you, Glen. I'd like to be alone now. You know the way out."

Accepted his hug reluctantly.

Waited until she heard the front door close before racing over there and turning the deadbolt, throwing the chain lock.

At a window, she peeked through the blinds.

Watched Glen ease into his car and head off before calling, "He's gone. It's safe."

CHAPTER 14

Instead of the station house, Sothern had headed for The Garden of Eden, where Gerry Cotton greeted him like an old friend, wondering if Chief Mount was also on his way over.

"By my lonesome, Gerry. Looking for a place to hang my hat and call home."

Cotton was telling him how they were fully booked for the duration when Roxy Colbraith materialized from somewhere saying, "It's all right, Gerry. I'll take care of Mr. Sothern."

Roxy motioned for him to follow her.

Took him by the hand, and started in the direction of her office.

Changed her mind.

Steered them up a narrow stairway squeaking and groaning under a rose-colored lane of posh carpeting.

On the second landing, she guided him toward the door at the end of a corridor full of doors. "It's our special room for special people, Mr. Sothern. Presidents, princes, and potentates; others who we privilege just because."

Coughing his throat clear to make room for the question: "Because what?"

"How did they always put it on *The Mickey Mouse Club?* Because we like you. Yes. Because we like you." Her voice purred with innuendo. "We like you, Mr. Sothern. Go on in. The door's not locked."

★ ★ ★ ★ ★

The room was twice the size of an average living room and unmistakably designed for loving, the centerpiece a circular bed dressed in virgin-white satin and a mountain of decorative pillows and stuffed animals. Large enough to host a squad or two of soldiers. Breathing room to spare. Overhead, a mirrored ceiling and a chandelier straight out of Buckingham Palace. Walls not lined with mirrors hiding behind burgundy floor-to-ceiling drapes hinting at pleasures to be revealed at the pull of a draw cord.

Roxy followed Sothern inside and locked the door behind her.

Flipped a switch that converted the bright lighting to a glow and made him aware of the perfumed air. It wasn't a smell he knew, but nothing that set off any of his allergies.

Another switch.

Mood music from invisible speakers, an orchestral rendition of something he recognized as Sondheim, although he couldn't conjure up the title, preoccupied with looking at Roxy looking at him with the suggestive stare she had used on him last time.

Whatever else, Roxy Colbraith wasn't the most subtle woman he'd ever encountered.

She aimed a finger at the bed. "Nobody's ever needed a chair in here for long."

He pushed aside some pillows and settled down on the rim, his bruised Nikes flat on the patterned pile carpeting, a bright avenue of forms and colors that reminded him of a Mondrian painting he'd seen at the Museum of Modern Art.

Another switch, and a set of draperies glided open to reveal a small, fully stocked bar.

"Name your poison," she said. "If it's primo, we have it."

"Jack Daniels."

"Primo. Jack D. The Breakfast of Champions. Rocks or . . . ?"

"Neat would be neat."

Roxy poured a tall glass for him, one for herself, and headed over. Kicked off her heels and used a foot to dump enough plush animals on the floor to settle alongside Sothern, her leg heating up his. Handed him a glass that tinged a note of pure crystal meeting hers and toasted: "Cheers! *A votre sante! Kanpai! Oogy wawa! Za vash zdorovye! Zivili! Zum whol!*" She slugged down half her Jack and brushed her lips. "Here's to me and here's to you, and here's to love and laughter. I'll be true as long as you, and not one moment after." Her shrill laugh buried the music before she took another gulp and urged him to match her.

"You trying to get me drunk, Mrs. Robinson?"

"Great flick. Anne Bancroft. My kind of woman. Yeah. Just in case."

He was happy to oblige. The Jack D passed through his throat like the old friend it was. "Just in case what?"

"Just in case you're prejudiced?"

"Prejudiced?"

"Against women of a certain age? My age, say? You can tell me yes. I'll understand, but you need to understand I won't stop there." She patted his crotch. "Nice puppy," she said.

Shane Vallery, who was older than him, was none of Roxy's business.

He said, "I've never given age much thought."

"Then maybe it's time to think about it. Your puppy's telling me it's waking up and growing up. Kids, these days. Always in a hurry."

She stood and passed him her glass, moved to a spot midway between the bed and the bar. Raised her arms like she was about to be nailed to a cross and did a full twirl. "Tell me what you think, Jack. Don't be bashful." Her gray eyes on him like magnets.

They were intense and interesting, but not her best feature.

Roxy Colbaith had no best feature, except maybe legs, shapely enough for hosiery ads, on display under the coal black silk wrap dress that fell a few inches shy of her knees. The v-neck hit low enough to suggest modest cleavage and show off a diamond pendant that sparkled too gaily for costume jewelry. Her waist was thickening, but acceptable on a fifty-something-year-old frame his eyes measured out at about five-five in her bare feet. A butch-cut crop of silver-streaked hair, that monotonous bean soup brown shade that came in a bottle.

The word for her face was "plain," nothing worth a second look, but at the same time one that was unable to resist. A face that didn't exactly beg for attention, so much as demand it. A face bearing the visible signs and mostly invisible scars of a hard history. A face that had stories to tell hidden inside a puncture-proof demeanor. A face he found challenging and intriguing.

He said, "In your case, I think you're aging like a fine wine."

Roxy nodded agreement and sent him a wanton look. She undid the catch on her dress and opened it wide, like the doors on a display cabinet. She was naked underneath. "Ready to test the vintage?"

Sothern heard his puppy barking.

She noticed and showed off two rows of perfectly aligned teeth.

"Jack, when *was* the last time you had a woman?"

"You go first, Roxy. When was the last time you had a man?"

She glanced away, then back. "A little innuendo there, Jack?"

"First time I was here, even allowing for the way you seemed to undress me with your eyes—"

"We weren't alone, so best I could do at the time, hound

dog. Woof!"

"Even the way you seemed to undress me with your eyes, I had the impression you were Maggie Collins' woman."

"Aren't we the observant one . . . that, also. I'm trisexual."

"You mean bisexual."

"Trisexual. I'll *try* anything once. Twice if I like it. Then and now, I'd like to *try* you on."

Sothern said, "I don't believe in casual sex, Roxy."

"Okay. We'll organize it." She briefly held him in her eyes, dropped her dress to the floor, and moved on him, ordering, "Drink up." She chugalugged her glass, swiped his empty, and sashayed to the bar, demonstrating a tight ass that defied the actuarial tables. "A little more Jack Daniels for Jack Sothern, then lots of Sothern comfort for Roxy Colbraith," she said. She refilled their glasses and moved on him. "Bottoms up before bottoms up," she said. She snapped the bandage off his nose, causing him to wince, and ran her tongue over the bruise. "Get ready for the ride of your life, Jack," she said, pressing his glass to his lips.

Drinking was easier than objecting.

Roxy straddled him and began unbuttoning his shirt, pushing her tongue into his ear and making promises he barely understood, the words dissipating into a jigsaw puzzle of sounds.

His eyes beginning to sight her in triplicate. The room moving like a carousel, a slow ride that quickly accelerated into a whirling dervish of a ride.

His mind frozen into a state of indifference, his body inert to her touch, the glass of Jack D slipping from his grip; finally, all of him wrestling with the angel of darkness in a contest he couldn't win.

CHAPTER 15

"So that I understand what you're asking," Chief Vernon Mount said, "you're asking me for the millionth time since you traipsed back in here from her place to okay a twenty-four-seven vigilance around Maggie Collins, that so, Detective Traylor?"

"What I'm asking," Glen Traylor said, readjusting himself on the chief's desk.

"Sothern agree it's necessary?"

"Maggie didn't want him around. I don't know where he disappeared to."

Vernon shooed Glen off the desk and adjusted file folders back into the neat stack Glen had disrupted. He said, "You do remember we're talking an eight-man force, counting you and me? Do the math, I think you'll come out same as me, with three eight-hour shifts, two men per shift. In the meantime, what do we do about protecting the rest of our city, the citizens who pay your salary and mine, especially mine?"

"I don't expect it to be for more than a day or two. By then Boone should be here and we're onto him for better answers. Confirmation. Or Maggie will have been contacted by the piece of shit who has Tracy and—"

"Instead, maybe we stumble over a body in the bushes, a shallow grave somewhere, and so much for your theory." He absorbed his detective's cold stare. "No matter how you work your theory on me, Glen, this boils down plain and simple to you being worried about your lady. I understand, but protecting

Maggie on a whim is not in the budget."

"I'll put in a double shift off the clock to help with some of the load. Work traffic during peak hours."

"Man's a saint, an absolute saint," Vernon announced to the room.

"We fill in with some of your reserve officers."

"The gang that couldn't shoot straight? Maggie's a whole lot safer without them in the loop. You remind me of your pop and how he had to be restrained from acting on some of his far-fetched notions."

"One of his notions saved your life."

"Granted, but the only problems I ever had with LAPD, Internal Affairs came from your pop good-guessing me away from common sense, like you seem hell-bent on doing now. Your guess could cost me my job, the taxpayers got on to how I was spending the money on anything less than probable cause. *Personal* cause more like it, so, Glen, do it on your own dime. You're sleeping with Maggie. Takes care of the overnight detail right there. Park your service revolver under the pillow and your ear cocked, too."

"Vernon, how many times I have to tell you? I'm not sleeping with her!"

"And the earth is flat, right?" He filled his cheeks with doubtful air and puffed it out. "Damn, boy, that's as fine a reason as any to start parking your pecker under Maggie's blankets." He signaled wait a minute with an index finger and went searching in the pencil drawer. "Here's what's good for whatever alarms you," he said, flinging a string of beads at Glen.

Glen made a one-handed catch and looked at Vernon for understanding.

"Genuine worry beads," the chief said. "Picked them up on the cheap from eBay, a down to the wire bid. Greek variety, called Komboloi, but they go back all the way to the beginning of ancient Chinese culture."

The detective held them like a riddle to be solved in his palm, nineteen olive green glass beads divided by silver spacers on a black nylon cord.

Vernon said, "That thingamabob that dangles off the knot is a solar tassel charm, a traditional symbol that wards off the evil eye." He grew his eyes to the size of half-dollars. "You work 'em right, rolling 'em in your hand, they take away your stress, bad temper, any high blood pressure. They even help smokers quit, so it's like trading a bad habit for a good one. In your immediate situation, a cure for any knots in your stomach over Maggie."

He pulled a second strand from the drawer and began working them. "My backups. Same as yours, only Mediterranean blue in color, the beads, to match my eyes. Don't know about you, but I'm feeling better already."

His detective pushed up from the visitors chair, plopped the beads on the desk, and stalked off, Vernon calling at his back, "You don't watch after yourself, Glen, that tension's gonna be the death of you yet."

When he was sure Glen was out of the station house, Vernon got on the phone.

He said, "Listen, a little problem with my detective that we best discuss one-on-one."

Vernon was about to leave for the meeting when he got the news about Jack Sothern.

He broke his own speed record making a beeline to The Garden of Eden, parked in a reserved slot around the side of the building, and was buzzed through the private entrance after his usual wave to the security camera. Gerry Cotton saw him round the corner and called across to him, "Roxy said for you to head on straight upstairs to her room, Vernon."

He took the steps two at a time and, on the second landing, was halfway down the hall when the door at the end burst open.

Roxy Colbraith, her dress loosely strung and barely hiding her meager assets, waving him to hurry in. She locked the door. "Over there," she said, pointing to the bed.

Jack Sothern was comatose under the covers, looking more dead than alive.

"Damn woman, what'd you do to him?"

"Never had the chance, Vernon. He was fine one minute, the next—worse than you see now."

From habit, Vernon checked him for breath and a pulse. "Slow but steady. What did the doc say finally?"

"Thinks it could be a brain aneurysm, some signs pointing in that direction, like the way he is now. Sothern said something about a headache, I figured it for the booze we were guzzling, like Prohibition would be back in an hour. Something about the room doing cartwheels. Then, bingo! I called the doc. I talked to you. The doc wanted me to hurry up and call the ambulance, get Sothern to the hospital for tests and whatever, but I held off, waiting for you to get here."

"Before he zoned out on you, Sothern say anything about Dan Boone still being alive?"

Roxy looked at him like she didn't know what he meant.

He knew better.

What he needed to know now:

Was Traylor an isolated problem or did the problem extend to Sothern, who could blow everything sky high by taking the news about Boone public?

He dipped his hand into the flap pocket of his buckskin jacket and began fondling his Komboloi. "Just heard it myself, Roxy. From Traylor, who heard it from Maggie, who said she'd already shared the secrets with you. 'Fess up. Did Maggie? And also

118

about her husband on his way up to the Highlands because of Tracy?"

"I was priming Sothern to get answers, Vernon, only we never got that far."

"Quite a prize you were ready to give up to him. Why your interest?"

"Don't go dumb on me. My interest is Maggie's interest, the way it's always been between us. If I'd have learned Sothern was here to do Maggie harm, the way he did all those years ago in Germany . . ." The rest of her thought trailed into silence.

"Only his seizure or aneurysm or whatever put him in that stupor beat you to it," Vernon said, stroking his mustache, patting down the ends, and cruising through his goatee.

"Something like that."

"You're sure."

"I'm sure."

"Before you got an answer out of him."

"Before I got an answer out of him."

"The way it looks, whatever Sothern's answer would've been won't matter anymore'n another annoying flea in my mutt Mutt's shaggy hide." He chortled at his next thought. "Hair today, gone tomorrow. Catch that, Roxy? Hair as in h-a-i-r."

"You're a million laughs, Vernon."

Vernon adjusted his ten-gallon against a determined breeze sailing in from the Pacific, already strong enough to sing through the trees and make their branches dance. He watched the ambulance take off for Eden Highlands Memorial Hospital, its red bubble flashing in harmony with the whoop of its siren, Roxy a passenger, promising to call him with an update on Sothern's condition as soon as she heard.

He wheeled around and swaggered back inside to the reception desk.

Gerry Cotton looked up from the computer. "So, what do you think, Vernon?"

"About anything in particular, Gerry?"

"The paramedics parading out of here the way they did, wheeling that Sothern fella out on a gurney. Good for business or bad for business?"

"Time'll tell better'n me, Gerry." He checked his watch. It was still about twenty minutes before they were supposed to meet. "I'm going on up to the VIP suite to do some follow-up on what happened at the accident scene. Anyone show his face asking after me, you send him there, got that?"

"As sure as I got me another honey from off of EvolDotCom. Anyone in particular you expecting?" He smiled at the name. "Oh, yeah. Him."

CHAPTER 16

Before setting off for his meeting with Vernon Mount, he wandered back to Tracy.

He stroked her hair.

She flinched at his touch.

Undaunted, he bent forward and kissed her on the cheek.

Her arms flew up and wigwagged, like she was warding off the devil himself, then she fell back onto the bed, defeated by the weight of her effort.

"I have to leave you for a bit," he told her, aware he could just as easily be talking to himself. "But first it's time for more medicine." He used his thumb and index finger to wedge open her mouth and drop in the gelatin capsule.

Her teeth clamped down and caught the edge of the index finger, deep enough to draw blood.

Reflexively, shouting in anger and pain, he backhanded Tracy across the face. Her head snapped and would probably be sore later, swollen, not that she would feel it, but that appeared to be the extent of the damage.

"I apologize," he said, not that she understood, even if she were conscious enough to recognize he was addressing her. "Accidents do happen, my beautiful little girl, and my finger will assuredly survive the wound you've inflicted."

He breached her mouth again and ran the damaged finger around her throat, to be certain she'd swallowed the capsule. It felt so. For insurance, he slid a hand under her neck and elevated her head before pouring a half cup of water down her throat from the tumbler on the nightstand. "Good girl. Good, good, good."

He rested her head back on the pillow.

"I apologize again for next what comes," he said, "but once again one cannot ever be too careful." With that, he undressed Tracy, treating each article of clothing like a work of art as he folded it and placed it in a plastic bag from the supermarket. "Nobody will see you this way, and only until I return and can dress you back, so don't think too ill of me."

He studied her inert form, feeling ill about himself and the urge that always came over him when presented with naked girls of this age. That he was as sexually corrupt as he was always filled him with self-contempt, but never enough to consider trying to alter the licentious habit of a lifetime.

Unable to resist temptation and opportunity, he touched Tracy, but only for a fraction of a second, only long enough for a hint of the gratification he might seek after the girl's usefulness to them was exhausted and he had no further need for her.

He closed his eyes and aimed his chin for the clouds, contemplating the joys to come, the silent moment of anticipation marred by a faint gasp of satisfaction realized.

CHAPTER 17

"You're late," the chief of police announced, exhibiting his wristwatch like a street corner hustler. It was a cheap watch, just as everything about Vernon Mount had reeked of the bargain basement from the day they met, after he tracked him to the Drinks 'R' Us Tavern and quietly inquired, "Would you like to earn a hundred thousand dollars?"

Back then, that first encounter, the chief had laughed his putrid skunk breath in his face and said, "Who do I have to kill?" Making enough noise to draw brief notice from the few other midday tipplers in the bar.

He'd joined in the laugh and slid into the booth across from Mount, saying, "That would be my job, Chief Mount. Yours a whole lot simpler." Signaled the overripe waitress for a round, two of whatever the chief was drinking, which turned out to be well bourbon, straight.

The chief looked at him hard. "Why don't I think you're joking me?"

"I'm not one for small talk, Chief Mount. In my country we get right to the point."

"Then point me in the right direction."

"Dan Boone."

The chief weighed the name. "Maggie Collins' husband? He's been dead for years."

"Not necessarily."

Mount finished his bourbon and wiped his mustache dry.

Threw a belch across the table. Planted an elbow on the table and used a fist to bench his cheek. "You got my attention," he said.

When he was through explaining, the chief said, "So all's I have to do is look the other way after you, shall we say, *borrow* Tracy for the duration?"

"Excellent choice of a word, Chief Mount."

"That's going to draw Boone out if, like you say, he's still walking the planet."

"The indication has always been he's a devoted father."

"Then how do you explain him being a candidate for a milk carton all this time?"

"I don't."

"No harm comes to the girl. She goes back to her mother same-day fresh."

"A little shaken up, maybe, but you know the saying, Chief Mount, how time will heal the wounds."

"But she's back in one piece."

"As good as new."

"And what about Boone?"

"Boone will be out of your life as quickly as he appears."

"You make it sound ominous, little man."

Little man.

Hearing Mount address him that way—

If he didn't already dislike Mount, that would have guaranteed it.

He forced a smile and said, "How it sounds will matter far less to you when your hundred thousand dollars is delivered, Chief Mount."

"You drinking that?" Mount said, indicating the well shot he had barely touched. Without waiting for an answer, he made it his own. Finished it in a swallow. Belched his satisfaction. Finger-dried his mustache. Reared back like indignation was his middle name. "What would ever lead you to suppose I'd buy into your kind of proposition?"

"Your service record with the police department of Los Angeles. My people, we do our homework."

"Nothing still there for anybody's prying eyes."

"So, then maybe I'm making up that part of your life."

Mount laughed, drawing that barfly attention again. "Ain't you ever the sly one," he said. He let the waitress know they were ready for another round. "My hundred thousand. I need half up front, before you borrow Tracy Collins. The balance when—"

"Whenever you say, Chief Mount. All of it delivered in front, we also can do that, if it suits you. Cash? Untraceable bills of low denomination? An account we open overseas for you, or deposit to your secret accounts that already exist in Las Vegas and Chicago? Whatever it takes to engage your trust in us and have you fulfill your obligation."

The chief slammed his ham fist on the table, swiping his fresh bourbon from the waitress' service tray. "I'll drink to that. Damned, if I don't like the way you do business, little man."

"Cheers!" he said, answering the chief's raised glass.

Thinking, *The greedy fool. If he only knew we were prepared to go much higher than one hundred thousand.*

Mount was less enthusiastic a week and a half later, at a meeting he demanded after the two girls were murdered and Tracy Collins abducted. The chief was deep into his liquor and every whisky-soaked word spilled from his mouth like a poisonous gas leak.

"Little man, nothing we ever agreed on called for killing those sweet young children," he had said.

"Unavoidable, Chief."

"I don't buy that."

"It was not the intention, Chief. The girls were there by chance. The operation was too far in motion to quit because of that unfortunate inconvenience." He reached inside his jacket for his box of English Ovals, quit when he remembered the damned law against smoking. So much for the country's famous freedom of choice.

"Horseshit. Nothing worth the out and out murder of those two innocents. Decent kids from decent families."

"Arrest me while you're at it, if you're supposing it was me who pulled the trigger before driving off with Tracy Collins. Or accomplice to murder? Either way, most certainly, for bribing an officer of the law and inducing him to participate in the commission of a felony. Two murders brings an automatic death sentence after the guilty verdict, what I understand the law to be for all the participants, but perhaps leniency for me in exchange for my testimony?"

Mount covered him in revulsion, tapping his boot in syncopation with the tune his fingers drummed on the table. "Tell me about Tracy," he said.

"She's unharmed, as I told you she would be. She'll remain unharmed throughout her visit with us. That was our arrangement."

"Tell me something else."

He showed Mount his palms.

Mount checked the tavern to make sure they were still outside anyone's hearing.

"As inconvenient as Betsy and Amy were, was there even a moment's hesitation before you slaughtered them, one, then the other?"

"A story, Chief. A joke you bring to mind . . . A secret agency that we could call the CIA has an opening for an assassin and they are down to two candidates. For the last test, they take the first candidate to a thick metal door in an underground room.

They hand him a pistol and tell him, 'Your wife is inside sitting on a chair, waiting for you. Go in and kill her.' The candidate is horrified. He says, 'You can't be serious. I could never shoot and kill my wife.' He is dismissed. Taken away and disposed of as a security measure.

"Next, it becomes the other candidate's turn. The same room, the same door, only this time it's his wife on the other side. Into the room he goes. A shot is heard. Then more shots. Silence, then screaming, crashing noises, banging on the walls. Then, silence again. The door opens and out comes the candidate, sweating profusely. He holds up the pistol and says, 'The gun was loaded with blanks. I had to beat her to death with the chair.' You see, Chief? In my line of work, once you go through the door, you do what you must, or you raise the probability of it being done to you."

Mount worked his hand over his mustache and beard and sought out a place to land his eyes. He said, "Two hundred thousand."

"You are asking for another hundred thousand dollars? Hardly cricket, Chief. We have been honoring our arrangement for the one hundred thousand dollars. We expected you to be a man of your word."

"Our arrangement was on Tracy and my looking the other way. You changed the game, so the rules of the game change with it. Not another hundred thousand I'm asking for, little man. Two hundred thousand more. One hundred thousand to cover covering up the murder of Amy Spencer. The other hundred thou for covering up the murder of Betsy Wheatcroft."

"And if I refuse?"

"You're a dead man, as sure as you're sitting here. As sure as I got my Beretta under the table aimed at your balls."

He gave it a moment, then shrugged. "You are a shrewd and persuasive bargainer, Chief Mount."

"Damned if I ain't, little man. Damned if I ain't."

"You're late." The chief of police tapped the watch's crystal face and repeated himself. "You are late, little man, hear me? Again. Seems to be a habit with you, like you're one of the kind could be late to their own funeral."

He gave Mount a contrite face, thinking, *Or yours, stupid man, definitely yours.*

"Late, yes, Chief," he said, checking his own watch and raising his arms in surrender. "My apologies. From force of habit I went to our usual rendezvous, the Drinks 'R' Us Tavern. Then, delay downstairs, that gab jockey at the reception desk carrying on about women he finds on his computer, one better than the last, and all going to fall madly in love with him, make him rich. His newest, a mongrel with money to burn, I just was hearing."

Mount said, "Nothing ventured, nothing gained, partner," and motioned for him to close and lock the door, settle anyplace. "Getting rich is part of the American way or you and me, we would never be meeting anywhere at all."

Absent chairs, he elected against sharing the giant bed with Mount and angled himself against the wall, directly opposite the chief. His eyes danced around the room. Only that door in and out, unless there was other access behind one of the drapes.

He said, "What made this meeting so urgent, partner?" *Partner.* Using the designation in the interests of good business etiquette, loathing the concept of a partnership with this sad and ugly excuse for law and order.

"Since our last huddle, your cat's come creeping out of the bag," Mount said, and did this thing with his hands, like he was opening the bag, pulling out a cat and holding it up for view.

He responded with an inquisitive eyebrow.

Mount said, "You have two problems, the way it's looking to me. First off, a writer who showed up in Eden Highlands knowing who Maggie Collins is, a shit load of history about Dan Boone and her, wondering how Maggie got out of East Berlin and here to the Highlands after her supposed murder. Smelling a news story as sweet as Chanel Numero Cinco. Even knew enough to drop your name on me, Emil."

"The writer, does he have a name?"

"Jack Sothern. Says you met him when he went to Berlin to hook up with Boone in the Commie days. You helped him across Checkpoint Charlie."

Emil Grass took the news casually.

He found his box of English Ovals and lit up with the eighteen-karat gold flame lighter that was a thank-you gift from Shane Vallery.

He said, "Sothern. The name means nothing to me. I met and helped a good many people back before the Wall came down."

"Like helping Maggie Collins go East to West?"

"This Sothern, how would he know that?"

"I don't know that he does. I'll have to ask when he's up and kicking from the hospital."

"Hospital?" Grass saw the chief didn't intend to explain. He filed away the information, ate a mouthful of smoke, and managed another drag before urging him to continue.

Mount said, "Problem number two after Sothern raised some interesting questions, little man. They led my detective, Glen Traylor, to go after more history from his lady friend, Maggie. Glen's now onto ideas that could tie you to the murders tighter'n Houdini in a straightjacket if he sticks with them. Meanwhile, he's on me to put a twenty-four-seven safety watch on Maggie."

"Have you?"

"Thought we should have this little buddy-huddle first."

"So, what are you telling me exactly, Chief?"

"What I just told you. This ain't no River City, but you got trouble past where I can help you out for much longer."

"River City?" Grass didn't understand the allusion.

The idiot waved it off and said, "This story blows sky high because of some writer who's trying to reclaim his old hotshot status or because there's one damn fine detective on the scent, I don't figure to blow sky-high with it, partner. Better all around if you get Tracy back to home in one piece and be on your merry way."

"The dead girls?"

"They won't be the first unsolved crimes in our files."

"The money we've paid you."

"Services rendered and, you figure there's some surplus due back, consider it my bonus to keep, for losing my memory the second you're gone from here. Any argument, report me to the IRS. For damn sure nothing I'll be doing."

Grass looked around for an ashtray. Finding none, he deposited an inch of cigarette ash in his palm and finger-rubbed it into oblivion, visualizing the chief. He said, "Who else knows of this?" Mount's gesture said he had no idea. "Tracy's mother? Does she know about me?"

"Only if you told her."

Grass said, "I'll take your suggestions under advisement with my people."

"Do better than that, you'll be doing both of us a favor."

He gave Mount a half-bow and turned to leave. Mount stopped him with his name.

"I have the impression you were working one side back when and you're working the other side now, little man. Which side is the now?"

"Always the same side, *partner,*" the word sizzling on the roof of his mouth. "The side that pays the most."

Their meeting over, Grass raced past Gerry Cotton without acknowledging his wagging wave. Outside, he fumbled for his cigarettes, lit up, and leaned against the building with one foot on the wall, alternately catching his breath and shooting out clouds of burnt smoke, reflecting on the removals that would be necessary as a security measure before he left Eden Highlands.

Sothern—

As good a starting point as any.

He ground out what remained of his English Oval and returned to the reception desk.

Gerry was racing letters onto the computer screen, his tongue glued to the side of his mouth. "Hey, Mr. Grass. Got me another one I'm going after," Gerry said, without looking up from the keyboard. "A genuine fox." He pounded away for another minute or so before clicking the mouse on Send. "A lawyer who owns three McDonald's franchises and apartment buildings in Santa Barbara. . . . So, wondering how we're doing with a room for you?"

Grass twitched his head, gave his mouth a grotesque stretch, and clutched at his stomach. "Suddenly I have this terrible pain, Gerry. I think I should have it looked at. Is there a hospital close by?"

"Close enough. Eden Memorial." He scribbled an address and directions on a sheet of memo paper and handed it over. "Curious how you're the second one here today with what ails you. Earlier, a guy named Sothern, meeting with Roxy in the VIP room, same as you and the chief. He wound up needing an ambulance to Eden Memorial . . ." Cotton pressed a palm to his chest. "Dear Lord, I hope we don't have no epidemic starting up. I got hot dates depending on me."

CHAPTER 18

Grass reached the hospital inside of ten minutes and parked his rental on a side street two blocks away. The traditional mission-style main building fit into the tone and temperament of the community, less so the adjacent, flat-faced glass annex rising five stories.

He hurried inside wearing the concerned face of a patient's relative. The rent-a-guard at the security station had less than a quick glance for him, more interested in his magazine than the few people coming and going.

Grass crossed the lobby to the untended information counter. A framed sign told him how to locate who or what he was looking for on the courtesy computer. To himself, Grass applauded the thicker cloak of anonymity ushered in by modern technology.

He typed in the name Jack Sothern and a minute later was following a green-lined path to the corridor that would take him to the Eden Memorial annex.

The pamphlet he'd picked up at the counter explained how the corridor had been blasted out of a steep slope and solid rock, achieved without disturbing the hospital's daily routine. He counted off every step and reached three hundred before he got to the elevator bank in the annex, two hundred of them in the corridor.

The annex was intended mainly for patients. There were no administrative spaces, except for the nurses' stations on each of the floors, serving sixty-four bedrooms, four two-bed rooms and twenty single rooms on three of the five floors. One floor was given over to the surgical theaters. The uppermost floor was unfinished, the needs of the Eden Highlands population and the surrounding communities more than satisfied by the existing amenities.

Stepping off the elevator on the third floor, he was hit up the nose by the astringent odor that recalled other hospitals he'd visited in years past, almost all of them as kindergarten-easy to crack as this one. It could have been as tough as a bank vault, but that wouldn't have mattered to anyone who had passed back and forth through the Berlin Wall as often as Grass.

The linoleum floor was drying from a recent sanitizing, bright orange cones urging caution. A sign directed visitors to check in at the nurses' station, an arrow pointing the way.

Grass headed in the opposite direction, determined to be noticed by as few people as possible, checking for Sothern's room number along the way.

He made a right turn onto another aisle and was halfway down when a wheelchair flew out of one of the rooms, blocking his progress.

The woman, in her late seventies or early eighties, had hair the color of a fire engine and a voice to match, addressing him like Grass was the root of all her problems.

"Are you my doctor?" Her eyes as empty as a condemned building. "Are you my fucking doctor?"

"No."

"Don't go lying to me. Where the fuck are my meds? Where the fuck are my meds? Where the fuck are my meds?"

He stepped around her and continued down the aisle.

She spun around and tracked after him, her wheels coming close enough to cause Grass to stumble. He managed to keep his legs under him and caught a wall with his hand, to help bring him to balance.

The woman was undaunted.

She aimed her chin at him, demanding, "There's more where that came from, baby, you don't get me my fucking meds and get me them damn quick."

"You've become quite an annoyance," Grass said. He reached into a pocket, as if he had something for her. "Here," he said, bending over.

"Damn fucking about time, baby, instead of—"

As far as she got before the side of Grass' flat right hand had judo sliced into her windpipe. She made a modest gagging sound and her head sagged. He brought the next chop down hard and quick onto the back of her neck. Her body jerked reflexively. Fell forward. Her hands slid off the wheels.

That was that, Grass thinking, *Stupid woman. None of this necessary if you were not drugged out of your mind already. A problem I didn't need.* He checked around, left and right. The aisle was empty except for them. No one had heard the woman protesting or, as likely, cared, burdened with problems and ailments of their own.

Quickly, he resettled her in an upright position with her head angled on her broken neck, as if she were taking a nap. He moved behind the wheelchair and started down the aisle with it.

A top-heavy nurse with binoculars for eyeglasses rounded the corner and gave him a queer look. He answered her with a smile and leaned over to tell the dead woman loud enough for the nurse to hear, "A nice stroll, my darling, and then we'll find the doctor and get you your meds." The nurse harrumphed understanding and continued on her way.

Grass turned the aisle at the next intersection and, three doors later, arrived at Jack Sothern's room. The door was open. He pushed the wheelchair inside and waited for some reaction that would determine how best to proceed.

Hearing nothing, he stepped inside, for insurance calling, "Mrs. Marx, have you got yourself into the wrong room again?"

Still nothing.

He closed the door.

The wheelchair had butted to a stop against the frame of the bed closest to the door. It was empty. Not so the bed nearest the window. Sothern was under the covers, asleep, his back turned to the door, his breathing steady and marked by a modest snore.

Grass rapped on the bathroom door and got no answer.

He opened the door.

The bathroom was empty.

He maneuvered the wheelchair inside and left the woman there.

He fished his precious Kemmerick HuntChamp from a pocket, musing over how easy it remained to get dangerous weapons into the country while deciding which of the blades would work best. He couldn't decide between the punch blade and the screwdriver on his quiet way over to Sothern.

He hesitated briefly, checked Sothern's breathing pattern once more, not anxious to be surprised a second time and have Sothern shouting for help or pushing the bedside panic button or—

Anything that might stand between him and sudden death.

Hamper a clean getaway.

"Mr. Sothern? Jack?"

No reaction.

Grass moved closer to the bed and angled over, moving his mouth to Sothern's ear and whispering his name again.

No reaction.

Dead to the world, but not as dead to the world as Sothern would be momentarily.

Holding the knife like a corkscrew, he dug the long, lean

punch blade into Sothern's ear, as deep as it would go. Pulled it out. Drove it in again, only this time aimed higher into his head. A third time at another upward angle, for good measure. The first time, hearing a pop. The next two times, a sound like air leaking from a tire. Each time observing blood tinting the blade. He knew from experience every thrust was deep enough to cause fatal brain damage. The one time he had failed, his intended victim was reduced to a vegetable.

That would work here, if by some chance he'd lost his touch.

Hardly, Grass told himself. It was not without justification he prided himself on his workmanship. His record, were it known, would testify to that. Wishing as he had often done over the years that there was some way to erase the blemish of that one vegetable.

He padded back to the bathroom and washed the blade thoroughly before closing it back inside the HuntChamp. Returned the knife to his pocket. Washed and dried his hands. Gave the dead woman a few farewell pats on top of her mound of flame-colored hair and shut the door after him.

"*Auf wiedersehen,* Jack," he said, adding a two-fingered salute at the temple. "Nice visiting with you after all these years."

He left the hospital as unobserved as he had arrived, hungry.

Killing always left him hungry.

He decided to stop at the taco place that had served an especially delicious hot tamale last week. Also buy one for Tracy. A hot tamale for the hot tamale that she was. He ran his tongue around his lips. Yes. The idea definitely appealed to him. A hot tamale for the young and tender hot tamale in his keep.

CHAPTER 19

Maggie saw Traylor staring back at her through the spy hole.

He was bouncing from foot to foot and stabbing at the doorbell with an impatience that said he wasn't going to leave. Her car was in the driveway, so no chance he'd conclude she was gone.

She turned, mouthed Traylor's name, threw her hands into a *What do we do?* gesture.

The gesture back advised, *Let him in.* He was still engaged in the call that had triggered his cell phone a few minutes ago and moved him away from her to quiet conversation, a hand cupped to his mouth.

"You're sure that's a good idea?"

He nodded approval, turned, and disappeared back inside the living room.

"You took long enough," Traylor said, entering. He pulled at his jacket to shake off the cold. The way he was studying her said he had more on his mind than her answering the door.

"I didn't know there's a time limit or a penalty on answering doorbells, Glen. Are you going to ticket me?"

He ogled the ceiling and reached out for her, saying, "Jeez, I'm sorry, Doll Face. I didn't mean to come on like that. It's just . . ." His voice trailed off.

Maggie stepped away, out of his reach. "Just what, Glen?"

"When I was here before, something I saw. It didn't add up

to four on the two plus two we were talking about. Been bother-ing me since."

"Just what, Detective?"

"C'mon." He headed for the kitchen, past the arch into the living room, checked to be certain she was following him, and pulled up at the fridge. "There, Maggie. This." Glen tapped his finger on the door panel.

"Tracy's seventh-grade report card? The best grades she's ever gotten. What about it?"

"Not the report card." *Tap, tap, tap.* "This. The drawing she made."

"First grade. Straight out of kindergarten. Her artwork has improved since then."

"Then why not something better up there?"

"I guess I just never thought about it, got around to doing anything. . . . Glen, I'm too upset to go through another inquisi-tion with you. If you're going to turn insensitive, do it somewhere else with someone else. Please."

She turned to walk away from him.

He reached over and grabbed her arm. "I want you to look at the drawing, Maggie, then tell me something."

She didn't like where this was leading, but she looked anyway, as if she didn't know what was on the paper or what it represented.

"A happy drawing, wouldn't you say?" She gave him a blank look. "A house with a roof much like yours? The three stick-figure people standing outside on a bright sunshiny day, their scribbled hairdos, their sizes suggesting a mommy and a daddy and their little girl?"

Traylor released her arm. He'd been gripping it tighter than he probably realized. She rubbed the spot where it ached and would probably be bruised. "Typical for someone that age. So what?"

"So, if I were to speculate, I'd say this little girl was express-ing her happiness over finally seeing her daddy. Seeing her mommy and daddy together."

"Or, maybe, wishful thinking? A longing for the father she'd never seen?"

"I like my theory better."

"Why's that, Dr. Freud?"

"The drawing is too happy for what would have to be a sad circumstance for little Tracy, just as you've made no secret about it being a source of sadness for you, Doll Face. It was, I'm super-inclined to think you wouldn't be keeping it on display all these years, a constant reminder of the pain brought about by the main man missing from your lives."

"So what? So what if that's so, Detective?"

"So, before, you told me you didn't see Boone after you left East Berlin. The two letters, period. So, what else have you been fibbing to me about? About him never coming back to you after that? Maybe more than just that one time? About Tracy not knowing who her father is? About what else, Maggie? What more?"

"Maybe better that I answer your detective friend, Maggie." Glen's head swiveled faster than hers toward the kitchen doorway. "My name's Crews, Detective Traylor. Burt Crews. I believe Mrs. Collins mentioned me when you were here before." He snapped his cell phone shut and slipped it into a trouser pocket.

"You were here?"

"And for quite some time, Detective Traylor. Why don't we head on in to the living room, get ourselves comfortable, and you straightened out on the facts. . . . Mrs. Collins, a chance for some coffee for the detective, the usual tea for me?" He reached into his jacket and withdrew an ID wallet. Flipped it open to reveal a badge. "Your tax dollars at work, in case you're wondering."

"I'm going to give it to you in a nutshell, Detective. How's that?" They were sitting opposite one another, in the easy chairs at either end of the coffee table. Maggie, too hyper to settle down, moving about behind the couch, wondering just how much Crews intended to tell Glen. At the same time, wondering how much of it Glen would believe, coming as it would be from someone who looked more like everyone's favorite college professor than a government agent.

She'd had trouble recognizing Crews when he showed up on her doorstep, almost didn't let him in, challenging the badge until he shared his name with her and flashed the perfect teeth that had appeared too perfect for somebody in his late forties, but now more like what a liberal dental plan allowed for somebody in his sixties.

The other shadings of age had also disguised Crews. He'd seemed to have slipped an inch or two in height. His generous mop of hair had reduced to topside strands of gray, a snowy white on the shaggy fall hiding his ears and lapping over his shirt collar. Dangling earlobes and a sinking face terminating in a generous turkey wattle he was unable to resist playing with. Maybe as an act of vanity or a show of resistance to time, the heavy horn-rimmed frame she remembered from Berlin had either been supplanted by contacts or his hazel eyes corrected through laser surgery.

He was wearing a plain brown corduroy jacket with leather buttons that matched the cracked elbow patches over an equally subdued vest stretched to the limit by a belly grown generous with age, the same outfit he'd worn every day since he turned up. Now, unbuttoned. Giving him quicker access to the fishnet holster under his left arm and the .22 automatic he said was necessary to carry at all times, the first time Maggie saw it, while reassuring her, "Only as a precaution, Mrs. Collins. Our net's been cast wide and you're well protected."

"Well protected from what, Mr. Crews?"

"A subject I'd be more comfortable discussing with you inside, than here on your front porch," he said, in the quiet, unfettered tone he was now using with Glen, his voice smooth as the honey he was stirring into his cup of tea.

"Learned to appreciate tea during my hitch in the U.K.," he said, kicking off his leather-tasseled loafers and wriggling his toes. "High tea, it's like a religion there. They ever outlawed high tea, a hundred-to-one all of England would shrivel up and sink to the bottom of the Atlantic." He worked his cup to his mouth, pinky extended, took a sip, and beamed. "Perfect. . . . So, where were we, Detective?"

Glen said, "Nowhere."

Crews shifted his eyes to Maggie, saying, "Everything the lady has been telling you is an honest accounting."

"Then you explain—"

"Tut-tut." Holding up a hand. "It's what she didn't tell you where I fill in the blanks, and I'm positive she'd like you to know that whatever she's held back today and before has been at my urging. That so, Mrs. Collins?"

"It's your nutshell, Mr. Crews."

He showed he liked that and, catching Glen by the eyes, said, "You're an excellent sleuth, Detective Traylor. Your logic tying Dan Boone to the tragic murders of those dear young girls and the spiriting away of Tracy, your analysis of Tracy's artwork on the fridge, pure Sherlockian. If you're ever interested in moving up the chain, think about calling me to help clean out the weeds in your LAPD jacket and bringing you through my department door."

"I can make giant rings with the smoke you're blowing up

my ass, Crews."

"Quite." Another grin, broader than the last one. "See, Mrs. Collins? Apparently not much gets past Detective Traylor." Crews settled the teacup and saucer on the coffee table. Clapped his palms and rubbed his hands briskly. Lost the grin. "This has all been a plot to lure Dan Boone into the open, Detective. Boone did call his wife to say he was on his way. Not my assumption or hearsay. We've had a tap on Mrs. Collins' phones for months, since we first got wind of the plot. His call is on disk and no doubt it's authentic; it's him. If they get to him before we get to them, he's a goner, Tracy is a goner, and—" looking at Maggie—"frankly, nobody's safe. Maybe not even you. To get in the way is to be in the way. Why I am Mrs. Collins' boarder for the duration. Why Mrs. Collins has been close-mouthed with everyone, not only you."

"Is there a *why* to this?"

"Of course. Dan Boone's name wasn't picked out of a hat."

"Pick it out of the nutshell."

"Not if you expect to use the information to go getting in our way, Detective."

"Out of the nutshell or I guarantee you I'll be in your way."

"Better we have you working with us, don't you think so?"

"I'm your Siamese twin."

Crews recapped what Glen knew, from time to time giving Maggie a look that asked for verification. After she'd provided them with refills and Crews had judged his tea for satisfaction, he said, "Now, Detective, to fill in the blanks, including a spot or two of truth Mrs. Collins will be hearing for the first time, not all of it pleasant . . ."

He began with Shane Vallery.

Shane was also a government agent, Crews said, who used sex

the way the men who took their direction from her used their weapons—

As necessary.

Sex got her where she wanted, who she wanted, what she wanted, and when she wanted it.

Her trigger was the *why* of it.

When it wasn't being squeezed for her by Washington, she squeezed it herself, sometimes recklessly, but more often with good cause, often motivated by spur-of-the-moment decisions in circumstances that couldn't wait for questions and answers to creep up and down the chain of command.

At the risk of her own life, she exposed herself as an agent to the Stasi, East Germany's Ministry for State Security, the octopus of political despotism that tossed thousands into prison, in a way that brought her to the special attention of the boss, Erich Mielke.

Mielke had personally assembled one of the world's most powerful secret police and espionage services, comprising a force of eighty-five thousand full-time domestic spies, a hundred-seventy volunteer informers, and a coveted group of turncoat double-agents that came to include Shane.

She achieved that by leading the ruthless Mielke to believe she was obsessed with his power and all its trappings. What she didn't make happen with her mind and body, he allocated to himself through his ego.

A few of his confidants viewed the potential for his downfall in their affair, but none was inclined to express an opinion that might inspire his wrath and their summary execution. Shane, with the freedom to come and go as she chose, always returned from a stateside visit with some shard of real or manufactured information calculated to help her lover enhance his status with GDR bosses like Ulbricht and whoever was running the U.S.S.R. on any given day.

143

Burt Crews said, "In turn, Mielke got increasingly freer with his pillow talk and—"

He stopped and looked at Maggie as if he were unsure of how to treat the rest of the thought. She encouraged him to continue, although certain by the way he'd quickly averted her look and adopted a pained expression that it was nothing she would like hearing.

After a few more seconds of self-doubt, he said, "It was about then that Washington decided it could be a powerful propaganda victory for the U.S. if the Turncoat Rebel, Dan Boone, denounced Communism and returned to America. Shane was ordered to get the job done—in any manner necessary—and they stamped the order 'Priority One.'

"A short time later, learning from Mielke that Boone was being sent to Hungary to bolster the cause of Communism against increasing threats of an uprising and overthrow of the Hungarian Socialist Workers Party, Shane managed to be there when Boone arrived. At the government's elaborate welcoming reception that evening, she did the tricks that caught him in her spider's web. By the time they returned to East Berlin, their affair was as torrid and secret as the one she was conducting simultaneously with Mielke."

Crews stopped again to gauge Maggie's reaction, apology written all over his face.

Maggie had no intention of sharing her thoughts with him or with Glen. Besides, in that moment she had no idea what her thoughts were. "It changes nothing, Mr. Crews," she said. "Tell the rest of it."

He played a brief game of adjustment with his fluffy bow tie and continued: "The way she told it to me, Shane got more than she'd bargained for in convincing Boone it was time for him to come back here to the States, where he could be as big a star in America as he was in the Communist countries. Her ace in the hole was the baby Mrs. Collins was expecting, and why growing up the child shouldn't be denied the advantages freedom had to offer his family."

Glen said, "More than she bargained for, you said?"

"Yes, Detective Traylor. For the first time in her life, Shane had fallen in love with her prey." He scanned Maggie again. She bit down hard on her molars and willed herself to show no emotion. He said, "It makes it easier to picture what Shane started going through, her emotional turmoil, the night Mielke revealed that he knew all about the escape planned for Dan and Meg Boone."

Mielke and Shane were in the bedroom of the secret hideaway the spy chief kept a few blocks removed from the Brandenburg Gate, a building all to himself where he could enjoy from an upper story window the sight of guard tower lights dancing across the ugly Wall he had come to treat as his personal toy and prized possession.

Mielke liked his sex rough. Sometimes he worked off his frustrations on Shane, but as a rule he preferred taking on the role of the submissive in their bondage-discipline or domination-submission routines, always cracking the same joke: *See how it is, creature of mine? They say we Communists are against God and religion, the Bible, but here I am, proving I only do unto others what I would have others do unto me.*

That night, remarking about the Boones, Mielke made it sound like he was making idle conversation, doing his usual bragging while he worked his way into a nun's habit, his role, where Shane would play the priest in the confessional.

She sensed a difference tonight, like Mielke was revealing that he also knew about her role in the escape plan, her affair with Dan Boone since Hungary.

She had an instant vision of tonight's sex game ending with

him putting a pistol to her chin and plowing a bullet up into her brain, his preferred method of execution and one he had committed dozens of times in this very room, he said often and proudly. Afterward, he'd have some of his most-trusted goons come in to clean up the mess, sanitize the room, then dispose of the body in a manner that would forever defy discovery.

Aware this was no time to lose her nerve, she said, "What's the game you have in mind for us this time, you devil?"

Mielke ordered her to strip to her skin and smacked her around a bit before demanding she settle on the bed, on her back. He cuffed her hand and foot to the bedposts, tested them, then climbed onto the bed himself and used her face for a cushion.

He screamed names at her, drained himself on her body.

Screamed more.

Applied a silk tie around her neck, drawing the simple knot tighter, cutting off the air to her windpipe, gloating with satisfaction as her face turned red, turned blue, and her eyes grew fearful, certain the vision of Mielke's ugly, evil face gloating with satisfaction would be her last on this earth.

As darkness closed in on the circle of light now reduced to a pinhole, Mielke pulled the tie away.

Shane exhaled the balloon of trapped air while her body ran through a last set of struggles against her restraints.

When he saw she was settled, Mielke took the cigarette he had lit, a Lucky Strike, his favorite American brand, and moved it close enough to her eyes that she felt the heat and heard an eyelash sizzling; then, another eyelash.

Certain he was sending a message that needed no words, she said, gambling: "What is it, Erich, my lover? Have I done something to offend you?"

He dismissed her question with a wave, settled on the edge of the bed, and used the Lucky Strike to outline her face. "Tell me everything you know about Dan Boone and his escape plans," he said.

"Nothing, my lover. Nothing. I met him in Hungary for the first time—"

"And you fucked him there for the first time. You screwed Boone every color of the rainbow and many times since. Cough it up, the truth."

"Whatever makes you think that?"

"One of your associates, a friend who's become a better friend of mine than yours."

"Whoever he is. Name him. Bring him here. Take me to him and I'll call him a liar to his face."

"And I call you one to yours, right now," Mielke said. "You weren't excellent with what services you perform for me, you'd be breathing your last this very evening. I would miss you. That's the only reason we're having this little conversation."

"What do you want? What do you want me to do?"

"Several things, if you're interested in possibly living to a ripe old age."

"Tell me."

"You go to Dan Boone. You tell him what I know. You tell him the Soviet Union, but especially the GDR, has no desire to lose him now or at any time. He belongs to us and with us he stays. You tell Boone, if he does not go along with this urgent suggestion, I aim to gift him with a most painful death for the wife he loves and his unborn child, seeing to it that she knows while turning on the wheel of pain and suffering that he'll have his whore of a mistress to nurse him through the darkest of times. Do you understand this?"

"Yes."

"You carry my message to Boone and make it the last time you see him. You are my property exclusively. Fortunately for you, you have a talent for perversity beyond any I have experienced with any other of my animals, my best reason for abiding by the words of the wise man who said, *Keep your friends close, but your enemies closer.* Words to live by, or—" He slit her throat with a finger. "Do you understand this?"

"Yes."

Mielke said, "And if you need to be reminded—"

He extinguished the Lucky Strike on Shane's left wrist.

She refused to scream for him.

Meg Boone was safely out of East Berlin shortly thereafter.

Mielke knew but didn't seem to care, at least, not enough to make it an issue with Shane.

In fact, he had reversed himself about her affair with Dan Boone, saying, "Make him want you and need you more than ever. Enough so that any thought of following his wife out of the GDR will grow more distant with each fuck you administer. Both of you will remain under my constant scrutiny, but your eyes will be closest to him and you will report to me his every thought, his every mood. Anything and everything that smacks of a renewed longing to leave here. You comprehend?"

"Whatever you wish."

"I wish."

That was the night Mielke played their game for real, beating her bloody and into the hospital for a week and a half. She emerged with an eye the doctors barely managed to save and a passion for revenge.

She knew how to get it, but she needed Mielke to initiate the opportunity.

He did so months later, deciding to resume a game that had been a favorite before the business with Dan was revealed to him by the rat of a turncoat she had not yet been able to uncover.

Shane proceeded to handcuff Mielke to the whipping post that rose like a wooden phallus from the middle of the bedroom floor. She applied the ankle chains and secured the blindfold and waited for him to say *Forgive me, father, for I have sinned* before she ripped the nun's costume from his body.

The action got its usual response, a whine of ecstasy accompanied by an erection the size of a toothpick.

She vigorously applied the cat-o'-nine-tails to his hairy chest and buttocks while he cried out one recent criminal act after the next and begged for absolution, which she gave him in the usual manner, by fondling his cock and causing him to ejaculate. She caught the sperm in her free hand and used it to administer the sign of the cross on him.

While Mielke sobbed for joy and recaptured his bearings, she found what she was looking for and transferred it to her shoulder bag, wrapped in a pair of bloody panties she had been carrying against this night. For all the blood Mielke enjoyed spreading like jam on bread, she'd learned from experience that this was the one type that repelled him. The panties proved an unnecessary precaution, with his bodyguards as well as with Mielke.

Crews buried his nose in his teacup, as an actor might use it as an excuse for the audience to catch its breath. Traylor pushed up from a slump and settled into a posture-perfect position, arms folded across his chest, and started tapping his foot. Checked to see if Maggie shared his impatience. Said, "So I'm asking, Crews. What the hell did Shane Vallery hike off with?"

Crews smiled and finger-stroked Glen a point in the air.

"A diary so dangerously important that Mielke didn't trust it anywhere but on his person at any time. In the past, he'd shared the secret with Shane more than once. He'd even let her see it on one occasion, when he had cause to jot down some new information."

"Why important? What kind of information?"

Crews shrugged. "You'd have to ask Shane that, were you able. It's something she played close to the chest. Washington knew of its existence and value, but that was all. She never told us more than that until she had the diary in her possession and safe. Where, she said, no one could ever find it without her direction."

"Her hammer," Glen said.

"Hammer?"

"The tool Shane used to blackmail Mielke into turning his back while Boone got out of East Germany."

Another air-stroke from Crews.

"Precisely, Detective, but it did not come without a bargain. Mielke demanded that Boone never resume his career or otherwise go public with his defection." Turning to Maggie: "In a manner of speaking, your husband gave up the life he so coveted in order to be reunited with you, Mrs. Collins. And why Mielke went to such lengths to fake Boone's death, murder Shane Vallery for her treachery, and use her death to help turn Boone from a Commie hero into anyone's worst villain, exclusive of himself."

Glen waved him quiet. "He didn't go back to Maggie, not for five years, and then not ever again." He passed her a puzzled look, which Maggie turned away from, satisfied with the story Crews was telling.

"Washington of course wanted to get him in front of the news boys fast, but Shane nixed that. She knew she was destined for problems with Mielke, but she also didn't trust him not to go after her—" Crews started to say her *lover,* but caught himself. The word came out *Boone.* "She also used the diary as a bargaining tool with Washington to get Boone into Witness Protection and in hiding, even from Mrs. Collins and the child she bore them."

"You're saying Shane Vallery gave Washington the Mielke diary as a tradeoff?"

"No. It stayed Shane's *hammer*—" acknowledging Glen for the word—"so long as Dan Boone required safekeeping. Five years of separation was all he could stand. He forced the boys to allow him to visit Mrs. Collins and spend time with the daughter he only knew till then from surveillance photographs. Although brief, it was a joyous occasion for all parties concerned. Am I correct, Mrs. Collins?"

"Yes," she said, underlining the word with a wistful smile.

Glen said, "And not after that?"

"No."

He looked at her like an atheist considering the Bible and asked Crews, "Where's the Mielke diary now?"

"Where it's been from the day he left East Berlin, with Boone. Are you beginning to see the light now, Detective?"

"Ramp it up for me, Crews."

"The truth began to surface after the Wall and Mielke fell at about the same time, but it wasn't fully unraveled until Mielke's death in 2000, something the German people cheered about, so despised was he by his countrymen that Mielke was buried outside the memorial in Berlin's Zentralfriedhof Friedrichsfelde where other famous Communists are laid to rest. Mielke sent his dogs after Dan Boone, but the search did not heat up until his papers revealed a belief that Shane had given Boone the diary for safekeeping and talked of secrets worth millions of dollars to any government, but especially the United States."

"What kind of secrets?"

"If I knew they wouldn't be secrets, Detective. What I do know—Washington somehow got wind of this years before it came out in Mielke's papers. Ten years or so ago. Boone found out before the question could be put to him and abandoned Witness Protection. He disappeared into the night, made himself as invisible as a grain of sand on the Gobi Desert."

"Until Boone learned the news about Tracy."

"Yes, exactly." Crews rewarded Glen with a third chalk mark. "Why we're here and why we're primed to bring down whoever it is that set up the situation in a way so brutal, it has all the earmarks of an old-line Mielke man. In fact, we're calling this operation 'Operation Milkman.' " Giving "Milkman" a slight Germanic twist.

"Any better name to put to the Milkman?"

"Yes. We suspect it's the same person who originally blew the whistle on Shane's plan to get Dan Boone out of East Berlin. The rat associate. Like me, one of her trusted lieutenants, only he had originally been brought over from the other side. A true traitor's traitor."

"He have a name?"

"His code name was 'Lawnmower.' The name on his birth certificate: Grass. Emil Grass."

A cell phone sang out, interrupting whatever Crews intended to say next.

Maggie watched as he and Glen drew their cells out, like gunslingers on a Main Street showdown. It was Glen's. Whatever he was hearing disturbed him. He flipped the cell closed and said, "Chief needs me at the hospital. We got two more homicides on our hands."

CHAPTER 20

"Damnedest thing," Vernon Mount said, leading Traylor off the elevator and into the hospital room. Doc Ayers was conferring with an assistant county coroner while criminalists worked the scene, cautioning paramedics on their handling of the two bodies being readied for removal, one bagged and zipped on a gurney, the other an elderly woman being eased out of a wheelchair. "No rhyme or reason for her," he said.

"Who?"

"Evelyn Blemish, remember old Evelyn, or was she before your time? A whack job. Always barging into the station, demanding we arrest some neighbor, who she swore a blue streak was out to murder her runt of a runt dog, Darling, a fur ball dyed to match Evelyn's dye job, a blazing blue back when, before she tippled one too many tranqs and swan dived from her balcony into a wheelchair. Happened a week after Darling got free of her leash on a pee stroll and took off, some saying it was because even she was tired of Evelyn's ranting. Quite a foul mouth on her, Evelyn, not Darling, but nothing about her bad enough to wind her up like that. Besides, no apparent reason for her being in this room. Not hers and no evidence she had cause to come visit the other victim."

"She's nobody I ever saw," Glen said. "Who's in the bag?"

"Somebody you do know," the chief said, momentarily holding onto the name like it was the key to the kingdom. He shook his head. "Pablo Mora."

"The councilman?"

"You know another Pablo Mora? Coroner says it looks like a brain drain through his ear the cause of death. Definitely nothing you can pin on the surgery Pablo checked in here for the first place, your basic hemorrhoidectomy, unless the surgeon didn't know up from down."

"Politically motivated?"

"Pablo did not have an enemy in the world. Besides, that still wouldn't explain Evelyn Blemish, unless maybe she heard Pablo was here and came to demand the City Council try and do something about Darling, who's still missing in action. A Pomeranian, her dog. I think that's what they're called."

"The other bed?"

"Empty as the killer's conscience. Pablo wanted a room to himself and got a little pushy when he heard all the singles were taken, so they fixed this one up for him. Didn't want to make any more a show of his lard ass through the dressing gown than necessary. Ain't that so, Doc?"

Doc Ayers excused himself from the assistant county coroner, tucked his clipboard under an arm, and joined them. "Heard you about Evelyn. Always haunting my waiting room, that one, with a list of what ailed her. Mostly imaginary. Swore like a sailor's parrot. Got herself hooked on pills of one sort or the other, but not by my hand. She had a neighbor who brought the shit in for her from Tijuana. Bruises on the neck tell what done her in. Not any pills. Something about her likeable, although I'm hard pressed to tell you what. . . . Ain't what so, Vernon?"

"About Pablo Mora wanting a room all by his lonesome."

The doctor nodded. He said, "Otherwise, that Jack Sothern fella could've also been ripe for autopsying, I expect."

Vernon watched Glen's face fall farther than his own.

"What's that about?" his detective said, challenging Doc Ayers.

"Vernon, he doesn't know?"

"No chance to share the particulars, Doc."

"Here's your chance," Glen said.

Doc Ayers picked up the story after Vernon had explained about Sothern's collapse at The Garden of Eden, saying, "They got him up and running in the woo-woo wagon and the ER and programmed him into this room, but there was a last-minute switch because of Pablo that put Sothern one floor up." He recited the room number. "We ran a battery of tests on him and may need more, so I'm keeping Sothern overnight, maybe longer."

"He as bad off as you were thinking, Doc?"

"Maybe. What Sothern was telling us about his head going into a tailspin before he passed out. Loss of feeling in his face. Problems with his eyes. Blood pressure high as the national debt. Everything points to a cerebral aneurysm. He's had the signs before, he said, but never this severe. Said he's had relatives die from cerebral aneurysms, couple of others off the Automobile Club."

"Automobile Club?"

"Triple A, Vernon. AAA. Stands for abdominal aortic aneurysm. Same as what took Albert Einstein, Lucille Ball, and Conway Twitty, although Roy Rogers survived it. These aneurysms are genetic. I judge this to be an early case that needs better looking after, but that doesn't rule out surgery. We'll know better a day or so."

"No surprise about Roy Rogers beating it, him being the King of the Cowboys," Vernon said, stroking his goatee. "Glen, you take over here, while I go on up and see how your partner is faring."

Vernon held his composure until he was out of the room, then grabbed for his cell phone and tapped in the number he had for Emil Grass.

No pickup after a dozen rings.

He disconnected, then tried the number a second time.

Same result.

He found Sothern's room and fixed a smile on his face before entering.

The first bed was occupied by a sixteen- or seventeen-year-old boy whose legs were buried knee-to-ankle inside elevated plaster casts. His attention was riveted on the TV set mounted on a wall platform sending out pictures of kids around his age horsing around on a beach in skimpy bathing suits, guzzling beer, groping body parts, and trading words that once were hard to find on public toilet walls.

Vernon recognized him as Betty Skidmore's kid.

He stepped over to the bedside serving table, took the remote, and clicked off the set.

The boy made a noise and glanced up at him, but quit before translating into words the irate look flashing in his distressed brown eyes.

"Chief Mount?"

"Your mother know you watch dirty pictures on the television, Larry?"

"It's not what you think, sir."

"Well, well, well. And you're a mind-reader, too. You better not let me catch you again watching filth like that, Larry, or it's straight to your mother I go, and you know how that's going to sit with her."

"Yes, sir," Larry said, unconvincingly.

"What's with the legs? Football again?"

"Broke 'em up pretty bad flying my board over at the skate park, Chief Mount. A double loop that didn't work out the way I wanted."

Vernon found his wallet and dug out a twenty-dollar bill. He set it on the serving table, using the clicker as a paperweight.

"Treat yourself to something," he said, moving on to Sothern, who'd been tracking him since he walked into the room.

"What say, Vernon. No box of candy or flowers for me?" Sothern said. "A get-well card to tack up on the wall like your young friend over there?"

"You're pretty chipper for someone who came this close to crossing the border, and by that I don't mean Berlin, Jack."

"My passport'll expire before I do, Vernon."

Vernon, thinking *You don't know how close you came,* said, "This happen to you before, the blacking out and all?"

"The blacking out and then some. A family thing, genetic. Who was it first said, 'Live fast, die young, and leave a beautiful corpse?' "

He shrugged. "Beats the living b'jeebers out of me."

Larry Skidmore called across to them, "James Dean. It was James Dean."

"What's an old country boy singer who made his fortune making sausage into a ripe old age know from that?"

"He means the actor, Vernon. James Dean, not Jimmy Dean. Killed himself driving a Porsche like he owned the road. You ever see *Rebel Without a Cause?*"

"See it? I lived with her in my flaming youth, up until she flamed out." He pulled over and straddled a visitors chair, his arms resting on the back. "Jack, what I think you should do is get yourself back home the minute Doc Ayers says you're okay to travel. It's the stress of what's going down here that caused your condition and could kill you yet."

"Kill me like the two homicides downstairs?"

"You heard, then?"

"Nurses administer equal parts medication and gossip. . . . The room I could have been in, but for the grace of a city councilman practicing the concept of *Rank Has its Privileges*. What's that all about, Vernon?"

"Investigation's underway. I got your partner on the case even as we speak."

"Traylor couldn't solve a crossword puzzle that came with the answers already in place."

"Don't sell Glen short, Jack. I'm thinking, if the doctor lets you go, today or a day or so, you're better off in the big city, L.A., where they can really take care of you, you get into serious ailing."

"The where of it doesn't matter, Vernon. This thing doesn't give advance warning. I'll be fine one minute, then—a little bulge, it balloons out of part of the wall of a vein or an artery in the brain, and the next time my name appears in print it's in the obituary column." He found the bed control and elevated the back. "Meanwhile, why do I get the impression you want me out of town before sundown, cowboy? I don't suppose I was meant to be one of those two homicides."

"I don't suppose it either," Vernon said, rising to leave. "Get yourself better, and you also, Larry. Say hello to your mother for me when you see her."

Walking down the corridor to the elevator, he tried Emil Grass' number again.

Still no answer.

The debate with himself began on his way to the car and, as usual, with him cursing himself for trading in what was left of his soul after finishing his twenty with the LAPD for a chief's badge in a town where it became too easy to look the other way on any crime that came with a handout attached from some member of the suspect's family, some friend of the family, mostly some attorney who knew money speaks louder than the law when you got right down to it, especially with a cop who never had enough left for himself once one of his exes got through breaking his balls in a divorce action.

Oink, oink, Vernon, you aging pig.

Nothing like a bottomless pork barrel, right?

Oink, oink, Vernon, wearing the silly cowboy rags like you're one of the Saturday matinee heroes you idolized as a boy and for a lot of years afterward: Tom Mix. Roy and Gene. Sunset Beaudry. Hoppy. Duke Wayne and Randolph Scott. The Cisco Kid, Duncan Renaldo, and his Pancho, Leo Carrillo. You, the good guy in the white hat, although you knew it was only a costume to hide the bad guy buried inside you and begging to come out. No. Not buried. Asleep in an open grave. Red Ryder. The Lone Ranger. Who'd you ever think you were fooling, besides yourself, Vernon? Besides you. Never in a million years Glen's pappy. Bill Traylor was a decent man, a fine cop, greater than you ever were or Glen would ever become. Bill was a standup guy whose only lying came late in his career and then only to save the exposed ass of a partner who had started taking where the taking was good. When Bill had his second thoughts in the months following his retirement, when he came to you and said, *Vernon, I can't live with the stink on my shoulders, I got to go to IA and tell those shit heels all I know, but I wanted you to know it first. Bill, you said—*

"Bill, you do that, you don't just bring me down or just yourself. There are people who won't take kindly, who won't want that to happen."

"How are they going to know, Vernon? You going to tell them?"

"Of course not."

And, of course, he did tell them. And they said forget about everything, leave everything to them, and inside the envelope is a thank-you bonus. *Treat yourself to something nice, Vernon.* And that was how he came to be looking the other way the day Bill planned to show up and spill to IA, bring down Vernon and maybe even himself; cost Vernon his pension and maybe even get him, both of them, indicted, and—

How Bill came to be killed.

Gunned down.

A drive-by.

The part they didn't tell him, but—

He knew.

Treat yourself to something nice, Vernon.

Deep down he knew what they had planned for Bill Traylor, a better man than he ever was or ever would be.

No, Vernon. Bill Traylor did not get himself killed, dammit. There's a traitor in us all, Vernon. You got your partner killed. You traded away your fears on your partner's life. You—

Oh, Jesus F. Christ, Vernon. Stop doing this to yourself again. Bill Traylor set his own destiny in motion by making the decision he did. How long is it going to take you to recognize that?

Forever, Vernon, and that may not be long enough anymore. Not now. Now that you've managed to outdo yourself.

Amy Spencer and Betsy Wheatcroft murdered.

Pablo Mora and Evelyn Blemish murdered.

A good chance Jack Sothern still a target.

Then what, Vernon?

Then who?

Tracy?

Maggie?

For certain, Dan Boone.

You can't let this happen, Vernon.

Enough.

It's over.

No more deaths on your watch.

He wheeled into the Drinks 'R' Us Tavern parking lot and parked illegally at the red-painted curb by the entrance, acknowledged the usual greetings from the usual drunks, and settled on a barstool in front of the double shot of well bourbon the barkeep set up without asking.

He gulped it down, swiped his mouth with the back of a hand, signaled for another.

Said, "Lee, my boy, you see anything today or lately of the gent I been doing time here with?"

"You missed the little guy by five, maybe ten, Chief. He warmed that stool over there, nursing a pull draft and helping himself to the trail mix, hanging on the TV news until his cell phone started singing. After, he retreated to the john for a couple minutes, hardly long enough to take a piss, trapped a fiver under his glass, and split."

"You overhear anything about where he might be heading?"

"All's I heard was him telling me, 'Keep the change.' "

Vernon, so drunk the full moon resembled a listless yellow cutout in the pitch black sky, clutched the steering wheel like it might sail off at any second and alternated between eyeing the speedometer—a steady fifteen miles an hour—and the rearview.

He sang to stave off his desperate need for shuteye, "On the Road Again," bellowing the words like he imagined Willie Nelson would to a packed Super Bowl. As good as Willie or, if he wanted to be perfectly honest with himself, better than Willie; hearing his every cracked note as pitch perfect; missing the slur that made the lyrics an undecipherable pile of sound.

The Garden of Eden came into view.

He applauded himself for getting there in once piece, got his hands back on the wheel in time to avoid sideswiping a car parked curbside at the lip of the driveway entrance, and worked to get control of a fishtail that ended with the car jumping the curb and the rear bumper crashing to a stop against the parking lot wall.

"Way to go, Vernon," he told himself and, slipping onto the sidewalk, gave the sky a victory punch and weaved his way to the house. Halfway there, a couple Marines approached, wondering if he could use a helping hand. Vernon responded by yanking out his Beretta and waving it threateningly.

They threw up their hands and, when he told them *Skidaddle*, they skidaddled, Vernon shouting after them, "Gimme your left your right your left. Gimme your left your right your left." Cackling into the soft wind dancing in from the Pacific, "Halls of Montezuma, shores of Tripoli." Singing the words the way he imagined Willie Nelson would sing them.

Only better.

He watched them disappear through the entrance, then sank to the ground and burst into tears. He pounded the asphalt with a fist, fumbled for his cell phone, and tried dialing Emil Grass' number for—what?—the thousandth time?

No answer.

Entering The Garden of Eden, Vernon was greeted by Gerry Cotton's lavish smile.

"Hey, Chief, how they hanging? Do something for you this evening?"

"Only if you're a beautiful woman, Gerry."

"Hardly, but how's this rank as a sight for sore eyes?" He shifted the desk monitor so Vernon could view the screen.

"What about her?" Vernon said, playing along. Even squinting, there was no way he could read the image.

"This fox, 'Good Time Gal,' came and went from my life about a month ago. Met all my rigid requirements, she did, and the more we got to talking back and forth, email first, then the phone, seems I played right into her specifications."

"A woman of discrimination," Vernon said, not so drunk he couldn't be nice to the kid.

"No, sir. 'Good Time Gal' said she liked me for who I was and what she was seeing, so much so that I went straight and narrow with her and told her the truth about my circumstances and all, working here and all."

"Gallant of you, Gerry. Honesty, the best policy. Takes practice."

"It excited her, somebody telling the whole truth and nothing but. She gave me one of the wildest rides of my young life, an all-nighter that stretched into morning. Amazing for somebody old as she had to be. Older than me, but also richer. A woman of the world, for real. Telling me about all the places she's been around the world while we were going round the world ourselves." He turned over his hands and blew out a sigh.

"Gerry, I could use a woman right now myself. I don't suppose you got any laying around from the good old days? All she's got to be is breathing."

"Gone forever, those days, Chief, like I thought for a time 'Good Time Gal' was. She up and disappeared after that, until about two hours ago. Two hours ago. Two hours ago, she's in my email telling me how I put a raging fire between her thighs that she hasn't been able to get out of her mind. Why she resisted seeing me again. Now she wants to, and not only that— she's on her way and can't wait to get me out of my Speedos, she said. She's got flaws, but don't we all?"

"Don't we all. Damn right, Gerry. Don't we all." He dug after his worry beads, filled his palm with them, squeezed and rolled them for comfort. "Gerry, I get the picture. Any empty bed and a jar of Vaseline, how's that?"

He felt his legs too tired to support his weight any longer and grabbed onto the reception desk for support.

"You okay, Chief?"

"Hell, no," Vernon said. "A rotten son-of-a-bitch, that's what I am, Gerry. A miserable bastard."

CHAPTER 21

Roxy's lids snapped open at the unfamiliar noise. It took another moment to remember she was in Jack Sothern's room at Eden Highlands Memorial Hospital. Sothern as trapped in sleep now as when she got back here from The Garden of Eden. Betty's boy, Larry, was also asleep, the TV screen casting his sweet young face in varying shades of light and shadow.

When she padded into the room with Glen Traylor, Larry at first saw only Glen.

He broke into a smile and raised a high five that quickly fell to the bedcover in response to her smile.

It was Larry's unforgiving acknowledgment of who Roxy was, that mean woman at The Garden of Eden, who'd fired his mother for no good reason.

How was she ever supposed to correct that, by telling Larry Betty was fired after Roxy caught her getting butt-fucked by Vernon Mount in one of the guest suites?

Better to live with the blame.

How many times had she wanted to rage at someone, "I am not an evil person. I have a job to do. I do it well. I run the business like a business. Health insurance, God damn it. Profit sharing and retirement benefits, God damn it."

Better, though, the scorn for her than for Maggie, the possibility of it filtering down to their precious Tracy.

God, how she loved Tracy.

As much as she loved Tracy's mother.

Maggie, always consoling her when some particular sting or overheard barb drew blood, taking her in her arms and re-assuring her, *"You're better than any of them could ever even aspire to be. Just walk with your head high and you'll never even notice them."*

"It hurts to the quick not to be loved, Maggie."

"The only people who matter are the ones who do love you, Sweet Thing."

The noise was the night nurse, grunting under the weight of the elephantine body packed inside her uniform, her nurse's cap with its taffeta borders and butterfly bow at the rear sitting askew on her mound of frizzy bleached blonde hair. Faye, her name, who'd got through nursing school eight years ago on wages earned at The Garden of Eden.

Faye used a penlight to check the chart hooked to the end rail on Larry's bed, then moved over to Sothern's chart. Turning, she realized Roxy was still in the visitors chair at the opposite wall.

Faye signaled a greeting and whispered, "You comfortable strung out that way, Roxy, or you need me to get you a pillow? A blanket?"

"Fine like I am," she answered, drawing her arms tighter across her chest.

Faye shook her head. "No. I think I'll come back with a blanket and a pillow end of my rounds. Air-conditioning in here's enough to freeze piss in a bed pan."

"How's the patient doing?"

"Still alive. Always a good sign."

"Going to keep him that way?"

"Looks to be. From what it says here on his chart, he could be good to go tomorrow or the next day, unless test results still out say otherwise."

"Hal still standing guard outside?"

Her head swung left and right. "Now it's another one of Vernon's reserves by the door. Tom Almond? I remember him from high school. Tom, as nuts as his name. I remember how he was always reminding me the 'l' in Almond was as silent as a fart in a blizzard. A wild man, that one. Don't know how he can be trusted with a gun, unless it's shooting blanks, same as him when we were going steady our junior year."

Faye blew her a kiss and oomphed her way out.

Roxy found a new way to lean in the chair, rearranged her legs and her grip on herself, and closed her eyes to the world.

CHAPTER 22

The Howard Johnson's restaurant at the San Diego Freeway rest stop was twelve minutes down the hill from Eden Highlands. Grass arrived early for a change. He was settled over coffee and a peach-filled pastry in the back booth they both liked—half-hidden from view, an excellent sightline to the entrance and the busy, well-lit parking lot, cars and a variety of freight trucks and other road-hoggers constantly pulling in and out—when Burt Crews arrived.

Crews was full of apology for his tardiness as he slid onto the tired mint green naugahyde bench across from Grass. He ripped off a piece of Grass' pastry without asking and devoured it like somebody coming off a fast. Washed it down with Grass' glass of water and flipped open a menu, scanning it while explaining, "Had to lay in time before making my getaway. It wouldn't have been wise to race away too quickly after that damn detective was called about the hospital murders."

"What did you tell her?"

"Call to me was government business, hush-hush and all that crapola. Shame. She had a nice meatloaf cooking in the oven. What's good?" His finger stopped. "The chili dip. Tasty last time I tried it." He finger-smacked a kiss. "Maybe some fries on the side. Put my cholesterol to a real test." He scouted for a waitress. "You?"

"Cheeseburger. You can have my fries. What do you think?"

"I'll take them . . . or do you mean your stunt at the hospital?"

"Stunt? I told you on the phone. Jack Sothern here and snooping, he could have ruined everything for us if he kept blabbing about Boone the way he was doing or, *Gott bewahre*, print the story someplace and bring the whole world down on us probably."

"If *Gott bewahre* anything, God forbid you making *eine neue groBe scheiBe.*"

Grass reared back at the insult. *"Eine groBe scheiBe?"* A big fuckup?

"GroBe." Big. Crews put two feet of space between his vertical palms. *"GroBe, GroBe, GroBe."* Extending the space another foot.

Speaking German had drawn attention.

They quit conversing until a waitress had taken their orders, then resumed at a level so low both were leaning forward and close to touching noses, despite the difference in their height. Shoulders hunched. Fingers tightly laced.

Grass said, "You mean the old woman?" He dismissed the idea with a gesture and told Crews, *"Hauab!"* Fuck off! Almost a hiss. "She put herself in the way. Better luck for her in her next life. I got to Sothern and sent him off on his way. All that should matter to you. Silence is golden, you know? Keeping the coast clear for us."

"Not that."

"What then?"

"Sometimes, Grass, instead of being early to action and late to appointments, you should try the reverse."

He said, "Don't talk to me in riddles, Crews." Thinking, *You swine. Like you're so perfect.*

"You don't know, do you?"

"What? Know what?"

They sat quietly as the waitress settled their orders in front of them.

Crews took a healthy mouthful of his chili dip sandwich, gave it a thumbs-up and added two fries from Grass' cheeseburger.

Grass lifted the top of the bun to inspect his order and, without a test, added heavy doses of salt and pepper and a thick glob of ketchup. Then he tried the burger. It was excellent. It would have been excellent even if it tasted like shit. Killing always brought on his appetite. Working the words around his stuffed cheeks, he said, "So, already—what am I to know?"

Crews said, "It was on the radio news driving down."

"I listen to music. It soothes the savage beast in me."

"Well, the savage beast in you got the wrong man at the hospital. You went to the wrong room and visited your extreme prejudice on some city father in addition to the old woman, not Sothern."

Globs of food burst from Grass' mouth onto his plate and their water glasses, almost caught Crews' shirtfront. He toweled off his mouth and chin with the napkin and answered the amusement beaming from Crews' eyes with reserve, even after Crews took to deriding him, saying, "You don't very often make mistakes, I grant you that, Grass. But when you do, they're lulus. This city father, his murder has stirred up a hornet's nest."

Grass struggled to keep his composure. "Accidents happen. Have they linked it in any way to Sothern?"

Crews rinsed his throat with Grass' coffee. "Not on the radio. Nothing I heard from the detective before he went running off to the hospital. Maybe I'll hear something when I get back to the Collins place, and that should be quickly." He checked his wristwatch and gave it a nod. "I think what you have to do is go back to the hospital and finish what you started, don't you? Let them believe there's some serial killer in their midst, distract them further, like the two dead girls, while we wait out Boone's arrival."

"The two girls. The two at the hospital, soon to be three.

Definitely that money-greedy *scheisse* chief of police. Maybe, probably, his detective, Traylor. The lesbian lady running The Garden of Eden. Boone. Then his wife and daughter . . ." He had been doing the count with his fingers. "Eleven. I'm out of fingers."

"Figure on eight for you. I'll take charge of the detective and Boone's wife. We'll share disposing of Boone. Don't look so concerned, Grass. I remember past missions, where you also ran out of toes."

"You really think what we're doing here is worth so many, maybe more than eleven before we leave?"

Crews let a grin snake up his face. "Are you developing a conscience, Grass?"

"Don't be a crazy man."

"We're here about Dr. Mielke's diary, Grass, so you tell me. I don't even know why you bother to ask."

"It's only a question. From curiosity."

"Once the diary is in our possession, we can retire rich men. Pursue our dreams."

"And if Boone won't surrender the diary?"

"Think positive, comrade. He's coming and he understands we're holding his child in escrow. The diary for the daughter. Will he suspect treachery? Yes. Will he be prepared for it? Probably. But Dan Boone's heroics were always just pretending. A movie star acting. Killing is second nature to us. Death is a way of life. And one other thing . . . ?"

"*Jah?*"

"The music station you picked on the radio. What one? I'll give it a try."

Seeing a police unit parked outside the hospital didn't surprise Grass, not with a homicide investigation in progress. Seeing the uniformed cop parked outside Sothern's room on the fourth floor did. It told him somebody had connected Sothern to the two killings downstairs.

Sothern was being protected, as flimsy as the protection was. Hick protection.

Real protection and they'd have thought to delete Sothern from the computer, not declare his new room number. Made it difficult for someone to freely wander the halls the way Grass had now done twice.

Possibly another cop guarding Sothern inside the room?

So what?

Still flimsy, two hicks.

Candidates for Number Twelve and maybe Number Thirteen.

Grass was confident he could take them out in the twitch of an eye.

He had faced bigger odds in the past, only last year with that Rosica business in New Jersey. No hicks there, and not any more time than now to either work a strategy or simply plunge forward.

Grass thinking—

Come up with a ruse to get the cop out of the corridor, onto his feet, into Sothern's room.

Break his neck. A quick twist, and that's that. You could even call it *a snap.* Hah, funny, my joke.

Auf wiedersehen, Number Twelve.

If there is a second cop, who gets his service weapon drawn and aimed fast enough to put me on the defensive, he'll be too confused and nervous to fire at once. He'll shout some nonsense about hands up, instead. These hicks always do.

Charge at Number Thirteen using Number Twelve as a buffer. If Number Thirteen does manage to get off a shot, it's Number Twelve who takes the bullet, his body serving as a silencer. In those same seconds, quickly maneuver to take out Number Thirteen with the long blade from my HuntChamp.

A stab or two—or three or four—to do the trick, then—

On to Sothern, quickly, no time to waste, especially if he's awake and groping for his summons button.

Another patient in the room?

Pffft.

Number Fourteen as unlucky as Thirteen.

Auf wiedersehen to all of you, and—

Gone.

Out of there.

Emil Grass, once more the invisible man.

The picture he had painted for himself excited Grass. His heart was pounding, trying to leap from his chest. He held a hand perpendicular to the floor to test his nerves. Steady as a rock. He dug out the HuntChamp and found the blade. Palmed the knife up his sleeve.

He would get this done and celebrate later, maybe pick up one of the whores he'd noticed a few times prowling outside the row of bars on Father Couts Drive that catered to all types.

Work off the steam.

Killing and sex.

Sex and killing.

They had more in common than most people might suspect, would ever know or experience. He could write a book on the subject. Two books. Maybe one day he would. Wouldn't that be something? His mother and father would have to finally be proud of him when that happened, from wherever the damn fools were looking up at him.

Grass had ducked out of the cop's sightline, back around the corner, but now he stepped out and started toward the cop, modulating his breath to control his excitement, focusing his eyes and his mind on the mission at hand.

The linoleum had been freshly washed and the smell of a pungent disinfectant lingered on the wet surface and in the air, transported by the relentless air conditioning.

The bitter taste drifted into his mouth and clogged the base of his throat.

He coughed it out.

The cop stirred at the sound, checked around, and saw him approaching. He eased his chair onto all four legs, got to his feet, and dropped the magazine he had been holding onto the leather-cushioned seat. His hand moved toward his hip holster while he gave Grass a cautious onceover, as if anticipating a problem.

"Help you, mister?" he said.

Grass sized him up. The cop was two heads taller and had at least fifteen years and two hundred pounds on him. Built like a wrestler. Not the easy target he'd first appeared to be. He quickly reevaluated every move he had in mind and worked through adjustments that would be necessary to keep the kill clause viable.

Stepping up to the cop, Grass said, "Yes, Officer. I believe you can."

CHAPTER 23

In a swift, single move, Grass dropped the knife into his palm and slashed it across the cop's throat. The cop's hand moved reflexively to the cut. Blood drained out between his fingers and his eyes grew immense, trading surprise for open-mouthed fear over what had happened to him. He fumbled for his revolver, but only for a few seconds before he tried to grab Grass, who had now dug the blade in and out of the cop's soft belly.

Grass stepped away. He looked up at the cop and smiled with delight before plunging the blade into the cop's midsection two more times. The cop staggered back, banging hard against the wall, and slid to the floor with a look that said he realized he would never know tomorrow.

Grass knelt beside him.

"You have my sincere congratulations, Officer. There is honor in dying doing your job."

He patted the cop on the head and stuck him one more time for insurance, removed the blade from the cop's chest and wiped it off on his shirtfront.

Now there was no time to waste, not with a body here in the hall and the possibility of someone coming along any second.

Grass jumped to his feet.

He pushed open the door to Sothern's room and hurried inside.

The shaft of light from the hallway was the only illumination aside from the flicker of a TV set.

"That you, Tom?" A boy's voice, groggy from sleep. "Tom? The noise woke me up was what?"

Grass thinking, *Ficken! So there is another patient in the room.*

"Faye? I think it's Faye, Larry."

Another voice, this one female.

Grass thinking, *Scheisse, what goes on in here? A convention?*

"Faye, that you?"

"Larry?"

The boy sounding straight ahead and off to the left, in the first bed.

The woman, farther back in the room. The second bed?

Christus. What this time? Had they again moved Sothern to a different room or, maybe, was the listing on the computer a ruse to draw him out?

Grass switched the knife to his left hand and used his right to pat the wall after the light switch. He found a dial, but before he could turn it, a hand settled hard on his arm and pulled it away. An arm clamped across his chest, trapping his left arm.

He yanked his right arm free of restraint, retrieved the knife, and thrust the blade backward, over his shoulder, over his head. Into the arm restraining him. Again. Over and over, until his body was freed.

He turned around and saw the cop, not as dead as the cop should have been, a mountain of red on knees about to collapse. He shot the blade up under his chin. Punctured his heart. Sent him stumbling backward, back into the hallway, loudly gargling death.

"Tom, what the hell?" The boy again.

"Larry, call for a nurse." The woman.

"Have," this Larry person said.

Grass saw the red call light outside above the door reflected on the opposite wall.

Blinking for assistance.

No time, no time, no time, he thought.

And fled before anyone would find him there.

Celebrating with some mangy whore, out of the question now.

Grass was too disturbed.

All he could think about the entire drive back to the trailer park was what Crews would have to say to him about this.

Eine groBe scheiBe again? What is it with you, Grass? Losing your touch? Age finally catching up with you? Reflexes not what they used to be? What else can I think?

That's how Crews would treat him, not waiting to hear the facts, prejudging him, the way Crews was always doing, as if he were in charge.

Crews' way, smug and superior.

Grass screamed into the windshield: *Well, you arrogant schwanzlutscher. Es is mir scheiBegal. I do not give a fuck what you think. Es is mir scheiBegal. Maybe when this is all done and we don't need each other anymore, I'll show you who has lost his touch.*

Grass turned up the radio, kept changing stations until he found the kind of loud noise that passed for music nowadays. Turned it up higher, hoping to drown out Crews' voice in his head. Crews stayed louder and more revolting than the music.

Happy Homes was a sad-looking trailer park on the edge of town, just outside the city limits. Most of the aging motor homes were permanently installed. They sat on a slab of cement that passed for a foundation in order to qualify for certain tax advantages under California state law, about two hundred of them, many with carports of canvas on rusted aluminum piping and fenced-in patches of weed-ravaged brown lawn being used for patio furniture and the obligatory butane-fired barbecue.

At the rear of Happy Homes, about a hundred yards from the main entrance, with an entrance of its own, was Temporary

Town, which accommodated about twenty-five or so vehicle owners after rental stays of short duration, mostly overnighters. Grass was one of them, paying by the week, the nondescript trailer in which he was holding Tracy Collins prisoner lost among similar trailers at the outermost point, where Temporary Town abutted the Father Melchoir Couts Memorial Park and Hiking Trail.

He came and went with bare notice among the other renters in the tightly cramped area, most of them balding and blue-haired older people spending their retirement dollars on cross-country travels or military wives waiting out a reassignment. Not the best motor park around, but far less expensive than those right off the freeway exits.

For Grass, it wasn't a money consideration.

Temporary Town was perfectly situated for his needs.

When his work was done, he'd be able to slither off as quietly as he had arrived, leaving the trailer behind and no evidence he'd ever been there at all—

Except for Tracy.

Grass pulled the car into an empty slot in the parking lot, climbed out, and took a few final drags off his English Oval before mashing it under his heel, then hurried across the noisy gravel to the trailer, book-ended by a modest trailer home that was there the day he arrived and a mammoth red SUV on giant wheels, with blue and white pin-striping and a rear bumper full of stickers, that sometime today had replaced a dusty two-story camper.

THE GENE POOL COULD USE A LITTLE CHLORINE.

That bumper sticker gave him his first reason to smile since the hospital.

CHAOS. PANIC. DISORDER. MY WORK IS DONE HERE.

That one gave him a start, as if it were addressing him specifically.

Even more startling was what the bright full moon revealed about the door to his trailer as it escaped from a bank of pregnant rain clouds that seemed on the edge of delivering.

The door was wide open.

Scheisse.

This shouldn't be.

He had locked the door securely and tested it before heading off, of course.

Grass broke into a trot.

At the trailer door, he caught his breath, hands resting on his knees, before easing up the platform steps.

He paused to survey the darkness inside, listened for some sign of activity, wishing he were carrying his .22 instead of only the knife. It was inside the trailer, clipped under the dining counter.

After another minute, the dark silence seeming safe enough, he took his first careful steps inside the trailer. Spent the next minute motionless, except to get the knife and ready it for use again.

"Hey, up there? Looking for your daughter?"

The question startled Grass, but it had come with a cordial patina.

Still, he exercised caution, palming the blade up his sleeve as he turned slowly, a false smile plastered on his face, and looked down at the man settling on a front fender of the SUV. He was dressed for summer, cutoffs and a t-shirt with the silkscreen image of a bumper sticker reading ARTIFICIAL INTELLIGENCE BEATS REAL STUPIDITY, clutching a bottle of beer that fit his thick voice, bulldog face, and smear of five o'clock shadow. Somewhere in his early to mid-forties.

Grass held his composure. "Why do you ask?"

"She went scooting out of there about the time we were pulling our joy rig in, like some little bat out of Hades," he said. He pointed at the sky and the threatening clouds. "I called after her about coming back for a jacket or a coat, anything warmer than the skimpy outfit she had on. Rain opens up, she's in for some drenching. Not even a turnaround, but I seen you and thought you should know. Give her what-for when she gets back."

"Yes. Thank you. What-for, for certain. Children, you know how they are. Bad weather never anything to occupy their minds, and my little Elsa already coming down with a dreadful cold."

"Not surprised. Elsa seemed a little wobbly on her feet."

"You notice the direction she was going?"

The man pointed toward Happy Homes.

Grass gave him a look that said he understood. "Probably the supply store. Silly little girl knew we need more orange juice and soup. Aspirin. Wanted to surprise her father, I'm betting."

"How old's she?"

"Fifteen and a half."

"Yeah, my two the same at that age. Fifteen going on fifty more like it. She into t-shirts?"

"What's that you're saying?"

The man thumped his chest. "T-shirts. Don't let me pull out of here tomorrow and not leave one or two for you. Some bumper stickers, my real line. Got hundreds of them and fresh ones being added daily. I sell mostly through the Internet and trade shows nowadays. Who needs the overhead when four wheels and a wanderlust are cheaper and work just as well for Dan-Dan-the-T-Shirt-Man?"

"Yes, of course," Grass said. "Thank you. I should get her heavy jacket and go after her myself." He flipped on the trailer lights while backing inside, to verify Tracy was not there and pick out something warm that looked meant for her, to play out the lies he'd told so well to that damn fool with his stupid bumper stickers.

Most of all, he had to find the girl before she got to anybody or anybody found her or, if he was too late for that—

Grass freed the .22 from under the dining counter and stashed it inside his belt.

In case the knife wouldn't be enough.

He was halfway to Happy Homes, hoping it wasn't too late to catch her, that Tracy had not stumbled into people somewhere in the mass of trailer homes or beyond and cried out who she was and where she had been—what had happened—when he quit his jaguar-paced run and held his hands in the air like he'd caught a sudden realization to go with the puzzled look freshly chiseled on his face.

He had let alarm taint rational thought in those moments of dread after discovering the trailer door open and being told by Dan-Dan-the-T-Shirt-Man how he had seen Tracy fleeing.

Now, with thinking room for more than panic, Grass recognized the man's lies.

Even if he had neglected to medicate her before leaving earlier today—and he was sure that hadn't happened—or, given that he had been gone longer than anticipated and the drugs were wearing off, she would still be too woozy, too disoriented to locate her clothing in the darkness, fish out the plastic bag, and get dressed. Find the trailer door. Work the lock and manage the door open. Get down the steps on unsteady legs lacking the strength necessary to run off like—how did Dan-Dan-the-T-Shirt-Man say it?—*Like a bat from hell.*

Run like a bat from hell?

Scheisse!

Nein.

No, no, no.

181

Grass' face hardened.

His eyes narrowed to a more likely truth.

He did an abrupt about-face and dashed back toward the trailer.

The SUV was inching out of its parking slot.

Grass knew he had to stop Dan-Dan-the-T-Shirt-Man before he got away, certain Tracy Collins was with him.

Chapter 24

The SUV was having difficulty angling around the speedboat hitched to the even larger, bulkier SUV parked to its immediate left, on the driver side. Dan-Dan-the-T-Shirt-Man pulled forward, then started another slow move out, the angle slightly varied from the last time.

He stopped and tried it again, the reverse angle more acute this time, but still not enough to fully clear the speedboat.

He began another forward crawl and must have spotted Grass racing toward him in the rearview.

The SUV suddenly accelerated. It bashed into the side of Grass' trailer, then raced into reverse, hit the speedboat hitch hard enough to dislodge the boat, noisily scraped past the sharp edge of the boat hitch, and made it onto the access lane.

Grass adjusted his course and dashed to a spot about ten or fifteen yards in front of the SUV before it began moving again.

He whipped out his .22 and broke into a one-handed shooter's stance, using his free hand as a shield against the SUV's brights. Aimed squarely at Dan-Dan-the-T-Shirt-Man.

For a moment he thought Dan-Dan-the-T-Shirt-Man meant to run him down.

He got off a shot that cracked the windshield on the passenger side, barely missing Dan-Dan-the-T-Shirt-Man, as he'd intended, but close enough to frighten him into braking to a full stop.

Grass hurried over and signaled Dan-Dan-the-T-Shirt-Man

to lower his window.

"Hey, pal, that shot's gonna attract attention you don't need," Dan-Dan-the-T-Shirt-Man said.

"A backfire, maybe, pal. Noises like that all the time and nobody pays attention, not at this time of night especially, this weather. The next noise they'll ignore will be the death of you unless you quickly unlock the doors."

Dan-Dan-the-T-Shirt-Man studied Grass' face and the .22 and did as he was told. Grass opened the passenger door and jumped in behind him. He pulled the door shut and commanded, "Drive. *Schnell.* Fast. Get going."

"Someplace in particular?" Dan-Dan-the-T-Shirt-Man said, trying to make light of the situation, but the crack in his throat betrayed his fear.

Grass had Dan-Dan-the-T-Shirt-Man drive deep inside the Father Melchoir Couts Memorial Park and Hiking Trail. Approaching a narrow service road on the downside, the gate of the brush-encrusted chain link fence hanging open by a hinge, the sign PARK EMPLOYEES ONLY barely legible under layers of dirt cakes, he ordered him to turn in.

Unlike the main asphalted roadway, this road was all dirt and rocks, potholes deep enough to bury a skunk or squirrel in and no tire tracks to suggest recent use. Turns came up abruptly and unexpectedly, requiring Dan-Dan-the-T-Shirt-Man to brake to a crawl or risk driving them into the drain ditches or ravines that followed the course of the road on both sides.

"Where in hell we heading to, pal?" Dan-Dan-the-T-Shirt-Man said, friendly-like, as if they might be lost on their way to a company picnic.

"Just keep your eye on the road," Grass said, having no better answer.

The SUV bumped along for another quarter mile or so, into

darkening shadows caused by tall trees tilted after years of battering from winds that sweep in from the ocean or down through the mountain ranges to form a natural roof and a sky approaching nightfall.

Dan-Dan-the-T-Shirt-Man switched on the high beams.

Grass whipped his arm with the .22 and ordered them turned off.

Dan-Dan-the-T-Shirt-Man flinched. "You crazy, pal? I'm no stunt driver."

"I'm crazy, pal." He shoved the gun into Dan-Dan-the-T-Shirt-Man's side. "Obey me. Do as you're told."

Dan-Dan-the-T-Shirt-Man took a noisy breath. "You're the boss."

"I am, yes," Grass said.

But not crazy.

He spotted a shoulder turnaround a few yards ahead.

Ordered Dan-Dan-the-T-Shirt-Man to pull in.

Dan-Dan-the-T-Shirt-Man shifted the SUV into park and nervously gunned the motor a few times before switching off the ignition and handing over the keys at Grass' command.

He angled himself between the seat and the door, wondering, "Are you going to explain what this is about? I'm uncomfortable as all hell staring down at that peashooter of yours."

Grass adjusted himself against the passenger door, the .22 level on a plane with Dan-Dan-the-T-Shirt-Man's chest, ordered him to turn on the overhead light, and said, "Where is she, the girl?"

"The girl? I told you where's the girl, how she—"

"No."

"What do you mean *No?*" Stuttering a bit.

Grass waved off the question with the gun. "Tell me now the truth."

"Like I said, she flitted out of the trailer like—"

"I know. A bat from hell. Only dressed, but she couldn't be a dressed bat from hell. How do you explain your telling me the bat from hell was dressed when she couldn't be?"

Dan-Dan-the-T-Shirt-Man answered with a silent stare.

Grass groped for the knife in his pocket.

In a blink, he had it out and swiped across Dan-Dan-the-T-Shirt-Man's right cheek.

A thin line of blood about two inches long appeared.

Dan-Dan-the-T-Shirt-Man howled as his fingers snapped to the wound, while his other hand stretched defensively between them.

Grass stabbed the palm with the blade, causing a second howl. "Next time a bullet, unless you tell me now the truth," he said. Nodded agreement with himself.

Moon rays were cutting down through the trees and through the windshield, two or three striping Dan-Dan-the-T-Shirt-Man's face and bringing out a glossy fear playing in his eyes. He took his fingers from his cheek and studied his blood. The blood leaking down his cheek glowed a rich ruby red where it had been caught by the moonlight.

"Are you going to kill me?"

Grass didn't answer him.

Dan-Dan-the-T-Shirt-Man wiped off his hands on his naked thighs, then across his t-shirt. He tilted his head toward his left shoulder, as if that might curb the flow of blood, but it only reduced it to a trickle. He said, "I cracked your door, like dozens before on the road. In and out in a flash with pickings ripe for pawning. The girl was a bonus."

"What does that mean?"

Dan-Dan-the-T-Shirt-Man looked like he didn't want to answer. Grass made like he was going to bring the blade down on his thigh. Dan-Dan-the-T-Shirt-Man twisted his legs away and waved him off.

"I usually snatch them from outside a bus station, street corners, playgrounds, out front a school, but never in campgrounds where I'm parked. That's like shitting in your stew pot, if you know what I mean?"

"You mean you're a pervert who preys on young girls."

Dan-Dan-the-T-Shirt-Man took quick offense. He reared back against the door and stroked the air repeatedly with his forefinger. "What's that make you, I mean, Jesus, the pot calling the kettle black?" An arrogant smile, exposing his bad teeth. "You got some naked kid back there in your trailer, drugged out of her mind, her breath smelling like a medicine cabinet, and who knows what's been going on between you and her, or how long?" He engaged his arms across his chest and challenged Grass with his uplifted chin.

"She's my property. What I'm doing with her is none of your business."

"You kill them when you're through with them? That part of your game, pal? Not me. I love 'em and leave 'em. I solve the mystery for them. I teach them the wonders of growing up. I deposit them better than I found them, with a fresh t-shirt of their choosing to keep as a reminder of their glorious awakening, not that I expect you to understand."

"I do, though. You're a pervert, Pervert."

"What name do you give yourself?"

"Not *Pal*," Grass said, and sloped the blade into Dan-Dan-the-T-Shirt-Man's thigh, eliciting a fresh howl. "And the name I give you is *Dead Man*, dead before you know it if you don't talk up fast. Tell me what you've done with the girl."

"Tell me what *you've* done with the girl, how's that?" Dan-Dan-the-T-Shirt-Man said, summoning the courage that Grass had witnessed many times before in people who recognized how close they were to dying. "Maybe we can do it together. I teach you and you teach me. What say?"

"*Gott bewahre!* I say you tell me where she is before I reach the count of ten or I'm going to blow your balls off."

"You would, wouldn't you?"

"A man of my word. One . . . two . . ."

"I tell you, you'll let me go?"

Grass pretended to think about it. Shrugged. "Our business is finished here, I have the girl again, why not? I don't think you'll go to a police station anytime soon, except to register as a sex offender. Three . . . four . . ."

"They never once caught me. Not once." Proudly, like he was applying for a medal. "I lost count how many times, how many states years ago. Got some pretty souvenirs could show you, except not taking them on the road with me anymore is part of being careful."

"Five."

Grass had the count to seven before Dan-Dan-the-T-Shirt-Man threw a thumb over his shoulder and said, "She's in back there, on as comfortable a mattress as you'll ever find anywhere on the road. I had your *property*—" saying the word so Grass caught his sarcasm and contempt—"laid out nice and comfy, primed for her lesson, when I spotted you out the rear window on your way back for the trailer. I got her covered up nice and good under the blanket and some t-shirts from the stockpile for good measure and me out onto the fender just in time to send you after the wild goose."

Grass threw a fast look behind. All he could see over the backrest of the bench seat were bundles of t-shirts stacked on shelves mounted on the sides of the cabin shell; what appeared to be bundles of bumper stickers; boxes and tins of food; some toiletries on one high shelf set aside for that purpose. He said, "Drop down the seat so I can see for myself."

"Can't reach the release from here." He demonstrated his words.

Grass said, "Get on your knees and reach."

"That'll have me spilling more blood on the leather upholstery than I did already. It don't clean out that good and getting the upholstery replaced, an arm and a leg nowadays."

Grass held the knife threateningly. "There can be more where that came from."

Dan-Dan-the-T-Shirt-Man winced. "The Red Cross blood bank know about you?" he said. Freed himself of the safety buckle and maneuvered onto his knees, facing the back of the SVU.

Stretched forward, lifting himself enough to reach the backrest release.

The backrest fell, exposing the mattress in the center of the floor, a hump about the size of Tracy Collins on top, covered by a thin blue wool knit blanket mostly hidden under a top layer of t-shirts.

"Damn. Look at what I meant about the blood spotting the leather?"

"I want to see under the blanket."

Dan-Dan-the-T-Shirt-Man stretched his mouth taut with resignation and grumbled something undecipherable. He pushed forward several more inches, an arm a few inches more than that, got a hand on the blanket and flung it aside, enough for Grass to recognize Tracy.

"Satisfied now, pal?"

"A wonder you didn't smother her."

"Hurrying aside, I was careful about that. Whatever else I'm into, necrophilia isn't one of my Joneses."

"We all have our virtues."

Turning to face Grass, he said, "What's yours then?"

"A merciful death for people I despise even as much as I despise you," Grass said. He shoved the barrel of the .22 up under Dan-Dan-the-T-Shirt-Man's chin and squeezed the trigger.

Besides the fact that dead weight is dead weight, Dan-Dan-the-T-Shirt-Man was bigger and heavier than Grass to begin with. Bulkier. It took a good half hour for Grass to pull him from the SUV, drag him to the side of the service road, and pitch him down into the gully.

Finished, he settled against the side of the vehicle. He lit up an English Oval and, one hand supporting the elbow of the other, which held onto the smoke three-finger style, he stared off into the dark distance, inhaling both the smoke and the satisfaction of knowing he had rid the world of a creature as evil as Dan-Dan-the-T-Shirt-Man.

He himself was not without fault.

Grass could acknowledge that, but—

As much as he fancied Tracy Collins, he was no Dan-Dan-the-T-Shirt-Man, who pursued these young girls as an end unto itself, the antidote to a sick urge that respected no limitations. Tracy was bounty, nothing more, his for the taking if he chose to take once the business with Dan Boone was concluded.

Maybe yes, maybe no, before the sad goodbye he found it necessary to administer to anybody who might be able to identify him. That was fair, that was just, but to send some poor little girl who'd been used as a sex toy off with a souvenir t-shirt—

Ugly, ugly, ugly.

Grass blew out some smoke rings that dissolved in the darkness. He flicked away the cigarette with indifference toward the dry brush, and laughed uproariously at what he'd been thinking. "You can lie to others, but not for long to yourself," he told the slight wind drifting up from the flatlands. "If it were a contest with Dan-Dan-the-T-Shirt-Man, you'd win in a stroll.

You are as sick as he was. As ugly as he was. Uglier. Still alive and kicking, Mr. Emil Grass, so with the means to grow even uglier. So, she's young. So what? You've had them younger. If not for the business here in Eden Highlands, you'd have had her already. Admit it. . . . Okay, I admit it. Does that make me uglier than the world itself? Sicker than the world itself? To who, then? Not to me. Not to me, God damn it. Not to me. Me? *Es ismir scheiBegal.* I don't give a fuck what anybody else thinks. Not anybody. No one."

He'd have preferred sending the SUV down the gully, as well as the pervert, knowing it would be days, maybe even weeks, before discovery, by which time he would be long gone, not that there was anything they'd find to connect him to the crime, not DNA or a fingerprint match or anything. Grass had been many places over the years, but never in any official files that could still come back to haunt him, even if they knew where to look.

He would have to drive back to Temporary Town, quickly get the girl back into his trailer, and then deal with unloading the SUV under cover of night. These hills provided a hundred and one places where he could do that successfully, so he wasn't going to give it a second thought until later.

Before starting off, Grass climbed into the vehicle to give Tracy closer inspection. He used his fingers against her neck to check for a pulse. Carefully pulled open her eyelids to verify the drugs were still working. Her glassy stare said they were, but a gargling sound from the base of her throat told him she was coming out of it. Much time had passed since he'd administered her last dosage. She would require a fresh fix once he had her safe and sound in the trailer, maybe a nice warm sponge bath to ease any discomfort of the last few hours.

Tracy was no longer naked.

The pervert had clothed her in an oversized t-shirt that

worked as an ankle-length nightgown, silkscreened with a bright yellow smiley face and underneath it the words GO HARD OR GO HOME.

Go Hard . . .

The thought set him off immediately.

He wagged his head against the urge, ordering himself:

Not here. Not now.

Grass ran his hand over Tracy's body, the way someone would pamper a pet, telling her, "Don't you fear, my beautiful little girl. Uncle Emil will see you to home safely." He brought up the blanket and tucked it securely under her chin and over her shoulders, gave her a kiss on the forehead, and assured her, "I've taken care of that dreadful man. You're safe with me," as if that were the truth.

From about a quarter mile away, Grass saw the people milling about Dan-Dan-the-T-Shirt-Man's rental space, flashlight beams dancing over the damaged section of his trailer and dissecting the speedboat that the pervert's erratic driving had knocked off its hitch into a forty-five degree angle. He cursed them for choosing this time rather than waiting until morning to assess the damage. To arrive now would have him answering questions that didn't need asking, like what was he doing with the SUV and where was its owner and was that blood they were seeing and—

Scheisse!

What's that there in the back? Let's have us a look, and—

Grass glided the SUV into the first empty slot he came across in the parking area. Said, "Your Uncle Emil has to leave you for a while, my beautiful little girl, but don't you worry. He'll be back." Climbed out of the van, clicked the door locks, and headed for his trailer.

★ ★ ★ ★ ★

Grass was gone almost an hour, sharing information, outrage, and ignorance with the trailer park manager, a jittery type who tried to assign blame anywhere but with the park, an insurance adjuster making copious notes with a pencil he kept wetting with his tongue, as if it were a lollipop, and the speedboat owners, a respectable-looking middle-aged couple whose demands inched closer and closer to threats of litigation.

He made no special demands of his own, doing his best to blend into the shadows, the less remembered about him later the better. He shook hands all around before stepping into his trailer and waited patiently until certain everyone had left, then headed for the SUV.

What he saw stopped him in his tracks. Sent his pulse orbiting to Mars.

The rear panel door was open.

Grass raced to the SUV and scrambled inside, fearing the worst.

Found it when he drew aside Tracy's blanket and discovered all it covered now was a pile of t-shirts.

The girl was gone.

CHAPTER 25

When the ruckus pulled him free from the sleeping crap the nurse had laced him with, Sothern was having the recurring dream that always had him edging toward total disaster—like was always happening in the Saturday matinee serials he used to collect on videocassette—being menaced by someone cloaked in shadows, who could be either male or female and always spoke in a language he didn't understand.

He'd be lost somewhere, an empty city on a barren landscape or in a hotel constructed like a maze, maybe trapped in an elevator, the walls and ceiling closing in on him—Chapter Eleven, *The Crawling Claw*—and desperate to save himself, but before he could—

CONTINUED NEXT WEEK.

Usually startled awake by the black-and-white pictures of impending doom, even though he knew death wasn't possible in your own dream, just as it was not possible to dream in color—proven scientific fact, absolutely, no matter what some claimed; he'd once researched this for a piece commissioned by *Other Worlds Monthly;* the same way holding onto the dream was like trying to hold a moonbeam in your hand, he was telling Roxy Colbraith.

"*The Sound of Music,*" Roxy said.

"What?"

"*How do you hold a moonbeam in your hand?* The song about Maria in *The Sound of Music.* Oscar Hammerstein the Third wrote that lyric." She sang the line to the Richard Rodgers melody. "You think it was something you wrote?"

"I wish. I was only trying to describe my dreams to you. How lousy they are."

"Why? You survive to live another chapter."

"I suppose, although I never get to the next chapter, so I can't be sure. . . . You knew that about *The Sound of Music*. I'm impressed."

"Yeah. Surprise, surprise, a brain to go with the body." She took a hand off the steering wheel and dismissed him with a flying flutter.

They were on their way to The Garden of Eden. Sothern had released himself from the hospital on a waiver of responsibility after they failed in their urging to keep him at least another day.

In another room, of course, Mr. Sothern. It's for your own good to stay.

Him telling them: *Listen, if somebody's out to get me, I don't aim to make it two out of three attempts here. Haven't you heard? Third time's the charm. I have a better shot at death by natural causes anyplace but here.*

The cop's body by then had been removed by somebody from the county coroner's office, Traylor had run out of questions to ask Roxy or the boy, Larry Skidmore, who'd been on his cell phone forever, excitedly describing every detail of the investigation with friends.

Nobody knew anything that pointed to a suspect or came up with better reasoning than Traylor's idea that Jack Sothern was the intended victim.

On that they had agreement.

On Traylor again saying how he'd be well off hurrying the hell out of Eden Highlands and going home—

No agreement, and—

None likely, partner.

He was sitting on a story that could resurrect his career, one he'd become a part of for some inexplicable reason—why else the two attempts on his life, assuming that is what they were?—and he wasn't quitting before he got to the next chapter and the chapter after that and after and after, and the final chapter that would reveal—

What?

Reveal *what*, Sothern?

He TiVo'd what he'd seen and heard that brought him here in the first place, from Dan Boone in East Berlin, before the wall came tumbling down, to the kidnapping sixteen years later of Tracy Collins. Meg Boone had resurfaced as her mother, Maggie Collins, so what about her father?

Did Dan Boone commit suicide or did he get out of East Berlin and, as he'd hoped, back to the States?

If that wasn't Meg Boone in the boat—and clearly it was not—who was it?

If he'd guessed correctly and Tracy had been abducted for a reason—

What was the reason?

Now, add to the conundrum:

What did he know that he didn't know he knew that had set people on his case with his murder on their mind? What was happening or set to happen that these parties unknown didn't want him to discover?

CONTINUED NEXT WEEK?

No.

CONTINUED HERE AND NOW.

Beginning with Roxy.

Sothern was certain she could fill in some of the history, plug some of the holes, given her closeness to Maggie.

Would she share with him what she knew?

Coming on to him as she had, before his seizure and now,

196

was there a bond Roxy was trying to build between them or was she only angling to screw information out of him, acting as Maggie's loving protector?

Roxy had no reason for hanging out in his hospital room or offering him a room at The Garden of Eden—a "hideout," she called it—when Traylor said there was no place safer for him than the hospital. A goodwill gesture to settle him where she could keep an eye on him, was that it, maybe? *The best way to play a game like this is by making up the rules as you go along,* he told himself, but—

The problem was he had developed a liking for Roxy, special feelings he thought he was beyond having after Shane Vallery. He'd tried. He'd tried again. It never seemed to work out, him always the reason for a failed date or short-lived entanglement. It wouldn't work out here, either, special feelings aside, but at least this time there were good reasons for sticking with it.

The story.

The glory that would come with an exclusive.

His life and his career on track again.

He clicked back to the car, Roxy waiting out an answer to her question about him being surprised she had a brain to go with her body. Not wanting to tell her he was finding more to admire about her brain, he said, "Definitely not surprised, Roxy. More amazed at how much we have in common."

She swung a wide turn, saying, "Besides an interest in Maggie?"

"Traylor's your competition in that department, not me . . . I mean how you seem to know your musicals. Before that, the movies. Anne Bancroft. Mrs. Robinson. Before you were born, *The Graduate,* wasn't it?"

"It won't take flattery to get you everywhere with me, Jack." She reached over and patted his thigh. "Once I get you settled in a room at The Garden of Eden, don't go sick on me and I'll show you what I mean."

"And, I'm discovering, a sense of humor. Not many women I've known had a sense of humor."

"I've known my share." He paid her a laugh on that one, appending a rim shot drummed on the dash and a thumbs-up. It pulled the half-smile from her face. "I use it like a shield, Jack. It wards off the hurt and the humiliation that made me run away from home, only it turns out I ran to more hurt and humiliation. If not for The Garden of Eden and Maggie, you could be talking to a tombstone in Eden Highlands Cemetery."

"How'd that come to pass?" Sothern genuinely interested, not trying to be polite or move deeper into her good graces.

"What can happen when you're illegitimate in a family of overachievers, who wear the mask of respectability to hide worse sins than my mother's? She died in childbirth, so I became the anointed black sheep. When you're treated like dirt long and often enough, you become dirt."

"Your father?"

"Hah!" She took a quick swipe at her eyes. "I could tell you stories about him, only I won't. He showed his face here once, out of the blue, found me and tracked me down out of curiosity. Looked around and said he had a favor to ask."

"Money?"

"He was richer than Midas. No. He wondered, since I was running the place and he was family, maybe I could extend him a family discount. Want to hear the worst part of it?" Roxy didn't wait for an answer. "Damn me. I comp'd the cheap bastard our best suite. . . . When he left the next morning, it was without so much as a thank you or goodbye. That was eleven years ago. I could give you the date. Last time I ever saw him in the flesh. About a year and a half later, I heard on the news he had suffered a fatal heart attack in Congress, in the middle of a fire-and-brimstone speech supporting, wouldn't you know it, some pro-abortion bill. All this time and he was still trying to get rid of me. . . . Me, I'm a right-to-lifer, even after all the dirty tricks life has played on me."

"Your father was in Congress?"

"House of Reprehensibles. Public service is a family tradition, going all the way back to Henry Wilson. You ever hear of him?"

"There was a talent agent by that name. He represented Rock Hudson, Tab Hunter, Troy Donahue. Always gave his clients funny first names."

"This Henry was originally Jeremiah Jones Colbraith. I took back the name after I set out on my own. He was an indentured farm boy who learned the shoemaking trade and eventually owned his own factory. He was a leader in the anti-slavery movement. Went from the Know-Nothing party to the Republicans, became a United States Senator from Massachusetts and then eighteenth vice president, General Grant's, in 1872. He suffered two strokes two years later and died in office." She blasted the windshield with laughter. "Jesus, I have no idea why I'm foaming at the mouth like this."

"Because you sense I'm interested in you." He stated it as fact.

"And here we are," Roxy said, turning into the back entrance to The Garden of Eden, breaking into lyrics from *Midnight Cowboy*. Everybody talking about her, not hearing a word she's saying. Breaking off to tell him, "Everybody thinks Nilsson wrote it because he sang it, but it was Fred Neil, you ever hear of him? He died a junkie's death." Not pausing to let him answer. "Roy Scherer, Merle Johnson, Jr., Arthur Andrew Gelien, who they really were, Rock Hudson, Tab Hunter, Troy Donahue. . . . You can change your name, Jack, but never who or what you are."

Mirthless laughter.

Her shield was up again.

"Got Chief Mount cleared out and gone from your room maybe half an hour ago," Gerry Cotton told Roxy, while switching his monitor from a screen-load of women's portrait photos to a Simpsons screen saver. He gave Sothern a nod of recognition. "The chief, ornery over his being disturbed until I passed on what had happened at the hospital to his man."

"He didn't know about Tom Almond?"

"Didn't remember any call-in from Glen Traylor telling him so. When he heard it from me, he sobered up real fast, went white with grief, and headed for some hair of the dog from your bar. . . . Got the room all nice and prettied up again, the way you said for Mr. Sothern here."

"What else, Gerry? Anything?"

"The business appointment you said might be turning up? Turned up, so I did like you said if he turned up. He's in Maggie's and your office waiting, settled over a coffee. I couldn't sell him on the doughnuts, though, so helped myself to the cream-filled ones."

Sothern gave her an understanding smile. "You go on. I know where the room is."

Gerry held up two ringed keys. "Ready and waiting for you, Mr. Sothern. The bigger key takes care of everything but the special safety lock that also shuts down the silent alarm. Do that one first in and last out."

Sothern reached for the key ring.

Roxy capped his hand and pulled it back, saying, "It can wait. Join me."

"Your business is none of my business. What I can use is a hot tub."

"The hot tub later," she said, looking at him like he had no

200

choice. She tightened her hold and started for the office with Sothern limping along behind her. Typed in the touch pad numbers that freed the door locks, stepped aside, and nudged him in ahead of her.

Her business appointment had made himself comfortable on Maggie Collins' side of the partners' desk. He looked up from the magazine he was hunched over and offered a kind of smile that could mean anything.

A stranger, but at the same time something familiar about him.

Late forties to early fifties. A pasty white complexion on a face falling to a wattle that bled into his thick neck. Day-old salt-and-pepper whiskers. Half-moon glasses on a rope chain, resting at the base of a bump-riddled nose, magnifying eyes the color of wet earth that studied Sothern as if he were some specimen under the microscope. Coarse steel gray hair lapping over his ears, and thick matching eyebrows full of unruly strands.

He stood and Roxy hurried to his outstretched arms.

He was shorter than he'd appeared seated, the illusion of height suggested by a head meant for someone taller and, as Sothern's mind catapulted backwards to another time and place—

East Berlin before the Wall came down.

The gold pirate's earring dangling from his left lobe had become more visible as he drew Roxy closer to him and turned his head, settling his blue lips on her cheek. Sothern remembered it clearly from their meeting in Café Munchausen, how his wife had worn its twin in her right ear. It was one of those details a good reporter spots and clings to.

Missing was the athletic body that made him look like Superman. He seemed to have withered away inside an outfit that suggested his next stop was the golf course. A sloped back. Sagging shoulders. Sunken chest. Boone had been taken prisoner by old age. Only memory remained of the infamous "Turncoat Rebel."

Sothern had to ask to be certain:

"Dan? Dan Boone?"

Dan Boone shifted his attention from Roxy to say, "In a manner of speaking, Jack," like he also knew what he had become. He released Roxy, eased her aside, and rushed a fist to his mouth to take on a horrendous cough disinclined to quit.

He cleared his throat into the fist tunnel and wiped off the residue on his red, green, and gray plaid slacks, then settled down again in Maggie's chair, urging Sothern to take the visitors chair.

Roxy moved to her own chair, angled her elbows on the surface of the desk, laced her fingers, and covered her mouth with them, as if locking out any temptation to speak.

Boone didn't look so anxious, either, so Sothern said, "You're looking well, Dan."

Boone snorted hard enough to make his chest jump, and that set off another spate of coughing.

When he'd recovered, he said, "Still the liar, are you, Jack?" Eating into him with his eyes, but signaling compassion more than anger. "Short a lung since last time we were together. Only one remaining between me and what's left of my life, and a new tire gets a longer warranty than that one's been given by my doctor."

"I'm sorry," Jack said.

"For my lungs, you mean? The rotten state of my health?"

"For what I did to you. You put your trust in me and—"

"Bygones, Jack. Bygones. I'm not the one you'll have to answer to on that score, but we can talk redemption, if that's of interest to you. Roxy, you think redemption might be of interest to him?"

"I told you, Danny, he came for a story."

Sothern said, "Redemption how, Dan?"

"My daughter, Jack. Tracy. We desperately need your help if we're going to get her back safely and—" He couldn't finish the word "alive." "Unharmed," he said.

Sothern didn't have to think about it. "What do you need me to do?"

CHAPTER 26

Dan Boone said, "I need you to understand what you'd be getting into, Jack." In broad strokes, he told him everything that transpired from the time Sothern's exposé ran in *Glamour World Weekly* to the present.

If he was trying to alternately surprise, shock, and sadden Sothern, he had succeeded even before he was finished describing the circumstances behind the reported murder of his wife Meg and his own suicide by drowning.

It got worse when Sothern recognized it was his exposé that kept Dan and Meg apart for most of the last sixteen years. Led to the murders of two innocent high school girls. Caused the deaths of the three people yesterday at Eden Memorial Hospital, people whose only sin was wrong place, wrong time.

"And Tracy," Boone said. "I have to keep believing she'll be safe at least until the trade is made." His eyes betrayed his worst fears. "The killing isn't going to stop until they get what they want, Jack. They're after you, they're after me, God knows who else, but I'll be damned if they're going to harm my child. I'm getting Tracy back, whatever the cost."

"The Mielke diary. What made it so valuable, keeps it valuable sixteen years after the fact? The Berlin Wall is history. Erich Mielke is dead and good riddance. Germany's united. Communism as it existed is as dead and buried as Mielke. Russia's an ally. The wars being waged today couldn't be more distant from all that, and—"

"You're certain, Jack? I'm not."

"Why?"

"Because people are dying all around us and my child may be next. Doesn't that tell you something?"

"Without answering my question."

"What goes around comes around. History repeats itself. However you choose to put it, Jack. Mielke saw the end coming, that's what I think. I think Mielke was preparing himself for a new beginning that would include Mielke. I think the diary contains information—names, dates, places, events, financial resources—that he could one day bring into play and cement his place in some new order somewhere. He was a survivor who always planned for the future. He survived Stalin's purges and Stalin himself. He survived imprisonment by the Vichy government in France during World War II. He survived over three dozen attempts on his life when he was heading the Stasi and not a few more after that by countrymen who despised him. He survived the theft of the diary and managed to live past ninety, probably while working on a plan to survive his death. He's done it, hasn't he? This business, this conversation. It keeps Erich Mielke alive."

"And the diary has kept you alive."

"You call this living?" Boone managed a groan and a forlorn grin. "It got Meg safely out of Berlin. It got me past Mielke and back to the States under the worst of circumstances. It kept the government at arms' length and put me into Witness Protection instead of a prison for traitors. I gave up my career, my life, for a different kind of prison, the hell of having neither until I could not stand it any longer. I sneaked away. I came here to Eden Highlands to see my baby girl, then disappeared into a new life where I could be miserable on my own terms."

"And you never tried seeing Tracy again?"

"Not so anyone would find out if they came looking, and I'm

sure they never quit looking for me, my own government as well as Mielke's disciples, because of the diary."

"You say Mielke listed names, dates . . . financial resources."

"More than enough to mount a revolution. Scattered all around the globe. Banked with more secrecy than even the Swiss provide."

"You learned this from reading the diary?"

Boone shook his head. "I read the diary, but what I've been telling you wasn't in the words. Coded somehow inside the words. Inside symbols as twisted as Mielke's sick mind. I learned the secret of the diary from—" Almost reluctant to say her name. "Shane Vallery. She knew it firsthand, from Mielke himself. How Shane knew to steal the diary and use it to get me out."

"Nothing happens for years, then suddenly—"

"I know where you're going with your question, Jack. I don't have an answer. All I know is it didn't take a genius to decipher the message they were sending me when they couldn't find me. Taking Tracy wasn't enough. They had to do something drastic to make sure the message reached me wherever I was."

"Killing her two friends."

"Killing her two friends. I understood at once—"

"And called your wife."

"My ex-wife. I made her promise to divorce me, start leading a new life of her own, the time I sneaked here to see Tracy. When I learned the news about Tracy and the girls, I phoned her, yes, to let her know I was on my way. Ever since, though, all my contact has been through Roxy." They exchanged warm smiles. "But now what needs to be done calls for you, Jack, unless you'd like to change your mind."

"A few more questions first?" Boone turned his palms up. "It wasn't you who committed suicide, so who was it?"

Palms up again. "Someone Mielke felt was expendable, which

means it could have been anybody. Mielke was judge, jury, and executioner rolled into one."

Next, the question Jack really wanted to ask, the one he had been desperate to ask and at the same time afraid to ask since Boone used her name: "Shane Vallery? The lake. Was she . . . ?" He couldn't bring himself to finish the question.

Boone understood and nodded. "She beat Mielke at his own game, didn't she? He wasn't about to let her get away with that. A very special lady, Shane was. Brave beyond imagination."

"For a fact? You know that for a fact?"

"Or I would have heard from her, Jack, but not once in all the years."

Sothern pushed up from the chair. He briefly wandered the office, spent another minute or two staring aimlessly out the window at a dark sky yet to keep its threat of rain. Turned to wonder, "Who is it you think is responsible for what's happened, Dan? Who are the people you say never stopped looking for you?"

"One man in particular. Tell Jack what you told me when I phoned this morning, Roxy."

Roxy said, "He worked for Shane Vallery, earned her trust and became a key player, but all the time he was one of Mielke's stooges. He's the one who got word to Mielke about how she planned on getting Danny out of East Berlin. His code name was Lawnmower. His real name is Emil Grass."

"Emil—" Jack's eyes jumped to the ceiling. "I remember him. Grass met me at Tegel Airport, drove me to Checkpoint Charlie. A little guy, silly mustache. Spouted on and on about democracy. Emil Grass. Jesus . . ." He returned to his chair, sank into it. Didn't quite know what to do with his hands. "You know that for a fact, Roxy? How?"

"Learned it from Maggie, who got it direct from the federal agent sent out here to stay with Maggie and look after her twenty-four-seven. Do whatever it takes to help find Tracy and bring her home safely."

Dan Boone said, "The agent. Another name you may remember, Jack. Burt Crews."

Sothern didn't have to think for long. "My welcoming committee on the Red side of the Wall. Pointed me in the direction of Café Munchausen and you."

"And the agent who helped guide Meg out of East Berlin to freedom, Jack. Bless him. Crews and Grass are both here in Eden Highlands, but this time on opposite sides of the Wall, metaphorically speaking. All they have in common is a desire for Mielke's diary. Grass for the millions he can get from the highest bidder. Crews for the secrets it'll let the government unravel once the code is broken."

"And you in the middle."

Boone shook his head violently. "No middle ground, Jack. I don't want to be called a traitor to my country again; be hounded by the government again; maybe put on trial and tossed into prison as living proof there's no statute of limitations for treason. But I will not let anything happen to my little girl. Only Tracy matters now. Not me, if it came to that. No one and nothing else. Why I need you, to stand in for me on any negotiations, on the exchange, the diary for my daughter, starting with Burt Crews."

Sothern felt compelled to remind him, "I screwed up and let you down last time, Dan."

"What second chances are all about, Jack."

CHAPTER 27

Burt Crews was one of those people who hummed into the phone while thinking. To Sothern, listening in on an extension in the conversation area of the office, it seemed to go on endlessly after Roxy reached the fed at Maggie's and told him there was somebody he should meet with, only—

"I can't say who," Roxy said.

"How perfectly mysterious of you," he said, finally. "How about why or about what?"

"Also not for me to say," Roxy said.

Crews began humming again, like a kitten purring. Finally: "I'm betting it has to do with Tracy."

"I didn't say so, Mr. Crews."

"I'm aware you're Mrs. Collins' best friend and confidante, thus you certainly know why I'm here. So, that would have to be what your call is about—Tracy. Mrs. Collins, if I ask her, will she know what this proposed meeting is about?"

"Yes and no."

"What's the no part?"

"The Mielke diary."

Lots of humming. "You'll have to tell me more to get my full attention, or come visit and we'll get to know one another better over a cup of Mrs. Collins' excellent coffee. Strong, the way her former husband preferred it brewed."

Roxy checked for direction with Dan, who was eavesdropping on Maggie's phone. He shook his head. "Some other time,

Mr. Crews. Let me know if you change your mind." Sounding like she was in the process of breaking the connection.

"Wait," Crews said, his voice rising. "My blind date. When?"

Boone held up three fingers, then made it two.

"Two hours from now," Roxy said. "My office."

Burt Crews stepped through the door, eyes bold with delight, his toothy smile as bright and perfect as Sothern remembered it from East Berlin. Fatter and showing his age. Horn-rimmed frames replaced by a stylish pair of simple circular rims. The voice huskier. Dressed out of a Target holiday clearance catalog.

He approached the conversation area with his hand extended, calling out Sothern's name as if to prove his memory was sharp as ever, no matter what aging had done to the rest of him. "Mr. Sothern, I heard you were here in Eden Highlands, but a surprise seeing you now. You're not who I expected, not at all." He glanced back at the door. "Will we be joined?"

Sothern shook his head.

Crews accepted the news like it didn't matter, but his eyes briefly sparkled less. He took the armchair across from Sothern and showed delight at the coffee and tea service on the table. He filled a Garden of Eden souvenir mug with hot water and let an organic tea bag steep, while Sothern refilled his mug with coffee and took a cautious sip that burned the tip of his tongue. "Cheers," Crews said. He settled his mug on the table without bothering to try the tea. "I also heard you were in the hospital, but here you are, so it was nothing serious?"

"Not this time."

"This get-together, though—serious?"

"Serious."

"About Erich Mielke's diary, Miss Colbraith told me. What news could you possibly have for me that makes this meeting so urgent and necessary?"

"Not news," Sothern said. "I have the Mielke diary."

There are eight hundred muscles in the human face. All of them appeared to go into motion on Burt Crews' face, not quite sure on which expression to settle, finally landing on affable surprise. A giant smile accompanying an orgasmic hum.

"You have it?"

"I have it and you want it. How's that for necessary?"

"Not me. Our government wants it, Mr. Sothern. How did you happen across it?"

"You already know that answer."

"And why would Dan Boone turn it over to you, a journalist who debased his trust and therefore logically could be expected to do it again?"

"To help him help you."

"Help me?"

"Bring home the diary and become a big hero, maybe get yourself promoted once you've done what's necessary to reunite Maggie Collins with their daughter."

"Boone couldn't do this with me for himself? I never let him down before, or his wife."

"I got the impression that Boone mistrusts our government more than he mistrusts me, and that includes you, Mr. Crews."

Crews burst out laughing. "I never said Dan Boone was a stupid man. Crazy for going down the dead-end road to Communism, but not stupid. What, then? How does he see this working?"

"Not complicated at all. He knows you're expecting Maggie Collins to be contacted by Emil Grass—"

"So Boone also spotted Emil's dirty hands in this?"

Jack dismissed the question. "An exchange is arranged. Grass hands Tracy over to me. I hand Grass the Mielke diary. You're nearby. The instant Tracy is out of harm's way, you move after Grass and the diary. Everybody wins."

He got an incredulous look from Crews.

"You should go into the Swiss cheese business, Mr. Sothern. So many holes in this less than brilliant plan from Dan Boone. It's a wonder he's managed to stay out of our reach all these years."

"You have a better idea?"

Crews nodded. "It's my business, after all."

It was exactly the kind of response Boone had told Sothern to expect.

"Try me," Sothern said.

Crews said, "You saw Emil once. I saw him a million times, worked with him a million times, helped expose him as more of a traitor than our Dan Boone will ever be in his lifetime. I know Emil's ways. How he moves. How he thinks. What makes him tick. When he phones Mrs. Collins, as he most certainly will, let me deal with him one on one. Arrange the trade for Tracy. Any statements that ring false, any scheming on Emil's part, I'll recognize it for a fact, where—no offense—it will surely go unnoticed by you."

He converted his face into a question mark.

"Good as far as it goes, Mr. Crews, but I won't hand over the Mielke diary to you or him or anyone until we have Tracy Collins."

"Of course not," Crews said. "Emil will have my word on that. He'll hem and haw and wheedle, but in the end he'll come around. History has taught him that lines I draw in the sand don't disappear or move. Another reason it should be me and not you."

"You'd actually give him the diary?"

"Let me put it to you this way, Mr. Sothern: What happens once Tracy is safe need not concern you." He threw him the smothering smile of a doting parent. "*Qué sera, sera,* but I can promise you this: My report will describe the contribution of

Dan Boone, as well as yourself, and recommend that Mr. Boone's file be wiped clean of any suggestion he was ever a traitor. More a patriot in disguise."

"Go public with that?"

"Make it part of the exclusive story you'll write to regain your own reputation, once this sad affair with its terribly tragic overtones reaches a satisfactory conclusion."

"Can you guarantee it?"

"Authorization from a grateful government is as close as a phone call."

"In writing? Boone deserves to have it in writing."

"Once you've proven to my satisfaction you do have Mielke's diary and this hasn't been a pie-in-the-sky waste of time. Will you show it to me?"

Sothern studied his coffee cup and counted off ten to himself.

"No," he said.

Anger flashed behind Crews' eyes, but it was gone in a blink. He smiled and threw a forefinger at him. "Absolutely the right answer, Mr. Sothern. I would have been surprised and amazed if you'd said otherwise." He put down his cup on the bench and stood to leave. "I'll be in touch the instant we hear from Emil. His call could come at any time. Where do I reach you?"

A few minutes after Crews left, Roxy pushed Sothern into her BMW and headed for First Church of Eden Highlands, for the joint memorial service scheduled for Betsy Wheatcroft and Amy Spencer. Gerry Cotton, in the backseat, couldn't stop fretting over the possibility that his lady friend might arrive before they returned.

"It's hardly a way to greet the love of your life," he said, "but no way I'd not show my respects to their mothers. Eleanor and Phyllis, always pleasant on me. No way not, but it is the love of my life on her way down here, Roxy. Tell me I'm doing the right thing about Good Time Gal. I am, aren't I?"

"She'll be smart enough to understand when she hears or she's not for you, Gerry."

"I suppose. I could tell right off she was no slouch in the brains department. She'd studied up on the Highlands, The Garden of Eden, even before we had our first date. Shows how smart she is, doing that to impress me. Say all the right things, ask all the right questions, so I suppose you have a point, Roxy. What do you think, Mr. Sothern?"

Sothern said, "She's picked herself quite a guy in you, Gerry." He caught Roxy trying not to reveal she had caught the underlying meaning of his remark, stifling a laugh inside a cough to clear her throat.

Gerry heard it as a compliment. "You bet, but I picked her first, and you can't begin to believe some of the doozies who've shown up on EvolDotCom. I mean, I'm talking here about women who run pictures that's not them and lie about their age and being well-off and that, just to attract some unsuspecting candidate for a walk down the aisle."

Roxy said, "Gerry, haven't you done a bit of that yourself?"

He shook his head. "First off, it makes it so I can weed out the deadwood if they're worth it, by springing my true facts of life on them. Second of all, I'm a man, so there's the real big, big difference right there. Wouldn't you say, Mr. Sothern?"

"Sounds a little chauvinistic for this day and age, Gerry."

"Exactly, thank you, and also card-carrying Methodist, which is what I am."

Most of the townspeople had turned out for the service. There also were people from the surrounding communities, as well as a smattering of TV news crews from San Diego and L.A., whose tech trucks lined the street outside, reporters outside staring sad-faced into cameras and reciting details behind the deaths of

Betsy Wheatcroft and Amy Spencer.

The chapel was filled to capacity, a modest overflow spilling out onto dozens of folding chairs set up on the porch and a vast section of tented lawn. Loudspeakers were carrying organ music into the air, too loud to suit some of the TV sound jockeys, whose faces showed their indignation at having to compete with "Nearer My God to Thee."

The mortician's son, Weldon Beldon, Jr., wearing the same black suit he'd worn to his junior high school graduation, greeted them with awkward familiarity as they approached the chapel entrance. He stepped aside to let them enter, indicating where three places were being held for them, off the center aisle in a series of bench rows filled with Eleanor Wheatcroft and Phyllis Spencer's co-workers at The Garden. Cotton moved in first. Roxy followed, leaving the aisle seat for Sothern.

Maggie Collins was sitting up front, the first row, flanked by Vernon Mount and Glen Traylor.

"Making her own statement," Roxy said. "The two moms may hate her because her daughter didn't die with theirs, but like me—nothing was going to keep her from paying her respects today. You know how Maggie has to be suffering? More than Phyllis and Eleanor. They're getting some closure, a stupid word for something that'll never go away, but Maggie's got nothing going for her except nightmares about Tracy never turning up at all. Where's the closure in that? You tell me what's worse?"

Sothern nodded agreement.

Cotton said, "The biggest wreaths over by the easels, Amy's picture and Betsy's? From us, Roxy. Like you told me to arrange for. Roses up the gazoo."

The organ music faded on the closing bars of a devotional Sothern knew from the years when he attended church. He couldn't give it a name. It had disappeared altogether from memory by the time the minister took to the pulpit, waved somber greetings to familiar faces, tapped the microphone and adjusted it for height.

He appeared to be in his late hundreds, bald as a basketball player and shrinking inside his vestments, nondenominational, except for a cleric's collar nine sizes too large. He gripped the podium tightly as a hedge against falling down and to control the palsy in his hands that matched the quiver in a delicate soprano that gained strength once he was past some mumbled quotations from the Bible and began describing the two girls he'd known since their birth.

The minister's tears were real.

Many in the congregation quickly joined him, creating a symphony of sad noises, sniffles, and noses being blown, none louder than the sounds emanating from Gerry Cotton. The woman alongside him moved closer and placed a comforting palm on his cheek.

Classmates were heard from, every voice choked with the emotional outpourings of children learning first hand for the first time that life is not forever.

Songs were sung by the high school glee club, nothing Sothern recognized, all to an up-tempo beat he guessed was rap or whatever they were calling it nowadays.

The two mothers were escorted from a private curtained room to the right of the pulpit and hugged each other for strength as they recalled their dead children.

One of them faltered on her way back to the private room and seemed on the edge of collapse.

An apprehensive noise rose from the congregation.

Vernon Mount jumped to his feet, steadied himself and two-stepped up the stairs and onto the stage to help her. Glen Traylor was right behind him. Once Traylor had her secured, Mount crossed back to the podium and gently eased the frail minister aside, holding him from collapse with a hand around his waist. His other hand played with his Komboloi worry beads as he leaned down into the microphone and fixed his eyes on the stained-glass skylights running the length of the chapel.

He said, "I swear to those dear, sweet women and to their grieving husbands, who I also know, although not as well as I know Eleanor and Phyllis—Phyllis a little more than Eleanor— and to all of you here right now and all the TV people and the world watching us. The rat who murdered those darling girls in the giant pictures over on the easels there and there, he will be caught. He will be brought to a swift and just justice. By me. Yes, by God, by me. Your duly elected chief of police, Vernon Mount. As God is my witness."

"Amen," Roxy said under her breath.

As thoughtless, foolish, and hung over as Vernon Mount had sounded, something made Sothern believe the chief. He added his "Amen" to hers.

CHAPTER 28

Emil Grass was fidgeting in their usual booth at the Howard Johnson's restaurant, toying with his apple pie a la mode, when Burt Crews arrived, tripping in like Gene Kelly on steroids, his Cheshire cat smile lighting up the dining room and adding to the volcanic migraine that had been exploding at Grass' temples since Tracy Collins disappeared.

He'd searched for her through the night and, except for a couple hours' sleep in the car, most of today, covering miles in all directions on wheels and foot, large chunks of the Father Melchoir Couts Memorial Park and Hiking Trail after scouring the Happy Homes trailer park twice.

Tracy couldn't be more missing and, given her state of dress and the rain showers that came and went in the hours before dawn, a leading candidate for pneumonia or some other complication. He didn't mind her growing sick and dying—that would save him time and effort later—but not now, not yet, not before the Mielke diary was in their hands.

Meanwhile, how to break the news to Crews?

He'd intended to sound the alarm when he phoned Crews earlier, catching him as he left some kind of meeting at The Garden of Eden, but was cut short, Crews saying, "I have excellent news to report. Meet me at our place." Ordering him about, as usual, as if he were the *fuehrer* himself, this aging rotter of an *Amerikaner*.

Crews slid into the booth across from Grass, picked up a

fork, and went after a healthy cut of the apple pie. Devoured it vigorously. Permitted himself a second helping. Settled against the backrest with his hands clasped schoolboy fashion on the table after picking out something that had stuck between his teeth. Revealed the giant smile again. Said, "The diary is as good as ours."

Grass used a napkin from the dispenser to pat away the sweat bubbles on his brow and nodded politely.

Crews' expression challenged his lackluster reaction. He pushed his glasses up and angled over the table. "I didn't expect applause, but more than that from you," he said.

Grass pretended a smile. "How did this all of a sudden happen?"

"The Colbraith woman. I was summoned to a meeting at The Garden of Eden, where you reached me. Our old friend Jack Sothern was there in her office, not quite as dead as we'd hoped to have him by now, and a good thing he's still among the living."

"How so?"

"Sothern has the diary. Given to him by Boone. He's prepared to trade for the girl once you've made contact with Mrs. Collins and arranged the details. I convinced him to allow me to be the designated intermediary. Control, Emil. We control the situation." He slurped up another chunk of apple pie. "I may have to have one of these for myself," he said, "only with a scoop or two of chocolate."

Emil waved for their server, anything to delay sharing his news with Crews.

She waddled over.

Crews returned her greeting and ordered apple pie a la mode, but immediately changed his mind and asked for the fresh peach cobbler a la mode; then, decided against the chocolate ice cream in favor of the creamy vanilla. A pot of tea, the teabag on the side.

Grass signaled he was fine, except for a coffee refill. Black, no cream or sugar.

She gave him a look that meant she already knew that about him.

Crews waited for the server to leave, then finished telling Grass about his meeting.

"The way we'll work it, you'll designate a secure place for the exchange," he said. "If I understand how the mind of a Jack Sothern works, and trust me I do, he'll want to be my shadow instead of entrusting the diary to me alone. I object hard enough to convince him of my concerns for his safety, then relent. How do you like it so far?"

"Nothing we haven't done before, but listen, Crews . . . the girl is a goner."

"Of course." He drew a line across his throat. "Sothern hands over the diary to me and you take her, then him, however it works best. Why do you even have to say it? You afraid I might think you're going soft on me? Partner of mine, we've played at the Burt and Emil Show too long for that insulting thought to ever cross my mind."

The server delivered Crews' peach cobbler and tea and exchanged Grass' coffee cup for a fresh pour.

Crews gave it a few security seconds after she left.

He said, "That dumbbell police chief, the detective. Anyone else you think is able to put two and two together and come up with us, Emil—" He raised his eyebrows and repeated the line across his throat. "Nothing left to chance, even though we'll be long gone to an area code nobody will ever guess. Millions of dollars richer and ready to live happily ever after in the lap of retired luxury."

Crews paused for a mouthful of cobbler and ice cream after

several more notes of self-admiration, the kind he was always pestering Grass with, how he was as reliable when it came to planning as Grass was when it came to execution. Laughing and pointing out his clever play on the word execution.

Grass nodding agreement, laughing along, all the while thinking how nice it would be to have for himself the millions of dollars the Mielke diary was going to bring on the open market.

Why would he need Crews anymore—really—once Sothern delivered the diary?

He wouldn't.

A plan?

Crews wasn't the only one who knew how to plan.

Grass decided not to say anything more to him about Tracy Collins.

Crews finished sketching out the first steps of his plan.

Treating him like a child, he insisted Grass repeat them, saying, "No offense, Emil. Only to be sure you and I are in perfect harmony." His smile a wonder of teeth.

"Like the Vienna Boys Choir," Grass said, burying his irritation and repeating the steps, rather than rile Crews or raise suspicion about where his mind might be going.

They agreed on a time for the phone call to Maggie Collins.

Crews left first, as usual.

Leaving Grass to pay the check, as usual.

Grass finished his refill over thoughts of a plan that would make more sense than what he'd heard from Crews, discarding one idea after another while making idle doodles on a paper napkin yanked from the table dispenser.

Nothing sounded better than anything Crews had said.

Grass worked on other possibilities driving back to the Father Melchoir Couts Memorial Park and Hiking Trail for another try at finding Tracy Collins. He parked in the visitors lot and

221

tramped down a couple muddy trails familiar from last night, pausing to reconsider one he had quit because of the downpour and a posted sign warning of danger from snakes and coyotes. He checked under his jacket, at the small of his back, for the .22 he was packing in a leather snatch-holster. He fondled the HuntChamp in his pocket.

He moved past the sign and began hunting for any evidence of the girl having come up this way.

Nothing.

He worked his way back to the main road, wondering where to search next.

CHAPTER 29

Tracy woke up momentarily unsure where she was, cold, hungry, and, in the next instant, as her memory kicked in and came crashing down on her, frightened. She felt the tears welling. Ordered herself to quit. She was no baby. The tears rolled down her cheeks anyway.

She felt her cheeks on fire.

Her forehead.

She was shivering cold and burning up at the same time, huddled here in the corner of the secret cave she had discovered years ago with Amy Spencer and Betsy Wheatcroft, when they were little kids and often explored the off-limits areas of the memorial park and the hiking trails named after her lots-of-greats-grandfather, Father Melchoir Couts.

The cave, which Betsy, Amy, and Tracy christened "The BAT Cave"—after the first letter in each of their names—was three-quarters of a mile up a tricky, thicket-heavy slope that started fifty or sixty feet from where one of the hiking trails quit at a posted warning sign about deadly snakes and untrustworthy coyotes.

Warning signs were for adults, of course, and besides, they had never once come across anything more deadly than washboard-thin dogs with desperate eyes that had been discarded like week-old leftovers by people from Temporary Town down below.

After the first time, they always packed extra food and

canteens, so they could feed any hungry dog they came across on their climb to the cave.

Going to the BAT Cave wasn't Tracy's first thought when she stumbled out of the SUV and shook her head clear enough to recognize familiar landmarks that told her the dreadful man who had murdered her two best friends in the entire world in cold blood—maybe her next—had parked in Temporary Town.

She fought to stay awake, as she had been doing since she felt his clammy hands on her body, his slobbery lips on her forehead, and feared what he might want to do to her next if she opened her eyes.

"Don't you fear, my beautiful little girl. Uncle Emil will see you to home safely," he had said. "I've taken care of that awful man. You're safe with me," he had said.

What awful man?

He was the awful man.

Him.

She stayed as still as silence and worked at resisting the mountain of confusion in her head while the wheels turned under her and she heard the hum of the road for what seemed like hours.

After the SUV stopped moving, after he said, "Your Uncle Emil has to leave you for a while, my beautiful little girl, but don't you worry. He'll be back," after she heard the creak of a door opening and closing, the click of the door catch, she waited another eternity before daring to get out of bed.

Tracy's legs were heavy and didn't want to cooperate.

She fought back and won.

She peeked out a window and spotted him down the drive, inspecting a boat with some other people. Quickly, she grabbed bundles of t-shirts, molded them so they looked like a body under the blanket on her bed, hoping he'd mistake it for her if he checked before driving off to wherever was next. She'd seen the trick work a lot on television.

Tracy willed herself to the door, took the deepest breath of her life, and exited the SUV, uncertain which way to turn to for help. Hardly any lights on anywhere in the park. All the vehicles around her dark behind drawn shades and thick curtains, making it impossible to know where the competing sounds of music and TV shows came from.

She thought about banging on doors, yelling for help, but the killer would definitely hear her, and that would be that. She felt the first drizzles of rain on her head and her shoulders and, after another moment, soaking through her t-shirt. She drew her arms across her body for warmth and comfort, without success.

The killer half-turned in her direction.

She ducked out of sight.

She couldn't stand around like this much longer. The cold and the wet were cutting into her body. The Temporary Town trading post or the Happy Homes convenience store compound? Both closed this time of night. Where then? What now?

Tracy felt her mind slipping away. Her knees growing useless under her.

She pressed her hands against the SUV for support.

Dared a peek.

The killer was shaking hands. He turned to head back to the SUV.

Tracy dropped to the ground and rolled under the camper next to the SUV, then did three similar rolls that took her as many more vehicles away, praying she'd make no noise that gave her away. She heard the killer approaching, his every step on the wet gravel path a cause for alarm.

He stopped a few feet past her, like something had caught his attention. Seconds later, his shoes became visible. They weren't moving. What would she see next, his face inches from the ground, his hand reaching in to catch her again?

Her pulse tore through her temples.

She covered her nose and mouth, held her breath, setting off a black whirlpool in her head.

She thought she was going to pass out.

The killer muttered some words in a foreign language—it sounded like German—then moved on.

She shook her head clear and waited a few minutes before easing out from under the cabin cruiser. Next door, a trailer had strung out two rows of clothing on a portable clothesline, either not expecting the rain or figuring on the rain to do a cheap overnight wash job.

Tracy grabbed a pair of stonewashed blue jeans, tennis sneakers hanging by their knotted laces and a heavy turtleneck sweater from the line. She saw a navy pea coat on a milking stool by the trailer door and swiped that, too.

She charged into the darkness, heading away from the killer's SUV, aiming for the closest gate through to her great-ancestor's memorial park. She had to stop every fifteen or twenty feet to catch her breath and slap her face to keep the rest of her awake. Behind her, she heard a door opening, caught a flash of light, and knew—just knew—the killer had learned she was gone and now was coming after her. Her mind panicked, but the adrenalin rush that kicked in pushed her body ahead of every pain.

She kept running until she was safely lost inside the underbrush, thrown off course once when she tripped over a sleeping black cat and nose-dived to the ground yowling as loud as the fleeing cat and attracting some trailer noises and lights.

She heard what she thought was a distant voice wondering her name. That got her up and running again, wincing whenever her bare feet caught a rock and her body suffered scrapes and scratch wounds from sharp branches, which was often.

She reached a small clearing and stopped to dress.

The jeans were three sizes too big, but she made them work. The turtleneck and the Navy pea coat were closer to her size, the tennis sneakers maybe half a size too small and pinching her toes, but better than what she'd been suffering barefooted.

A San Diego Padres cap had been stowed in the pea coat. She slapped it on as the drizzle started up again and instantly turned into a heavy shower. She lifted her face to the sky, shut her eyes, opened her mouth wide, and drank the rain. Stood motionless while showering off however many days it had been since she, Amy, and Betsy had gone for pizza. She cried until she couldn't tell her tears from the rain.

The park was growing with noises from creatures scurrying for refuge.

The sounds bounced out of the brush and echoed off the hillside.

A coyote howled in the distance.

Closer, the sound of a dog in distress.

Another coyote.

More of them.

A multiplicity of dogs sending out their messages of discomfort; a protest Tracy couldn't identify as well as the slither of snakes in the underbrush, maybe squirrels or possums.

She stood her ground, enduring the rain while waiting for the clouds to surrender a new look at the half moon.

When it appeared, she used it to get her bearings, then moved in the direction of the BAT Cave.

She took it slowly, carefully, but not without stumbling or tripping along the way, more so when she started the climb up the hillside. When every muscle in her body begged her to stop, she drew new strength from an image of the killer closing in on her.

She reached the cave and dove inside like it was a return to her mother's womb.

She crawled to the back wall, a distance of about twenty-five feet, and was asleep within seconds, a prayer of thanks still on her lips.

A fading daylight filled the narrow mouth of the cave, Tracy's only indication of how long she had slept.

Through the night and most of the day.

Or, maybe more than one day.

Too weak to walk, Tracy crawled to where the cave angled off and formed a modest cul-de-sac, where she, Amy, and Betsy kept the three picnic hampers and two coolers they used for supplies and the assorted munchies they devoured during their gabfests. There was also their emergency sleeping bag, the emergency always being what was necessary if one of them ran away from home because of some parental infraction, a possibility they reviewed and argued over endlessly.

Tracy worked open the cooler latches. The first one was empty, except for melted ice water. She scooped out handfuls and splashed her face in an effort to cool down the fever. The other cooler also was full of water, but fishing around she caught a carton of orange drink. She fought open the spout and finished the drink in a gulp. It was warm and had a bitter taste, maybe spoiled, but nourishment she knew she needed. She rescued a second carton and set it aside while she checked out the hampers, coming up with empty bags. Potato crisps. Bagel crisps. Buttered popcorn corncakes. Cheese puffs. A box full of vanilla wafer crumbs.

She found beef jerky dog treats in a plastic container and a bag of dog biscuit treats the girls always kept handy on the likelihood of coming across a lost dog as hungry as she was now. She chewed her way through a half dozen jerky strips, a handful of the biscuits, washing them down with the second carton of orange drink.

Whether the meal was too much or too exotic, after ten or fifteen minutes her stomach began to ache, then rumble. She vomited, the puke shooting from her mouth like a scene she remembered from the movie *The Exorcist*.

Tracy got the sleeping bag unzipped and squirmed her way inside, closed her eyes, and fell asleep with images of herself as that little girl in *The Exorcist* who was possessed by the devil, only in her case she was being pursued by the devil.

He looked like the killer.

He was winning the race.

She heard herself screaming for help from her mommy.

However long afterward, Tracy was startled out of a nightmare by the sense she was being observed. Too frightened to open her eyes, she prayed she was still dreaming and tried burying herself deeper inside the sleeping bag.

She wasn't dreaming.

She felt a presence beyond her own, with an outdoors smell that challenged the cold earth odor of the cave and her own sweat and puke, traces of which had hardened around her lips and chin.

The guttural sound she heard was low, intense, and threatening.

She resisted daring so much as a squint, felt her heart racing out of control as the harsh sound came closer and the odor intensified and—

A slobbering tongue lashed her forehead, flew across her eyes, and worked over her mouth.

The sensation was familiar.

She dared a squint and found herself staring into the determined black marble eyes of King Kong, the name they'd given last month to the desperately hungry Rottweiler that struggled into the BAT Cave, growling menacingly, its powerful jaw open wide, showing off strong teeth sharp enough to cut through to the bone. It was two or two-and-a-half feet tall, coal black, with a gray spot over each eye and on its cheeks, trailing down on both sides of its muzzle. A gray undercoat formed two triangles on either side of its breastbone. The same gray marked three of its four feet, the exception being the solid black left hind foot.

The girls' panic at being confronted by the formidable animal abated as the Rottweiler, maybe sensing friendship, settled on its haunches, hung its massive head, and looked to them for rescue. It made quick work of a five-pound sack of dog food, all of the biscuits, and a handful of the jerky strips before backing away and padding out of the cave.

The next time they came, so did the Rottweiler.

He showed up minutes after their arrival, leading Tracy, Amy, and Betsy to suspect King Kong kept a home nearby. They fed him. He packed in the dog food and the treats, successfully begged after some of their munchies, circled around, and scrambled out of the cave, only to return every time they did.

By the fourth visit, it was ritual.

King Kong was staying longer, moving faster, and looking healthier and heavier, his weight probably up fifteen or twenty pounds to somewhere over a hundred or hundred and twenty-five pounds. Before leaving, he'd nuzzle up against the girls, one and then the next, to show appreciation and take their stroking, patting, and scratching to his dewlap and arch before disappearing.

"Hey, Kongie, how goes?" Tracy said, her voice weaker than a whisper. "Only me here this time and not doing so well."

The Rottweiler lay down beside her, one ear cocked, as if he wanted to know everything.

Tracy worked an arm out of the sleeping bag and struggled

to pull the bag of dog biscuits and the beef jerky container closer. "Here's what you're wanting, right, Kongie? Made me sick, but fine for you, right?"

She waited, as if expecting him to answer. Then, as if she'd received one, she said, "Your other girlfriends won't be coming anymore, Kongie."

King Kong gave her the look that always meant: *More treats, please.*

She peeled off another jerky strip and fed it to him. It was gone in a bite.

He settled his chin on the sleeping bag and seemed pleased to feel her stroking and scratching from his dome to the crest of his neck. He purred, sounding like Betsy's pussy cat, Puddy Tat.

"A bad man, he did bad things to Amy and Betsy," she said. "They're in Heaven, but I don't suppose you know where that is, Kongie, do you? No, I didn't think so. I think he was trying to do the same thing to me, Kongie, but I got away from him and that's why I'm here. You're going to protect me, Kongie, aren't you? Sure you are. That's a good boy, Kongie, but I think I have to sleep some more now, okay?"

King Kong lifted himself up and followed his tail several times before settling down approximately where he'd been, only now he was facing the entrance to the cave—

The last thing Tracy saw before her eyelids became too heavy to keep open and she lapsed back into sleep.

However long afterward, she was startled awake again, only it wasn't a nightmare this time, but a voice calling, "Someone in there?" King Kong was still at her side, on all fours, making rumbling noises, the tight hairs on his sway back at attention, his powerful forepaws poised to attack whoever was casting a shadow inside the cave. "Hello?"

A flashlight beam was making patterns that bounced from

the side to the back wall, but couldn't penetrate the cul-de-sac, keeping Tracy hidden from discovery.

King Kong growled and moved forward.

The shadow halted.

The flashlight beam caught the Rottweiler noisily holding his ground and ready to spring at the slightest provocation.

"Easy there," the voice, a man, said, picking up a slight cavern echo. "I'm leaving, so easy. Easy. Nice doggie. Nice doggie . . . Easy . . ."

King Kong let him know what he thought.

Seconds later, no more shadow.

No more flashlight.

King Kong relaxed, turned, and plopped down beside her again.

Tracy said, "He's found me, Kongie. I know it was him. It was the killer. I can't stay here anymore. What am I going to do?"

Instead of answering, King Kong went to work with his tongue and teeth on an itchy paw.

Tracy had visions of the killer lurking somewhere outside in the underbrush, waiting for the Rottweiler to show himself. He would catch Kongie off-guard and shoot him, maybe with the same gun he had used to kill Amy and Betsy. He killed them— girls—so how much could a dog matter? Then, he'd be coming after her again.

A different thought:

Why didn't he shoot Kongie before?

Aim the flashlight at Kongie and fire away.

Because he didn't have a gun?

Yes. That could be it. Had to be it.

No gun, or—

Something else:

He had no intention of killing her.

If he had, wouldn't she be dead already, same as Amy and Betsy?

Thinking:

He abducted her because he needed her alive for some reason.

What, girl? What reason? Think. What, what, what?

Money. Wasn't money what kidnappings were always about? She'd seen enough movies and television to know that.

He'd probably already sent a ransom note to Mommy, but he couldn't collect the money without her. No, wait. Send Mommy some proof he had her, that's all that was necessary. Proof, and then he didn't need her anymore.

Or—

What if he was demanding more money than Mommy had? They were well-off, she supposed, although not millionaires, not by a long shot.

What was the word Mommy was always using to describe their situation?

Comfortable.

They were *comfortable.*

Or—

What if he had already collected the ransom money, and now he intended to kill her, which was easier and safer than turning her loose? Turn her loose? He didn't have to come searching for her if he planned on turning her loose. Just forget about her and leave Eden Highlands with the money.

It had to be something else.

That she had seen him long enough to memorize his face and could identify him?

She squeezed her eyes tight and drew a perfect picture of him on the insides of her lids.

Had to be that, or what else?

Her mind racing now, exploring possibilities until they

became one big jumble, but always drawing her to the same conclusion:

He'd come after her and he'd found her hiding here in the BAT Cave.

She needed to get away from him, but—

Was she brave enough? Did she have the courage to try?

She remembered something her father had said to her once, more than once, when she was growing up, in one of their secret conversations, before he stopped coming at all. He'd never told her why they had to be secret, but she believed Daddy, the same way she believed him when he promised there would be a right time for them to be together again, some time, but not yet and maybe not for years to come. He'd told her:

"Courage is being brave enough and doing what you're afraid to do, Sweetheart."

"Why can't you have the courage and be brave enough to come back home to us now, Daddy?"

"Maybe because I'm too scared, darling. Some day you'll understand how much courage it's taking me not to be with you."

Tracy spent the next minutes thinking about escape and how soon King Kong always showed up at the cave whenever he smelled their presence. His own lair definitely had to be close by. All she needed was enough strength to get there and she'd be safe for the time being. Another day and she'd be able to get back down the hill and home.

But—

If the killer was outside, lurking until he was certain it was only some wild dog here in the cave?

She would have Kongie by her side, guiding her to his home, ready to pounce at the first threatening signs from a stranger. Protect his turf as well as her.

And if the killer had a gun?

"Courage is being brave enough and doing what you're afraid to

do, Sweetheart."

She decided she was scared, but not too scared to try.

Would her body cooperate, though?

Tracy pressed a hand to her forehead. Still burning. After escaping this far, the climb up the hillside to the cave, the lack of food, the upchucking, did she have enough strength to get out of the BAT Cave, much less to the Rottweiler's lair?

She reached for King Kong, who rolled onto his back and let her hear how much he welcomed her touch. "So, Kongie, think we can be brave together, you and me?" She wriggled and inched her way out of the sleeping bag and struggled to her feet. Propped herself up against the wall. Swallowed a deep breath full of sour air. Asked a second time, "So what do you say, Kongie? Want to show me where you live?"

King Kong rolled into a sitting position and found new fleas to attack.

"C'mon, Kongie," Tracy said.

The Rottweiler's ears perked up. She felt his eyes tracking her as she used the wall as a crutch to work out of the cul-de-sac. Her legs were wobbly. She locked her knees and walked stiff-legged to the mouth of the cave. She was relieved to see there was still enough daylight to safely navigate a path.

"C'mon, Kongie," Tracy said, again.

King Kong raced past her.

She called after him, telling him to wait, picked up her pace incautiously, caught her toe on a rock, and stumbled forward seven or eight feet, but sustained enough balance to keep from falling onto a pathway the rain had turned into one long, muddy slush-puddle. Fighting for breath, her hands cemented to her knees, she searched around for King Kong.

He had disappeared.

Tracy thought she heard a rustling in the underbrush, off to her left.

She turned, hoping to see Kongie.

Nothing.

She glanced in the other direction.

She saw the killer standing at the head of the trail.

CHAPTER 30

Except for the park ranger, Emil Grass might have missed finding Tracy.

The ranger was backing away from a barely noticeable cave uttering words of caution—*Nice doggie . . . Easy*—when Grass finally reached flat ground after an eternity of struggling up the hill on a barely existent mudslide of a trail, frequently grabbing onto a cluster of low-slung bush branches to keep from falling.

The ranger was stout, middle-aged, and silly-looking in a Halloween costume of a uniform that could have been inspired by the Canadian Mounties, a military brown with touches of lipstick red, epaulets, a belt strapped diagonally across his beer-barrel chest, a gun belt and holster, holding a cell phone instead of a weapon. A pair of mirrored shades, for effect, certainly not for protection against the modest light.

The ranger turned and spotted him emerging from the trail. He raised a hand like he was taking an oath. "Ho!" Grass duplicated the gesture, held his ground and a plastic smile as the park ranger approached. "You miss seeing the posts, mister? This area's way-aways off limits."

"Sorry, I am," Grass said. "Searching."

"Searching, huh? Don't suppose it's after a dog?"

"Why's that, Officer?"

"Ranger . . . Brute of one over there, that cave. Sounding like it was getting ready to tear me a new butt hole. Not what I expected to find, they called me to fill in today for the regular,

Eddie, laid out with this here flu going around."

"What or who then?"

It took the ranger a few seconds to understand the question.

"Some girls from down Eden Highlands, always hearing how they got this habit of turning up in that cave. Keeps Eddie busy sometimes shooing them out and to home. Took it upon myself to come on up here and see if maybe they were in there now, caught by the rain." The ranger shrugged. "Not a peep, unless one of them does a gosh darn good imitation of a dog." He tapped the golden shield on his chest. "Like I was saying, it's strictly n.g. for civilian-types here, so I got to ask you to descend the area."

"About the peep, you're sure?"

The ranger eyed him curiously. "Why so interested, mister?"

"What got me up here searching," Grass said, improvising furiously. "My niece has been gone last night and all day. I know about the cave from my sister. I couldn't return home without checking it out, the cave, for myself. You don't mind?"

The ranger appeared insulted by Grass' suggestion, as if his very manhood was at stake. He put on an officious face. "There's twenty-twenty behind these glasses. Besides, I know dogs when I hear them. Besides, you get yourself harmed, we get us sued for damages, I get my sagging butt fired from the stingy hours I'm always getting anymore."

"No offense, Ranger."

"None taken," the ranger said, not even trying to mean it. "In fact, I think it's best giving you some protection on down, possible damage control as far as the righteous trail, and you're good to go from there."

"Most generous of you, but I can see myself down," Grass said, anxious to lose the ranger; figuring to lose himself in the nearby underbrush until the ranger was gone. He had a feeling about the cave. He wasn't going to settle for this oaf's opinion.

The ranger shook his head. "Not only a dereliction of my duty, which I take letter-of-the-law serious, but it wouldn't not be courteous of me at all."

He eased around Grass and motioned for him to follow.

Grass sighed in anticipation of what the ranger was bringing on himself and fell in step. He stayed five or six feet behind while the ranger described the park and its attractions as if he were leading a tour. He fished out the HuntChamp from his pocket, worked open the big blade behind his back, and waited until they'd reached a modest shelf about an eighth of a mile down.

"Need to catch my breath," Grass said, moving forward.

"Enough cigarettes in my lifetime to know that feeling," the ranger said, turning around. He barely had time to show surprise before Grass' knife caught him in the hollow of his throat. The ranger slapped a hand over the blood spill. The other hand shot down, caught Grass by his throat, and began choking him, the grip tight and powerful enough to lift Grass inches off the ground.

Grass plunged the blade into the ranger's throat a second time. A bloody gargle spilled over the ranger's bloodstained teeth and down the corners of his mouth. Not satisfied, Grass rammed the blade straight and hard into the ranger's chest, below where the leather belt crossed his heart. The ranger released his hold on Grass. Grass landed on his feet, quickly moved into a pose that showed he was ready to strike again. The ranger gathered strength from somewhere and charged at him.

Grass sidestepped him with a matador's grace.

As the ranger passed by, he wheeled around and punctured him at the base of his spine.

The strike brought the ranger to his knees. He fell forward and landed face down in the mud.

Grass moved in to make sure the ranger was dead.

He wiped off the blade on the ranger's uniform and returned it to his pocket, shoved and rolled the ranger from the trail into the underbrush, pocketed his shades as a souvenir of the kill, and headed back up the hill.

Tracy was about twenty feet away from him, bent over with her hands on her knees.

She turned in his direction and at once cracked the air with a painful noise. Extended her arms palms facing him, as if that would be sufficient to ward him off. Began stepping backward, then wheeled about and ran as fast as the muddy path allowed, not fast at all.

Grass hurried after her, not wasting his breath on words, keeping pace, and confident he would momentarily have her back in his grasp. How to keep her under control while transporting her back to the trailer park, the bigger concern. He had no medication with him, no rope to corral Tracy like the delicious little calf she was.

He thought about the ranger's chest strap. That could contain her on the trip down to his car. The easiest solution: knock her out. Carry her slung over his shoulder like a sack of potatoes. He'd hoisted potato sacks that weighed more than her. So simple it was a last thought: show her the HuntChamp or his .22. She was no dumbbell that she wouldn't get the message.

Tracy slipped and faltered on the muddy turf.

Grass closed the gap between them. He was about to grip the collar of her pea coat when he lost his footing. He rotated his arms wildly to keep from falling. He called at her, "You can't get away, my beautiful little girl," unloading a heavy breath between every other word.

She shrieked at the suggestion and seemed to take strength from it. Gained a yard or two on him before hitting a pothole that caused her legs to skid out from under her. She landed on her buttock and squealed with pain. She tried working herself back onto her feet, but couldn't get the mud to cooperate before he reached her. She sank her head onto her chest and began sobbing.

Grass stood over Tracy, telling her, "You have been the naughty little girl, thinking you could get away from your Uncle Emil before he was finished with you. Shame on you for that. Shame, shame, shame."

He hunkered down and offered his hand to help her up.

She slapped it away.

He made a clucking noise. "Still playing a naughty girl, are you?" He rose, pulled the .22 from the holster at the small of his back, and pressed the barrel to her ear. "I want you to tell your Uncle Emil you're sorry and you'll behave yourself," he said, "or I may have to send you on your way to join your two girlfriends. Remember them?"

The fright he hoped to throw into her didn't take.

As if Tracy knew better, she fixed him with a deadly stare and said, "Go to hell, you pervert."

Brave, he thought, like her father always pretended to be. He banged her head with the gun barrel. "Foul words don't belong in a young lady's vocabulary. I taught my daughters to know that, every one of them."

"Screw you and screw every one of them, perv. Or have you already? Have you?"

He stepped away from her, angled his body and took one-armed aim, like he meant to make good on his threat, thinking maybe he would. Talking like that about his children. Her behavior had become despicable, the dirty-mouthed little tramp. What business was it of hers anyway, his relationship with his children? "I'll count to ten," he said, cocking the weapon.

The clicking noise drew a loud gasp from her.

Progress with the bitch, he thought, and began counting.

He was at seven when Tracy reached out a hand, calling, "Kongie!"

Grass glanced over his shoulder.

The ugly dog trotted to a stop within striking distance, its face a lesson in danger, eyes glowering with menace, humming a finely tuned warning growl. It had to be the one the ranger talked about. A Rottweiler, the kind of animal that came with a reputation for killing that was worse than his own.

Grass turned careful aim on the Rottweiler.

Before he could squeeze off a shot, he was knocked off balance by the little bitch, who had wrapped her arms around his legs and pulled.

The shot exploded and the bullet disappeared somewhere.

He lost hold of the .22 as his gun arm fell.

The Rottweiler leaped, catching him by the arm, its fangs biting through material and touching raw skin, drawing blood.

Grass screamed, flailing and kicking in his attempt to shake off the beast while trying unsuccessfully to get a hand on the HuntChamp. The struggle continued until the Rottweiler released his arm and appeared ready to lunge for his throat.

Grass dug a swift toe into the Rottweiler's underbelly.

The beast let out a howl and catapulted onto its side, quickly scrambled back onto all fours, and prepared to strike again.

Grass had the knife out now, waist high, and aimed at the beast.

He worked it in a circle while dodging left and right, skipping from one foot to the other.

The noise coming from the back of the beast's throat was deeper and more intense. His eyes checked after an opening.

Leading with the blade, Grass quick-stepped toward the Rottweiler.

The beast must have recognized the danger. It backed off.

Grass took another few steps. The beast again retreated. It moved into a circling tactic. Grass followed the beast's lead, sidestepping until he saw the beast settling into a protective pose alongside Tracy, who was sitting in a mud puddle, her knees raised and being used to anchor the two-handed grip she had on his .22.

"You come another step and I swear I'll shoot you," she said. "You harmed Kongie, you'd already be dead."

Grass thought to hold the HuntChamp at arm's length, close it with the flick of a thumb and shift it into a pocket, to suggest he was no longer a threat to her. For emphasis, he locked his hands behind his back.

The beast seemed anxious to charge.

The little bitch circled his neck with her arm. "Not yet, Kongie," she said, like Grass was supposed to believe the beast was taking orders from her.

"Such brave words from a brave little girl," he said, thinking through his options, eyes darting left and right, then back onto the little bitch and her damned pet. "Do I understand you would shoot and kill me if your dog doesn't eat me first, my beautiful little girl?"

"Don't call me that. I hate you," she said.

He didn't doubt her for a minute. "Of course. Am I supposed to believe you really know how to shoot a gun?"

"From my daddy. Aim and fire. Squeeze the trigger."

"And maybe hit something. Your daddy, was it? He knew how to shoot a firearm?"

"Knows how. He learned it for his movies and he taught me before he had to stop coming to visit. Sometimes. Hey, I said don't move, or else." Her voice rose on the threat, bringing on a mean growl from the beast.

The Rottweiler was the difference, or the little bitch would be his by now.

She could shoot, maybe, but would she?

Would she shoot to kill?

The little bitch was desperate enough, certainly, trying to keep the .22 steady, the beast ready to attack him if she let go of it, but—

Her eyes sent a different message.

He saw in them a teenager too scared to make a final commitment to the act of murder.

Could he turn his back goodbye on her and head away without suffering a bullet?

Only one way to find out.

He drew a heavy breath.

"I am going to leave you now," Grass said. "You are welcome to keep the gun. I have others."

"You do, you'll be sorry."

"I'm already sorry, but I must see a doctor about this arm and what serious damage has been done to it by your sinful pet." He held up his arm. Feigned a damaged wrist.

She followed his every movement with the .22 and a chin as recklessly aimed.

She said, "I'm going to shoot you, kill you, if you don't stop it right now. I mean it. I really mean it. You'll be dead before you know it."

"Yes, but think about this. . . . If I stay my ground, what are you going to do with me? I'm more of a danger to you here than if I go away."

"A lot of things, a lot of things I can do, you take one false move." She clenched her brow, forming deep furrows of uncertainty, her eyes taking on elements of confusion. "And Kongie here. He hates you as much as I hate you."

"I'll be on my way before it gets any darker," Grass said.

He turned and started toward the trail, ignoring the little bitch's shouted demands to halt, his back full of spasms brought on by the idea the little bitch might, in fact, fire.

Cuh-rack!

A shot splattered mud about five feet ahead and barely off to his left.

He'd felt the breeze as it passed.

Grass paused, blew out a bagful of breath, and continued.

The little bitch called another warning.

He ignored her and kept going.

Her next shot was closer, either because she was lucky or a better shot than he'd ever give her credit for being.

He reached the trail and increased his pace, careful to maintain his balance while waiting for the next gunshot.

It never came.

Within minutes, he was below her sightline.

He settled onto a boulder and fired up an English Oval.

The smoke was a welcome pacifier.

He pulled up his jacket and shirt sleeve to check where he had been bitten by the beast. Teeth marks and violated skin about three inches above his wrist, but probably no damage of a serious or long-lasting nature. If the beast had rabies, nothing he could do about it right now.

Grass wondered about waiting for nightfall and going back up after her, confident he could outmaneuver her and her damned dog. He inspected his wound again. Rabies. An ugly death if it wasn't treated quickly and properly.

Getting to a doctor made sense.

Where was the little bitch going to go anyway? She'd eluded him once, but he had found her. He could find her again after he and Crews put the next part of the plan in play.

Rabies.

An ugly, ugly way to die.

Grass ground what remained of his English Oval under a heel.

He flipped it into the brush and continued down the trail.

Yes. Get to a doctor, definitely the next order of business.

He checked his watch.

Palm-slapped his forehead.

He had been so caught up in the business with that stupid park ranger, then the dirty-mouthed little bitch and her filthy mongrel hound, it was now more than an hour and a half past the time Crews wanted the call made to Maggie Collins.

Grass reached after his cell phone.

Scheisse. Shit. Missing. Gone.

Maybe lost in his wrestling match with that damned Rottweiler?

The best of any possibilities, unless it had slipped from his pocket while driving.

He checked once more, to be certain. *Scheisse.* Damned Crews would be riding his ass again about always being late, like there was a Nobel Prize handed out for punctuality. How much more time would pass before he could get to a telephone?

Grass snapped his fingers and answered the question:

Minutes, only minutes.

The park ranger, he was carrying a cell phone in his gun holster.

Grass cautiously worked his way down the muddy slope another twenty yards, to where he had freed the ranger of any worries about his future. The ranger's body was half-visible in the roadside brush.

Another few minutes and he was dialing Maggie Collins' number.

She answered halfway into the first ring, her voice quavering, a study in apprehension.

"Mrs. Collins, we both have something the other wants. Are you ready to deal for your beautiful little daughter's safe return?"

"Let me speak to her. I want to speak to her."

"You haven't answered my question, Mrs. Collins."

Undecipherable noises on the other end before he was talking to Burt Crews.

"Emil, hello, hello, hello. Do you know who this is?"

"Crews, I need to tell you—"

Cut off before he could continue, Crews saying, "Yes, indeed. Burton X. Crews, himself. Surprise. Your old comrade-in-arms. A small world getting smaller by the day."

Noises that made Grass wonder if the line was tapped.

He asked.

Crews responded with the phony smile in his voice that could always disarm a stranger. "Tapped? Certainly not. I know better than that when it comes to dealing with you. . . . You hear a tap, you would disappear faster than farts in a wind tunnel. We certainly don't want that, do we, old friend?"

"You're positive, or I'll hang up. There's something I have to tell you that's most urgent."

Momentary quiet before Crews said, "Yes, of course, the agency deciphered your signal," like he was into a different conversation, to illustrate the line was clean. "The two killings and the abduction, how it linked to Mrs. Boone—Mrs. Collins. It certainly did not take a genius to decipher your handiwork. So close to that nasty business you once pulled off in Paris, wasn't it?"

"Monte Carlo." He couldn't put it off any longer. Crews had to be told before he followed the script and demanded the little bitch be put on the line with her mother, as a sign of good faith. "Crews, I've lost the girl. We don't have her."

An eternity of silence, then, "I don't need to hear that now, Emil. What I need before we discuss the Mielke diary is for you to allow Mrs. Collins to hear her child's voice. Do it for me, old friend? Show a modicum of compassion for the poor woman."

"Crews, you weren't listening? I said—"

"Yes, your surmise is correct. I've been authorized by Mrs. Collins to represent her, and it's with government blessing. Nobody else, no interference by other agencies, so I can guarantee we'll be able to work out an arrangement satisfactory to all concerned parties—but after you put Tracy on and let her speak with her mother. Humor me and do that now, Emil? Please?"

"Damn you, Crews. Damn you. *Verpiss dich!* Fuck off! That was never mentioned as part of the plan."

He snapped the cell phone shut.

CHAPTER 31

"Emil, it's not that at all. I've made it clear that if you say Tracy is fine, Tracy is fine, but—" Crews turned to Maggie with his hand covering the mouthpiece. "He's being difficult to be difficult, Mrs. Collins. That's his way, but he wouldn't lie about something like that, not to me anyway. I'd hear it immediately." His hand off the mouthpiece. "Emil, then how do you propose to satisfy Mrs. Collins about her daughter? Tell me."

Maggie watched him pace to another corner of the living room, all Crews had been doing since he took the phone from her, touring like an actor on stage, making gestures as broad as the horizon line to underscore his every sentence.

She remained frozen in the armchair alongside the sofa, every breath she released an assault on her chest, hands locked on her lap, laced fingers as blue as the veins snapping at her temples. She tilted her head up toward Roxy, standing behind her applying gentle thumbs to the muscle spasms torturing her back, and wordlessly asked her the same question.

Roxy leaned over and filled her ear with gentle assurance. "It's going to be fine, Sweetie Pie. Only a little longer before your baby is safe back home." She stroked Maggie's hair, resettled loose strands behind her ear. Leaned over and kissed the top of her head.

Maggie reached for Roxy's hand and squeezed it lovingly.

Crews was staring at the cottage cheese ceiling, like he was counting the lumps, telling Emil Grass, "That will have to work, if that's the way you want it. I think you're being overly cautious, but that's just me, isn't it?" A tight smile inching across his face. A burst of laughter. "And up yours, old friend." His hand back on the mouthpiece, calling to Maggie, "Progress." A smile to reach the balcony. "After that, what?" His head nodding to whatever Grass was saying.

Glen Traylor moved from the doorway leading in from the central corridor to the sofa he was sharing with Jack Sothern. He tossed Sothern one of the Budweiser Light cans he'd fetched a minute or two after the phone rang.

Sothern made a one-handed catch and gave Glen a thumbs-up. He sprang the top and took a greedy swallow.

Glen followed suit, but settled for a sip while throwing a look at Roxy that asked, *What have I missed?* She responded with a *Not now* gesture and went back to massaging Maggie.

Roxy and Sothern had joined Maggie and Crews at the house following the services for Amy and Betsy. Glen arrived twenty or thirty minutes later, after depositing Vernon Mount at Doc Ayers' office.

Stepping down from the church stage, the chief had tripped over his own unsteady feet, suffering what the doctor said could be anything from a bruised ego to a hip fracture.

"Won't know until I run some x-rays," Doc Ayers said, while Traylor and a member of the congregation hoisted Mount under the arms and got him into Traylor's car and stretched out on the back seat. "It's not that you fall and break your hip, it's the bones that wear out and cause the fall," the doctor said, denying Mount's complaints he was fine. "A good thing you didn't land on your head, Vernon, or they'd start mistaking you for a piñata."

Crews' voice took another turn.

His head-bobbing became twists of disapproval.

He said, "Can't do that, Emil. Not me. It has to be Jack Sothern. . . . Yes, him. One and the same. In the room with me, even as I speak." He turned to Sothern and said, "Emil says hello and sends his regards." Sothern showed him an animated middle finger. "Mr. Sothern sends his regards back, Emil."

Crews crossed to another part of the room, waving a hand like he was conducting an orchestra. "Thank you, Emil, I appreciate that. I've told Mrs. Collins as much, how you know you can trust me, but here's the point: Mr. Sothern has the Mielke diary, not Mrs. Collins."

Maggie and Traylor sent Sothern incredulous looks.

Sothern shrugged and set about analyzing the top of his beer can.

Crews said, "How that occurred, I don't know, but Mr. Sothern is resolute in refusing to work a trade through me or anybody. He's adamant about doing it personally, trading the diary for Tracy. . . . Emil, Emil, I'm no mind reader. . . . If I vouch for him, how is that? . . . If I accompany him?"

Sothern said, "Let me talk to the son of a bitch." He sprang from the sofa, reached Crews in four giant steps.

Crews clamped a hand over the mouthpiece, angled the phone away from Sothern, and gestured for him to retreat. For a few seconds, Sothern seemed ready to argue the point, but he wheeled around and resumed his seat. Consoled himself with several swigs of Budweiser Light.

Crews said, "No tricks, no gamesmanship my side, Emil. To be quite frank with you, my team lost interest in the diary years ago. We learned all its secrets from other sources. I haven't a clue why it's important to you and I don't care. Frankly, all I care about is the safe return of Tracy Collins."

Maggie couldn't stop the moan climbing out of her throat. At once, Roxy was at her ear, polishing her cheek with her fingers, promising a happy ending.

The expression on Glen's face was less certain.

Crews listened for what seemed to Maggie like an eternity,

several times moving the phone away from his ear for a second or two and showing exasperation. "Emil, I get it," he said, finally. "I don't have to repeat it back. We'll see you then. . . . Yes, yes, yes, I speak for them, Mrs. Collins and Mr. Sothern. We'll see you then."

Crews quit the connection looking like he had just won the grand prize on one of those hokey reality shows. He announced, "My friends, we've taken one giant leap closer to our goal."

Maggie made a noise and gripped her chest.

Traylor said, "Sothern has the Mielke diary? What else don't I know? Fill me in."

Sothern said, "The *Encyclopedia Britannica* would be a good place to start. How's that, partner?"

Traylor killed him with a look. Crews explained the situation.

When he finished, Traylor turned back to Sothern. "He hasn't said how you came by the diary."

Sothern said, "A good newspaperman never reveals his sources."

"Well, that lets you out. How'd you come by it, Sothern?"

"What's important is that I'm here, I have it, and nothing happens now without me."

"You really don't give a flying fuck about Maggie or Tracy or anyone but yourself, do you, Sothern?"

Maggie shouted, "Glen, let it be. I'm fine with whatever it takes to deal with Emil Grass."

"Whatever the arrangement is, I'm cutting myself in, Crews. Nothing goes down now without me."

"Then nothing goes down, Detective. I know too well what can happen with Emil if I deviate the merest fraction from the arrangement we just made."

"Which is what?"

"Which is not for your ears, Detective."

Maggie shouted, "Glen, if you care for me at all, if you care for Tracy, I'm begging you to let it be."

"So this hack writer over here gets himself a story making him out to be some kind of a hero?" Sothern let the challenge ride. "For this trash bag I'm supposed to step aside and pass up a chance to catch a cold-blooded, murdering snake?"

Sothern said, "That's Mr. Trash Bag to you, partner."

Traylor swept him into infinity with a gesture and began popping up a finger with every name he threw into the room: "Amy Spencer. Betsy Wheatcroft. Pablo Mora. Evelyn Blemish. . . . How many more people will get killed if we don't stop Grass? Once he has the diary—"

"Detective, that's not going to be the case," Crews said.

"Where's the crystal ball that news came in on?"

"That's not going to be the case, Detective," Crews said, as quietly as before, his face as emotionless as a brick.

Traylor rose and moved on Crews like a playground bully, so close it looked like their noses would collide. Crews' expression stayed firm and unimpeachable.

"We'll see what we'll see," Traylor said.

Without another word, he turned and fled the room.

Seconds later, the front door slammed loud enough to set some neighborhood dogs howling.

"Where do we go from here?" Sothern said.

CHAPTER 32

It was dark when Emil Grass arrived at the doctor's modest Craftsman-style two-story duplex on a quiet, badly lit neighborhood street sheltered by overripe trees and white picket fences. He was still fuming over the phone conversation with that damn Crews, but not enough to shortchange his concern about his arm, where the Rottweiler's fangs had drawn blood.

Admitted hypochondriac that he was, Grass was convinced the beast was rabid and he would need one of those treatments where the anti-rabies vaccine is injected into the stomach through an obscenely long needle, day-after-day for fourteen days, and then—

Who knows?

Rabies is deadly.

For all Grass knew, he could be dying already.

He had read up about rabies years ago, because of Herr Mielke, whose own interest was not in saving lives so much as destroying them.

One of Herr Mielke's favorite tricks was to threaten a tight-mouthed suspect with an injection of rabies-infused blood.

Often, after getting the information he wanted, he ordered the injection, then put the suspect on display as a warning to others in his secret holding pens.

Oh, yes. Yes. Grass had observed the progress of the rabies in its three stages. In the beginning came vomiting, a low-grade fever, headaches, and irritability. Within two weeks, the disease had involved the nervous system and the suspect began hallucinating. The third stage brought on muscle contractions in the throat, seizures, paralysis, breathing difficulties, a coma, and death.

As Doc Ayers snapped on the porch light and swung the front door open, Grass was feeling the fatigue, a sure sign of the disease. He hadn't eaten for hours, but he wasn't hungry. Another sign. The back of his hand was on his brow, verifying the unnatural heat that spelled fever brewing. Irritable? Grass couldn't recall the last time he was this irritable, but that, of course, was due in part to Crews, damn him.

"Rabies, is it?" the doctor said, leading him to a room off the corridor. "Strip down to your waist, good enough, and sit on the examination table."

"It was a dog did this to my arm."

Doc Ayers took his arm and inspected the gashes. "This hardly looks worth the price of a bandage. I've had Navy up from San Diego come in here, showing off worse than you from some whore they sailed into in some dark alley off Couts Drive. Wounds deep or large enough for stitches, not your rinky-dinks."

"A wild dog, a beast what attacked me, not any damned whore."

Grass slammed a fist on the examination table and barked and howled to illustrate what kind of dog he meant. He explained where and how he had been attacked, leaving out the parts about the park ranger and Tracy Collins.

Doc Ayers said, "Off limits, up there's off limits for a reason, but I still would bet on you surviving." He put a stethoscope to Grass' back. "Deep breath and cough for me. . . . Congestion I hear makes me think you're a smoker in more danger from losing a lung, you don't quit before it's too late."

"Let me worry about my lung."

"Deep breath and cough again. . . . Two lungs up for

grabs. . . . When was the last time you had a tetanus shot?"

"Never. I hate needles."

"Get yourself dressed while I go and fix up a needle for you. It's guaranteed to cure what ails you."

As Doc Ayers turned for the door, it opened. Vernon Mount stuck his head inside without so much as a knock, bloodshot eyes crawling out from behind uncooperative lids. "Doc, you got some animal in here or what? Damn noise just now woke me, scared the living b'Jesus out of me, so I—"

Mount realized it was Grass on the examination table. That popped his eyes. The look on his face bordered recognition with contempt. His mouth turned ugly. He said, "I didn't know you were with a patient, Doc. Apologies," and retreated, closing the door after him, as if Grass were a stranger to him.

"That was our esteemed chief of police," Doc Ayers said.

"That must be why he looked familiar to me," Grass said, playing the same game as Mount.

"Unless you've been on some of the barroom floors his face favors. He's been sleeping it off here from a fall down that busted a couple of ribs, but could have been as serious as a broken hip."

Grass was clicking open the SUV door, priding himself on not having succumbed to his fear of needles or shown any sign of cowardice while the doctor stung him with the tetanus shot, when he heard the shuffle of shoes closing in behind him. He turned to discover Vernon Mount five or six feet away, a little wobbly in a shooter's stance, aiming a .45 pistol like he meant to use it.

"Something I don't know?" Grass said, sounding nonchalant while his eyes roamed an inkwell of an evening broken only by the curtained lights of a dozen homes on either side of the street.

"You got that part in the plus column," Mount said. "Your taste for blood's taken me out of a game I never should've gone along with, little man."

"It was your taste for money that got you into it, Chief Mount. Is that what this is about? More money for the chief of police? How much?"

Mount waved off the suggestion with the gun, the movement so quick and broad it almost threw him off balance. "You blue suede-ed me into it, talked me out of it one time before, but not anymore."

"Your greed did the talking, not me. I ask you again, how much?"

"Not for all the tea in China. Four decent people dead, when it should be you stretched out in a box six feet down. Not part of our arrangement."

"The alcohol gives you short-term memory? I've never pretended to be more or less than I am, Chief. I do whatever my work requires of me. Tell me the amount. I'll have it over to you in the morning. Making it worth your while to make peace makes it worthwhile to me."

"Soft soap gets you nowhere. I phoned you and phoned you. You never once answered."

"If I hurt your feelings, I sincerely apologize. I must not have heard the telephone. I have been otherwise engaged in business matters."

"I waited until you left the Doc's because I didn't want him becoming another notch on your belt."

"Never. I owe him a debt of gratitude. He saved my life tonight. From contracting rabies. An encounter with a mad dog."

"An encounter with a mad dog. That pretty well sums up his opening the door to you. No more killings on my watch, little man. Them days is gone forever. Over and out. Kaput."

257

"Exposing me is to expose yourself at the same time. We've had this conversation before. Accessory to murder, that's you, Chief. No better than me." Grass drew a knife across his throat. "How much?"

Mount seemed to be thinking it over.

It didn't matter, though. Grass knew the chief's time had come.

He stepped forward, stretched out his arms and slapped his hands into a tight grip.

"Cuff me, Chief Mount. I'm your prisoner. Lead me to your jail. I'm game if you are."

"Hold it right there," Mount said, and stepped back. "Drop your arms. Put them behind your back. Move to the van and marry it with your body, you hear me, little man?"

"Or what?"

"Or I'll be shooting a prisoner in the act of trying to escape."

"In which case, I bow to your command," Grass said.

He lowered his arms, bowed, and instantly launched himself at the chief.

Mount's reflexes couldn't handle the surprise.

Grass' head butt caught the chief belt-high and caused him to drop the pistol.

The chief staggered backward and fell.

Grass was on him at once, his hands wrapped around Mount's throat.

"Such big and powerful hands for a little man, wouldn't you say so, Chief Mount?" Grass squeezed harder, enjoying the gurgling sound that might last a minute longer. "Are you saying your prayers, Chief Mount? Goodbye, Chief Mount."

Grass held onto the police chief's throat longer than necessary, ecstatic over how well the kill had gone, almost sorry it was over so soon. It might have taken longer if the chief were a younger man or had been less into his cups. Any longer, he would have had an orgasm, and not the first time. Years ago, he'd started keeping count, but the practice grew tiresome after a while, the same way he had difficulties now whenever he tried to recite the names of all the people he'd sent on the long journey. The pleasure he derived from killing almost made him sad to think that once he had the Mielke diary sold and his millions collected, it would all come to an end.

Grass rose and checked around. Nothing to indicate they had been observed. He had to make a decision, and quickly: Leave the body behind to be found or haul it away in the SUV, dispose of it elsewhere? This was no time for imprecision. When was it ever? Grass dropped to his knees and hunted for Mount's .45. It had fallen into the high-rise weed patch near the chief's body. He stuffed it inside his belt. With military precision, he opened the rear door of the SUV, then dragged Mount over by his ankles. He struggled and raised a healthy sweat getting the chief inside, dead weight being dead weight, all the while satisfying himself it was all in a good night's work.

Good?

Excellent, more like it.

All in an *excellent* night's work.

He drove off at peace about the rabies, feeling invincible, like he could live forever.

259

CHAPTER 33

Glen Traylor sat stewing outside Maggie's home, hunched behind the wheel of his Ford, wishing he had thought to grab a fresh brew before blasting out of there. Resenting the arrogance of Burt Crews, arbitrarily cutting him out of the loop like he was some snot-nosed kid who didn't know his way around an investigation.

Wasn't that just like any of those holier-than-thou feds, who were always tossing their weight around, shutting out local law enforcement in order to haul in the glory for themselves? Worse here. Vernon, his own boss, cutting in a discredited journalist, promoting him to amateur detective, for Christ's sake.

They had something going, the two of them, Crews and Sothern, that had to be it.

Sothern was in because any story he'd write would make out Crews the hero.

Vernon, also angling to be a hero?

That would be Vernon.

At least *hero* wasn't Glen Traylor's game.

Getting Tracy back for Maggie, that was his game.

Maybe, finally, lighting some sparks under Maggie, installing some love in the one-sided romance where he often came away feeling like he had delivered a charity fuck. He knew better than that, though.

Maggie cared for him, she did.

She gave him clues often enough, even if she never came

right out and said so.

So what if every so often she slipped in the midst of some especially erotic moment and called him "Danny"? It's hard giving up a cherished memory of long standing, that's how he heard it. So what, the role Roxy Colbraith played in Maggie's life outside of The Garden of Eden? The rumors and the side-of-the-mouth gossiping, true or not, so what? He could live with it.

What he wanted was to share a life with Maggie that was more than *Wham bam, thank you, Glen.* Maybe getting Tracy back for her would lead to the defining moment. He felt in his gut and, more important, his heart, that it would be. Yes, so damned if he was going to let Burt Crews or anybody ease him aside.

Traylor checked the dashboard clock. He reached for his cell, punched in the number for the LAPD Hollywood substation, and asked for Liam O'Ferris. Liam, who'd come up through the ranks with Vernon and Glen's dad and had been warming the graveyard shift's watch commander seat for as long as he could remember.

O'Ferris answered with his title and the Falls Road accent that always betrayed his point of origin in Ireland.

"Liam, still as crooked as they come?"

O'Ferris laughed heartily. "Still the one that got away, lad. How's it faring with you and that miserable excuse passing himself off as a chief of police?"

"Surviving."

"Beats the alternative. Couldn't ask for more for m'self. What do you need?"

"Maybe I'm calling to say hello, check up on your bones."

"And I'm His Holiness, the Pope. As my sainted mother used to say, 'Everyone lays a burden on the willing horse.' Lay it on me, Glen."

O'Ferris heard him out. He asked for the number he was calling from and said, "This may take a bit of doing, but don't stray too far from the phone."

Traylor hung in at Maggie's more from curiosity than for any reason he could ascribe.

After about a half hour, the porch light clicked on and Roxy and Sothern stepped out, pausing at the door for a few words with Maggie before heading down the pathway toward her BMW. They engaged in an animated conversation that had them both laughing like they were watching a Will Ferrell movie.

The car was parked a half block from Traylor's Ford, on the opposite side of the street. He ducked out of sight until he figured they had passed. He thought about the hug Roxy had given Maggie just now. Maggie hadn't hugged back. He appreciated that. She always returned his hugs.

Traylor killed time calling over to Doc Ayers to check on Vernon.

He was surprised by what he heard, the Doc telling him, "One minute here, next minute gone, that fool. Some broken ribs having to heal themselves, so no serious harm done, although I wanted him to stay the night, sleep off his one too many–two not enough."

"Vernon say where to, Doc?"

"No chance to ask. Last I saw of him, he had stuck his fool head into my examination room while I was mending some uptight tourist from Temporary Town who'd been bitten by a stray park dog and feared he was coming down with rabies. He ducked out just as fast, over to the jailhouse, maybe?"

Traylor called there on the two-way.

Andy Peck on the dispatch desk said there'd been no sign of the chief since the memorial service and nothing on the logs to say he'd checked in anytime after.

His cell phone sang out.

Liam O'Ferris calling to say, "Got half your answer for you, lad, although it may be one you weren't expecting." He recited Maggie's number. "That's where the call went?"

"Yes."

"Lasted ten or fifteen minutes, you said?"

"Yes."

"Not to that number, lad. I ran it up and down the phone company, every which way, and the last call-in received there was two minutes, not twenty. Two minutes and some odd seconds. From a satellite connection on relays, maybe from out of the country. Impossible to track it down for certain until come morning, if ever."

"You're sure? I was there. I heard the conversation. It was ten or fifteen minutes, not two minutes."

"True as the gospel. You consider, maybe, on your end was somebody in love with the sound of his own voice?"

"I am now, Liam."

Traylor was half-asleep, debating with himself about marching up to Maggie's now and confronting Crews head-on, throwing the question at him instead of continuing to wrestle with possible answers, when a car remote tweeted.

It was Crews, aiming at the Honda Accord parked in her driveway. He backed the Honda onto the street and waited until he'd reached the end of the block and was easing into a left turn downhill before switching on his headlights.

A minute later, Traylor was after him.

Crews had no business abandoning Maggie this time of night.

He was supposed to be protecting her, for Christ's sake.

Traylor kept his distance, navigating most of the tricky drive with his lights off, hoping Crews wouldn't notice he was being tracked. He took the last side avenue before the street hit the freeway access road, jigsawed his way to the road, and picked up Crews again.

The drive ended at the Howard Johnson's, its towering sign a beacon to truckers and other travelers making use of hours when the freeway lanes promise more than the bumper-to-bumper clutter of daytime traffic.

The counter was lined with road-weary drivers hanging over mountains of food. Several booths were occupied by singles and couples, some by families with young children asleep with their heads on the table, their arms for pillows.

Crews slipped into a vacant parking spot close to the entrance.

He walked over to the window and connected to it with his hand, looking for someone. Threw the hand away in disgust and returned to the Honda. Sat behind the wheel with the door open, half in and half out of the car, nervously tapping a foot.

Shortly, Crews pushed himself onto the asphalt and pointed an accusing finger at the driver who'd stepped out of an SUV parked in a dark spot across the access lane, under a pole lamp with a burned-out bulb.

They acted out words, Crews more excited than the driver of the SUV, gesturing wildly to emphasize whatever he was saying.

The driver of the SUV took it all with a smile while patting himself after a cigarette and torching it.

Moments later, instead of entering the Howard Johnson's, Crews returned to the Honda.

The driver of the SUV bombed the blacktop with his smoke, ground it out under his heel, and climbed back behind the wheel.

He headed away with Crews on his tail.

Traylor tossed aside the notepad in which he had jotted down the license number of the SUV. Gunned his motor. Checked the rearview and discovered his exit was blocked by a two-ton waiting for a space.

He watched the SUV and the Honda pull out of the lot, cursing mightily.

Traylor drove back to Maggie's, parked inconspicuously, and pushed himself into as comfortable a position as he could manage, in the corner between the passenger seat and the door. He called the station, learned Vernon still hadn't checked in, and recited the two license numbers he wanted run.

Then he waited out what remained of the night.

When he roused to the noises of morning, he discovered Crews' Honda back in the driveway.

CHAPTER 34

Crews had followed Grass north on the 405, flashing him over when they reached an empty stretch of overgrown weeds a mile and a half before a state weighing station, the sort of desolate spot most likely to yield wetbacks dumped to freedom from cargo vans or crossing into the country from Tijuana through elaborate tunnels the border patrols were never successful in finding.

They rolled to stops on the narrow asphalt shoulder, in front of a chain link security fence topped by razor wire. Somebody had made a three- or four-foot vertical slash through the rusted metal and shaped a modest crawl space at the base that was badly hidden behind pieces of cast-off driftwood and sections of newspaper fluttering in a light breeze sailing in from the Pacific.

Crews threw up the Honda's hood. Grass stepped up alongside him at the fender, where they resumed conversation while studying an engine neither understood, like they were trying to define a problem, not marking time until the traffic was sparse enough to let them take care of business.

Bringing Vernon Mount's body here for disposal had been Crews' idea back at the Howard Johnson's, after he arbitrarily overruled Grass' suggestion that they dump the police chief in Couts Memorial Park, same as Dan-Dan-the-T-Shirt-Man and the park ranger.

Feeding on his own smug, self-righteous arrogance, Crews had called Grass stupid, pelted him in the face with laughter that hit like spitballs, saying, "A brilliant idea. Start a collection of corpses where some other ranger can find the bodies you've already left to the coyotes and next thing you know, the park will be smothered by a million police beating the bushes for more victims before we have a chance to exchange the girl for Mielke's diary and disappear. You know, Emil, the girl we don't have? The girl you let get away from you? Who you should have kept hunting for instead of running off to a doctor like some scaredy-cat baby with a boo-boo that doesn't amount to a hill of beans?"

Grass' eyes had filled with venom. "*Verpiss dich!* Fuck off with that shit. It was more important I leave the ranger and look after myself for what might be rabies. *Gott bewahre* that should happen, even to you. And since when have you suddenly become my boss, Crews, telling me what I should have done?"

In that moment, how he wanted to take care of Crews, have him join Mount in the back of the SUV, but that would have been stupid. *A time and place for everything,* Grass told himself, and this was neither. For the duration, it was essential he continue to think of them as a team about to reap fabulous wealth and comfortable retirement once Mielke's diary was sold to the highest bidder.

Crews may have recognized the thoughts flashing through Grass' mind. He held up his hands in surrender and said, "You're right, and I apologize, Emil. It was rude of me and wholly out of place in our mutual admiration society. Rabies. Deadly. I would have done the same as you in that predicament."

He sounded about as sincere as a used car salesman, but Grass let it go. He flamed an English Oval to steady his nerves. "I suppose you have some idea better than the park?"

Crews nodded. "Remember when they had me working the Colombian mule train through Tijuana? Wetbacks whose bellies were being used as suitcases for the cocaine and heroin? You were off doing something nasty in Prague."

"A nasty in Salzburg. Two nasties. I sent you a postcard from Mozart's *geburthaus* at Getreidgrasse 9."

Crews said, "So you did, Emil. Thank you, again. There are places along the freeway I remember well from a nasty of my own." He described them. "We'll get rid of Mount at the one by the weighing station. Make it look like he spotted some illegals, who overpowered him, shot him with his own weapon, and took off in his vehicle."

"Why not?" Grass said.

Crews was doing more of his bragging while Grass probed the engine with the beam from a long-handled Maglite Dan-Dan-the-T-Shirt-Man kept underneath the driver's seat of the SUV, explaining the exchange scheme he pretended was coming from Emil after Emil hung up on him.

"And they all bought into it?"

"I was very, very convincing, if I do have to say so myself." A hum underscoring his words.

"They still believe the girl is with me?"

"Of course, but only Meg Boone's opinion matters. I don't exaggerate at all telling you she trusts me one-hundred-and-ten percent." More humming.

"Why not? What other choice does she have?"

"None, so long as she thinks I'm the difference in getting her precious cargo back to her."

"Sothern. Him?"

"An opportunist. Wasn't he always?"

"A regular *schwanz lutscher.* How could Boone ever even have considered turning over Herr Mielke's diary to him? It makes no sense."

"We only have Sothern's claim it's so."

"But no proof."

"We'll have our proof and the diary before he gets the girl—and whatever else we have coming to him."

"With my compliments," Grass said. He moved the Maglite, fiddled with the ring pull on a dip stick. "We should head to the SUV. Rid ourselves of that damn fool police chief and be on our way."

"Another minute, to be on the safe side. The gun?"

"Here," Grass said, patting his jacket, where he had slipped the police chief's .45 under his belt.

They were interrupted by a siren's repetitious whine and a burst of light.

They turned and saw a California Highway Patrol car had pulled up behind the Honda.

Grass used a forearm to protect his eyes against the glare of the whirling red roof bubble. "Why is it never simple?" he said, the words escaping out one side of his tightly drawn mouth.

"Don't do anything foolish," Crews said, making with the commands again. He flashed a smile at the patrolman easing out of the front passenger seat and gave him an arc wave.

The patrolman nodded and approached cautiously, working his beacon flash from their faces to the Honda, on over to the SUV, and back to them. He halted about five feet away with his left hand hovering over the Glock in his hip holster.

"*Buenos noches,*" he said, in a baritone that sounded too old for the cherubic face hiding under a scruffy two-day stubble and a Band-Aid of a mustache, spoken like he was testing their citizenship.

His older and beefier partner had moved out from the driver's seat, drawn his Glock, and was using the door as a shield while dictating into his shoulder mike.

"As American as apple pie, if that's what you're wondering about," Crews said. "A little car trouble is all. Good Neighbor

Sam here came to my rescue. Thinks maybe a leak in the power steering?"

The patrolman moved the beam onto Emil. "Your name 'Sam,' *compadre?*"

Grass squinted and nodded.

The patrolmen surveyed the surrounding area with his light, pausing briefly at the break in the fence. His strip of eyebrow raised and put rows of furrows across his brow. He said, "I suppose you have some ID to back that up? A driver's license, maybe?"

Grass nodded.

"And you, *señor?*"

"You can't drive without one," Crews said, full of nonchalance.

"Unless you don't qualify, eh, *muchacho?*" The beam roved back to the SUV. "Me and the missus, thinking about getting ourselves a rig like yours, do some cross-country sightseeing come the kids' summer vacation break. Mind my checking it out, have myself a peek inside?"

Grass recognized it for the lame excuse it was. "Nothing so special or exciting in there but my posters and t-shirts," he said.

"Your business? Posters and t-shirts?"

"Exactly. I'm Dan-Dan-the-T-Shirt-Man."

"Not Sam? I thought you said you were Sam." He threw his partner a fast check over the shoulder. "What you thought, Roy? How's it go? *I am Sam. Sam, I am.* My little one, she loves that Doctor Seuss."

The older patrolman waved him quiet. His shoulder was hunched tight to his ear, trying to catch whatever message was coming at him. Frustrated, he shook his fist angrily at the night air. A three-section trailer truck rumbled past, only the second or third vehicle since Crews had signaled Grass over.

"Shall we?" the young one said, his gun hand hovering over

the Glock like some frontier Marshal Dillon. "Worst can happen, I'll see a t-shirt or two to buy for the kids. Something hip-hoppity for the boy? Olson twins for my little sweetheart?"

Grass said, "Not what I specialize in, sir."

"Something else then," the patrolman said, wagging a directional finger at the van. "Maybe souvenirs from south of the border? Go ahead . . . Roy, you keep tabs on this other *muchacho,* maybe help him figure out what's ailing the Honda."

Grass sent Crews a questioning look.

Crews answered with the look that always signaled *Protect the mission.* He said, "Maybe what I should do is call Triple A? I bet a truck out here in no time, the freeway empty as it is." He went after his cell phone.

The CHP officer named Roy ordered Crews: "Hold it, *señor.*"

Crews moved his arms out parallel to the asphalt. "See? My cell phone."

"My weapon," Roy said, exhibiting the Glock, using the top of the door frame to steady his aim.

Crews laughed, the sound joined by white puffs of breath in the increasingly cold air. "Officer, do I look like a coyote?"

"Curious how you know what they call a wetback smuggler, but no. Take it nice and easy, anyway, while I sort out this damn fool problem with interference on my two-way."

"Here, feel free to use my cell phone," Crews said. He opened the phone and was at the car door before Roy could object. He angled the phone upward and sent a bullet smashing into the patrolman's right eye.

Roy's head snapped backward, the other eye registering surprise before he dropped the Glock and, seconds later, cracked his head on the door frame before hitting the ground.

Crews wheeled around and charged at Roy's partner, aiming the cell phone like it was a Jedi light saber.

At the sound of the shot, Roy's partner had turned his back on Grass.

He sized up the situation at once and had his Glock out before Crews was halfway.

He fired.

The shot caught Crews in the chest. He stumbled backward.

The patrolman's second shot hit Crews in the stomach before Crews slammed into the patrol car and pitched forward.

In the same seconds, Grass yanked the .45 from his belt and got off two shots in quick succession. Both hit the young patrolman between his shoulder blades. He danced forward and fell within feet of Crews, the landing accompanied by the sound of his nose bone cracking.

Grass moved on him and dropped to one knee.

The patrolman was moaning.

Grass put the .45 to the base of his neck and squeezed the trigger.

The patrolman's body arched. His spasms became more pronounced, then quit.

Grass took the Glock and hurried around to the other CHP officer. Crews' shot with the cell phone had done its work. Grass settled the mouth of the Glock below Roy's left ear and blew away half his head for good measure.

He stuffed the patrolman's Glock inside his belt, stored Roy's Glock in the small of his back, and raced back to Crews.

He didn't have to feel for a pulse to know Crews was dead as they come.

Grass checked the freeway. Headlights were approaching in both directions, maybe as close as half a mile and growing larger by the second. He'd have to hurry.

He rescued Crews' wallet and slid it into a hip pocket.

Removed the .22 and the fishnet holster from under Crews' left arm.

Snapped Crews' cell phone shut and studied it with admiration. He had laughed it off as an overpriced, impractical toy when Crews originally flaunted his purchase, calling the built-in .22 a backup weapon as practical and unobtrusive as a derringer in the head of a cane—

—four shots coming from a source nobody would expect.

Well, Crews had to be right about something at least once in his life, Grass decided.

Next, he did something he had always thought about trying: He ran his fingers inside Crews' half-open mouth and tugged at his snow white uppers and lowers.

All these years he had guessed wrong.

Those keyboards were real, not dentures.

"*Adios,* you dumb fucks," Grass said, rising and tossing off a two-fingered salute at his temple. "And that includes you, Crews. Sorry he saved me the pleasure."

He jumped behind the wheel of the Honda, tossed his .45 on the passenger seat, and seconds later was streaming down the freeway, checking for the first exit that would allow him to turn around and head back south to Eden Highlands.

He snapped on the radio and punched buttons until he came to a jazz station, music that always proved calming after an especially exciting night. He hummed along while he worked through the plan Crews had explained earlier, choosing the parts that would work for him on his own.

The one big switch: Forget about meeting Jack Sothern on Sothern's terms.

Grass had decided on a better scheme: When he reached Eden Highlands, he would be making a surprise visit to Mrs. Dan Boone.

When she opened the door, Grass saw she expected it would be Crews returning.

Her expression quickly shifted from anxiety to puzzlement, her lips forming the word *Who,* but the question went no further as her mind triggered the answer.

Her anger turned to fear. He half-expected her to try pushing the door shut. She fooled him by doing nothing, except stand like a stone statue, immobile everywhere but in eyes that glistened with hatred, further proof she remembered him.

Grass responded with a benign smile. "I'm not here to harm you," he said, in as gentle a tone as he could raise.

She closed her eyes, pushing more tears into the avalanche in progress, gripped the doorjamb to keep upright a body trembling with dread, Grass picturing her naked and thinking, *Still a body worth admiring under her robe, I bet.* "You have done that already, you bastard." Her voice was hoarse, harsh, the words struggling free between heavy breaths that kept her hidden breasts in motion. "Where is my daughter?"

"Where not even Herr Erich Mielke could find her, if these were the good old days and we were in East Berlin, Mrs. Boone." He corrected himself. "Or, I suppose I should be calling you Mrs. Collins?"

"Tell me Tracy's alive."

"Would I come visit otherwise?"

"Say the words. I want to hear the words."

"Tracy is alive. Your daughter is alive. There. So. Does that do it for you?"

"What do you want from me?"

"You know. You heard it from Burt Crews."

"Where is he? Crews. He said you had called him back. He had to meet with you. You had new demands."

"We met. We talked. I told him what it would take for Tracy's safe return. He said he'd present my needs to you when he returned. I gave him an hour to report. That was three hours ago, closer to four now. Finally, when I didn't hear—"

"How have they changed, your demands? I want my daughter back, you bastard."

"Crews didn't say?"

"I'm asking you. How have they changed?"

"Crews, he's usually so good about details."

"He's not here. Not since he left. How have they changed, you miserable son-of-a-bitch. Tell me, or so help me—" Her frustration raging, she slapped him on the cheek, her palm landing hard enough to promise him a nice bruise.

The pain excited Grass. He wondered if she'd notice and be at all embarrassed. Her robe had come undone, revealing enough of her body to make him desire more than a peek. He had to fight to put his delicious thoughts aside.

He said, "Maybe I'll come in and we can talk about it over a nice coffee?" She hesitated. "Or I could just go away and that would be that?"

She closed her eyes to his meaning, shook her head with denial.

He fed her a grim smile, half-bowed, and turned as if planning to leave.

"Wait."

The door hinges groaned.

Grass turned back as she stepped aside and made room for him to enter.

He brushed against her in passing.

He liked the sensation.

He liked it a lot.

Making love and making death, they had so much in common.

CHAPTER 35

Traylor was undecided:

March up to Maggie's place, confront Burt Crews about his sham of a phone conversation with Emil Grass—pressure him to cough up the truth—or wait for Crews to take off again, track him again, see where it led this time?

The decision was made for him.

The sound that caught his attention was Maggie's walking shoes squeaking as she headed down the path, followed by—

Not Crews.

Who, then?

Jesus A. Fucking Christ A-mighty.

It was the guy from the Howard Johnson's.

Where was Crews? Why wasn't he with them?

Maggie and the guy were getting into the Honda, Maggie behind the wheel.

Gear up and track them?

Negative, Traylor.

Maggie knows your car.

Too much daylight.

She'd spot you.

She's already hauling the Rock of Gibraltar on her back, on the edge of a nervous breakdown.

Don't risk upsetting her, contributing to her uncertainties, pushing her over.

Go with your gut, Traylor.

Go up to the house and button Crews.

Spring his answers about the phone call out of Maggie's earshot.

If what you learn dictates chasing after Maggie and the guy, chances are ten out of ten Crews will be able to tell you where they headed.

Traylor used his door key and went looking for Crews, calling his name.

Within minutes he knew he was alone in the house.

So much for his gut.

His cell phone hummed on the way back to the car.

Headquarters calling.

He keyed in the number, expecting it would be Vernon checking up on him.

He got Willie Quadflieg, sounding more out of breath than usual, reporting, "The CHP needs you right quick out the 405, Glen." He told him where.

"The CHP rules the road, so what's that about anyway? They say why?"

Willie said, "Nothing that you're going to like hearing, Glen," and started bawling the way he had for months after his pet Siamese, Miss Julie Newmar, disappeared.

CHAPTER 36

Roxy was waiting for them in her suite at The Garden of Eden, uncertain who Maggie was bringing over—she'd dodged an answer to the question—or why she wanted Jack Sothern here. Sothern was no help either, unless a shrug counted, pacing the room like a blush-tainted high school kid waiting to get his balloon busted for the first time. He'd been pouring the Jack Daniels like he owned the franchise, and his legs weren't as sturdy as they were a half-hour ago.

She credited that to the booze, not to their marathon sex last night, when they got back from Maggie's. Not lovemaking. Straightaway sex, more aggressive than passionate, resulting from the emotional tide brought on by Emil Grass agreeing to let the trade go through Sothern. Tension-relieving straightaway sex, broken only by a mutual laughing jag when both uncorked their champagne bottles moaning and groaning Maggie's name.

"It's probably Crews with her," Roxy called to him.

Sothern shrugged.

"I think it'll be Crews. He probably heard from Grass again."

"Pro'lolly," he said, and settled on a barstool to freshen his drink. He grabbed a handful of ice cubes from the bucket, plopped them into his glass, stirred them with a finger, and raised the glass to her. "*Salud* . . . Roxy, I ever tell you you hab a great ass?"

"Many times. I ever tell you you probably should slow down

with the Jack D, at least until after we meet with Maggie and Crews?"

"Semrall tibes," Sothern said. His skewed smile was as blotto as his eyes appeared to her. "And Samson slew them with the jawbone of an ass, Roxy." Shaking a power fist. Working out the words one-by-one. "Tha's me, Roxy." Singing: *Me-me-me-me-me*. His voice was as out-of-tune as his thinking. "Samson, for agreeing to go along with Dan Boone's plan. Asshole, more like it. But going to change, Roxy. Get Tracy. Get Grass. Get story. Get redemption."

Roxy thinking how Sothern seemed to have his liquor under control until yesterday.

Crediting the change to pressure Sothern must have begun feeling after committing to Dan.

Recognizing why Sothern and Vernon Mount had become so asshole buddy palsy-walsy so quickly. They were a pair of fugitives from AA, Tweedle-Dum and Tweedle-Dee, Vernon the cheerier of the two, either carrying less guilt than Sothern or hiding it better. If she were a betting woman, she'd guess the latter.

She'd always liked Vernon, but there was something about him she never trusted.

More trust in Sothern?

Yes.

Sothern never put her down, where Vernon often treated her like a big joke, calling her the "lovesick lesbo" sometimes when he introduced her to strangers, even when he wasn't on the sauce, so that had to be it.

The intercom buzzed. It startled Roxy out of the conversation she was having with herself and gave Sothern enough of a jolt to rattle his cubes. He took a quick swallow, like he needed it to steady his nerves, while she charged to the nightstand phone and punched the com line button.

"Maggie, about time. I was getting worried sick that maybe—"

"Roxy, Gerry here?"

"Gerry, is she on her way up—Maggie?"

"Not exactly."

"Meaning?"

"She's not here, only this gentleman who says he's here to see you this time."

"Who?"

"Mr. Raisin his name? Been coming around for a while, checking after availability of a room that suits his taste."

"Maggie's not with him?"

"Hold on." Gerry's voice became muffled, like he'd covered the mouthpiece. Another few seconds. "No, not. Mr. Raisin, he wants to say something, so here he is now."

Roxy took a deep breath and sent an anxious look at Sothern.

Loaded as he was, he appeared to comprehend what was happening.

He pushed his Jack D aside, gave himself a one-handed launch off the bar counter, and stumbled toward her. Got tangled in his shoes. Flopped face down on the unmade bed and rolled over on his back. Gave her a thumbs-up sign.

"It's not pronounced 'raisin,' like Gerry keeps saying, Miss Colbraith." He put a European spin on his name. Said it again. Explained, "As in *Rasen Betreten Verboten! You know what that means? It means *Keep Off the Grass. Der rasen.*"

"Emil Grass."

"Indeed. May I join you?"

"Where's Maggie? What have you done with her?"

"I asked, may I join you and Mr. Sothern? You'll want to hear what I have to say."

By the time Emil Grass knocked on the door, Roxy was ready for him.

Grass acted with mock surprise. He closed and locked the door behind him. "Please don't go melodramatic on me, Miss Colbraith. Put the gun aside, especially if you care at all about the safe return of your girlfriend and her daughter."

"Where are they? What have you done with them?"

"Shoot me and I guarantee you you'll never know. . . . The gun?" He turned his palms to the ceiling and waited her out.

She relaxed her grip on the 9 mm automatic and returned it to its hiding place on the side of the entertainment breakfront, whose door sprung open when she tapped it twice with the side of her fist. She kept the weapon there as a safety precaution, but in all the years had no occasion to use it. Leaning against the breakfront, her arms locked across her chest, she gave him a *What now?* look.

Grass acknowledged it with a half bow and crossed to the bed, shaking his head. He bent over Sothern, tapped him hard on the shoulder. Sothern didn't budge. Looking back at her, Grass held his nose.

"He's quite stinko. I'd heard Sothern's drinking could get out of hand," he said. "It's most unfortunate he picked this time to let it happen again."

"Meaning what?"

"He would hand over a certain diary of interest to me and I in turn would direct him to your girlfriend and her child. What could have been more simple than that?"

"Believing you would be more simple. I don't believe you. It's not the arrangement you made with Burt Crews."

"So? Is he here, Crews? I heard the same from your girlfriend. A meeting at the Balboa Park Zoo with Crews along for the ride? I changed my mind. A new arrangement I made last night with your girlfriend. Streamlined, like the new Jaguars I've had my eye on. You hearing any objections from Crews?" Cupping a hand behind his ear. "I don't."

He pulled a folded sheet of paper from an inside jacket pocket, briefly revealing a gun handle jutting over his belt. He held it out. "See for yourself what Mrs. Boone is asking of you."

She padded across the room and snatched the paper away from him. Grass moved to the bar, taking the stool Sothern had occupied. He scooped out a handful of mixed nuts from one of the crystal snack bowls, tossed it into his mouth, and began working his jaw like he hadn't eaten in a year.

Roxy unfolded the paper and saw there was no challenging the handwriting—

Maggie's—

Every letter a perfect example of penmanship.

She had written:

Dear Roxanne, I am with Tracy. We are fine. Mr. Grass will let us go after Jack Sothern gives him the diary. Then and only then will he tell you where we are. I beg you and Jack Sothern to meet his demands without delay, then come get us.

The note was dated today.

Grass said, "See how easy I've made it? I get the diary. I complete my end of the bargain, and you'll never have to see me again. The sooner the better, wouldn't you say?" He went at the nuts again, tossing the peanuts back in the bowl and finger-snatching more almonds.

"Try telling him that." She indicated Sothern.

Grass understood immediately.

He hurried over to Sothern, shook him aggressively, and slapped his face several times, demanding he wake up. When that didn't work, he ordered Roxy to bring him the water pitcher from the bar. He emptied it on Sothern's face. That got a stir out of Sothern. Nothing more.

Grass cursed the world and flung the pitcher across the room. It broke into a half dozen pieces.

He caught his breath and apologized. "Perhaps he let you in on the secret? Where he's keeping the diary?"

"I knew that, I'd already be on my way to get Maggie and Tracy."

Grass thought about it. "Of course, you would. So—I'm at the mercy of this fool."

"Sit it out until he wakes up and is sober enough."

"Give you a chance to try pulling the rug out from under me, I hardly think so."

"You think I'd gamble with the lives of my loved ones?"

"I love me enough not to gamble with mine."

"What's your better idea?"

Roxy saw he wasn't thinking that far ahead. He averted her stare and spent a minute studying Sothern, like he was measuring him for a coffin, then turned and looked to her as if to say he'd just bought the world for a bargain on eBay.

"I'm sure you have business to attend to," Grass said. "If you'll lend a hand getting Mr. Sothern downstairs, we'll leave you to your own devices."

"Hell you will. I won't leave their safety to a killer and a drunk. Go if you want, but I'm going with you."

"You forget I hold all the cards. I'm a man of my word. Sothern gets me the diary, you get your girlfriend and her daughter. I wouldn't push the issue I were you."

"Or what? You'll kill me?"

"Only if you insist."

"I won't get in your way. Sothern's just out of the hospital. All that booze could bring on a stroke, send him into convulsions. Then where would you be without a paddle?"

"Where the rangers would one day get around to discovering

the bodies of a mother and her daughter would be my guess, so what do you say we stop wasting more time. I think I can manage him downstairs and to my car with some assistance from you."

The phone rang.

Her private line.

Roxy reached for the receiver, then hesitated.

Grass threw her a *Be my guest* gesture.

It was Dan Boone. "Rox, go along with it," he said. "Not too fast or you'll have Grass wondering why the sudden change of heart. Understand?"

Roxy had switched on the spy-cams when she went for her 9 mm in the breakfront, but couldn't be certain Danny would be monitoring the meeting from wherever it was he had tapped into the system. He was keeping his distance and his secrecy, insisting: *Better you not knowing.*

Because?

Because better you not knowing.

Grass was studying her.

Roxy improvised: "I may be out the rest of the day, so I'm glad you phoned. When you know your schedule, call and tell Gerry. He'll know where to reach me . . ." She giggled. "Yes, don't I always know what to do, Admiral?" More giggles. "You, too. Damn the torpedoes and full speed ahead." She resettled the receiver. "I've been part of that man's Navy since he was an ensign," she said, and made a face that said everything and nothing at the same time.

"I'd been guessing you might go both ways," Grass said, excitement tilting his expression. He'd bought her act. "Like me."

"Except I haven't killed anyone."

"It's never too late."

Roxy turned the subject back to Sothern and argued why

Grass should allow her to go with them. Grass said nothing, only showed amusement until he signaled her to quiet and said, "You're covering old ground, Miss Colbraith. Either help me take him downstairs or prepare to accept responsibility for what misfortunes might otherwise occur."

Gerry Cotton saw them struggling toward the door with Sothern and rushed over to help, concern dotting his eyes, wondering, "Sick again? Better my calling to get the 911s on over than you getting him to the hospital?"

"Not that," Roxy said, grunting under the load she and Grass were maneuvering by the armpits, Sothern as helpless as a puppet without strings. "A little too much hooch and a little too much me."

"I recognized the smell. I should have recognized the look on his face," Gerry said, popping a grin. "Let me take over for you and Mr. Raisin with him. I can manage alone just fine." Neither bothered to correct his pronunciation.

Outside in the parking lot, Roxy said, "Where's your car, Mr. Raisin?"

Grass flicked her a look, started to tell her where, and abruptly changed his mind.

He said, "I'll take Mr. Sothern home in your car, if you don't mind my borrowing it."

"I could drive him then," she said, still playing a delaying game. "How's that?"

Grass made no secret of his annoyance. His smile was forced. "Don't you trust me with your car?" There was nothing pleasant about the way he said it.

Roxy's smile was no better. She said, "Gerry, I'll take over on Mr. Sothern while you fetch the BMW, please. Key's in the ignition."

The BMW passed out of sight.

Roxy, her shoulders as collapsed as her nerves, returned upstairs to shut down the spy-cams and retrieve Maggie's note, which she'd left on the nightstand.

Something about the note had troubled her. She read it again, then aloud, and knew what. She damned herself.

She should have picked up on it immediately.

Maggie had never called her Roxanne, never once, not even by accident. As much as she professed to adore her, she abhorred the name—without explanation—except to say she was no more a "Roxanne" than Maggie was a "Margaret."

Then, as an afterthought: "Besides, friendship doesn't need names, only emotions."

By addressing her as Roxanne, Maggie had sent a warning.

Telling her not to trust Emil Grass.

"Your Sweetie Pie wouldn't have anyway," Roxy told the room. "I didn't, Maggie, honey—not for a single minute."

She hadn't.

Not that it mattered.

Grass had taken off with Sothern, who'd eventually reveal he didn't have the diary, that it was a trick cooked up to smoke the bastard out.

Then—

Grass would have no further use for Sothern and that would be the end of him.

Then—

"No." Whispering the word. Shaking her head violently at a spy-cam. Refusing to acknowledge what it could mean for Maggie and Tracy.

The phone rang.

The private line again.

Dan Boone again.

Hearing his voice unlocked her tears.

He almost sounded worse than her. "We were fine until that slime switched cars on us, Rox. We had the tracking device mounted before you got Sothern outside, with time to spare. He'd have led us right to Meg and my baby."

"Damn it, Danny, you should have grabbed him the second he got here. Beaten the truth out of him."

"Sink to his level?"

"Below his level. Wherever."

"Yes. Except, I'm not there, Rox."

"Where are you?"

"You're safer not knowing."

"Who's *we?* Who's *us?* Who put the tracking device on Emil Grass' car?"

"I'll tell you when I see you."

"And if Grass sees me first? What do I tell him, Danny? That Dan Boone still has the diary? That you're somewhere in Eden Highlands, but I don't know where? That he can kill me next and I still won't know where you are with the diary?"

"I don't, Rox. I don't have the diary."

She quit breathing for a moment. "Then who?"

"My Tracy—my Tracy has the diary."

Her world stopped.

Before she could ask him the question, Dan said, "You know how I was always sending her gifts through you? Her birthdays. Special occasions. Valentine's Day. Christmas. Her grade school graduation. Middle school. . . . Any other way of getting them to her being too risky?"

"In case anyone on your ass figured to connect the dots by staking out Maggie."

"One of those gifts was Mielke's diary. I enclosed a note telling Tracy to hide it in a safe place and not tell anybody or show it to anybody, not even her mother. It was a special book, full of magic, I said, and one day Daddy would be able to explain why."

"Tracy never said a word to me about your gifts, Danny. They were her own private little treasure."

"As she is mine. . . . Her mother? Meg?"

"If Maggie knew, she'd have said something. We've never had any secrets between us."

"Except for me."

"Except for you. For her safety as well as yours."

"And it worked."

"Not anymore. . . . Explain something to me, Danny. Why involve Jack Sothern? What decided you to make him your stalking horse, put his life at risk?"

"Sothern was here already. He knew enough history to be useful to me. He had his own agenda, one I could play into, one that would give me time to maneuver in the background, get a bead on Emil Grass and let him lead me to Tracy. Take your pick. Think less of me for saying it, but Jack Sothern's life was the least and the last of my concerns. What I didn't count on was him being the lush he is. Sober, Sothern would have stayed with the game plan. I give him that much credit. He would have handed Grass the key to the bank safe deposit box that supposedly holds the diary and was the trade for my kid, and I'd be on Grass like a fly on flypaper."

"What now, Danny? Grass has Sothern and Maggie, as well as Tracy, and you're no closer to him than you ever were. What now? . . . Danny, you still there? Danny . . . ?"

Finally, struggling to get the words out, he told her: "We wait."

CHAPTER 37

Morning.

Rush hour.

Traylor, sitting behind the wheel of his unmarked in a parking lot of CHP vehicles on the 405, the freeway stalled to a crawl in both directions by a bumper-to-bumper parade of lookie-loos, couldn't bring himself to leave the crime scene.

Except to confirm an ID on Vernon Mount for the California Highway Patrol, answer some routine questions, and express condolences about the two dead officers, he was out of his jurisdiction and unnecessary to the investigation, they told him.

Damned interdepartmental rivalry.

Two sides to that street.

For lack of any on-site identification, pending a run of his photo and prints through the FBI, they were calling Burt Crews a John Doe.

Fine by Traylor.

Giving them a name to work with would have meant questions he wasn't ready to answer and information he had no desire to share, for fear of opening the Pandora's box that would bring the media circus back to Eden Highlands bigger than ever and possibly end any chance they had of rescuing Tracy Collins from Emil Grass.

Now, maybe, also Maggie.

He was sweating over the probability that the man who'd been in the SUV and left the Howard Johnson's parking lot with Burt Crews was Grass, which would make it Grass he had seen Maggie drive off with in Crews' Honda Accord before he got the call summoning him here.

There was no doubt in Traylor's mind that Grass was responsible for this massacre, no matter how strong a case the CHP was making for illegals or their coyotes, maybe drug mules, caught in the act. The way he read the clock, Vernon may already have been in the SUV. He'd have encountered Grass sometime after the memorial service for Amy and Betsy, the last time anyone appears to have seen the chief.

Why?

Maybe Grass met up with Vernon after leaving the Howard Johnson's, not before, this time with Crews along.

Still, why?

Was it something Crews arranged?

What reason could Crews possibly have for bringing Grass and Vernon together?

Why here on the 405?

Traylor followed the questions with a string of question marks after scribbling them down in his steno book, the freshest entries in his attempt to figure a timeline and work the puzzle that had occupied him while waiting for the crime lab guys to finish their basics and authorize the body buggy to move Vernon.

He had never forgotten hearing how Vernon had stuck with his father the night Pop was gunned down, refusing to leave him dead in the street, forcing his way into the ME's wagon for the long ride downtown; afterward, taking care of the funeral arrangements.

For all Vernon's warts, faults the size of the San Andreas, he was cream, and Traylor was going to give him the same loving care he gave Pop.

He would feel like shit leaving Vernon a corpse by the side of the road.

Traylor touched the tip of his ballpoint to his tongue and was about to add to his string of questions when the two-way crackled out his name—

Willie Quadflieg, still in meltdown over Vernon's death, bringing him up-to-date on the license numbers Traylor had asked him to check out.

"The Honda's a rental that tracks to a location at John Wayne Airport," Willie said. "Was issued to Irving Dunne on a New York driver's license that turns out to be questionable."

"Questionable?"

"A fake. A registration number doesn't exist. I had better luck with the SUV."

"How so?"

"Checks out to a Daniel Papermill of Salt Lake City, AKA Dan-Dan-the-T-Shirt-Man. Travels the country nine months of the year selling posters and t-shirts with funny sayings on them from out of the van. Tracked him back to his missus, who's angry at him for not calling to wish their four-year-old twins happy birthday. She said the last time he phoned it was to say he was here in the Highlands, at Temporary Town."

"Good show, thanks," Traylor said, appreciating Willie's effort more than the result. He was about to hit the off switch when Willie said, "One other thing, Glen. Roxy called in looking for you and sounding mighty anxious. She said she needs to see you ASAP. How it was urgent."

Traylor tried her private number and got no answer.

Gerry Cotton on the general line at The Garden of Eden said Roxy had instructed him not to put any calls through.

"She wanted me to call her."

"Sorry, Glen. She signs my paychecks."

"Let her know I'm on my way," Traylor said.

He spent the next fifteen minutes doing a drum solo on the

dashboard, cursing the ME's crew for taking its own sweet time loading the body bag into the wagon.

Traylor pulled into The Garden of Eden and ran the lanes looking for a parking slot close to the entrance. He thought he recognized the only Honda Accord on the lot and braked while checking the plate against the number he'd logged in his steno book. A match. It was Burt Crews' rental. He cut the ignition and left his unmarked there, angled to prevent the Honda from leaving.

He reached the reception desk at a gallop, startling Cotton, whose attention was fixed on a monitor filled with mini-photographs of women. Cotton quickly hit a key that converted the screen to an image of the Simpsons, broke into a smile, and started to say something about a new girlfriend.

Traylor shut him down with a headshake. He said, "Where is she?"

Cotton pointed to the ceiling. "Still in a Do Not Disturb *modus operandi*," he said, too late to make a difference.

Traylor was already halfway up the stairs.

He had his Glock drawn by the time he reached Roxy's room.

His lungs were ready to explode. He flattened against the wall, fighting to win back control of his breath, debating whether to knock and call for her or crack the door. If Emil Grass was in there, no telling which posed the greatest threat to Roxy. He flipped a mental coin. It landed on its edge. He flipped it again.

Traylor backed up the hallway a dozen feet, the Glock in a firm two-handed grip, and set himself to use his shoulder as a battering ram on a running charge.

He raced at the door.

It opened wide in front of him.

He was traveling too fast to stop and stumbled forward across the room. He hit the far wall with an *Oomph* and bounced off into an awkward dive onto the bed. A quick roll took him onto his back. He elbowed into a sitting position and navigated the Glock around the room.

No Emil Grass.

Only Roxy by the open door, looking worse than he felt.

"I saw you from the camera monitoring the hallway," she said. "Too late to stop you."

"Emil Grass, he's here somewhere?" Traylor said, still working the Glock.

"Was. How'd you know?" She closed and locked the door.

"The Honda outside in your parking lot," he said.

He gave her a fast briefing.

Only the news about Vernon pulled any emotion from her.

He said, "Why the emergency call? What do you have to tell me?"

Roxy began shaking, like she had been caught naked in a Big Bear snowstorm.

She hugged herself protectively.

"I know where Grass took them," she said. "I know where he has Tracy and Maggie."

Roxy settled into a chair by the breakfront. She told Traylor about her meeting with Grass and how he'd driven off with Jack Sothern in her BMW. All the while she fiddled with a remote deck that controlled a TV screen full of live multiple images monitoring the reception room, the staircase and the hallway, other interior and exterior areas of The Garden.

She said, "After, I had the sense Grass had said something important that I missed at the time, everything going down so fast, me just trying to deal with the situation and afraid Sothern would pull out of his Rip Van Winkle and say something stupid, or me, ending any chance of getting Maggie and Tracy back whole. I faked a brave front, but inside me it was like the ulcer that ate New York."

Something she did caused the TV images to fade and the screen to briefly go black before the monitor relit with a frozen full-screen picture that showed her with Grass and a dead-to-the-world Sothern on the bed.

Roxy said, "I had the spy-cams running. Once Grass was out of here and I'd settled my nerves, I ran the playback praying I'd find what it was, something, anything, the same way it took time before I figured out how Maggie was sending me a warning signal in her note."

"And you found it."

"See for yourself." Roxy pressed a button on the remote.

The freeze-frame wobbled and became animated, a venomous Emil Grass telling her:

"You forget I hold all the cards. I'm a man of my word. Sothern gets me the diary, you get your girlfriend and her daughter. I wouldn't push the issue, I were you."

Trying to talk him out of taking Sothern, she gives him a smart-mouth response:

"Sothern's just out of the hospital. All that booze could bring on a stroke, send him into convulsions. Then where would you be without a paddle?"

Grass isn't buying into it:

"Where the rangers would one day get around to discovering the bodies of a mother and her daughter would be my guess, so what do you say we stop wasting any more time. I think I can manage him downstairs and to my car with some assistance from you."

A phone ringing in the background. Roxy reaching for the receiver, and—

She pigeon-holed the TV picture again. "You catch it, Glen? You catch what I heard, or do you want to watch again?"

Traylor thought about it for a few moments and, uncertain, was about to ask her for a replay when—

With a snap of the fingers, he said, "The rangers. Grass threatening it would be rangers who found Maggie and Tracy. He let it slip. Maggie and Tracy are in the park. He has them in Couts Memorial Park. Sothern, probably him, too." His smile dissolved into grimness. "Only, where in the park?" He started pacing, casting off wild gestures, loudly examining the situation, more with himself than with Roxy. "To go in with a search team would not be smart," he said. "Grass gets wind we're closing in on him, he's the kind who'd turn desperate enough to kill the three of them." He looked at her for confirmation.

Roxy shifted her eyes uneasily and said, "I believe I know where in the park."

Traylor eased back his head and studied her over the bridge of his nose. "And what else? Why do I think you have more to tell me?"

"I won't say where, but I'll lead you there. We're going together or I'm going later—alone."

"You really think that's wise?"

"It's what I want."

"It's dangerous. Give me one good reason."

"You know I have two—Maggie and Tracy."

He took a deep breath and blew it back into the room. "Okay. Okay. Okay."

She rose, saying, "Give me five to get into something less comfortable. I'll meet you downstairs."

Roxy called it the BAT Cave.

Heading for Couts Memorial Park, she explained how she and Maggie had been sworn to secrecy by an exuberant Tracy before she took them there—once—to show it off, Tracy full of dancing explanations about its discovery and how she and her friends Amy and Betsy had made it their own secret world.

Traylor said, "So secret, why would Tracy reveal it to Grass?"

Roxy shrugged. "A million reasons, but I don't know one. Only a gut feeling. Grass, he got it out of her somehow, I don't know—" She pounded the dashboard in frustration, nodding agreement with herself. Shook her head in denial. Filled the cabin with silence and desperation breath for the rest of the short ride to the park. "There," she said, directing him to a visitors' lot with more empty slots than visitors.

Another few minutes and she was leading him uphill on a hiking trail, then higher still, cautiously, on an invented pathway in a restricted area that finally brought them to level ground, Traylor gasping for air.

He bent over, palms gripping his knees, and surveyed the area.

"The BAT Cave," Roxy said, pointing.

Traylor ordered her to stay back, out of the way, and cautiously approached the cave with his Glock drawn. He entered by inches, his back against the cold dirt walls, listening for sounds of life, hearing only his heart.

After what seemed like the day after eternity, he wheeled a sharp corner turn and in the dim light captured evidence of recent occupancy—a sleeping bag, empty orange drink containers, and discarded snack wrappers, but—

Nobody.

CHAPTER 38

"Courage is being brave enough and doing what you're afraid to do, Sweetheart."

Daddy's words to her when she was growing up, and she didn't want to disappoint him now, however certain she was the killer was still out there somewhere, waiting for her to reveal herself again, waiting for the chance to ambush her, spring out of the bushes from behind some tree, tie her up, whatever, and—

Hiding in a patch of mud-caked dirt she'd followed King Kong to, Kongie's home inside leafy walls roofed by a tangle of tree branches, the partial remains of field rodents and wayward birds evidence of the Rottweiler's usual diet—

Sitting on the damp ground with her legs crossed, fiddling with the .22 in her lap, a reminder of how she'd stood up to the killer and driven him away an hour or two ago, or what felt like a lifetime ago—

Daddy's words kept running through Tracy's mind like a playground dare.

She wasn't certain which scared her more, staying here until she sensed it was safe to maneuver down the hill to safety, sneak back to the BAT Cave and a few hours more of hiding, maybe overnight, or—

Or what? she asked herself.

The question reduced Tracy to tears again. Her body began twitching from the intense cold rising from the earth, the ocean breeze sifting through the bushes, or—

Was it from the fear she was living with, as hard as she tried to be brave for Daddy?

Kongie was stretched out beside her, making sleeping noises, an ear cocked against the sounds of life outside his domain—birds noisily trading gossip; the crackle of movement in the underbrush; noises of uncertain identity.

She shared her questions with him, massaging Kongie with gentle, circular motions that made him jerk when her palm glided over his hip. Instead of answers, the Rottweiler got up and stretched, followed his tail a few times, then wandered away with determined indifference; was still gone when darkness settled around her.

Tracy struggled for warmth against the mounting cold and an assaulting wind. Her teeth turned into mad castanets. Fingers pressed against her forehead warned of a fever on the rise.

Common sense told her it would be total madness to try making it through the night as Kongie's houseguest, but the killer knew about the BAT Cave. That's where he'd be most likely to lie in wait.

She'd have to be brave and try getting down the hill, before she ran out of strength.

She'd feel safer with Kongie at her side, protecting her like before, so she counted off what felt like fifteen minutes.

No Kongie.

Tracy stashed the .22 in her pea coat and, denying her body aches and the dizziness trying to fracture her skull, shifted onto her hands and knees and eased halfway out of her hiding place. She hesitated, searching for ominous shadows revealed by an early-rising full moon and straining after any sounds of movement, before starting on a cautious crawl toward the trail, sticking close enough to the bushes to duck fast if the killer showed himself.

Courage is being brave enough and doing what you're afraid to do.

The trail and the BAT Cave came into view at the same time and made her rethink her decision.

When the killer came at her again—

Wouldn't she be better off in the cave, protected on three sides, instead of heading down the trail, where he could emerge from anywhere, any direction, any time, any—?

No.

Asleep in the cave, and she didn't know how much longer she could keep her eyes open, she would have no protection. He could get to her then or, tomorrow, station himself outside and wait. Kongie back and looking after her? Nighttime or day, the killer would be ready to confront Kongie. Kill him. Bad enough, if she got through this alive, she had to go through the rest of her life blaming herself about Amy and Betsy. She wasn't going to be the cause of Kongie's death next, not if she could help it.

Courage is being brave enough and doing what you're afraid to do.

Tracy edged her way into the coppice alongside the park trail, taller than her by at least a head; no clear path to follow. Using branches for support, she got to her feet and began working her way down the slope. She used what little moonlight was available to sidestep rocks and slosh puddles. She moved her body sideways, like she was treading a stairway one step at a time, both hands on the banister.

An outbreak of noises rustled the underbrush and startled her, causing Tracy to misstep. She caught a sneaker on something and lost her footing. She whirled her arms trying to keep her balance, but her knees stopped supporting her weight. She pitched forward and landed on—

Not sure what.

Hard to make out.

Soft, wet to the touch.

She pushed and scrambled onto her hands and knees, turned after a closer look.

Eyes stared back, dead except for twin reflections of the full moon fighting through the cloud covering.

She screamed. The sound echoed like thunder breaking over the Highlands, louder than the killer's gunshot, the two shots she'd aimed at the killer; now, wishing she'd killed him dead, took her time, aimed more carefully, and watched him die, die, die, instead of only scaring him off, making it so he could come back after her.

The thicket vibrated with the sound of troubled wildlife.

Tracy threw a hand at her mouth to keep from screaming again. Her palms were wet and pasty, stained a dark crimson. She rubbed them off on her jeans, used a sleeve to towel her lips and cheeks.

Pee was showering down her thighs.

She was too scared to be embarrassed.

She half-welcomed its warmth.

Before she'd finished, she had the .22 out and was using it to survey every direction. She expected a confrontation with the killer any second. *This time I won't miss,* she told herself, then shouted it, setting off another burst of wildlife resentment.

She dared a glance at the body, saw it was a park ranger, saw the cell phone jutting from his hip holster. She swiped the cell away and thumbed in her home number, meanwhile, giving thanks for the divine twist that had provided her with a means of contacting Mommy and getting rescued.

Only—

There was no ring.

No anything except the fierce silence in her ear brought on by the dead batteries in the cell.

Tracy flung the phone away.

She watched the park ranger turn into a shadow bag as the moon once more slipped into hiding.

She whispered into the wind, "I'm trying, Daddy. I'm trying."

She aimed the gun at her invisible fears and cried, until she didn't have strength for even that.

She needed to rest for a while, not for long, only long enough to gather her strength for the rest of the flight down to safety, that's all.

Fifteen minutes, maybe twenty. That should do it.

She settled against the scarred trunk of a tree, made a blanket of her crisscrossed arms, and shut her eyes.

When she opened them again, it was daylight.

She had no idea how long she had slept.

She thought she heard voices.

CHAPTER 39

Emil Grass parked the BMW behind his trailer. Sothern was sprawled across the back seat, an arm dangling over the edge, no indication he'd budged an inch since Grass headed back to Temporary Town from The Garden of Eden.

He gave Sothern's shoulder several hard pats. "How are you doing, Mr. Sothern? You awake?" No reaction beyond a snarl of annoyance. "Brilliant. Stay that way until I return." He patted his cheek. Sothern's free arm reacting like he was swatting away a pesky fly.

Inside the trailer, Meg Boone's eyelids danced when he switched on the lights.

He had insisted she take the flunitrazepam before lashing her to the bed last night with the three-strand Manila hemp he kept with other supplies in the storage hamper.

She had tried arguing him out of tying her, taking the roofie, saying, "I am not about to go anywhere until I have Tracy back. Otherwise, why would I even be here, have come with you willingly, agreed to write that damn note to Roxanne?"

"Then you won't mind humoring me, will you?" he said, thinking, *Have come with me, how prophetic of her.* What he'd missed with the daughter, he intended to make up for with the mother before morning and a phone call to fix a meeting with Roxy Colbraith and Jack Sothern. "It's a mild sedative that will allow you a peaceful night's sleep and ensure my peace of mind."

She answered him with a poisonous look. "You think I don't

know what Rohypnol looks like, what it does?" she said.

"What it does is help bring you closer to seeing your dear child again, Mrs. Boone."

"You're a swine," she said, but opened her mouth wide for the roofie he settled on her tongue and watched her wash down with two shots of vodka.

"Good afternoon. Nice to see you awake, Mrs. Boone." He sat down on the bed alongside her. Ran a hand up and down her body to remind himself of the pleasures of their night together. Carefully peeled off the duct tape he had used to seal her mouth against outcries.

Her eyes focused on Grass. Her confusion turned into slits of contempt.

As if he didn't know what she must be thinking, he said, "I'm going to release you now, Mrs. Boone, to shower and dress. Then, come find me outside, the BMW like yours. Something else we need to do together. No tricks out of you, correct?"

Grass knew her silence was the best answer he could expect.

He fondled her once more.

Tossed off a three-fingered kiss of satisfaction.

Undid the rope, which had left harsh red reminders on her wrists and ankles

Within minutes, Mrs. Boone joined him, as if showering and getting dressed had been some sort of race. She was still jamming the hem of her lavender blue cashmere sweater into her deliciously tight pair of tan leather pants. Sneaker laces untied. Hair the Mixmaster mess he had made it with his pawing. No makeup, not even a dab of lip gloss, no attempt to disguise the black pouches under her eyes. Still sexy, though, so maybe he wasn't finished with her yet. Maybe next time he'd let her experience what she had been too drugged to enjoy about him last time.

She spotted Sothern in the backseat of the BMW, settled a look on Grass that demanded an explanation.

"Not dead, if that's what you're thinking, Mrs. Boone. Drunk and passed out, like I found him at The Garden of Eden earlier today, when I went to meet with him and your devoted friend, Miss Colbraith. I require your help getting Mr. Sothern into the trailer. He weighs a ton."

"Easy for you to say," Sothern said. He rose to a sitting position, as if Grass' voice had worked on him like an elevator Up button. Squinting against the afternoon sun. Forging focus by palm-slapping his forehead. Turning a frown into a smile when his eyes found Maggie Collins.

He licked his licks and said, "Have I died and gone to Heaven?"

"Not yet," Grass said.

"In that case, I could use a little hair of the dog. The whole dog, if it's handy."

Grass settled across from them at the dining table, on the cushioned bench seat that gave him a clear view of the trailer door, the silenced .45 within reach. He didn't expect to have need for it, but experience had taught him that it never paid to be too confident.

His hand drifted to an area just below his heart, where Will Morgan Johnson had caught him good with a pig-sticker. Another inch and a half and he wouldn't be here now. *Not to worry,* Crews told him beforehand. *Johnson is never armed. He leaves any dirty laundry to his minions.* Damn, Crews. Always playing at being so much damned smarter than him, than anybody, than the world, saying more times than he took a piss: *Emil, I am the brains of our operations and you are the brawn. The only muscle you never have to exercise while I'm around is your brain.* Well, his brains brought Crews to a dead stop on the side of a freeway, while Emil Grass' brain muscle was strong as ever and soon would bring him a diary worth a fortune he would not have to share.

Who does that make the real brains, Crews, who? he thought, the smile escaping to his face.

He told Sothern, "Have another before we move on to the business at hand." He refilled Sothern's glass from the vodka bottle and offered a pour to Maggie Collins. She shook her head again and continued drawing invisible circles on the Formica surface.

He resumed tossing the HuntChamp from palm to palm, making it appear like a nervous tic instead of a weapon he could have opened in seconds for a counterattack.

Sothern said, "Cheers, Emil, old buddy-buddy of mine." Emptied the glass in a swallow, pounded his chest, and belched. "When do you let me in on the secret?"

"Which one, Herr Sothern?"

"Why we're here, wherever here is."

"Temporary Town. A brief stop to pick up Mrs. Boone and put some rules in place before we leave to finish our business and get Tracy."

That got Meg Boone's attention. Her back stiffened. She locked her hands, moved them to her mouth and began gnawing at a knuckle.

Sothern said, "Rules?" He shifted his bloodshot eyes over to Meg Boone. "I don't need no stinkin' rules. You know who said that, or something like that?"

"Shut up, Sothern, and listen to him."

"I have rules," Grass said.

"Alfonso Bedoya. Said it in *The Treasure of the Sierra Madre*. I don't need no stinkin' rules. Something like that."

"Damn it, you drunk. Listen to the man."

Sothern made a *What can you do?* face. He said, "Spill your stinkin' rules. I'm all ears.'"

"You have something I want. I have something Mrs. Boone wants."

"Actually, she's Mrs. Collins."

Meg Boone slammed her fist against Sothern's shoulder. "Just listen to him, damn you. It's my daughter's life you're fucking with."

Sothern rubbed the spot. "Anybody ever mention you are a walking danger zone?" She slugged him again. "All right, okay. I get the message, Garcia." He raised his glass and framed a pout. "Aw-gone," he said, and reached after the vodka bottle. Meg Boone grabbed the bottle and pulled it away. Sothern said, "Not nice. Not nice at all." He wagged a finger at her and looked to Grass for relief.

"Let's satisfy Mrs. Boone first, Herr Sothern, and then we can celebrate," Grass said, as if he were talking to a child.

Sothern pulled his face into frustration. "Shoot." Weighed what he had just said. Shook his head vigorously. "I mean by that, what's on your mind? The stinkin' rules?"

"Rule One," Grass said. "You give me Herr Mielke's diary before we retrieve little Tracy for her mother."

Sothern angled his head and looked as if he hadn't heard correctly. "We agreed on Balboa Park, an equal exchange, and—"

"And nothing," Grass said, curiosity inching up on him. Sothern hadn't sounded as loaded as he had a few seconds ago. "That is Rule One. Also, Rule Two, Rule Three, Rule Four, and so on. Isn't that so, Mrs. Boone?"

Sothern looked to her for confirmation.

She closed her eyes to what she knew had become the truth last night.

Sothern's chin pumped oil while he worked through what he'd heard, began moving left and right. "I don't think so, buddy-buddy," he said. "Unh-unh. Stinkin' rules. Stinkin', stinkin', stinkin'. We have to talk some more about this."

"We don't."

"Oh, yes, we do. We do-do-do, all the doo-dah day."

"Sothern, don't gamble with my Tracy's life," Mrs. Boone said. Her voice was verging on hysteria.

Grass settled the HuntChamp by his thigh and moved the .45 from the bench seat to the table. "I would listen to her, I were you, buddy-buddy."

"Which you're not, so maybe you should listen to me?"

Grass arched an eyebrow. "Why do I begin to sense you've been playing a game with me and may not have Herr Mielke's diary, Herr Sothern?"

"Because maybe I don't?"

"Then maybe you better tell me something I'm going to like hearing, before I decide to kill you both, and then kill the girl." He moved his eyes onto Meg Boone. "Believe me, I will."

"God damn you, Grass," she said.

"Yes. That was guaranteed years ago, Mrs. Boone."

Chapter 40

Grass was correct about him playing a game. It was the one he had played for years, on all those close-the-bar nights when he'd somehow managed to drive home without one-stopping into a telephone pole or sharing time and space with some pedestrian confusing his right to cross at an intersection with Jack Sothern's determined effort to beat the signal.

Sothern had not let the DUI arrests stop him or the red flags from editors, not even his earliest seizures, modest bubbles of discomfort that briefly ripped his temples to shreds and had his eyes spinning like pinwheels. He was still at that age where people believe that death is what happens to everybody else.

Not anymore.

Nowadays, death was his next-door neighbor, always making friendly conversation over the backyard fence and angling for a dinner invitation.

Sothern's game called for him to psych out a problem situation and stall for time while he sobered up fast enough to worm his way through to a solution, as he was doing now with Grass.

He had been working at it since Grass slapped him hello and got his senses going again. They no longer recharged as fast as they had in the long ago, before he'd lost sight of himself, so all he could do was keep at it—play the fool—until he could buy time with an answer that would prevent Grass from adding them to his body count.

Giving him the Mielke diary was not a viable option.

It would not have been even if it weren't part of Dan Boone's scheme to flush out Grass, and he did, in fact, have possession, but—

Grass suggesting Sothern might not have the Mielke diary—

Grass had unwittingly opened the door for him—

Given him a much needed jolt of sobriety—

Given him the confidence to say Grass might be right about that, and now—

"Tell you something you'd like hearing?" Sothern said, keeping a little froggie in his throat, trying not to show he was clearing the last of the cobwebs from his head, and steering clear of Maggie Collins' desperate eyes. "The world's round. How's that? Do it for you?"

"When I kill the girl and her mother, you'll have no one to blame but yourself, idiot."

"I heard you right the first time, I'll be too dead to notice, Emil, buddy-buddy."

"Sothern, I pray to God. For the sake of my baby. Please do not do this to me. Let this madman have the diary," Maggie said, a wail to her words.

Grass said, "Not mad, Mrs. Boone. Merely determined to have my way."

"Don't get mad, get even," Sothern said, sensing his game was close to playing out Grass' patience, wondering if Grass understood how much truth he was putting behind the thought.

His head was clear now—clear enough to have found the answer he'd searched for.

He moved a hand onto Maggie's thigh and gave it a squeeze he hoped she'd understand was meant to say: *Don't panic. I have the situation under control.*

She pushed his hand away, looked like she was about to strike him, scream something at him, but must have read the clue in his eyes. She quit with her mouth ajar and settled her palms on the table, stared silently out the trailer window, her jaw flexing nervously against what might happen next.

Sothern held his hand high. He let go of the key ring he'd dug out of a pocket. It clanged onto the table. "You asked for it, you got it, Herr Grass."

"What kind of drunkard's game is this you're playing now?"

"Have I mentioned how I liked you better with the mustache you had when we first met? You should think about growing one again."

"I'm not amused," Grass said. His hand dropped out of sight and returned with a .45 he aimed at Sothern. "Recognize a silencer when you see one? Your death will be our little secret within the four walls of this motor home."

A strip of noise grew out of Maggie's throat.

Sothern patted the key ring.

He said, "I'm trying to tell you you'll find the diary there."

"Explain."

"Did you really think I'd have brought it with me to Eden Highlands? No reason for that, Herr Grass, not then and not until after I learned better from Burt Crews and you got around to showing your kisser."

Grass used the gun to signal him for more.

Sothern fingered through the keys until he found the one he wanted. He put it on display, saying, "To the safe deposit box at my bank. I've had the diary there ever since it was entrusted to me for safekeeping."

"Who would entrust anything to you?"

Sothern left the question hanging, as if the answer should be obvious.

Grass one-handed an English Oval from the flip-top box on the table and wedged it in a corner of his mouth. Ignited the cigarette with his gold flame lighter. Shot a dirty gray smoke cloud into Sothern's face. After another few seconds, a grin that

could have passed for a tic put wrinkles at the edges of Grass'
mouth. "Shane Vallery," he said.

Shane.

It was not what Sothern expected to hear. He had expected
Grass to throw Boone's name at him. He said, "Mielke had
Shane murdered after Shane stole the diary out from under his
nose and used it to get Dan Boone back to America. Drowned
in the lake, where Boone—"

Grass blew out a noise. "What's it? You think you Americans
are the only ones who can make up fairy tales?"

"You're saying Shane's alive?"

"You're saying she's not?"

"My understanding."

"From?"

"Crews. Crews told me that."

"A devoted student of the brothers Grimm, that Crews."

"Shane Vallery is alive, then?"

"How else would you have gotten Herr Mielke's diary, from
a corpse?"

"From Dan Boone."

"Ah," Grass said, and hit him with another cloud. "And how
recent is this?"

Sothern waved away the smoke, realizing he'd been played.
"Years ago," he said, his pulse moving into a gallop. "After
Boone made it back to the States. A favor he said I owed him—"

"For the great damages you'd caused in his life."

"Yes." He glanced at Maggie, who dodged his eyes. "Boone
told me what it was, its value. He said he'd be back to reclaim it
when he could. He never did."

"And all this time you've sat with the diary, recognizing its
worth, and never put it to your own gain?"

"I thought about it . . . I'd done enough damage to Boone
and his family. I took it to my bank, where it's been ever since."

Grass considered Sothern's words. Swatted them away. "I can't believe Dan Boone ever trusted you in the first place. Shane Vallery, she's another story. You had this thing for her, like most of the men she had occasion to use."

Sothern forced Shane out of his mind. "There's the key, no matter what you believe," he said. He worked the key off the ring and pushed it across the table to Grass, who inspected it at close range.

"And the safe deposit box, your bank, is where?" Grass said.

"Where I'll take you once you hand over Tracy to her mother."

"I told you already—you don't get the girl until I have the diary."

"Some reminders, Herr Grass. It doesn't matter where the bank is. You're going to need me there to sign in. To match up face and signature with what the bank shows in its computer index. Only after that do you get escorted downstairs to the vault, to the box, and fit in the key while a vault guard finishes the process with his key."

Grass snorted smoke out of his nose, dashed out the English Oval on the Formica. "You go. Take the BMW. Bring back the diary. Twenty-four hours. Any later than that, you'll find two deaths on your conscience."

"No. Tracy first, then you and me to the bank."

"You sound more and more like a dead man, Herr Sothern."

"And you like somebody who will never get the diary, Herr Grass." He reached after the vodka bottle. "What do you say? One more for the road?"

CHAPTER 41

Grass figured it would be awkward taking them to the cave, but he had no choice.

He needed to make it appear he was going along with Sothern's demand.

Anything less, Sothern might guess he didn't have the girl.

Grass knew that would mean—

All this time and effort, and nothing to show for it.

Scheisse, he thought. Shit.

He caught himself wishing Crews were still around.

With Crews, he'd have been able to pump Sothern full of Rohypnol, or the GHB he also carried in his toiletries kit, put Sothern to a long-distance sleep, and leave him in the trailer under Crews' watchful eye while he headed to the park and up to the cave with Meg Boone.

Under no circumstances could he leave her behind.

She was his stalking horse.

He need Mama to draw Tracy out of that damn cave or wherever she might be hiding in the park with that damn dog, unless by now—

Tracy was gone from the park.

Scheisse.

Also a possibility.

Then what?

Okay, since Crews was on his mind—

Mr. Big Man with All the Bright Ideas—

313

What would Crews say to a situation like that?

He heard Crews say it now: *Grass, think positive. Negative thoughts drain energy and can turn your brain into oatmeal if you're not careful. First things first. One step at a time. Step one, then step two, then—*

Ever treating him like a senseless child, but Crews was right about first things first, not that it was anything he didn't already know for himself.

"Where in the park are we heading, Grass?"

"Don't ask so many questions, Herr Sothern."

"That was my first."

"Already one question too many. Keep to the main road, Mrs. Boone. I'll tell you in plenty of time where to turn off."

Grass had her at the wheel of the BMW, Sothern in the passenger seat.

Beside him on the backseat was a paper bag with items he had pulled from the trailer storage hamper: duct tape, his coil of Manila, two pairs of handcuffs, roofies from the brown plastic prescription bottle in the toiletries kit, and the depleted bottle of vodka, into which he'd poured a generous amount of GHB.

The combination of vodka and the undetectable "Liquid X" would keep Sothern under control later, passed out and sleeping like Cinderella on the long drive back to Los Angeles, if he stayed with what he considered a reasonable step two—

Something even Crews would have endorsed, Grass was thinking, thinking—

Okay, you see, Mr. Big Man? It's not just you always in the ideas department.

Grass tapped Meg Boone on the shoulder and said, "Coming up there on your right, a road with a broken gate, a sign saying for park employees only? Drive down until I say to stop."

He issued the command when he gauged the BMW couldn't be seen from the main road. Absent-mindedly checked for his HuntChamp. Mount's .45. The Glock he had rescued from the highway patrolman.

Meg Boone's eyes flirted with the landscape, fingertips at her teeth, her breathing on fire.

Sothern said, "If you've been hiding that little girl in this wasteland, you want to know what I think?" Not quite the drunk he'd been earlier.

"No," Grass said. He rummaged the bag for the cuffs. He stashed one pair in a jacket pocket, angled forward, and dropped the other pair on Meg Boone's lap. "Mrs. Boone, get out from the car and lock one cuff onto your wrist and the other cuff onto the steel hitch under the rear bumper," he said.

She drew a breath that sounded like sandpaper rubbing against her vocal chords.

Sothern said, "No dice, Grass. Mrs. Collins, sit right there."

Grass let him see the Glock. He said, "This is not another negotiation, Herr Sothern. I can't control you and her on the trails to my satisfaction, so she'll remain here while you and I fetch her daughter, as bargained."

Sothern reacted as Grass had anticipated. He snatched the handcuffs away from Meg Boone and locked one onto his wrist. "She goes with you," he said. "We'll do our deal after they're back safe and unharmed." He bolted from the car and hurried to the rear before Grass could even pretend to argue.

Grass allowed himself a minute before telling Meg Boone to stay put.

He got the vodka bottle from the bag and angled out of the BMW, satisfied himself that Sothern was securely fastened to the hitch, and offered him the vodka. "A swallow or two for warmth and comfort until we return, Herr Sothern?"

Sothern took a healthy taste, wrinkled his face, and handed back the bottle.

They had barely started up the footpath to the cave when Meg Boone said, "I know where we're going." She had been moving sluggishly, her progress prodded by Grass' gentle pressing on her back, but now her pace quickened. She cast off what was left of the zombie-like state brought on by the roofies he had fed her and turned indifferent to the potholes on the steep dirt trail. "It's the BAT Cave, isn't it? That's where you have Tracy. In the BAT Cave."

The BAT Cave?

The cave had a name?

Grass' nicotine-blackened lungs had him struggling to keep up with her. "You'll see when we get there," he said, breathing hard.

Meg Boone didn't have that problem. "She took me there once, Roxy and me, after they found it, my baby, Amy, and Betsy," she shouted to the sky. "They were so proud of their own special hideaway. They made us promise we'd never go there without permission. How did you ever—?"

As far as she got with the question before her foot seemed to catch in a mud hole. She lost her balance, fell backward, and knocked Grass off his feet. Landed with her body prostrate on his. As they slid a few yards down the path, he felt her playing with his body. She rolled off him and scrambled onto her feet aiming his Glock at him like a divining rod. She had ferreted it out from his shoulder holster. Her arms were trembling, but the nervousness didn't extend to her words, resolutely telling him, "I will shoot you if I have to."

"Like mother, like daughter," Grass said, feeling stupid for letting the woman get the better of him, wondering how best to get at the .45 inside his belt that was now biting into the small of his back.

"What's that supposed to mean?"

"Nothing, Mrs. Boone, nothing at all," he said, surveying his options. "So, what do you intend to do? Kill me and go to the BAT Cave yourself and hope for the very best that she is there, your precious Tracy?"

Grass started to shift into a sitting position.

She stopped him with a shouted warning.

He folded his hands on his chest, like a corpse in need of a casket.

She said, "Tracy is, isn't she? She's in the BAT Cave." Grass shrugged. Shot her a glance. Her look had turned poisonous. "I saw you put handcuffs in your jacket," she said. "I want you to get them out and cuff your hands. Then, I want you to stand up—slow—and no tricks."

"I don't think so," Grass said. "Since it's clear I cannot trust you, you fetch them from my pocket and you put them on yourself."

"It's not going to work that way. I will kill you first." Her voice trapping an echo off the hillside.

"If Tracy is not in the BAT Cave, what then? Picture her the way I left her, Mrs. Boone. Alone and frightened, so full of roofies she could not possibly know who or where she is. Not that it matters, because I also left her bound and gagged. There are not a lot of hours before the weather and a weakened condition brought on by the lack of food or water eliminate any chance for her survival before you can find her and get her medical attention. *If* you can find her."

Tracy said, "I'm here, Mama."

She stepped out from the tall brush, aiming the .22 at Grass like it had become a habit, her hands steadier than her mother's, looking like only a miracle was keeping her on her feet.

She screamed, "Go ahead and kill him, Mama. Shoot him. If

you don't, I will. I will, Mama. I will."

As Tracy stumbled toward him, Grass had no doubt she meant every word.

CHAPTER 42

Meg Boone was shouting, "Baby, don't do it!" when Tracy's legs gave out before she had traveled more than a few feet. It was as if her daughter had hit an invisible wall. She stopped. Tottered. Grabbed for a subway strap in the air. Sank to her knees and tilted over into something resembling a fetal position.

"Oh, my dear God," Meg Boone said, investing the words with a mother's worst fears. She took off for Tracy, skirting around Grass, waving the Glock and warning him not to move.

She settled alongside her daughter and pressed a hand to her face.

Begged Tracy to be all right.

To say something.

Anything.

She dropped the Glock and used both hands to ease Tracy onto her back. Checked her for a pulse. Cradled her in her arms, bent into her ear, and cooed, "You'll be fine, sweetheart. Fine, my precious darling baby girl. Can you hear me? Tell me you can hear me. Tracy, it's Mama. It's Mama, Tracy."

In those seconds, Grass recognized he had stopped existing for her.

He leaped to his feet, pulling the .45 from the small of his back while advancing on them.

Sideswiped Meg Boone's face with the gun butt.

The force of the blow knocked her off Tracy and onto her back.

Grass scooped up the Glock and stashed it in his shoulder holster.

Meg Boone made a grab for his leg when he stooped to yank the .22 out of Tracy's tight grip. He shook himself loose and hammered her head with his fist, warning: "Enough is enough, you bitch."

He made like he was going to strike her again.

She threw up her arms defensively and pleaded: "We have to get Tracy to a doctor."

"First things first."

"I'm begging you."

"They always do at moments like this." He took possession of the .22 and shoved it inside his belt. Pulled out the handcuffs. Dropped them by her. "Turnabout is fair play," he said. "Only now, instead of you wearing the charm bracelets by yourself, share them with the girl."

"Can't you see she's sick?"

"I've seen worse. . . . The charm bracelets, and quickly, Mrs. Boone. I remind you there is nothing in my arrangement with Herr Sothern saying you must be part of the exchange."

Grass gave the .45 a lingering glance. She understood. She swooped up the handcuffs. Enclosed her left wrist and locked Tracy's right. "I feel more comfortable already," Grass said. He torched an English Oval. "Shall we be on our way?"

Meg Boone flagged her head left and right, arguing the suggestion. "Look at her, she's unconscious."

"I inspected the merchandise already, Mama. Tracy isn't so heavy that carrying her will pose a problem for you, able-bodied woman that you are. And, no doubt Herr Sothern will be delighted to see us returned so soon, unless he's still visiting the Disney World of his dreams."

She showed him she didn't understand.

Grass explained how he had flavored the bottle of vodka with

GHB. "One can't be too careful, can one?" he said. "Added insurance he'll be waiting for us when we get back to your auto."

She looked at him like he was the village idiot. "GHB and vodka, the combination can bring on a seizure and kill him," she said. "He just was treated for a cerebral aneurysm at the hospital."

"Then best you quickly gather up your daughter, so we can be on our way," Grass said, sounding as dumb as she'd made him seem. He flicked the cigarette into the brush. "And pray hard the seizure doesn't occur before we've completed our trade, Tracy for Herr Mielke's diary. That, I guarantee, would be the greater tragedy."

Meg Boone destroyed him with a stare.

She worked around the awkwardness of the cuffs, lifted Tracy, rested her over a shoulder like she was burping a baby.

They had barely started down the trail, Grass several steps behind, when the underbrush rustled with trespass—

—a noise full of dedicated anger.

Grass swung around to check—

Grunted untranslatable alarm.

A Rottweiler on the attack, noisily charging at Grass from a distance of about twenty feet.

Grass jerked himself out of the dog's way.

The Rottweiler grazed his thigh as it plunged past him.

It skidded to a halt, got its bearings, and came after Grass again.

Grass had wheeled around and was facing the dog, trying to steady his balance.

He took sloppy aim and fired.

CHAPTER 43

The gunshot had a distant sound to it, resonant and smothered. It catapulted off the hillside and bounced onto the interior walls of the cave, blowing Roxy's eyes wide with a question Traylor quickly grasped.

The noise was his excuse to leave, finally, after an hour humoring her insistence—discarded food wrappers and tossed drink cartons her proof—that Tracy had been here, had brought Emil Grass, Maggie, and Sothern here.

Traylor settled his jangled nerves. "A shot pop, for certain," he said. "No car backfire could travel up this far sounding like that." He motioned Roxy to follow him outside.

The park was full of the scatterbrained sounds of birds and animals complaining about the disturbance, a frenzy of motion in the underbrush.

Traylor sucked up a few pounds of air, hoping for the scent of an answer, but only pulled in dust-filled air that brought on a thick cough. He blew a wad of mucus into his fist, tossed it away, and wiped the hand dry on his shoulder.

"What say we go see what we can see back down the trail?" he said. "We're past due on doing ourselves any good here."

Roxy used her hands to swat away the idea. "What if Grass shows up with them again?"

"What if he doesn't?" Traylor said, playing along. "What if it was Grass fired that shot?"

"Oh, dear Lord Jesus, Mary, and Joseph."

"Maybe only a hunter spotting rabbits, a rattler," Traylor said, feeling sorry about the volcanic eruption of emotion he'd caused. "We won't know without checking." He turned his back on whatever she was saying and headed for the path.

They hit the main access road and were about to cross over to the parking lot when Traylor spotted Grass.

He was across the way, fifty or sixty yards ahead of them, angling toward a secondary trail on the south side of the road.

Maggie and Tracy were with him, Maggie hauling Tracy in her arms, but—

No Jack Sothern.

Roxy also saw them.

"Come on, let's go get the bastard," she said, urgently, stepping ahead of him.

Traylor leashed her wrist. "Not yet. He's armed. He's probably heading back to your car and to Jack Sothern. I follow him and hold down the fort while you haul your sweet ass over to my car. Use the two-way to call for backup, then lead them to the trail."

"I'm going with you."

"Negative. We've already done that number, Roxy."

It wasn't the answer she wanted.

She broke free of him and sprinted across the road.

Traylor caught up, lifted Roxy off the ground from behind with her arms trapped inside his. Her heels banged maliciously against his legs while she demanded he put her down.

He got her to the unmarked and settled her on the ground.

"Sorry, pal," he said, and—

Brought pressure to bear on her neck that shut off the flow of oxygen, long enough to send her into a swoon.

Managed Roxy into the back seat.

Grabbed the two-way.

Put in the call for backup.

Raced after Grass, Maggie, and Tracy.

It was a service road for park employees, not a hiking trail. The rusted gate looked like it had been cracked open years ago, but the tire tracks eating into the caked, not-quite-dry mud ruts and bumps were fresh, the shoeprints fresher.

Traylor worked his way down the road cautiously, using the tall brush in a narrow strip of shoulder for protective covering. After a few hundred feet, the road cut sharply to the south. The shoulder narrowed and now paralleled a drainage ditch fifty or sixty feet below, a nasty fall and broken bones, for certain, if he didn't watch his steps on the tricky sludge.

He didn't have far to travel.

Roxy's BMW was parked about twenty yards ahead.

Jack Sothern was stretched out on the asphalt, a wrist handcuffed to the bumper hitch.

No sign of Maggie, Tracy or Grass.

Traylor pulled his Glock and inched forward with the barrel ready to shift aim from the sky to anything that moved. Something crunched under his foot. A tossed beer can. The sound set off complaints from invisible brush creatures and birds. It also got Jack Sothern's attention.

Sothern struggled upright and searched for the source, squinting against the bright sunlight Another moment and he appeared to fix focus on Traylor. Shifted away, then back again. A third time, and a fourth. A fifth. Left and right like a speeding pendulum. Sending Traylor a message. Trying to signal something.

Traylor caught on.

Followed Sothern's tick-tocking.

Saw Emil Grass charging at him.

Grass was almost on top of him before Traylor could twist

around and get the Glock in firing position.

Grass shoved hard on his chest and sent him hurtling backward over the edge of the dirt shoulder, banging against the shoulder's slanted wall, a second time before plummeting the rest of the way; slamming against a barely visible tortoise shell of waste disposal pipeline; the sound of cracking bone buried under a meaningless gunshot, and—

Traylor sank into the muddy slime.

CHAPTER 44

Grass peered down into the ditch for a few minutes, satisfying himself that Traylor had been disposed of, then wandered back to the BMW humming an upbeat tune that put a dancer's rhythm into his steps. *In Munchen Steht Ein Hoftbrauh. In Munich Stands a Royal Drinking House.* How he missed those good times, Grass thought, but his to enjoy again as soon as this business with Herr Mielke's diary was successfully concluded.

He reached Sothern and kicked him in the thigh like he was Beckham going for a goal. He flashed a smile of pleasure over Sothern's cry of pain. Settled with arms akimbo, eighteen or twenty inches between his shoes. Leaned forward and barked laughter.

"Nice attempt at signaling *der schwanzlutscher,*" Grass said, "but you were playing to a foolish amateur compared to yours truly, Herr Sothern. He called himself a detective. I call him a fool, so sloppy I saw him coming before he saw me on the road. Did he know? I think not." A gesture of dismissal. "Back in a moment, so don't go anywhere," he said, and rewarded himself with laughter.

He sauntered around to the rear driver-side door of the BMW and checked through the open window. Tracy Collins was stretched across the length of the seat like a rag doll, her head in her mother's lap, the way he'd deposited them before hurrying off to dispose of Glen Traylor. He said, "I commend you for obeying my instructions and doing nothing stupid, Mrs. Boone."

Meg Boone returned his stare, but not his smile.

"Why so glum, Mrs. Boone? Our business is almost finished, so you and your child will be home soon. Back to your normal routine, with wonderful stories to tell about your exciting adventure."

She gave Grass a look that betrayed the fact she didn't believe him.

A smart woman, he thought, not that he was trying so hard to keep the truth from her. Living happily ever after can't be for everyone. Once Herr Mielke's diary was in his hands, the last thing in the world he'd need was people running around who could identify him.

"But first a visit to Los Angeles, the city of angels," Grass said. "Not exactly Disneyland, but you can wave as we go past the Magic Mountain."

He flamed an English Oval and took a few lung-expanding swallows hurrying back to Sothern, who appeared half-asleep, his hooded eyes weighted by the world. He squatted beside him, blanketed his face with gray smoke, and commanded him to pay attention.

"We have no more time to waste here," Grass said. "Traylor wasn't alone before. He was with your competition for Mrs. Boone's affections, the dyke who runs The Garden of Eden, and I expect she's called in the cavalry by now, so it's quick, quick, quick on to Los Angeles and your bank. . . . I'm going to free you, and I expect you to get into the car without incident. Mr. Sothern, are you paying attention to what I say?" Grass patted Sothern's cheek. When that didn't work, he slapped Sothern hard on both cheeks. *Scheisse.* Shit. No reaction. The vodka laced with "Liquid X" had done its work too well too soon. He hoped for Christ's sake it wasn't a seizure. Not God damned yet anyway. Not before they'd done their banking.

Grass filled his lungs one more time and flipped away the

butt, let the smoke drift out the sides of his mouth, his nostrils, as he dashed back to Mrs. Boone.

He pushed the key to the cuffs at her.

"I'm in need of your assistance getting Mr. Sothern into the car," he said.

Her mouth curled into one of those superior smiles the nuns were always lashing him with. "The GHB you pumped him full of, right? I warned you what could happen."

"And I warned you worse," Grass said. "Shut your stupid mouth and come help me, or I swear you'll watch what tricks I can play on your daughter before I snuff out her life, then your own." He showed her the .22 as an added incentive.

Meg Boone took the key and dug it into the keyway. "Bastard. I never suspected you could be this cruel."

"You never knew me long enough or well enough, bitch. Close the door quietly. We wouldn't want to disturb your little angel's sleep, would we?"

Grass was hovering over them, watching Meg Boone free Sothern from the bumper hitch when he heard the clunk. An Eden Highlands cop car, making the bend into view; no siren, no flashing roof bubble; trying to sneak up on him, but reacting noisily to a rut in the road. He had been right about the dyke, that Colbraith woman, calling in the cavalry, damn her.

With or without Meg Boone's help, there wasn't enough time to work Sothern into the car and move out of here.

There was nothing to be gained by holding ground and shooting it out.

He needed Sothern.

He had Sothern as long as he had the girl.

The decision made itself.

Grass giant-stepped around the car and jumped behind the wheel, triggered the ignition, and roared forward even before he had pulled the driver's door shut.

Meg Boone was on her feet, screaming for him to stop, banging at the air with her fists.

Grass hit the brakes after another fifty yards, but not because of her.

He knew how deep down he'd gone with Dan-Dan-the-T-Shirt-Man—how many curves and turns he'd counted off—but he didn't know how far the road stretched beyond that point or if he'd come to an exit.

He checked the rearview.

The cop car was slowing as it neared Meg Boone and Sothern.

She had stepped into its path and was wigwagging her arms.

Pointing out Sothern on the ground.

Twisting to point out the BMW.

Moving out of the way and waving the cop car to chase after him.

Grass imagined her squealing:

My daughter, my precious daughter, my beloved daughter, he has her. He has my precious darling baby. He has—

She had that part correct.

"Your mommy has that part correct," he called to Tracy over his shoulder. He elevated his pitch and recited the words like a bad actor as he worked the BMW into a turn. Gunned the motor a few times. Charged at the cop car, which was picking up its own speed on a single-lane side road wide enough for only one car at a time.

Grass made chicken noises:

Bwahk, bwahk, bwahk.

This wasn't the first time for him playing James Dean.

The last time? Two years ago. No, closer to three. Surprising Jannings on a four-lane section of the Autobahn in Stuttgart. Jannings, one of the few others who knew about Herr Mielke's diary and foolishly thought he could beat Crews and him to it. Stupid man.

How easy it had been taking him out, watching his Mercedes fly off the concrete, fold like an accordion before flip-flopping out of sight over the crash barrier. He was the last to go, leaving the field clear for Crews and him to reorganize their relationship and plot a strategy that would take them to the diary.

Bwahk, bwahk, bwahk.

The cop car showed no signs of slowing.

Grass had the gas pedal to the floorboard. He pressed harder, cursing the BMW to go faster. His heart was pounding, his throat dry with the thrill of the moment. His body gushed sweat that stung his eyes, salted his lips and tongue. Expectation was bringing him close to an orgasm as great or greater than any he had ever experienced.

The cop car was close enough for Grass to make out the cop's face. His eyes hid behind mirrored, blue-lens Ray-Bans, but his mouth spoke to his fears—lips so taut, Grass would not have been surprised to see bone bursting through flesh any second.

Bwahk, bwahk, bwahk.

Maybe six car lengths separated them.

Grass pushed back against his seat, gripped the wheel like a miser protecting his purse, wondering if this was an error in judgment he'd never know about, when—

The cop pulled a hard right and slithered past the BMW by inches, fishtailed into a series of pinwheel spins that propelled the car past the shoulder and, after stuttering in the air, dropped out of sight.

Bwahk, bwahk, bwahk.

Grass eased his foot on the pedal navigating around Meg Boone and Sothern.

He rejected the idea of stopping to load them into the car.

There might be another squad car on the way.

Meg Boone chased after him, a diminishing presence that disappeared entirely as he angled around the bend.

On the 405 a half hour past San Juan Capistrano, Grass heard Tracy making noises in the backseat. Grunts and groans mixed in with untranslatable dream state words, except for *Mama*. She said *Mama* several times and once or twice what could have been *Daddy*.

He spotted a rest stop, pulled in, and kept the motor running while he joined her in back long enough to tease a roofie down her throat. "To keep us both comfortable, my beautiful little girl, you and your Uncle Emil," he said.

Back on the freeway, Grass serenaded Tracy with a lullaby he'd sung to his children, a gentle melody full of sweet, comforting words. All these years later, he sometimes sang the lullaby to himself, on lonely nights when memories of what once had been and would never be again climbed into bed with him.

CHAPTER 45

When Emil Grass called, Roxy was giving Gerry Cotton focus and a frozen smile, feigning interest in what he was telling her, carrying on about the new woman he had met through the Internet, who came to join him in Eden Highlands.

Cotton was saying, "She sure fooled me, but only after I put her in the luxury suite I held back from anybody else until she got here. Next thing I know, she's holed up in there with some dude who shows up from nowhere, like he's known all along she'll be on her way."

"Shit happens, Gerry. The one for you is out there somewhere."

"Darn right there's more where she come from. EvolDot-Com sent over a fresh batch of faces only this morning. I'll find the true woman of my wet dreams yet."

Roxy was glad for the diversion. Her mind had been everywhere else for all of the two days since Grass got away again with Tracy and depression was tilting Maggie toward a full-blown nervous breakdown.

Grass was not exactly a serial killer like Ted Bundy or one of those other crazies, more an indiscriminate killing machine, the bodies falling around him like autumn leaves. It was a wonder the media had ignored what was going on in the Highlands, except for a few occasional references to Tracy still being missing.

She'd said that to Dan Boone when they spoke yesterday,

Danny phoning to ask how Maggie was, if there was anything new he should know about. Him guessing it was the feds, keeping a lid on the real story, especially since it was one of their own, Burt Crews, who got killed. Saying, "What Burt Crews was doing here in the first place is definitely not a question with an answer they'd want to share."

"This here's The Garden of Eden, Gerry Cotton speaking," Gerry said when the outside line lit up. "And hello back at you, Mr. Raisin."

Roxy jumped at hearing the name.

Raisin. Rasen.

Grass.

Cotton gave her a questioning look.

She nodded.

"She sure is, Mr. Raisin. Wait yourself a minute and I'll get Miss Colbraith on the line with you."

Roxy aimed an index finger at the ceiling and took off for her suite.

Grass cooed into the phone, "Good morning, Miss Colbraith. I expect you and yours have had a miserable two days."

"Screw you. Tell me about Tracy."

"I've got her cleaned up and into fresh new clothing. She looks cute as a button again. She'd like to go home to her mommy. I tell the little darling that's also my wish."

"Let me speak to her. Put Tracy on the phone."

"I wouldn't want to wake her. Besides, I didn't ring you up to play manservant. I need you to deliver a message for me to Mr. Sothern, assuming you know where to find him. I don't."

"He's at Maggie's. He almost died, thanks to you. Call him."

"He's still alive, thanks to me. Ring him up there, and how many strangers are still eavesdropping, expecting me to be stupid enough to call Mrs. Boone? I don't believe so. I consider you a safer channel, too wise to involve third parties who might interfere with my business with that rummy of a journalist. Do we understand each other?"

"Tell me what you need."

"Do we understand each other?"

"Yes."

"Say it."

"We understand each other."

"Excellent. . . . Listen carefully to what I tell you he's to do."

Grass spoke slowly and deliberately, like every teacher Roxy remembered from grade school. His tone was enough to bring on the kind of shiver chalk scraping the blackboard once gave her. He repeated key elements of his plan, pausing frequently to have her recite them back.

After the last test, she said, "Except for one thing—Jack Sothern is in no shape to drive. The vodka and GHB cocktail you fed him has him half-blind, bumping into walls and tripping over the furniture half the time, if he's able to get out of bed at all. Dizzy spells. Fainting spells. The doctor says it'll be days before he pulls out of it."

A drawn-out silence before Grass coughed out some throat gravel. "I do not have days," he said. "*You* drive him up here to Los Angeles. Today. This afternoon. In time to visit his safe deposit box and collect Herr Mielke's diary, after which we will rendezvous and conclude our business satisfactorily."

It was not what Roxy expected to hear. "Why me? Why not Maggie? She's desperate to be with her daughter."

Another long pause, then: "Desperation comes with its own problems. You meet my standard quite well enough. You and Herr Sothern. No monkey business. Bring him to Los Angeles. Do exactly as I've explained. I'll see you before you see me. Anyone else, I swear nobody will ever see Tracy alive again. Her life is now in your hands, and the clock is ticking. We still understand each other?"

"We understand each other."

"Excellent," Grass said, and clicked off.

Roxy moved to the bar and poured herself a tall Cuervo La Reserva, understanding the situation with Grass better than she was understanding herself. There'd been a moment when she wanted to tell him:

You don't need Sothern. I have the diary, not him. The story about him having the diary in a safe deposit box in a bank in L.A. Fabricated out of whole cloth. You only need me for the trade, Tracy for the Mielke diary; only me, Grass.

She didn't expect Grass would believe her. He'd call her a liar, presume to call her bluff by demanding she tell him something about the diary:

What does the cover look like? What color? What's on a page? Read something. I know it's written in German, so do the best you can. I'm no dummy that I won't understand or hear enough to know the truth.

Roxy debated another slug of the tequila, to steady her nerves and flush her head, wondering: What would telling Grass she had the diary accomplish? Keep Sothern out of the picture, if she were able to convince him?

If.

Not her, though.

Roxy Colbraith, still in the line of fire.

Grass capable of shooting her for sport.

Tracy, no closer to being reunited with Maggie.

How many times had she told herself, told Maggie in the wake of a magical moment together, that she was ready to give up her life for her? How many stars in the sky?

Now—the opportunity as real as her next breath—she wasn't so certain.

She didn't love Maggie less, but maybe she loved life more.

Roxy capped the Cuervo and pushed the bottle aside.

She used her private line to call Dan Boone at the number he'd given her yesterday, saying to use it only in an emergency.

Halfway into the third tinkle, a woman answered.

"Pronto?" The voice accented, throaty, and not quite awake. Roxy too surprised to answer before the woman said again, *"Pronto?"* Roxy wondering if she'd misdialed, while the woman said in a shifting European accent, *"Nanu? Was ist dehn hier los?"* Roxy about to hang up and try again, when the woman said in wide-awake English, "Hello? Yes? That you, Miss Colbraith?"

Roxy, lost in the moment, saying, "Who is this?"

The woman saying, "Hold on for Danny."

CHAPTER 46

Emil Grass eased the nondescript Volkswagen camper off the freeway and onto the exit lane that would take him over the bridge to the Museum of the American West in Griffith Park, whose Alamo-styled bell tower hung over the junction of the 5 and the 134 like a spacecraft not quite ready for launching. A giant canvas banner stretched across the concrete block compound wall advertised the current exhibition in the George Montgomery Gallery, "Legendary Cowboy Heroes of Fact and Film."

So very appropriate, he thought, his choice of location for the exchange with Jack Sothern, confident Burt Crews would have applauded and endorsed the idea, given how it brought full circle their business with Dan Boone, "The Turncoat Rebel," the Communist cowboy star of stars who most certainly would not be found among the legendary cowboy heroes on display at the museum.

"What do you say, Burt?" Grass asked aloud, on the off chance the dead had links to the living. "Do I get credit for being the clever rascal you never saw in me? I should still care what you think, Burt? Fuck you, Burt. *Leck mich am arsch.* Burt. Go to hell, Burt. Oh, I forget. You are there already." His laughter filled the cabin, causing Tracy to stir. She was strapped to the lower bunk bed and half-asleep. He called over his shoulder, "Didn't mean to disturb you, my beautiful little girl. Patience. This business will soon be concluded, and you back in

337

your dear mother's arms."

Wondering how sincere he sounded to her, not that it mattered anymore.

She wasn't going anywhere now—

—or later.

Grass traded middle fingers with the driver of a Chevy low-rider who squeezed ahead of him on Victory Drive and followed Zoo Drive about a mile to the parking lot on the south side of the museum. He chose a slot that had a clear view of the picnic lawn across the walkway.

The lawn was sprinkled with couples and families, children running amok, blankets and baskets spread out on perfectly manicured grass green as turtle soup. There would be hundreds more visitors arriving within the hour to take advantage of a Van Gogh sky, a temperature that was not expected to fall below the mid-sixties, and the free admission that was a weekly feature on Thursdays after four o'clock.

The camper's dashboard clock said almost three-thirty.

He had a half hour before Sothern and Roxy Colbraith would arrive with Herr Mielke's diary at the monumental statue of Gene Autry that occupied a place of honor in the museum's forecourt. His instructions to Roxy Colbraith were straightforward and uncomplicated:

—Drive Sothern to his bank.

—Once Sothern has picked up the diary, proceed directly to the museum, arriving no earlier than four-thirty.

—Park in this lot and use the picnic area entrance to proceed with the diary to the Gene Autry statue.

—Wait for him to arrive with Tracy, who will be in a mild state of disorientation, brought on by a combination of Rohypnol and a deadly poison that will kill her if she is not administered the antidote within fifteen or twenty minutes.

—He will inspect the diary for authenticity.

—If satisfied, he will reveal the location of the antidote he's hidden somewhere in the museum.

—While they race off to procure the antidote and save Tracy's life, he will quietly and irrevocably disappear from their lives.

The business about the poison would prove irresistible. It was a lie, of course, another of the admirable techniques he had learned under Herr Mielke, who borrowed it from Adolf Hitler's inspired propaganda minister Goebbels:

"The Big Lie."

The bigger the lie, the more people will believe it.

Grass' lie about the poison was as big a one as he needed this time.

These fools weren't going to gamble with the life of Tracy Collins.

He'd let them find the so-called antidote, saving for later the real surprise he had in store for them—

In a manner of speaking—

His farewell gift.

Grass savored a few more drags off the English Oval before jamming it out in the ashtray, tossed off a few sweet words to Tracy, and headed for the museum plaza.

Card tables and chairs had been set up to handle the crowd expected for a starlight concert by mariachi groups on the temporary stage next to the Autry Picture Palace. A double-bill of Hopalong Cassidy movies was scheduled for tonight: *Secrets of the Wasteland* and *Bar 20 Rides Again.*

He paused to study the Autry statue, the cowboy parked on a tree stump and gazing skyward while serenading his wonder horse, Champion, before wandering over to the gift shop to purchase the heroic ten-gallon hat he had admired yesterday, when he surveyed the museum. He was no longer able to escape the impulse to go back home with a modest gift for himself, a deserved souvenir of an exciting adventure that would allow him to retire in style and comfort.

He cruised the aisles until four o'clock, then joined dozens of others hurrying onto the glossy marble floors of the spacious main lobby to be among the first in line for free admission.

He sailed past the upper-level galleries with the plush dark red carpeting and dim lighting and downstairs to Heritage Court, where the galleries were less formal, wide open, and filled with permanent exhibits more to his taste.

At the set portraying Sheriff Wyatt Earp, his brothers, and Doc Holliday gunning after the villainous Clantons at the O.K. Corral, he checked to be certain no one was paying him attention before he transferred an inconsequential-looking package wrapped in brown butcher's paper from his pocket to a stack of prop hay bundles by the corral fence.

Returning to the Plaza, he bought an iced coffee from a cart vendor and settled at an empty table outside the Golden Spur Café. It put him within ten feet of the Autry statue and offered a clear view of the picnic area gateway and all the other museum entrances. The air smelled of fresh buttered popcorn, hot dogs, burgers, fries, and barbecue.

A group of mariachi musicians in traditional "charro" costumes congregated onstage to check the sound system. Their outfits were as much a part of the heritage as the music, the *traje* consisting of ankle boots, a sombrero, a large bow tie, a short jacket, tight trousers without back pockets, a wide belt, and shiny buttons on the sides of the pants.

He and Crews had learned the lingo and dressed like that in the early nineties, in Guadalajara, where they had been sent to remove an obstacle from future consideration.

How it was usually put to them:

To remove an obstacle from future consideration.

That, a name and a photograph.

Nothing else—

—not that they ever needed or wanted more in order to do their work properly and efficiently.

He and Crews were professionals, who understood it was always wisest to leave the politics to the politicians.

Grass smiled at the memory of the removal, remembering it was quick, clean, and efficient—his trademarks—and no recollection of who the obstacle was, except that he was playing a *vihuela* in the mariachi, the small belly-back guitar with five treble strings. No, the *guitarrón*, the larger six-string bass guitar–like belly-back tuned to within an octave and a half range. And, at the moment of truth, doing a nice job on *El Son de la Negra*.

What he was hearing now was strands of *El Rey*, another song that every group included in its repertoire, along with *Jalisco* and, of course, *Cielito Lindo*. He was half-tempted to wander over to the stage and ask the mariachis to also warm up on *El Son de la Negra*.

He checked his wristwatch.

Jack Sothern and the Colbraith woman were due any minute.

So, save it for another evening.

He powered an English Oval and pushed out one perfect series of crisp blue smoke rings after the next between sips of iced coffee. His fingers danced to the music when they weren't strumming an air-*vihuela*. The ten-gallon hat was on the table and he was stroking it like a pet when he spotted Sothern and the Colbraith woman arriving through the picnic area gateway. Give or take a few seconds, they were on time. He appeared unsteady on his feet. She was maintaining a tight grip on his elbow as they weaved through the plaza foot traffic.

Sothern was unnecessarily bundled against the weather, in a full-length coat and wide-brimmed Panama hat, a scarf hanging to his waist and sunglasses. The Colbraith woman also was dressed in overkill, a mint-colored turtleneck sweater and tight leather pants tucked inside flat-soled ankle boots under a full-length leather coat. Hair tucked inside a mint-colored beret. Retro sunglasses. A tote bag hanging from her shoulder.

Grass arranged the table to appear like he was off visiting the *herrentoilette*—an English Oval burning in the ashtray beside the cigarette box and his iced coffee, the ten-gallon hat parked protectively on a chair.

He lingered at the main entrance until they reached the Autry statue.

Satisfied they had come alone, he sped off to fetch Tracy.

She was awake enough to understand what he was telling her, although not quite out of the dreamland state that along with the restraining straps kept her from becoming a flight risk. He squatted by the bunk bed, pinched her cheeks, and pulled her face around so that her glassy eyes had nowhere to go but to his hard stare, which he quickly modified by breaking out a smile that showed off his teeth.

"You're almost on your way home, my beautiful little girl," Grass told her. "I want you to swear no tricks before Uncle Emil takes you to your Auntie Roxy. Yes?" He ran a hand over her hair, brushing it down, while waiting for an answer.

A drawn-out whisper: "Yes."

"Of course, yes." He leaned over to kiss her forehead, came away with his lips and the tip of his tongue coated with her perspiration. "First you need to take this," he said, and held up a roofie for her to see. "Open wide." She didn't respond. His smile quickened into a determined line. "Be a good girl, or your Uncle Emil will spank you again," he said. He pinched her cheeks hard enough to force her mouth open, deposited the capsule, and capped her mouth with his hand, urging her to swallow.

Satisfied, Grass loosened the straps and helped Tracy into a sitting position. He got her into her sneakers and fluffed up her hair a bit. Helped her to her feet. Tidied up the t-shirt and tie-dyed denims he'd changed her into after their arrival. Ran his hands over her body one last time.

"Let me see you walk," he said. She worked her way to the end of the camper and back to him, working her arms for balance a time or two. "Brilliant," he said. "Do you need to go potty?" She nodded. "Quick, then. We don't want your Auntie Roxy waiting any longer than necessary."

He used the minutes to recheck the loads in the .22 parked in the fishnet shoulder holster and the .45 in the small of his back. The jacket he was wearing had felt tight when he sat down in the plaza. He switched into a formless black jacket that he'd been swimming in last year, after he had lost all that weight. It fit better now, almost like when he'd bought it. He made a promise to go on a diet soon, appreciating that the word "soon" didn't come with a time stamp, while patting his trouser pockets after the feel of his HuntChamp and the marvelous .22 caliber cell phone he'd inherited from Burt Crews. He stepped over to the toilet door, pushed it open a crack, and called to Tracy: "What is it, my beautiful little girl? Have you fallen in and your Uncle Emil will have to come rescue you?"

CHAPTER 47

Using the toilet seat for leverage, Tracy scrambled up from her knees and to the sink. She had been vomiting, intentionally, jamming her fingers down her throat to coax out the last pill and whatever else he had been shoveling into her to keep her his mental and physical prisoner. "My period all over me, just beginning, and now I got to wash up," she said, making it sound as if she were still fogbound.

"*Scheisse!*" he said, buying her invention, and quickly shut the door again.

Tracy washed off her mouth, gargled, and spat. She kept both taps running hard while she explored the cabinet in a bathroom barely larger than the one on a jet plane she and Mama flew once to Las Vegas, for her thirteenth birthday. She hoped to find something that could help her escape from the filthy pig if he was lying about going to Roxy.

A spray can of underarm deodorant, which Emil Grass used as a substitute for showering. Too large to sneak past him. The slim tube of breath spray. Better. She stuffed it in a pocket. The nail file. Perfect. She got the file into a pocket as Grass yelled through the door, "It's not the Red Sea, you know?"

Tracy closed the cabinet and took a moment to check herself in the mirror.

Hated the ghoulish face staring back at her as much as she hated Emil Grass.

She stepped out to Grass advising her, "I didn't think you

were old enough."

"Had to plug me up with toilet paper," she said, letting the words drag. "Want to see? Show you." She started to fumble with the top button on her denims.

Grass turned away, saying, "Stop that. Don't be vulgar, you dirty little creature." After a minute, he turned back around. "I'll show you something now," he said. He revealed his shoulder holster and told her what was hidden behind his back. "You do anything but what I tell you and I intend to use them," he said. "Your Auntie Roxy will die and so will you. Anyone else who gets in my way. Do you understand that, Tracy? Say it? Look at me and say it."

Tracy tilted her chin upward and, arms dangling at her sides, her shoulders sagging, her eyelids drooping, and said—

Nothing.

Made like the demand was beyond comprehension.

"Look at me and say it, Tracy."

She thought about it. Eyes closed and lids blinking furiously. Teeth digging into her lower lip.

"It Tracy," she said.

It took Grass a second to understand. He nodded approvingly and patted her head, like she was a puppy who had obeyed her master's command. "Good girl," he said. "Take my hand and off we go."

Outside, it took Tracy a few moments to adjust to the daylight, sense where she was. Grass had kept the camper dark most of the time, except for a safelight; the shades always drawn. The picnickers came as a surprise, but explained some of the smells that had drifted inside the camper. The freeway explained the constant rumble and most of the exhaust fumes; the parking lot the rest of it.

The mariachi music grew louder as they approached the

Museum of the American West.

Grass must have read her mind, her thinking how easy it would be to break free and lose herself in the thickening crowd. He nudged her a foot or two ahead of him and gripped her by the shoulders, steering her toward the statue of some cowboy.

Through jumbles of people, she spotted Roxy by the cowboy's horse, her shades lifted onto her forehead, searching around anxiously, saying something to a guy standing next to her.

Impulsively, Tracy started forward.

Grass pulled her back with a warning: "Only if I say so." After another nine or ten feet down the narrow aisle, he released her. "Now, go join your Auntie Roxy," he said.

Still playing a role, Tracy stumbled ahead, calling Roxy's name over the music and the din of a thousand different conversations.

Roxy saw her, threw open her arms with excitement. She wrapped them around Tracy, swept her off the ground, hugged her almost tight enough to crack a rib. Kissed her endlessly all over her face. Asked over and over: "You're all right?"

Grass reached them. "Now it's your turn," he said, shifting his oily smile from Roxy to the guy. "I believe you have something for me, Mr. Sothern?"

The guy's head wandered left and right—

Sothern silently telling him otherwise.

Emil Grass' face turned to stone, like the faces Tracy saw in pictures of the tombs at Westminster Abbey. He reached inside his jacket. She was certain he was going after his gun. Trapped by Roxy's arms, there was nothing she could do about it, except—

Maybe cry out a warning—

Shout for help.

Only, fear had closed her throat beyond any sound at all.

CHAPTER 48

"I have it, not him," Roxy said.

She settled Tracy's feet on the ground, dug into her tote bag, and came up with a small cardboard box. She handed it over to Grass. "Now, you owe us something," she said, her voice polluted by tension.

"In good time," Grass said. "I inspect the merchandise first."

"It's the diary, damn you." She looked at her watch.

"Come, Tracy," he said, ignoring Roxy's demand. He turned from her, locked onto Tracy's wrist, and guided her to his table outside the café. The couple sitting there seemed to have materialized from nowhere. He gave them a false smile. "This is my table, if you don't mind," he said. He pointed out the cigarette pack and the remains of the English Oval in the ashtray, the glass of iced tea, its cubes in the last stages of meltdown, the ten-gallon hat he'd parked on the chair.

"You got a pink slip to show me?" the man said. He was fiftyish and half a head shorter than Grass, but carried twenty or thirty pounds more. Barrel-chested. Dark-skinned. A nose ring that matched his silver earring. A Zapata mustache. A greasy black pigtail that trailed halfway down his back. A sports jacket with frayed lapels and missing sleeve buttons. "You got no pink slip, you don't own this table, man."

The white-haired woman with him said, "Enriqué, don't start anything." She gave Grass a look that pleaded understanding. "You got to excuse him, mister. He don't mean nothing by it."

Her voice was earnest, throaty in a sexy way that spoke less to her age than to massive breasts climbing over the lace-trimmed ridge of a peasant blouse she wore off her shoulders. Green eyes equally majestic under thick, connected eyebrows the same dark shade as the hair fence running across her upper lip. A full skirt traveling down to her trim ankles, exposing thrift shop sneakers. "Enriqué, tell him you didn't mean nothing."

"Nobody got to do me no favors," Enriqué said, pushing himself up from the table. He yanked Grass' ten-gallon hat from the seat, plopped it down on Grass' head. "Ride 'em, Gringo," he said, and stalked off toward the picnic grounds.

The woman pleaded with Grass for forgiveness and chased after him.

Grass pointed Tracy to a chair and settled the cardboard box on the table in front of him.

Within seconds, Sothern and the Colbraith woman joined them.

Sothern edged himself with difficulty into the chair Enriqué had taken. The Colbraith woman held onto the back of the other chair, shifting from foot to foot, as if counting off the seconds with each step.

"Eleven minutes remaining before the poison assumes its mission, so no problem, Miss Colbraith, Mr. Sothern, unless, of course, I discover a problem once I've lifted the lid. Will I discover a problem?"

"Poison?" Tracy said, looking to anyone for an answer.

Roxy shook her fist at him. Eyes two storm clouds. Nostrils flaring. "God. Damn. You. Open the God damn box." Heads turned, and she drew curious stares.

Grass cautioned her with an index finger against his lips.

He rubbed his hands in anticipation and raised the lid high enough for a peek.

"Splendid," he said, lifting out the small volume, about the size of a Bible, but only a third as thick. He rewarded the Colbraith woman and Sothern with an approving nod. "Now, the real test," he said, carefully settling the book on the table after brushing off the area. He used his thumb to inch up the cover, slowly, cautiously. "*Wunderbar*," he said. "Herr Mielke's signature. How well I know it." He checked pages at random, pausing to study the script, the block printing. "*Jah*. Definitely Herr Mielke," he said. "My congratulations, Herr Sothern. You have not let me down."

"The antidote, Grass. Hand it over."

"Miss Colbraith, please." He returned the diary to the box. "I'm a man of my word."

"Make good on it now," Sothern said. He lifted the Panama hat he'd set on the table long enough to show Grass it was covering a 9 mm revolver.

"My, my. Not so helpless as first appearances suggested, are we?"

"Strong enough to shoot, pull the trigger, and put one where your heart would be, if you had one."

"Squeeze the trigger, Herr Sothern. Squeeze, not pull. You pull the trigger, the shot from your little cap pistol might go astray and deprive some innocent of his life."

The Colbraith woman said, "Jack, please. We don't have time to waste." Desperation masked her face.

"A bull's-eye with that thought, Miss Colbraith. Our little arrangement called for Jack to deliver me Herr Mielke's diary and, upon satisfaction, for me to direct you to the antidote for the poison and bid you a final farewell, correct?"

Grass started to rise.

Sothern signaled him back down, saying, "First the antidote to my satisfaction."

"Not playing by the rules, Jack."

Tracy said, "What antidote? Roxy, what antidote? What's

happening?"

"Why you little devil, you," Grass said. "So suddenly alert. You fooled your Uncle Emil better than most can ever do and get away with it."

"Screw you, perv."

"Yes, but I was going to keep that our little secret." Oblivious to the 9 mm, he lit up an English Oval and pushed a jet of smoke out the corner of his mouth, went after the iced tea, and raised the glass in toast. "May all of us live long, healthy, and prosperous lives," he said. Flicked a sardonic smile. "Mine to toast and yours to act upon, Jack. So, which will it be? You're running out of time, you know?"

"Jack, for Christ's sake," Roxy said, imploring him with her eyes.

Sothern said, "Here's the deal, Grass. You hand over the antidote and you're free to go. I won't try stopping you. You have my word."

"Your word? How good is your word, actually? Years ago, Dan Boone had your word. A hill of beans good it did him. Why should I expect any better treatment at your hands or, for that matter, his daughter expect better treatment than you gave her father?"

"Call it payback. Paying back Dan Boone by helping save Tracy's life. Right now that's more important to me than ridding the planet of your likes."

Tracy said, "Saving my life? How? Roxy, what's he mean, *saving my life?*"

The Colbraith woman settled a hand over Tracy's mouth.

"How so very noble of you," Grass said. "I'd rather have your weapon than your word."

"I don't think so," Sothern said. "First the antidote."

Grass made like he was thinking through the demand.

He turned his palms skyward and said, "Downstairs in the

museum, a Wyatt Earp exhibit. His historical gunfight at the O.K. Corral." He paused for a puff and smoke rings that dissolved as quickly as he intended to do away with Sothern's perceived upper hand. "At the corral fence, on the left side, are bundles of hay. Between the second and third bundles, I placed the package containing—"

The Colbraith woman didn't wait for him to finish.

She yanked Tracy from her chair and pulled her in the direction of the museum, ignoring Tracy's demand she be told what she didn't understand. Bumping into people and almost crashing into a popcorn vendor's cart before they'd reached the entrance.

Grass waited until they had disappeared inside before saying, "You don't really plan to let me leave, do you." Not a question. A declaration on which he anticipated a quick, affirmative acknowledgment from Sothern.

"That would take more courage than killing you, Grass. They get back, you're on your way to the cops."

"I know other people like you," Grass said. "They're no longer around." He mashed out his English Oval and fired up a fresh one. "While we're waiting, shall I share information to help complete the exclusive story you probably expect to write, about helping to apprehend this bad person name of Emil Grass? Single-handedly, a single-minded act of bravery on your part, if I accurately recall how you embroider the truth."

"A confession would be nice, starting with those two girls, Tracy's friends."

"And good for the soul. Shouldn't you tell me that?"

"You have one?"

"Collateral in a bargain I made with the devil years ago."

"Do you keep count of the people you murder, Grass? You must be into double digits by now."

"Your sense of humor, it's quite dark. I've never found

anything funny in killing, Jack. One does what one must." He squared the box containing Herr Mielke's diary. "Instead, I'll tell you about the poison I chose for Tracy. Triclofos. You've heard of it?"

Sothern's face went blank.

"A particular favorite of Herr Mielke," Grass said. "A clear liquid, so hard to detect and so reliable. Depending on circumstances, easily administered in either liquid or capsule form. I prefer the red-tinted gelatin capsule myself. What I chose for Tracy. Triclofos starts its deadly work quickly, by depressing the central nervous system. Soon afterward, a coma. After that—death. An ugly death. Nothing you'd ever really want to see, as you're about to, Jack."

"What's that supposed to mean?"

"It means the last person I ever trusted was my mother, and I didn't trust her much. What I deposited at the O.K. Corral fence was the poison, not the antidote. Two gelatin capsules, with instructions for Tracy to take both." He studied Sothern computing the news. "If you hurry, you may be in time to stop her. Otherwise, prepare to explain to her mother how you allowed Tracy's death by standing guard over me."

"You're lying."

"And you're playing Russian roulette with Tracy Collins' life," Grass said. He showed off his watch. "I'd offer to tag along, but it would only slow you down, Jack."

Chapter 49

Sothern hobbled through the plaza crowd and into the museum.

He worked down the staircase to Heritage Court on the lower level, half-hopping on a leg soured by a bolt of pain every time it hit another step, holding onto the railing with both hands to prevent a stumble from turning into a nose dive.

He misread a directional sign.

Turned in the wrong direction.

Wound up in the Conquest Gallery instead of the Cowboy Gallery.

He cut back through the central lobby, bucked the crowd through Trails West, and—fatigue pummeling his body, struggling for breath, pausing half a minute to collect himself—Sothern tracked down the O.K. Corral.

Found Earp and the Clantons shooting it out, but no Roxy or Tracy.

Neither visible in the heavy traffic working both sides of the gallery's viewing aisle.

Sothern headed back to Heritage Court fueled by panic and adrenalin.

Turning the corner, pausing to let a dizzy spell pass, hanging a hand on a wall to keep from falling, he saw them across the way:

Roxy perched over Tracy, who was bending over the water fountain.

The thick conversational buzz of visitors trafficking in the

Court drowned out words he couldn't raise above a disjointed croak—

Telling Roxy not to let Tracy take the antidote.

Roxy spotted him through a break in the crowd.

She floated across a smile, held up a brown vial like she was Lady Liberty showing off her torch.

Pointed at Roxy.

Gave Sothern a high five that she instantly converted into a thumbs-up.

CHAPTER 50

Grass aimed for the picnic lawn exit, the fastest and most direct route back to the camper. He delighted in imagining the pain the girl's death would inflict on Sothern and the Colbraith woman. They would not soon forget Emil Grass.

He zigzagged across the lawn and was almost to the pavement, the box containing the diary packed under his arm like a football, when Enriqué sprang from somewhere and blocked his way.

"You wasn't so nice with me inside there," Enriqué said. His woman came up behind him and implored Enriqué not to do anything foolish. He gave her a shove and worked his face up to Grass'. His whiskey breath was repellent. "I'm as good as you, Gringo. Better." He poked Grass in the chest. "You want to make something out from it?"

The woman said, "Enriqué, enough. Not again this time."

"Shut up, you," he said, not taking his eyes off Grass. "What you saying to that, *Choco,* or don't you got the *aguacates?*" He tugged on the brim of Grass' ten-gallon hat.

"Enriqué, *por favor.* No more of this."

"I ask you, *almeja?*" He wheeled around to confront her. She backed away, turned, and fled. "So, now it's up to me and you, *Choco.*"

Grass scanned the area.

Making a scene made no sense.

He moved away from Enriqué and quickened his steps.

Enriqué called after him: *"Chinga tu madre!"*

"Aviente." Same to you. The answer slipped out louder than Grass intended.

"Fuck my mother? Come back and say that to my face, *Cabrón.* You faggot, you."

He charged after Grass. Clutched his shoulder and yanked him around, challenging him in two languages, his face as ugly as a pus infection, until he realized Grass had jammed a .22 under his chin.

His bravado quit at once.

His angry eyes graduated to fear.

He tried a backward step.

Grass moved with him.

Enriqué's hands zipped up in surrender. "Hey, man I was only joking you," he said.

"Next time try somebody with a sense of humor," Grass said. "Now, go. Leave while your head is still attached to your shoulders."

Enriqué stumbled away.

Grass waited until he was a safe distance before continuing on to the camper.

Unlocking the door, he heard shuffling footsteps approaching.

Thinking it might be Enriqué back, he dug his hand inside his jacket, going for the .22 again, and swung around.

"No, *señor, por favor.* Please." It was Enriqué's woman. "I only come to apologize for my husband," she said, stepping forward, her arms entwined and giving support to the heavy breasts that burst from her blouse, hypnotizing him again. She shuffled closer, explaining, "He becomes a different person when he's had too much drink. An ugly person, and something else I need to tell you."

"Not necessary," Grass said, his eyes moving to her face, then back to her breasts.

"Necessary," she said. She eased apart her arms to let him see the .38 short-barreled revolver her breasts had helped her to hide. "Get the door open and get inside," she said, her English not as scraggly as it had been.

She twirled a finger in the air, a signal for Enriqué to join her.

They were quite efficient and professional, working without words passing between them while Enriqué relieved him of the .22, found the .45 patting him down, then propped him at an awkward angle against the toilet door. All the while, his woman kept her .22 on him, nothing on her face to make him think she wouldn't use it if he made a false move.

Grass studied them carefully, trying to decide what that might be.

The first rule, always, was to get a sense of motive.

He figured it for money and valuables, not a kill shot, although the possibility was there once they had what they were after. Thieves like these were on a low rung of the ladder, between purse snatchers and carjackers, who given the slightest cause could panic into making the wrong move. Fireflies were brighter.

Enriqué had taken the box with Herr Mielke's diary from him. It was now sitting on the dashboard, alongside his ten-gallon hat. He doubted they'd have cause to leave with it, even if they checked it for content. Neither looked the reading type, the greatest element of relief the situation had to offer.

Grass said, "Money's in my billfold, in my hip pocket. Two or three hundred dollars. Best I can do for you. No jewelry except for the watch." He showed it to them. "A knock-off I picked up in Thailand last year. Sixty dollars. You'll be lucky to pawn it for six. Run the camper and all you'll find of value is the color TV on the desk. Picture-in-picture but not the flat screen that's so popular now."

The two of them traded the kind of laughs circus clowns get.

"We already have what we came after," the woman said, no longer any trace of an accent. She pointed at the box with the diary.

"And my daughter, out of your murderous hands," Enriqué said, accent-free.

"Your—?"

"Daughter, Emil. Tracy."

"Boone? Dan Boone? That's you?"

"Somewhere under the makeup and padding. Closest I've been in years to *Zapata Rides Again,* one of my biggest films. And, say hello to another old friend of yours." He indicated the woman.

She said, "Emil, you treacherous prick—the way you were lapping at my tits, I thought for sure they were going to give me away."

"I told Shane they'd distract you too much for you to think about anything but coming," Boone said. "You were always the tit man, and Burt Crews was the ass man."

"*GroBer Gott!* Shane, it can't be," Grass said, erasing the idea with his hands. "You are dead. I know for a fact. I was there."

She gave Grass the kind of superior look he had always hated about her. "The lady drowned in the lake wasn't Meg Boone, and it wasn't me, either," she said. "A diplomatic arrangement worked out by two governments that didn't concern you at the time, or now."

"Enough wandering down Memory Lane," Dan Boone said. He dipped into a jacket pocket and extracted a roll of duct tape. "I'll just bundle you up nice and tight, and we'll be on our way."

"Somewhere to kill me?"

"Another diplomatic arrangement would be a kinder, more gentle way to put it."

Grass couldn't tell if he meant it.

A cell phone sang out.

Boone's.

Boone flipped it open, said: "Got him, Jack. Tell me about Tracy."

Within seconds, any sign of victory had fled his eyes. Grass grabbed it for himself, certain of what Boone was hearing from Sothern. He shot a self-satisfied grin at Boone and Shane Vallery.

"Danny, what?" she said.

Boone clamped the phone to his chest. "It wasn't the antidote. It was the poison this double-dealing shit just traded for. They're on their way with Tracy to Glendale Memorial, Central and Los Feliz; five minutes away. Jack's already called ahead to say they're coming."

"Tell Jack through the park, not the freeway. It's rush hour."

Boone repeated her words into the phone.

Shook his head.

"Too late. They're on the 5 and it's fast going bumper-to-bumper. Radio saying it's the hour and Dodger Stadium early birds."

Grass studied his watch. "How unfortunate, time running out like that."

Boone clicked off and charged at Grass. Grass crossed his arms in front of him to ward off the blows he knew were coming. Boone fooled him. He brought up a hand from below and tightened a grip on Grass' throat, lifting him an inch or two off the floor while he rummaged Grass' pockets for the keys to the camper.

Boone demonized the one-way road through the park that fed

out onto Griffith Park Boulevard at Los Feliz Boulevard. He turned left and fudged every yellow light through the Atwater District and across the Glendale city limits sign that put Glendale Memorial in sight.

He parked illegally at the red curbing outside the hospital's entrance and got on the cell phone again, desperately begging the rings to turn into Jack Sothern. "Come on, come on, come on, come on," he demanded. "Answer me, God damn it, Jack."

Finally: "Jack, we're at the hospital. Where are you? Still on the freeway or—?" He took the phone from his ear and gave it as dirty a look as he'd been giving Grass. "The fucking phone quit on me."

Grass seized opportunity.

He said, "Try mine. Same pocket as the keys."

"March it over," Boone said. "On the double."

Shane kept the .38 aimed at him while he dipped into his pocket and pulled out the cell phone, his hand already clutching it in shooting position, silently thanking Burt Crews for this deadly toy right out of a James Bond movie.

Grass stepped forward, figuring to take Boone with the first of the four bullets the cell phone carried. The gunfire would startle Shane, throw her off balance. The second bullet would be for her. Then, he'd be on his way to Happily Ever After with Herr Mielke's diary.

When he was within two feet of Boone, he said, "Your battery's not the only thing dying today."

The .22 slug ripped into Boone's midsection and pushed him back hard against the wheel.

Grass spun around from the hip and, in the same motion, fired blindly at the spot where he visualized Shane standing.

The bullet caught her off-center, in the gut, sent her into a clumsy pirouette before she dropped the .38, hit the camper wall, and glided to the floor.

Grass went after the diary. Boone's gripped fists came up from nowhere and caught him under the chin. Sent him reeling backward. He grabbed onto a support pole to keep from falling and got off a shot.

The shot struck Boone in the chest.

Boone flew backward with his arms flailing for balance, Grass demanding, "This is no movie, you swine. Die!"

"You first," Shane yelled, scrambling after the .38.

She couldn't quite get it gripped.

Grass took careful aim at her and squeezed the trigger.

Scheisse!

He'd neglected to count in Burt Crews' shot that killed the highway patrolmen.

His three shots plus Burt's.

The cell gun was empty.

By the time Shane had a grip on the .38 and was going for aim, Grass had managed open the camper door. He leaped out barely a step ahead of the bullet that sailed past, close enough for him to feel the breeze.

Grass raced south on Central, his legs pumping hard, his lungs threatening to burst, not even daring to check over his shoulder to see if he was being pursued. He spotted signs telling him an Amtrak station was a block away. He turned at Cerritos, made another right turn onto Gardena. It deadheaded him into the station.

In the descending light, he made out the badly lit mission-style terminal. Fewer than a dozen scattered cars and vans were in the parking lot. A posted notice advised that this was an unattended pickup-and-delivery location. His footsteps echoed on the tile flooring as he passed through to the boarding platform. He stuck to the shadows, a lone figure waiting for a train to—

Anywhere.

Whatever train showed up, that's the one he was hopping.

Safety first.

The diary would have to wait.

Why not?

It had waited for him this long, so what difference did a few more days make?

Or a week or a month.

The weather was turning chilly.

He wished he still had the ten-gallon hat.

CHAPTER 51

"See her, the one going upstairs?" Gerry Cotton said. " 'Good Time Gal.' She's the one what took advantage of my good nature. Lied to my face. Took up full time with another man almost to the minute she got here to The Garden of Eden."

Sothern, studying her as she glided to the landing, said, "There's a woman like that in every man's life, Gerry. You'll get over her."

"Knock wood," Cotton said, knocking on the desktop. "You sound like you're a voice of experience." Sothern nodded confirmation. "How long did it take you to get over your woman?"

"Never, Gerry. I'm still working on it," Sothern said. He lifted the key to Roxy's suite and dangled it. "You need me, you know where to find me."

"Good Time Gal" was waiting for him.

Sothern guided her inside the suite.

She wheeled around, pulled him to her, and laid a kiss on him that shared her lips and her tongue in equal proportion.

It was like no time at all had passed between them.

He wanted more, but the moment he moved a hand to her breast, Shane Vallery broke away, saying: "Only a thank you, Little Boy."

Little Boy.

Shane was the only one who had ever called him that.

363

"Don't read anything more into it," she said. She crossed to the bar, poured herself a double Cutty, and offered to make him one.

He waved it off.

"You're not drinking? Since when?"

"Right now, would rather get drunk on you."

"You wouldn't want the hangover, Jack."

"Been there, done that," he said. "There never was a moment I stopped thinking about you, Shane."

She refused to let him trap her eyes. Found a corner of the ceiling to study.

Sothern said, "Gerry Cotton thinks you done him dirt."

"I did. Same as I did you."

"A leopard doesn't change her spots, that it?"

"I change my spots. You were Los Angeles. Gerry was Eden Highlands."

"And Dan Boone was East Berlin."

"The world, Jack. Wherever that takes me. Then and since."

"I will have that drink," Sothern said. He crossed to the bar and took the stool next to hers. Poured himself half a tumbler of Cutty.

"You want ice with that?"

"I've got you, Babe."

Shane reached over and patted the back of his hand. "It hasn't been enough years for you to forgive and forget?"

"Forgive and remember, that's my motto. . . . Cheers!"

She answered his toast, settled the glass on the bar top. "I never meant to hurt you, Jack. It was business. I never had the chance to apologize. Please. Take my word for that. Getting Danny out of Germany and, later, afterward, getting Washington to settle accounts with him—that's what it was about."

"And taking him from Maggie, keeping them apart from then to now, don't forget that."

"And keeping her alive, getting her out of Germany, don't you forget that. It almost cost me my life, but I did it for Jack, for his unborn child."

"Either of you ever explain that to Maggie?"

"They were never really together, Jack. Can't you tell that from Maggie and Roxy? They have a depth of love that Danny couldn't find until he found me. Danny makes every risk I ever took worthwhile. That includes courting Gerry Cotton to make sure of a room here. It gave us a base of operations, where Danny could stay close to the action and be invisible at the same time."

"Roxy knew?"

"Only that Danny was somewhere in Eden Highlands, come to rescue his daughter or die trying. Not that Danny was hiding out in the guest room Gerry was holding for me. Not that we'd managed to tie into The Garden of Eden's monitoring systems, so we could take quick action on any situations that developed. The rules changed when Grass called Roxy to demand you deliver Erich Mielke's diary to him at the museum. She phoned Danny at once. That's when she revealed she had possession of the diary all along."

"Roxy had the diary?"

"When she said that, Danny sounded as incredulous as you do now, because Roxy had told him Tracy never described any of the gifts he had sent. It was the truth, Roxy said, except about the diary. Danny wanted to know why the diary, why Roxy hadn't said anything about it before this. Roxy said it was because he had told Tracy not to tell anybody that she had it, that the book was full of magic and she should hide it in a safe place. Tracy felt she was betraying her father, so made Roxy swear she'd keep it their secret. Then, Tracy decided to read the diary. Nothing made sense to her, not the German, not the combinations of letters and numerals. She got frustrated and dumped the diary in Roxy's wastebasket, saying she didn't believe in magic anyway. After Tracy left, Roxy retrieved the diary and stashed it in the company safe. She told Danny she was certain Tracy would eventually regret what she did with her daddy's gift. That's when Roxy would surprise her with it."

Sothern said, "Something else. He told me he's dying. Lost a lung. Not a lot of time left."

"Danny doesn't tell a lot of people."

"It's true?"

She considered the question. "Who would lie about something like that?"

"Dan Boone. You."

"I've never seen the x-rays. Maybe, if you ask, Danny will show you."

"When he dies, then what?"

"Ask me that when he dies."

Sothern wasn't getting straight answers, but he wasn't going to let her off the hook.

Musical raps at the door beat him to the next question.

He downed a healthy swallow of Cutty and headed for the spy hole.

It was Dan Boone.

Boone pulled him close after Sothern took his handshake.

He wrapped an arm around him and pounded his back, saying, "My kid would be dead it weren't for you, Jack. You got Tracy to the hospital nick of time, the doctors said. They pumped her stomach and whatever, and now she's sleeping comfortably." He threw a wave at Shane over Sothern's shoulder. "I'll head back there to hang for a while longer with Maggie and Roxy, but I want to clean up some business with you before Shane and I do our disappearing act."

Shane said, "Grass?"

Boone crossed to her shaking his head, planted a casual kiss on her lips, and took the barstool Sothern had been occupying. Borrowed Shane's Cutty and sampled it. Broke out a hacking cough. Wiped his mouth and hands. Used another shot of Cutty to clear his throat. "MIA. I doubt he'll try again so soon, knowing we're here gunning for him."

Sothern said, "He's already done crazy things coming after the diary."

"Grass is crazy, not stupid," Shane said.

Boone disagreed. "Both, Angel. If his bulb was brighter, he'd have figured we were padded in Kevlar and aimed for our faces." He thumped his chest. "How about that, Jack? Shane's idea, fixing ourselves up as Enriqué and his fat mama. What comes of having an ex-spook in the family. Knows all the angles."

"All the angles," Sothern said, toasting Shane.

His sarcasm wasn't lost on her.

She nudged Boone. "Time to go, Danny."

"You forgetting something? First things first," he said.

Shane ran a hand down his cheek and, without a word, hurried from the room.

She was back in minutes, carrying Erich Mielke's diary.

She offered it to Boone, who shook his head and pointed at Sothern.

"It was your plan, so you give it to him yourself," he said. "The unfinished business I was talking about, Jack."

Sothern took the diary from Shane and settled down on the bed, coveting it like a lover he was surprised to have, but had no intention of giving up. "Do I get to hear why?"

Boone made a *Why not?* gesture.

He said, "You go on the hell home and write up what's been happening here. The diary is your Exhibit One, some editor accuses you of making up the story like you did some of those others. I won't be surprised if you get a book deal out of this, come out a millionaire. Just give me your word you'll share it fifty-fifty with Tracy. Put it in a trust fund for her."

"I broke my word to you once before."

"You saying you'll do it again?"

"I'm reminding you."

"I didn't need the reminder, Jack, anymore than I'll ever need to be reminded you helped save Tracy's life. Once you take the story public, Washington will come knocking at the door, demanding the diary or your ass. Hand the diary over to them and we can stop worrying about Emil Grass. He becomes the government's problem."

"Once the feds have the diary, they can go after you again."

"Better the feds after me than Emil Grass after my daughter. Besides, so what? In my condition, it's going to be a short race no matter what, Jack. . . . We have ourselves a deal? What say?"

Sothern thought about it. "If Grass thinks I still have the diary, he'll come after me, not Tracy."

"All the more reason to get the story out as soon as possible."

"Jack, do yourself a favor and listen to Danny," Shane said, trying to sound like some goddess of wisdom. Sounding like she knew more than she wanted him to hear. Her tight eyes and taut mouth sending him the same message.

CHAPTER 52

Sothern hit MacArthur Park every morning for the two-mile trot his doctor said would help keep his heart as sturdy as his legs, a supplement to the handful of pills he downed with his breakfast oatmeal; twenty-seven pills and counting, most with names he couldn't pronounce; all meant to help prevent another one of his seizures.

He was winded, whooshing air and sweating a rainstorm when he got back to Westlake Court, intent on taking a quick shower and settling at the computer with a few bottles of brew for as long as it took to defeat the paragraphs about the Mielke diary and its deadly aftermath that had plagued him late into the wee hours.

Sothern wanted the pitch to be letter-perfect before he called around to the majors about the story he was offering exclusively to the highest bidder.

In Sothern's mind, it was a surefire natural for a *Newsweek* or a *Time*, and—

Could the book offers be far behind?

He stepped inside and held up the wall with his hand while he finished catching his breath, unaware of the intruder in his bungalow until Emil Grass said, "How very nice to see you again, Jack."

Grass was relaxing on the sofa, legs crossed, resting a silenced automatic on his knee.

He flashed a sliver of a smile. "You know what I'm here for."

"I don't have Herr Mielke's diary, Grass."

"You're a bad liar, Jack. Not what I read, or I wouldn't have been in such a hurry to see you again."

"Read? What do you mean, you *read?*"

"The current issue of the *Eden Highlands Courier.* I went back there yesterday to find you, and I found the newspaper instead. A front-page story about you." Grass reached for the newspaper on the coffee table, flipped it in half, and chucked it to him. Sothern caught it one-handed. "How you came to possess a diary you plan to share with the government. How the diary will help identify and bring to justice the party responsible for the horrible murders that plagued the community." Grass bowed, a hand over his heart like he was gratefully receiving some honor. "The reporter credits this to his exclusive source, saying how he's been unable to reach you for confirmation or comment at your home in Los Angeles. What got me on the road here, so I owe him a debt of gratitude for pointing me in the right direction. Your address I got from a place where few think to check nowadays, the modern miracle known as the telephone book."

"The phone company charges extra not to be listed. I couldn't afford it."

"Your misfortune was bragging to a guest at The Garden of Eden about Herr Mielke's diary, 'Good Time Gal,' as she identified herself, the reporter's otherwise anonymous exclusive source, who clearly couldn't wait to do you dirt, looking for her fifteen minutes of fame."

Sothern located the story and skimmed it.

Shane had done it to him again.

Only worse this time.

She was someone he had loved, who had put a target on his back, trading his life for the safety of her man's kid. She knew exactly how to manipulate him. *Do yourself a favor and listen to Danny,* she had said, knowing it would be her voice he heard, not Dan Boone's. Knowing that was all the convincing he'd need to leave Eden Highlands with the diary. Knowing Grass would show up to get it, kill him, and that would be that, good-bye, Jack Sothern, while she and Boone would be back to living happily ever after somewhere, oblivious to any consequences caused by Grass peddling the diary to the highest bidder.

Fuck it.

Everybody dies sooner or later.

Sothern's jaw tightened with resolve.

He tossed the newspaper back at Grass and—propelled by fear—flew at him over the coffee table.

Grass raised his arms reflexively and pushed aside the paper, getting off a stray shot that thudded harmlessly into the wall before Sothern landed on him and batted the automatic out of reach.

They grappled onto the table. It crashed under their weight.

They rolled onto the floor, trading aimless whirlwind punches, Grass screaming his murderous intentions, Sothern having a hard time breathing.

Grass elbowed free, scrambled into a sitting position on Sothern's belly and beat him about the chest and face before managing a two-handed strangler's grip around his throat.

Sothern was coughing on blood leaking down his windpipe since a blow to the nose and what sounded and felt like bone cracking. Struggling to breath. Drawing on a reserve of strength he prayed was there, he crashed both fists against Grass' ears, then his cheeks. Grass howled and released Sothern's throat.

Sothern pushed him aside and got to his feet. He spotted the automatic and headed for it. Grass sprang after him and threw him aside. Sothern crashed backward against the bookcase, causing it to topple over. He regained his balance as Grass wheeled around and charged at him with a knife he aimed like a bayonet at Sothern's chest.

Sothern's memory geared into lessons he had taken years ago, researching a story on self-defense. He angled his body, exposing his left arm instead of his chest. *Always the weaker arm,* he remembered. The blade sank deep with Grass anchored to his grip. Sothern seized the seconds to shift and bang the side of his open palm against Grass' eye, trying to blur his vision and bring on disorientation.

Grass yowled and arched backward.

Sothern's next blow caught him on the throat.

Grass dropped the blade and moved his hands there.

Sothern stiffened his fingers and, with all the strength he could muster, rammed them into Grass' abdomen. Grass tripped backward on his heels. Spitting blood, Sothern moved on him. Got Grass good on the side of the neck. Connected a shoe to Grass' balls.

Grass screamed again, louder now, and in German, words Sothern knew weren't praise for his opponent's skills. Refusing to fall, he pushed Sothern aside, struggle-stepped after the blade.

Sothern leaped onto his back, causing Grass to fall to his knees and slop forward, his hand struggling after the few inches needed to get hold of the knife. Seconds later, he had it gripped. He arced his arm around and dug the blade into Sothern's thigh. A second time. A third.

Sothern rolled off him to escape.

Grass managed onto his knees and crawled over. Straddled him. Clearing his eyes of sweat, he raised the blade, but before he could bring it down—

A hand captured his wrist.

Sothern heard the thwack of a muted gunshot.

Grass made a little noise and pitched forward, trapping Sothern in flesh, bone, body, and blood.

Before lapsing into darkness, he heard a voice telling him:

"You're going to be fine now, Little Boy. Everything's going to be fine."

Reassured, Sothern dropped off the edge of the world.

After the paramedics had patched him up and the cops had taken his statement and the media had raced off to make their headlines and deadlines, Sothern eased himself into a sitting position on the side of the bed. He used the aluminum crutches the 911 team had left behind to make it onto his feet and gingerly crossed to the desk. He worked onto the chair, wincing at the pains every error of movement caused his wounded arm or thigh, and fumbled open the locked bottom drawer where he kept the Mielke diary. He needed to know it was there.

It wasn't.

Chapter 53

Sothern heard from Shane Vallery a few weeks later.

The email from "Good Time Gal" was among the hundreds of spams that blitzed his computer every morning. He almost zapped it along with them, more angry about her theft of the Mielke diary than he was grateful to Shane for saving his life.

He'd earned his redemption, and possession of the diary had promised him a fresh start in the news business.

Without it, the future offered nothing that made the present worth living. Not that he was suicidal, nothing like that. Not yet, anyway. He would still rather kill a bottle than himself. Fuck it. What did he have left to lose?

Shane had written:

Danny and I have been following the news and see where you're being made out a hero, for the way you tracked the mass murderer who'd been terrorizing a small Southern California community; how you tricked him into coming after you and narrowly escaped with your life. We weren't surprised to see the facts made bigger and truer than they ever were, in order to hide greater truth the feds still have no interest in sharing with the public, about the Mielke diary. Neither did we, as you must have figured by now. The diary, so long as it's in our possession, it's still our best bargaining chip with an unrelenting and unforgiving government that would rather see the "Turncoat Rebel" dead than red. Why after all this time? I don't have the answer, do you? Did you get any sense at all after you learned no one wanted the story? I'm guessing about that. I'm also guessing my guess is the correct guess, otherwise the truth about Grass would have appeared in print by now, somewhere. I would have come across news somewhere that you had made a book deal or a movie deal. Nothing like that, though. Nothing. The feds can't be beat when it comes to spinning the facts to a press corps that used to dig for the truth instead of helping to bury it. Your career hit a dead end back then, when you were caught lying. Now, it's in vogue. Jesus, Jack. You were light years ahead of the growing pack as a purveyor of prevarication. You were a prophet without honor, and that is the truth. If only you had known. Mielke's diary, if you had it now to back up what you were unable to sell, could put you on a new track. The truth as truth. What a startling concept. Maybe for another day. Maybe, maybe, maybe, Little Boy.

Sothern read Shane's email a second time, then deleted it.

He reached for the bottle of vodka he kept within arm's reach of the keyboard and took a healthy cut straight from the lip. Backhanded his mouth, rubbed his palms to warm them up for the creative juices he was positive would start flowing today, and studied the paragraph he had been working over the past three weeks, striving for perfect pitch:

The four high school girls waltzed into Luigi's Pizza Parlor as they had three times a week since the seventh grade, Mondays, Wednesdays, and Fridays, no way of knowing one of them would never walk out again.

The name "Luigi," he didn't like it as much as he had yesterday.

Back to "Dino's," he decided.

Better.

"Dino's Pizzeria."

Better than "Dino's Pizza Parlor."

Maybe only two times a week, though. Keep the pizza a treat. Three times, one too many. Two times a week since the seventh—

No, the ninth grade.

The *ninth* grade.

Mondays and Fridays since the *ninth* grade.

Yeah. Felt right. Felt better. Felt honest.

Sothern knew he was cooking now. His creative juices flowing. He rewarded himself with another slug of vodka. *Since the ninth grade, Mondays and Fridays, no way of knowing one of them would never walk out again.*

Excellent, Jack.

He exercised his fingers, working out the kinks while his mind wrestled with the next sentence.

He knew.

Yeah, *He knew.*

Outstanding.

The four high school girls waltzed into Dino's Pizzeria in Eden Highlands as they had two times a week since the ninth grade, Mondays and Fridays, no way of knowing one of them would never walk out again, but—

He knew.

Three high school girls, not four.

Only three.

The three high school girls waltzed into Dino's Pizzeria . . .

Sothern's head hurt. He ignored the pain.

ABOUT THE AUTHOR

Robert S. Levinson is the bestselling author of seven prior novels: *In the Key of Death, Where the Lies Begin, Ask a Dead Man, Hot Paint, The James Dean Affair, The John Lennon Affair,* and *The Elvis and Marilyn Affair.* His short stories appear often in the *Ellery Queen* and *Alfred Hitchcock* mystery magazines. He has won *Ellery Queen* Readers Award recognition three times and is regularly included in "year's best" anthologies. His articles have appeared in publications including *Los Angeles Times* magazine, *Rolling Stone, Written By* magazine of the Writers Guild of America–West, and *Los Angeles* magazine. His plays "Transcript" and "Murder Times Two" had their world premieres at RiverPark Center's International Mystery Writers Festivals in Owensboro, Kentucky. Bob served four years on Mystery Writers of America's national board of directors. He wrote, produced, and emceed two MWA annual "Edgar Awards" shows, as well as two International Thriller Writers "Thriller Awards" shows. His work has been praised by Nelson DeMille, Clive Cussler, Joseph Wambaugh, T. Jefferson Parker, Heather Graham, John Lescroart, David Morrell, Gayle Lynds, Michael Palmer, James Rollins, and others. He resides in Los Angeles with his wife, Sandra. Visit him at *www.rslevinson.com.*